The only child of a schoolteacher and a circus clown, Christina Jones has been writing all her life. When her father gave up clowning, he travelled with various fairs and Christina spent her school holidays manning hoopla stalls and playing the fairground organ. The gallopers were such a huge part of her life that she had her own horse – Uncle Sam – on Irvin's roundabout, to whom this book is dedicated. When not writing full-length fiction, Christina contributes short stories to magazines, and writes for the *Daily Mail*'s 'Femail' page. She is also a regular panellist on TVFM's topical humour show, *Week at the Knees*. *Going the Distance*, her first novel, was chosen for WH Smith's Fresh Talent promotion. *Running the Risk* is her second novel. After years of travelling, Christina now lives in Oxfordshire with her husband Rob, daughter Laura and seventeen cats.

RUNNING THE RISK

Christina Jones

ORION

An Orion paperback

First published in Great Britain in 1997
by Oriel
This paperback edition published in 2001
by Orion Books Ltd,
Orion House, 5 Upper St Martin's Lane,
London WC2H 9EA

Printed and bound in Great Britain by
Clays Ltd, St Ives plc

For Don Marshall – my second Dad – with everlasting love
and gratitude

Acknowledgements

To everyone at Orion for their friendship, help and professionalism in nurturing my ramblings into Real Books: to Jane Wood and Selina Walker for being brilliant and kind editors and for becoming such good friends; Susan Lamb for her time, advice, and every kind of support; Joanna Carpenter for absolutely everything (especially the racing tips); and of course Sarah Yorke, publicist-extraordinaire, for always looking after me, for setting up all sorts of mad shenanigans, and for making me laugh.

To Sarah Molloy, my agent, and all at A. M. Heath, for simply being wonderful.

To Hilary Johnson of the RNA, for being there whenever I needed her with guidance and friendship – not to mention food and drink – and to Katie Fforde and Norma Curtis for looking after Rob so well.

To my mate, Marilyn Fountain, who lived every minute of this book with me.

To Percy Dearlove for everything.

To all at Rapier Employment, especially Tim Dackombe, Harvey Townson, Sally Roycroft, John Bailey and Charlotte Evans, for their readiness to answer my most unintelligent questions, and for helping me to understand the vagaries of the agency driver.

To all the lorry drivers who bought me drinks and talked to me for hours and didn't seem to mind me prying into their most intimate habits. Special thanks to the gorgeous Andy Rhodes, Paul Spooner, Stan Street and Frank Cox – all of whom could give up trucking and join the Chippendales.

And a very special thanks to my darling Rob for all those days (and nights) on Britain's motorways in the cab of whichever lorry came to hand. I learned a lot.

CHAPTER 1

On Saturday evenings the John Radcliffe's Accident and Emergency unit was obviously a popular venue. Georgia, narrowly missing being crushed in the automatic doors, winced at the tailback of wheelchairs and trolleys. Row upon row of plastic seats were occupied by people in various stages of drunkenness, the noise was deafening, and the merry little digital message board – which wouldn't have looked out of place in Leicester Square – announced that there was a two-hour wait for non-urgent cases.

Looking at the bloodied faces and grazed knuckles, Georgia wondered who was brave enough to determine non-urgent. And, more to the point, which poor junior nurse had to tell them so. The heating, however, was a plus. It was pulsing at tropical, and whatever cost-cutting methods had been applied by the newly-appointed hospital management board, none of them had reached the thermostat. Georgia felt herself defrosting damply like a cheap pizza.

It was hardly a salubrious end to the Chamber of Commerce Dinner Dance, she thought, as she elbowed her way through to the reception desk. One minute everyone lambada'ing wildly, the next all leaping into cars and belting off up the A34. Someone was bound to call an extraordinary committee meeting to complain.

Squinting at the rows of woebegone faces she heaved a sigh of relief. No one else from Upton Poges had arrived. Yet. There was a serious risk, she knew only too well, that the rest of the workforce would pour into A and E wanting up-to-the-minute information. Diadem Transport were a closely knit bunch.

'Name?' The receptionist didn't look up.

'I'm here for –'

'Name, dear.' The receptionist raised her head, took in Georgia's vibrant tangerine evening dress and her general air of panic and nodded. 'Name. Address. Take a seat. Unless –' she peered closer, 'it's drugs.'

'No.' Georgia was shocked. 'It's –'

'I can't make a diagnosis, dear. I just take your details. Name?'

'Georgia Drummond. I'm a co-director of Diadem Transport in Upton Poges and –'

The receptionist, obviously waiting for her coffee break so she could nip outside and have a Marlboro, sucked longingly on her biro. 'It's not *This Is Your Life*, dear. Just your name will do nicely.' She tapped into the screen. 'So, it's Georgia Drummond, and what's the problem?'

Georgia could feel the tangerine silk clinging to her body as the heating grew ever more effective and wished she'd worn a bra. 'Well, we were at a dinner dance and Jed, he's one of our drivers, collapsed, and –'

The receptionist stopped sucking the biro and tapping her keyboard, and drew her brows together. 'Brevity, as I'm sure you're aware, is of the essence in these circumstances. Am I to understand that you're not the patient?'

'No. It's Jed Thomas.'

With a glower that would have silenced a far less anxious customer, the receptionist leaned from her cubby-hole. 'And Mr Thomas has been brought here, has he? By ambulance?'

Georgia nodded. 'With his wife. Trish.'

The receptionist beat a tattoo with the biro. 'But you do know that casualties from Upton Poges would be taken to Reading? To the Royal Berks?'

'No.' Georgia shook her head. She couldn't, simply couldn't, drive all the way to Reading. 'I was sure this was

2

where the ambulance was going . . . To Oxford. My grandmother said it was,' she finished rather lamely. Cecilia had sworn she'd heard it on the paramedic's radio. Cecilia, grandmother or no, was going to suffer for this.

A second receptionist leaned over at this point, stared at Georgia, then at the screen and whispered something. Georgia's receptionist looked a bit miffed. 'Oh. Right. It would have saved time if you'd said that straight away, dear.' She double-checked the screen. 'Apparently there's a major emergency at the Royal Berks. We've had to take some of their overspill. Mr Thomas has been brought in here and is being seen now. Are you a relative?'

'No, but –'

'Take a seat then, dear. Preferably not by the drinks machine unless you want to be trampled to death when the rush starts. Next.'

Georgia stumbled away.

Sitting as far away from the drinks machine as possible, Georgia tried not to stare at her neighbours. A very young boy with floppy hair seemed to be holding his fingers together in a blood-soaked towel, while on the other side a girl with a writhing bundle on her lap twitched.

The hands on the functional clock seemed to have become paralysed. Was it only an hour ago that she'd been inexpertly dancing with Alan Woodbury? An hour ago that Ezra Samuels and his Latin Lovers had been trumpeting across Upton Poges Masonic Hall? An hour since she'd watched in horror as her grandmother shimmied her little black Jean Muir against Spencer Brimstone's dinner jacket? An hour since Jed had groaned and slid beneath the Diadem table? Georgia tried to arrange the tangerine silk more decorously and stared at her feet.

The girl with the writhing bundle nudged her. 'I don't suppose you could do me a favour and hold this, could you? Only I'm bursting to pop to the lav.'

3

'Well, I'm not sure. I'm waiting for someone and they might –' Georgia recoiled slightly from the bundle.

'Oh, it'll be all right.' The girl was already on her feet. 'It won't be our turn for ages yet. If they do come and call me – the name's Sabrina Yates – just come and give me a yell – OK?' The bundle was thrust without further ceremony into Georgia's arms and Sabrina fled towards the Ladies.

Overcome by curiosity, Georgia peeled back the bundle's covers. A newish baby sucked its fist and cooed at her. Instinctively she cradled it against her, rocking rhythmically, and smiled. The baby smiled back, gurgled, sucked harder on its clenched fist, and drooped long dark eyelashes over navy-blue eyes. It was the most gorgeous thing she had ever seen. 'Your mummy won't be long,' she whispered. 'Then you can go and see the doctor.'

The baby, apart from being rather grubby, seemed healthy enough. Perhaps its mother was the patient, Georgia thought, still rocking. Maybe the twitching Sabrina had a bladder problem. She had certainly been a while in the loo. Any further conjectures were brought to an abrupt halt by an eruption at the automatic doors. The Diadem reinforcements had arrived.

Cecilia, Georgia's grandmother, looking glamorous in an astrakhan coat slung casually over the Jean Muir, her blonde bobbed hair still managing to gleam in the unflattering light, teetered across the reception area.

'Good Lord!' Cecilia peered down at Georgia. 'What's that?'

'A baby. Its mum has gone to spend a penny.' She stared over her grandmother's shoulder. 'Did you come on your own?'

Cecilia sat elegantly in the absent Sabrina's seat and tickled the baby. 'Kenny drove me in. I'd had several of Mikey Somerville's dubious cocktails during the evening.'

4

Georgia was relieved. Just her grandmother and Ken Poldruan. It could have been worse. 'And where's Ken now?'

'Trying to park in a non-wheel-clamping zone. So, is there any news of Jed?'

'He's being examined. I haven't seen Trish yet. I was just told to wait.'

Cecilia looked at Georgia with some concern. 'Didn't you wear a coat, darling? You must be frozen.'

'Not any more. I've got all my wrappings in the car. I just didn't have time to put them on.'

'Make sure you do then,' Cecilia said with grandmotherly concern, 'before you go home. We don't want to lose another member of the workforce, do we? Ah goody – Kenny must have found a parking space.'

Ken Poldruan, Diadem's spare driver, mechanic, yard manager and Cecilia's sometime lover, picked his way through the rows of seats towards them. Sporting a white tuxedo, man-tan and a black moustache, he looked exactly like Engelbert Humperdinck.

'Nice baby.' Ken draped a protective arm round Cecilia's shoulder. He looked even more Mafioso tonight, Georgia thought. It was probably the lights. 'Where did you find it?'

'Its mother has gone to the Ladies,' Cecilia said, 'so Georgia's looking after it . . . Oh, and here's Trish!'

Trish Thomas, Jed's wife and Diadem's secretary, flew towards them. Her hair was dishevelled, her midnight-blue evening dress was badly creased and she'd cried off all her make-up. 'It's a ruptured appendix. They've taken him straight up to theatre. Oh, God!'

Ken tightened his squeeze on Cecilia's shoulder and flashed very white teeth. 'Well, that's a relief. Appendix. Great.'

'What?'

Georgia, Cecilia and Trish all stared at him. Trish's lips were trembling.

Ken nodded cheerfully. 'Back at the Masonic they were saying it was probably food poisoning. Salmonella could have got us all.'

Cecilia glared at him and Trish burst into fresh floods of tears.

'Sit down,' Georgia patted the seat beside her. 'Come on, don't take any notice of Ken – he's just sulking because Gran spent so much time with Spencer Brimstone tonight.'

Trish turned her back on Ken and sank down next to Georgia, dabbing at her eyes. 'They say it's serious – but they reckon they've got it in time. God knows how long he'll be in the theatre. Oh, he's got to be all right.' She sobbed on to Georgia's shoulder.

'Of course he'll be all right. He's in the best place, none better. He'll be fine.' Georgia uttered the stock platitudes, feeling completely helpless.

'Shut up, Georgia, please.' Trish groaned, studying the baby for the first time. 'Who does he belong to?'

Georgia, knowing that Trish and Jed were desperate for children and had been saving for IVF, wasn't sure that this was the right time to be indulging in substitute therapy, but went through the story of Sabrina and her bladder again.

Trish's tear-stained face became wreathed in smiles. 'He can't be more than a few months old. Can I hold him?'

'If you take him I think I'll go and see if his mother is OK.' Georgia passed the baby to Trish. 'She's been ages.'

The ladies' cloakroom, with its harsh strip-lighting and putty-coloured walls, was deserted. Pushing open each cubicle door, Georgia frowned. How many loos were there in a hospital this size? She hadn't actually seen which direction Sabrina had taken. She hurried back out into the waiting area. The floppy-haired boy had gone. Trish was cooing over the baby and Ken and Cecilia were holding hands. Georgia went to the reception desk.

'You were here for Mr Thomas?' The receptionist was less flustered now, having had her cigarette break and got her urgents and non-urgents satisfactorily sorted. 'I believe he's gone down to theatre.'

'Yes. Thanks. Actually, it's about another patient.'

The receptionist looked suspiciously at Georgia. 'How many did you come in with?'

'Well, none actually. There was a girl called Sabrina Yates. I was sitting next to her. She's got a baby – well, I've got it now. Has she gone in?'

The receptionist flicked patiently through the screen and shook her head. 'No Yates. No Sabrina. No baby, dear. We always give babies priority.' She leaned across the desk and peered at Trish whispering over the grubby bundle. 'I expect she was waiting for someone too, dear. Give her a few more minutes. The nightclubs'll be out at any time and it starts to get hectic, so I'd sit down if I were you.'

Georgia, buffeted by a throng of girls in skin-tight Lycra and heavy make-up dragging a comatose boy with a bloody nose, fought her way back to Trish, Ken and Cecilia. 'Are you still all right here?'

'Fine.' Cecilia crossed shapely legs. 'Have you found the mother?'

Georgia shook her head. 'Not yet. Are you OK with the baby a bit longer, Trish?'

Trish gave a weak smile, her eyes bright with tears. 'Yeah. It keeps my mind off Jed. Take as long as you like – we'll probably be here all night.'

She sincerely hoped not. Cecilia would never last until morning without her Estée Lauder night cream. They'd have to send out for emergency supplies.

Georgia rushed past the cubicles where ever-cheerful nurses and one harassed doctor were zooming in and out, past the snaking queue for X-ray and into a quieter complex of dimly-lit corridors.

She was beginning to have serious doubts about Sabrina Yates. What had she looked like? Young, with unkempt black-rooted blonde hair, faded jeans and a pink cardigan, was all Georgia could recall. And she hadn't had a coat. On one of the coldest nights of the year, Sabrina Yates hadn't had a coat . . . Oh, God! Georgia clapped a hand to her mouth. Did that mean she'd wandered into the hospital on the off-chance, looking for somewhere to leave the baby? Was that why she'd disappeared? Surely she hadn't simply abandoned it?

The doors at the end of the corridor crashed open and a trolley, liberally hung with drips and attachments, made a Grand Prix entrance.

'You shouldn't be down here.' The porter who was steering glared at Georgia. 'This is off-limits. Emergency theatre only. Go back to Admissions.'

'Is there a cloakroom?' Georgia pressed herself back against the wall, trying not to look at the wired-up heap on the trolley. 'Apart from the one in Reception?'

'Outside X-ray.' The porter bringing up the rear hissed over his shoulder, 'But it's for patients only.'

The trolley crashed like a ghost train through the second set of swing doors, and shakily Georgia retraced her steps. The overpowering smell of antiseptic and fear was choking her. Somewhere in this labyrinth Jed was being operated on. Somewhere – please God – Sabrina Yates was waiting to be reunited with her baby.

The cloakroom in the X-ray department was far busier than its reception counterpart. Perhaps X-rays made people nervous. All eyes were riveted on Georgia in her zinging orange frock. Ignoring the interest, she tiptoed up to each cubicle, peering in as the doors opened, trying not to look like a voyeur. Sabrina wasn't there.

She almost ran back into the corridor, then remembered an episode of *Casualty* where it had been stressed that no one

8

ran in a hospital, not even when it was life or death, and slowed to a walk. Bloody Sabrina Yates! She'd probably made up the name anyway. Dumping her baby – how could she? Georgia pushed through yet another set of swing doors and was almost deafened by the rattle of cups and the scrape of forks on plates.

Squinting across the canteen, past off-duty staff who were drooping into their minestrone and sad little family groups, she saw a skinny figure in a pink cardigan, her variegated hair shielding her face.

Oh, joy! Georgia practically vaulted the tables.

'Sabrina!' she shouted. 'Sabrina Yates!'

Heads turned. Sabrina looked up from her mug of soup. 'Bugger!'

'What the hell do you think you're doing? We've still got your baby!'

'I'm sorry.' Sabrina looked up with doe eyes. There was a trace of soup outlining her mouth. 'Have I been ages?'

'I thought – we thought – that you'd left him!'

'Nah,' Sabrina drained her soup and staggered to her feet. 'I wouldn't do that. You looked nice – and I really did want to go to the loo and –'

'You weren't even ill!' Georgia hissed, tugging Sabrina out of the canteen and heading for the safety of Accident and Emergency. 'Were you?'

'Nah. I was cold and tired. I quite often come in here for a bit of a warm and a kip. I didn't mean to dump Oscar on you for so long. I went into the lav and when I came out I could smell the soup. It's dead cheap in here. He's all right, isn't he? Oscar? Nothing's happened to him?'

'He was fine and being made much of last time I saw him. But don't you – I mean, haven't you got a home?'

Sabrina gave Georgia a look of deep pity. 'If I had a home I wouldn't be here, would I? Nah, I'm in bed and breakfast. It's OK, but we have to share and it's pretty cold and at least here

I can see a bit of life. And Oscar – I worry about his chest. We have to walk about all day, see, and –'

'But what about your parents?' Georgia was appalled. 'And Oscar's father? And your friends?'

'I don't have the first. The second dumped me when he found out Oscar was on the way. And the third are all in Devon.'

Georgia bit her lip. Sabrina rubbed her bleary eyes. 'It's a bit of a bugger when you're pregnant and you work in a hotel and your accommodation goes with the job. I lost the lot when Oscar arrived. I came to Oxford because Oscar's dad was a student here. I thought I could trace him.'

'And you couldn't?'

'Not a hope in hell. The colleges can't do much with "his name's John and he's got blue eyes".' Sabrina smiled. 'So, I've got a really nice social worker and she found me the B and B. And that's about it . . . oh, look, he's awake!'

Sabrina hurried through the crowd and removed Oscar from Cecilia's arms. Georgia, feeling shell-shocked and exhausted, made brief introductions and then realised Trish wasn't there.

'They've taken her upstairs.' Ken looked extremely relieved that Georgia had found Sabrina. 'Jed will be out of theatre shortly, and there's a relatives' room where she can wait.'

'We're going to wait, too.' Cecilia wiped away traces of Oscar's saliva from the front of her Jean Muir. 'So you can go home, Georgia. There's nothing else you can do at the moment. And if one of us has some sleep tonight then we'll be more help tomorrow.' She glanced along the row of seats to where Sabrina was preparing to breast-feed Oscar. 'Is everything all right there? He's such a darling baby.'

'It's so sad.' Georgia swallowed. 'She's homeless, and the baby's father dumped her and –'

'Georgia.' Cecilia frowned. 'Not another lame duck.'

'No, I suppose not.' Georgia always had to turn off the

television when there was any mention of abandoned animals or babies. 'I just wondered . . .'

'Well, don't,' Cecilia said firmly. 'Now, you drive home safely, darling. Turn the central heating up to full when you get in, and get some sleep.'

'And don't bother with a hot-water bottle in Cecilia's bed.' Ken grinned wolfishly. 'She won't be needing one.'

CHAPTER 2

'Bloody hell!'

It was like being plunged straight from the hot wash into an ice-cold rinse. The white brilliance of the January night dragged the moisture from Georgia's lungs, freezing it into plumes. Wrapping her arms tightly round the inadequate evening dress, she slipped and slithered towards the car park.

Having unlocked her elderly MG with fumbling fingers, Georgia tugged on the layers that would have to prevent frostbite on the A34. The thick black tights, tartan socks and fluffy purple mules gave little warmth at first, but she knew from experience that there'd soon be an improvement. The knee-length sweater embroidered with an inebriated-looking pink elephant felt damp but covered the coldest parts of her. She pulled on multicoloured woolly gloves and, with chattering teeth, heaved the car in the direction of home.

The A34 was fairly quiet. Despite the absence of a heater and the fact that bits of her were being subjected to piercing draughts through gaps in the flapping hood, Georgia was feeling quite snug by the time she reached the turn-off for Upton Poges.

She accelerated and thought about Jed and Trish, and Sabrina and Oscar, and all the other people who were suffering on that stark night. It didn't matter how hard she tried not to worry about homeless people and animals, somehow they always crept in. Slowing down to negotiate the Upton Poges bends, she thought of Cecilia and Diadem and security and a warm bed.

She turned on to a straight bit of road and pushed her foot down. And she had the best friends in the world. So what if there was no man in her life? She considered Alan Woodbury, transport manager of the Kon Tiki Superstore and her Chamber of Commerce partner for the evening prior to Jed's collapse, and shook her head. No, he certainly wasn't the man in her life – or anyone else's. Poor Alan. Since his divorce, he'd become a serious party animal, turning up at the opening of an envelope if there was a drink attached. And his clothes . . .

Georgia changed down again and winced. Alan Woodbury had been the only person to ignore the black-tie bit on the Chamber of Comm invitation, and turned up in canvas trousers, T-shirt and baggy linen jacket. Apparently it had been his attempt to emulate Don Johnson after a rerun of *Miami Vice* on UK Gold. If it had been anyone other than Spencer Brimstone in the chair then Alan would have been sent home to get changed. As it was, Spencer Brimstone had several good reasons for wanting to keep on the right side of Georgia – most of them to do with her grandmother.

Stopping at a deserted junction, she remembered that amidst the panic she'd had no time to say goodbye; she'd have to ring Alan and apologise. Cecilia was going to have to apologise too, not to Alan Woodbury, of course – but definitely to the Brimstones. God knows how her grandmother's flirtatious dancing with Spencer Brimstone would have progressed if Jed hadn't tumbled under the table at that opportune moment.

Spencer and Beth Brimstone ran Upton Poges's one employment agency, and were vital business colleagues. Whatever shenanigans Cecilia and Spencer indulged in during their private moments, most of the Chamber of Comm had been pretty shocked at the goings-on on the dance floor. None more so, Georgia recalled with a shudder, than Beth, Spencer's long-suffering wife.

The roads had narrowed into switchback lanes and the houses dwindled away into one or two small cottages. Her rambling thoughts were pierced by the sudden appearance of headlights behind her. There were no streetlights now, so the startling bright beam illuminated only skeletal trees and the occasional sheep.

'Jesus!' Georgia slowed on a bend as the following headlights danced dazzlingly in her driving mirror. 'If he gets any closer he'll be in here with me.'

The headlights dipped, brightened again, dipped and flickered out completely, before full-beaming into the MG. The vehicle behind was large, possibly a lorry, and obviously hopelessly lost. No one knowing the area and driving something of that size would have dreamed of straying from the A34.

'Sod off!' Georgia growled as the light show began again. 'Pass me if you have to, but just get off my tail.'

Pulling the car into the next available gateway, Georgia watched with malevolent satisfaction as the lorry rumbled past her. He'd be completely stymied by the time he reached Potter's Farm. The track along there was about wide enough for an extremely careful bicycle.

'Oh, bugger.' Georgia swallowed. The lorry had pulled to a halt in front of her, completely blocking the road.

Quickly locking the MG's doors, she crunched the gears into reverse, panic rising for the first time. 'Don't be stupid,' she said to herself, peering over her shoulder through the tangle of her hair. 'No one ever got hijacked in Upton Poges. There hasn't been a rape in living memory, and no one has been murdered since Bert Nicholson shot his mother-in-law seven Christmases ago.'

Nevertheless, she wished she'd refrained from reading the more ghoulish articles in Cecilia's *Sun*. By the time the MG, used to a more leisurely age, had decided to mesh into reverse, the driver had jumped from his lorry cab

and was striding towards her through the glittering darkness.

'Tough,' Georgia muttered, pushing the accelerator to the
floor. 'You've pick on the wrong lady here – oh, shit!'

The MG stalled.

The driver loomed large and dark. Adrenalin zoomed
hopefully round Georgia's body, but finding her unpoised for
flight, subsided into shivers and a beating heart.

As he tapped on the window, Georgia scrabbled in her
handbag and closed woolly fingers around her salvation.
'What do you want?' she mouthed warningly through the
window. 'I've got a mobile phone. I can call the police.'

'Good idea,' the driver's voice echoed from outside. He
must have been shouting very loudly. 'They might be able to
tell me where the hell I'm supposed to be.'

'You're lost?' Again, her mouth opened and closed exaggeratedly through the window. 'You want directions?'

He nodded. He still looked huge and bulky and threatening, and had now bent almost double to peer inside the car. 'If
you could just open the window and stop the goldfish
impersonations, I'd be extremely grateful.'

The window, with its layer of melted ice, scrunched open
to halfway. The lorry driver looked about eight feet tall and
six feet wide and had a lot of fair hair like a thatch. He'd
never get through the gap.

'I've got my phone,' Georgia repeated, clutching the oblong
object like a talisman. 'So no funny business.'

'Funny business is the last thing on my mind. I'm cold,
hungry, knackered and trying to find some godforsaken place
called Milton St John. I was sure I'd followed the right
signs –'

'You did,' Georgia said smugly. 'Except you ignored the
one that said "Not Suitable For Heavy Goods Vehicles".'

'I didn't see it.' His hair had fallen across his eyes
which, like the rest of his face, was darkly shadowed. He

looked like an Old English sheepdog with attitude. 'Where was it?'

'Actually, it's a bit hidden,' Georgia admitted. 'I mean, we all know it's there, but I suppose foreigners could easily miss it.'

'I've come from London, not Tibet.' He sounded irritable. 'And I'm not a bloody mind-reader. So, how do I get there from here?'

'You'll have to reverse all the way back along the lane. Then turn left on to Upton Poges High Street. You can't drive along it because there's a weight limit – so take the second exit from the roundabout where it's signposted Newbury. Milton St John is just off the A34. It's quite easy.'

'It sounds bloody complicated, not to mention about three times as far.' He shook his hair away from his eyes. 'And I'm nearly out of hours.'

'There's a pub in Milton St John that does bed and breakfast.' Georgia decided that she felt quite sorry for him now. 'It would be better than sleeping in the cab on a night like this. The Cat and Fiddle stays open – er – all night for the locals. It's fairly lively, you can't miss it.'

'I probably can,' he said mournfully. 'I can drive in central London with no problems at all. I can cope with cities. Cities make sense. All these little roads seem determined to spook me.'

'Haven't you got a map?'

'I'm a lorry driver. Of course I've got a map. I've got bloody hundreds of maps. I've probably got more bloody maps than the Ordnance Survey Archives –' He stopped and shrugged. 'Sorry. I shouldn't bawl at you. You've been very helpful. Yes, I've got a map – but it seems a bit short on cart-tracks and goat paths and whatever else passes for roads around here.'

Trying not to smile, Georgia again scrabbled in her hand-bag and produced a much-folded piece of paper. 'This shows

Upton Poges, Milton St John, even Tiptoe . . . but don't worry about Tiptoe – no one ever goes there . . .' She looked at his white face and weary eyes. 'Look, I'll show you a quicker route. You'll still have to go back into Upton Poges, but I'll point out the best roads. It'll be quicker than the A34.'

As he didn't seem likely to be a rapist, murderer, or any other sort of molester, Georgia cautiously opened the door of the MG. The wind had been waiting for just such a moment. It snatched the door away from her and slammed it back against the bodywork. The interior light snapped on, displaying Georgia in all her glory.

To give him his due, Georgia thought later, he didn't laugh openly. But there was certainly a twinkle of mirth in the eyes that were fleetingly visible through his hair. His gaze flickered over the knee-length sweater and the tangerine dress, the thick tights and the tartan socks, without his lips moving. However, the fluffy purple mules seemed to fascinate him.

'Here.' Georgia jerked at the flapping map in irritation. It really was bitingly cold. At any minute her nose was going to run. 'If you reverse back up the lane, take this turning, then off the roundabout here, follow this road and it'll take you straight into Milton St John. They're all suitable for HGVs.'

'Are they?' He raised his eyes from the mules. 'It's very clever of you to know that.'

'Oh – er – I drive a lot round here.' Georgia's teeth were chattering.

'Really? In slippers?'

'Mostly.' Georgia pushed the map into his hands. He was still bent almost double and seemed even bulkier at close quarters. 'So if you'd please reverse so that I can get home, I'd be awfully grateful.'

'Of course. You've been very kind.' He stepped aside as she slid back into the MG. 'And extremely trusting under the circumstances.'

'As I said,' Georgia slammed the door, 'I would have telephoned for help if necessary.'

'On that?' He raised his voice as the MG behaved itself and roared into life first time. 'Really? You must be very hi-tech in this part of the world. We don't have things like that in London.'

Georgia was blushing furiously as she pushed her purse back into her handbag, vowing that she would remember to pick up her mobile next time she left home.

The lorry, lights flashing and hazard horns blaring, reversed carefully past her. The driver sketched a salute from the cab, and disappeared backwards into the darkness.

It was nicely done, Georgia thought grudgingly, watching the manoeuvre with a critical eye. She couldn't help it. Even off-duty, she judged everyone's driving standards by her own. Mind you, this wasn't an exercise she'd want to attempt – and definitely not in the pitch dark on unfamiliar territory. She was very aware of the difficulty involved in reversing any large vehicle, the careful control, the absolute co-ordination between hands, feet and brain while steering something forty feet long in the opposite direction to that which you felt it should be going. The lorry was an articulated Mercedes, certainly not the easiest of vehicles to reverse along Upton Poges's twists and turns, and he handled it with smooth skill, judging the locks of the steering wheel with complete precision. He had managed the whole blind-side reverse unaided – using only his mirrors and, she guessed, a fair bit of instinctive trucking intuition. She had hoped he would at least scrape the cab on the overhanging branches or teeter off into the bushes as fair retribution for the purse and the mules, but he did neither.

Squinting through the darkness, Georgia couldn't decipher any name on the lorry cab, but the phone number was from inner London. No doubt he'd taken the job thinking it an easy option – fresh air, open fields, minimal traffic. Georgia grinned as she headed the MG towards home. By the time he found Milton St John he would probably never want to drive through the wilds of Berkshire again.

CHAPTER 3

Diadem House stood four-square and comforting in the glittering night. Georgia locked the MG and paused for a fleeting second on the frosted cobbles. She was always glad to come home. Home . . .

Diadem had originally belonged to her grandfather. A lorry driver and an inveterate gambler, Gordon Harkness had been given a hot tip for a hopeless outsider in the 1953 Diadem Stakes by a drunken Irish ex-jockey in a pub. Absolutely down on his uppers, and despite Cecilia's misgivings, he had lumped everything he possessed on various each-way bets on his travels round the country. The horse had come in obligingly at 100 to 1, and Gordon had moved Cecilia and their five-year-old daughter Morag – Georgia's mother – into an abandoned farm on the outskirts of Upton Poges. He had bought two futher lorries, and Diadem Transport had been born.

Georgia checked quickly that all the lorries, huge, powerful, top-of-the-range lorries these days, were standing shadowy and secure. The cluster of outbuildings and cottages on the far side of the yard were also in darkness. There was no light in Marie's window. Barney and Marie both drove for Diadem, and Barney had been caught up in a road-snarling dispute in France for two weeks. Marie was beginning to think he was enjoying it. Georgia shivered inside the elephant jumper and picked her way carefully across the cobbles.

When Gordon died in 1980, Cecilia, who had been taught to drive lorries at the tail end of the war by a succession of lonely American airmen, had assuaged her grief by taking over Diadem in its entirety. Georgia, who had always travelled with her grandfather, was able to double-declutch while other children were still wobbling on their stabilisers. At eighteen she was made a director of Diadem; at twenty-one had gained her HGV1, followed by her CPC. Now, six years on, she was able to tackle any job in the transport industry. She had always considered it something of a pity that she was less adept at tackling men. Still, she thought with a wry smile as she fumbled for the keys, one man-eater in the family was possibly one too many. She wondered how Cecilia would be explaining her behaviour with Spencer Brimstone to the ever-attentive Ken Poldruan.

Untouched for a hundred years, the farmhouse had been divided into two for Georgia's twenty-first birthday. Ignoring her own front door, Georgia slid Cecilia's key into the lock and was greeted by the usual massed volley from three dogs and a furry assault from the five cats who had all picked the snuggest spots and resented the intrusion.

After patting and stroking and explaining the night's activities, she turned up the heating and switched on the kettle for a hot drink. Embers still glowed in the grate. She riddled them into life and curled up by the hearth, allowing the warmth to seep into her. Two cats clambered hopefully on to her lap and proceeded to knead the bright orange dress. It really had been a pig of a night. She peeled off the woolly gloves and the tartan socks, replacing the purple mules. Cecilia had long ago given up trying to coax Georgia into a wardrobe of classic black, navy and cream.

She gave a luxurious shudder as the heat soaked into her toes – and felt immediately guilty. She hoped Sabrina and Oscar had found some cosy corner in Admissions. She hoped Jed wasn't in too much pain. She hoped Trish wasn't too unhappy. She hoped the lorry driver had found the Cat and Fiddle . . . and that all the world's stray animals had found a warm bed for the night.

The scrunch of tyres on the frosted cobbles heralded

Cecilia's arrival. Georgia scrambled to her feet. The cats, furious at the disruption, glared at her with baleful amber eyes and stalked away, tails erect. Not wanting to be sitting around like a spare part when Ken and her grandmother, flushed with amorous intentions, made their entrance, she scuttled through to the kitchen.

She was at the door leading to her part of the house when Cecilia, pink-cheeked, floated in.

'Lovely and warm in here, darling.' Cecilia shed the astrakhan coat and fondled whichever animal came to hand. 'And you've got the kettle on. How super. I'm awash with that plastic stuff from the machine in the hospital and I could really do with a –'

'Where's Ken? I thought he said –'

'Yes, he did. He thought an invitation to the Chamber of Comm included bed and breakfast. Silly boy.' Cecilia eased off her high-heeled black patent Pierre Chupins which were immediately seized by the senior dog who disappeared under the kitchen table. 'I couldn't be doing with all that nonsense tonight. So he's gone home to sulk.' She patted her immaculate blonde hair. 'Now, were you just disappearing or have you got time for a cosy cuppa and a chat with your old gran?'

Georgia laughed. Cecilia could never be described as an 'old gran'.

'I was going to bed. I didn't want to be a gooseberry.' Georgia poured scalding water into the teapot and glanced at the clock. 'Jesus! Look at the time!'

'Sunday tomorrow, darling.' Cecilia took the green and white cup and inhaled the steam. 'We can all catch up on our beauty sleep. Jed was still unconscious when we left. Trish is staying at the hospital for the night. And that scruffy girl and the baby had disappeared. She'd probably gone home.'

'She couldn't.' Georgia stirred her tea. 'She didn't have a coat or transport or anything. She wouldn't walk through Oxford in the early hours with the baby. Oh, poor girl . . .'

'There are a lot of Sabrinas in the world, Georgia.' Cecilia sank into a Windsor wheelback chair and rested her ten-deniered toes on the dog. 'Sadly. You can't hurt for all of them, darling. We got Barney and Marie and all those children when their house was repossessed. Ken after his divorce. Trish and Jed after the redundancies at Ashers. And all those second-hand dogs and cats – not to mention that bad-tempered horse you insisted on rescuing.' She looked tenderly at her granddaughter. 'You can't take on all of life's waifs and strays, you know.'

Georgia knew. It didn't stop her wanting to.

'They've all worked out well, though,' she said. 'And Tumbling Bay will win races one day. You wait –'

'I'm waiting.' Cecilia smiled indulgently. 'It was one of your grandfather's dreams, too. Being a racehorse owner . . . I was always waiting for Gordon to turn me into another Susan Sangster.'

'We're not contemplating Ascot.' Georgia giggled. 'Maybe a selling hurdle at Windsor. Drew Fitzgerald is a brilliant trainer. The best in Milton St John. He'll make Tumbling Bay a star, I know he will.'

She nearly added that Charlie Somerset had said Tumbling Bay was coming on nicely in schooling and then thought better of it. One mention of the pulse-racing jump jockey would only set Cecilia galloping off on her prospective grandson-in-law tack.

Instead, over the soothing tea, Georgia told her grandmother about her run-in with the lorry driver.

'What sort of rig?' Cecilia was instantly professional. 'Anyone we know?'

'Mercedes artic from London.' Georgia let the heat from the teacup warm her fingers. 'Very much a foreigner.'

'And did you tell him why you knew so much about the best routes for HGVs?'

'No.' Georgia hauled a fat tabby cat on to her lap. 'He

23

probably wouldn't have believed me anyway. You know what men are like about female lorry drivers.'

'Only too well.' Cecilia sighed happily. 'In my day they all seemed to find it most attractive. Almost an aphrodisiac.'

Georgia raised her eyebrows. She had never been able to reconcile her femininity with her masculine job as easily as Cecilia. She had always felt that maybe there was something just a little odd about even wanting to. It had nothing to do with equality in the workplace. But there was a part of her that worried about whether it was her overtly male occupation that meant she so rarely found a man to take her seriously. Not that she wore the lorry drivers' badges of eau-de-diesel and oil-ingrained fingernails, but somehow every man she met *knew*. It seemed to frighten most of them.

'Well, this one wouldn't have found it a turn-on, I can assure you.' Georgia grimaced as the cat clawed her thigh. 'He was big and angry at being lost. Although,' she conceded, 'he was quite sweet in the end.'

'Oh?' Cecilia's brows rose in a porcelain forehead. 'How sweet?'

'You'd have loved him.' Georgia lifted the cat up to her shoulder. 'After all, he was male.'

'Tut-tut,' Cecilia said without rancour. 'He probably thought you were a Newbury by-pass protester. Honestly, darling –'

'Attracting a stray lorry driver in the middle of the night was not uppermost on my mind.' Georgia tucked her purple mules more firmly out of sight beneath the senior dog.

'But you haven't been out with anyone for ages,' Cecilia continued, innocently examining her red-frosted nails. 'Have you?'

'I have. There was Simon Capley. And Alan tonight and –'

'Oh, darling!' Cecilia's eyes were reproachful. 'You can't

count Alan. He's business. And much as I hate to agree with boring Elizabeth Brimstone on anything, you do have to admit, Alan Woodbury is rather a clown.'

'He's kind,' Georgia protested. 'And a good friend. I know people laugh at him – but so does he. He doesn't mind. That's why I like him.'

Depositing the tabby cat firmly in her grandmother's lap, Georgia stood up. Any minute now Cecilia would launch into marriage and babies, and how Georgia stood no chance of either if she insisted on wearing her hair in the same shoulder-length bob as she had at sixteen and dressing like a rainbow explosion.

She took the teacups to the sink and turned on the water.

'Georgia – I'm sorry.' Cecilia encircled her with her arms and a cloud of Joy. 'I just want you to be happy.'

Georgia wiped energetically round the cumbersome taps. The kitchen, indeed the whole house, was almost exactly as it had been when her grandfather bought it, with very few concessions to modernisation. Every penny Diadem earned went back into the business or into Cecilia's wardrobe. 'I am happy, but I'm also completely shattered. You may be still firing on all cylinders – but those of us without the benefits of HRT start to droop not long after midnight. Can we leave any further discussion of my love-life until morning?'

Cecilia laughed. 'What love-life? Which reminds me, I'll have to spend some time with Spencer on Monday as we're now two drivers short. We were discussing a replacement for Barney this evening while we were dancing. After all, Diadem can't operate efficiently on short-manning, can it? Whatever Elizabeth and Kenny may have thought, I was merely asking Spencer to sort me out a good temp.'

Georgia sighed. It sounded likely. She knew it wasn't.

True, Barney was caught up in the French farmers' dispute and stranded outside Calais. True, Brimstones supplied

25

agency drivers. And if it hadn't been for that little incident just before Christmas when she'd arrived home early and found her grandmother stalking around the sitting room in a basque and high heels and Spencer sneaking off upstairs wrapped in Cecilia's white lace negligée, she may well have believed it.

'I can take on more driving,' Georgia said. 'Agency drivers are expensive –'

'You do enough.' Cecilia, still in full grandmother mode, patted Georgia's hand. 'And Diadem can afford it. Spencer's always happy to negotiate with me.'

Georgia changed the subject. 'Have you thought about the play? Jed was your leading man, wasn't he?'

Cecilia was a stalwart of the Poges Players. Georgia was roped in as prompter, scene-shifter, programme seller, and anything else that was needed.

Cecilia pulled a face. 'I'd forgotten. What a bore! And droopy Alan is Jed's understudy! Christ! He's nobody's idea of a romantic hero!'

'You'll have to drag out your casting couch.' Georgia hung the dishcloth across the throbbing radiator. 'And then what will Kenny have to say?'

'Oh!' Cecilia's eyes snapped open. 'That reminds me! Guess what snippet of goss Kenny told me tonight while we were waiting for Trish.'

Georgia shook her head. She wasn't sure she wanted to know.

'He said he'd heard on the grapevine that the Vivienda Group have made an offer for Ionio in Newbury – and Ionio is even smaller than us.'

Georgia sucked in her breath. The Vivienda Group was notorious for moving in on small thriving companies, offering to invest huge sums to enable them to expand, and then withdrawing their financial support just at the crucial moment, leaving Vivienda with the cream of the contracts, the firms struggling, and a complete takeover the only way out.

'Surely not? I mean, Ionio is the only other independent transport company for miles – and it's been in Claude Foskett's family for generations. Why on earth would Vivienda be interested in Ionio?'

'God knows.' Cecilia shrugged. 'The bastards. They'd better not try to get their mucky paws on Diadem. I'd rather die than be put out of business by a multinational – and certainly not a bunch of asset-strippers like Vivienda.'

Georgia grinned at her grandmother's venom. 'I'd like to see them try to asset-strip you. They wouldn't know what had hit them.'

'Your grandfather and I had to fight off takeovers a lot in the early days. Thankfully, since we've all become share-holders I haven't had that problem. But if Kenny's information is correct and Vivienda have got serious designs on Ionio – they might well want us out of the way. They could employ all manner of dirty tricks. We'll have to watch the situation very carefully.'

'Don't you have some ex-lover in the Vivienda Group who could pull strings?'

'Sadly, no.' Cecilia tried to prise the astrakhan coat from beneath three cats and lost. 'I did have hopes of entrancing Sir Greville Kendall when he became Vivienda's chairman. He was a sensationally handsome man – very much like Clark Gable – but I never got any further than twenty tables away at the Café Royal luncheon. Of course, he's dead now, and I don't know any of the new regime. Maybe it's just a rumour.'

'Let's hope so.' Georgia yawned. 'And now I really am going to bed before I collapse.'

Parting from her grandmother at the dividing door with an affectionate kiss, she staggered upstairs.

Not bothering to remove her negligible make-up, she

tugged off her clothes, pulled on her winceyette pyjamas with the Day-Glo teddy bears – a Christmas present from Trish and Jed – and tumbled beneath the duvet.

CHAPTER 4

'How's Jed?' Alan Woodbury leaned across his higgledy-piggledy desk on Monday morning. 'Any improvement?'

Georgia nodded. 'Vast, thanks. I went in to see him with Trish last night. He's still very sore and grumpy, of course, and he won't be able to work for a couple of months. But he's going to be fine.'

'Thank God. He scared me to death on Saturday night – just keeling over like that. Ken Poldruan said it was possibly salmonella poisoning, and as Kon Tiki had supplied most of the food it wouldn't have done us any good at all. And I was worried about you. I couldn't find you. Then Cecilia said you'd gone to the hospital and I thought –'

Alan paused to suck in his breath. Since his divorce, he had taken to wearing mock Armani suits as well as growing a moustache and redesigning his hair. He still didn't look quite right. Georgia itched to stretch out and straighten his crumpled lapels and loosen his tie from its vicious little knot.

'Well, Ken was wrong. It was definitely a ruptured appendix. I don't think anyone will blame you for that.' She smiled kindly and picked up her copies of the Kon Tiki delivery notes. 'Will you be needing Diadem for any other runs today? Only I've left Cecilia to organise a couple of agency drivers – an excuse to have lunch with Spencer Brimstone – so she might be gone for the rest of the day, and we're pretty pushed. Unless Spencer can come up with two drivers straight away I'm afraid I'll have to do your Bristol run again tomorrow.'

'I'd have no objection to that.' Alan stood up. 'You've covered everything excellently – as usual. Actually, now that we've got the business out of the way, I was going to get on to the pleasure. About Wednesday . . .'

Georgia blinked. Wednesday? What on earth was happening on Wednesday? Jesus – was Alan asking her out? Had she given him some signs of encouragement on Saturday night?

'Am Dram night? The Poges Players?'

'Oh, *Wednesday*.'

'We're supposed to be having a read-through.' Alan tightened his tie's stranglehold. Any minute now he'd garrotte himself. 'And – er – with Jed out of action there'll have to be some recasting.'

'Oh, yes,' Georgia gabbled in relief. 'I suppose as Jed's understudy you'll have to step into the breach. Er – are you OK with that?'

He might be, Georgia thought, Cecilia sure as hell wasn't.

'Fine. Word-perfect, actually.' Alan tried to look coy and failed. 'And we'll probably have to find someone to replace Claude Foskett as well.'

'Why? Is he ill, too?' Georgia had visions of the whole of the Poges Players succumbing to some virulent bug. It would play havoc with *Inherit My Heart*. 'I thought that he –'

'No, he's fine, but he won't be around any more. He's sold Ionio to the Vivienda Group and is intending to retire to Florida.'

'What?' Georgia's mouth gaped. This was even worse than an outbreak of food poisoning. 'When? Ken only mentioned it to Cecilia on Saturday night. Surely, nothing could have happened that quickly?'

Alan tapped the side of his nose. 'Take it from me – they made a very good offer for Ionio. And Claude has no one to pass the business on to. The deal's been imminent for some time. I reckon the ink was already drying on the contract by Sunday. Don't look so worried – Kon Tiki won't switch their allegiance. We've been let down by big companies in the past.'

Georgia shook her head. The Vivienda monster had taken a giant step forward.

Alan continued to beam. 'Forget about it. I'm sure Diadem is quite safe. No one in their right mind would try tackling Cecilia. Anyway, about the play –' He looked as though he was going to melt in a pool of excitement. 'We could go to the Seven Stars first and try some more of Mikey Somerville's cocktails. Those Blue Lagoons he made on Saturday night were seriously good.' Alan was really getting into the swing of thespian life. 'And they might give me a bit of Dutch courage.'

'Lovely.' Georgia thought they were far more likely to give him alcohol poisoning. 'I'll meet you in there about eightish, shall I?'

'No, I'll pick you up at the house.' Alan held the door open for her. 'The roads are treacherous and they're forecasting snow. I wouldn't like to think of you risking your neck.'

Georgia didn't bother to remind him that she'd been risking her neck since three in the morning, driving a forty-foot articulated lorry to Bristol. Alan Woodbury obviously saw her as fluffy and helpless in her off-duty moments. It was one of the things she liked about him. He was among the few men who thought of her as a woman first and a lorry driver second.

'Great, then. I'll see you on Wednesday. No, don't come out into the yard. I'm in a bit of a rush. There's something I've got to do.'

She shuddered in the biting wind and hauled herself into the lorry's cab. It's probably one of the most stupid things I've ever done in my life, she thought.

The sky was hanging low and yellow across the town, and Alan's snow forecast seemed to be becoming more and more likely. Georgia had mixed feelings about snow. The child in her delighted in it. There was always this surge of excitement as the first flakes fell, and a sense of wonderment as familiar

31

landscapes became transformed beneath their white eider-down. As a lorry driver, she absolutely dreaded its disruption.

Georgia steered the black and gold Magnum, with its distinctive emblazoned silver crowns and the Diadem logo, carefully away from Upton Poges's weight-restricted High Street. Away from Diadem. She knew she really should go straight back to the yard and carry out all the unglamorous, mundane tasks that still remained at the end of a delivery. Things like refilling the lorry with diesel ready for the next run, washing down the whole unit, and then handing it over to Ken for a quick service check. She knew she really ought to help Trish in the office before the afternoon appointments with potential customers – Cecilia's lunch with Spencer could lead to dinner and heaven knows what else. And she had to tell them about Vivienda. She really should go back. And, of course, she would, she told herself as she pulled the lorry off the roundabout and on to the A34, just as soon as she had salved her conscience.

She drove with unconscious ease, slotting the lorry's length into the fast-flowing traffic. These were the moments when she felt happiest. Alone in the cab, sitting up high above the road in her glass cocoon, completely in control. It never failed to give her a sense of immense satisfaction. The view was magnificent, and despite the misconception that something weighing as much as a sperm whale must be the very devil to drive, Georgia found it remarkably easy. The steering was light, the dash-board only slightly more complicated than that of a car, and once you'd got the hang of the fifteen or so gears, driving a lorry was really a piece of cake. She grinned to herself as she cruised towards Oxford. It wasn't something she told people very often. If they thought it was second only in complexity to piloting Concorde, who was she to disillusion them? Aware of the admiring glances from male motorists in standard hatch-backs, she switched on the radio and began to sing.

*

The harassed Social Services' staff were fairly reticent. They didn't give out information about their clients, they explained to Georgia. Not for any reason. No, they couldn't possibly tell her where Sabrina Yates and Oscar were living. They hoped Georgia realised that Upton Poges didn't even come within the Oxford catchment area. Well, yes, they supposed they could pass on a message.

Scribbling briefly on the back of one of Diadem's cards, Georgia popped it inside the Social Services' small buff envelope and thought that Sabrina would probably dismiss it as yet more authoritarian gobbledegook and rip it up without opening it. Still, she'd tried. Smiling her thanks, she pushed her way out of the office.

''Ere!' a gruff voice bellowed behind her. ''Ang on!'

She paused at the opulent swing doors with a sigh. Was it a traffic warden incensed at having Oxford's overloaded streets congested even further by the lorry? A forty-foot Magnum was not the easiest thing to park, but even so, she thought she'd kept within the law.

She turned with a placating smile. 'I'm awfully sorry. I'm just going to move it. It's not on double yellows or anything is it? Oh!'

Unless the city's traffic wardens had suddenly adopted a new uniform, the man hurrying behind her, slithering on the acres of burnished linoleum, was not interested in her parking practices.

'What?' He screwed up a weather-beaten face. 'What you say?'

'Nothing.' Georgia shook her head. 'I thought – oh well, it doesn't matter. Did you want to tell me something?'

'Ah.' The man nodded his greasy grey head vigorously, making dust and debris dance from his shabby overcoat. 'I was going to say – if they won't 'elp you, there's a good 'ostel just down by the river. It ain't the Ritz, of course, but they 'as a delousing system and you gets a smashing cup of tea. Nice warm beds, too. 'Course,' he surveyed Georgia severely, 'it's teetotal. You 'as to leave your bottles at the desk.'

'Oh, right. It's – um – very kind of you. Thanks. Thanks very much.' Georgia wasn't sure whether to laugh or cry. 'I'll bear it in mind.'

She was still giggling when she pushed open the door of Diadem's office.

'Share it, please.' Trish looked up from her screen. 'I could do with cheering up.'

'Not bad news from the hospital?' Georgia sat down at her desk and picked up her post. 'Not Jed?'

'No, he's doing nicely.' Trish was inserting information on to the screen with speedy dexterity. 'It's just that I've realised how long I'll have to go without sex.'

Georgia snorted with laughter.

Trish glared. 'Oh, it's all right for you. And I'm not thinking of pleasure-zone levels. I'm thinking of baby-creating.'

'Oh, yes. Sorry.' Georgia bit her lip. 'I've never got that far. Will it screw up your IVF thing?'

'Bound to.' Trish bit into a fat sandwich, still staring at the screen. 'Bit of a bugger all round, really. Still, at least I will eventually get a shot at it. You're still on home base.'

Georgia reached over and helped herself to a sandwich. 'Since we're discussing sex, I assume Gran is still lunching with Spencer?'

'Oh, yes . . . sod!' Trish clenched the sandwich between her teeth and deleted furiously. 'Yeah, she phoned. They've fitted us up with two drivers from the agency. That adenoidal one we had before who couldn't find Birmingham and a new bloke called . . .' she riffled through the papers on her desk, 'Faulkner.'

'As long as he's got a Class One I don't care what he's called.' Georgia started to check through the mountain of letters on her desk. 'We'll put Adenoids on the multi-drops and

Mr F on the Bristol trunk. I can do the locals then, and spend more time in the office and drumming up new business. Does that sound OK?'

'Whatever you say, boss.' Trish snatched the last sandwich from the pile and grinned. 'I need it – I'm emotionally disturbed and deprived of my marital comforts. I need some sort of substitute.'

Georgia shook her head, unlaced her Doc Martens and slid her toes into her fluffy mules with a bliss-filled sigh. 'So they're both starting tomorrow, are they?'

'Adenoids is.' Trish washed down the sandwich with a mouthful of coffee. 'I've asked Mr Faulkner to come in this afternoon. We need someone to run down to Southampton. Marie's in Hull and you've got appointments all afternoon. He didn't seem to mind.' She glanced at the clock. 'He should be here soon. Do you want to give him the once-over?'

'Professionally or personally?'

'Well, both.' Trish grinned. 'He might be a bit of all right.'

'He'll be married, have a lorry-driver's gut and be devoted to the greatest hits of Box Car Willie.' Georgia deposited her post in Trish's in-tray. 'So we'll just hope he can drive. OK?'

'That's a bit sexist – not to mention elitist and stereotypist.' Trish opened a packet of chocolate digestives. It always amazed Georgia how she managed to stay stick-thin. 'After all, Diadem employs two not unattractive female drivers, my Jed is a stunner and Barney looks like Gregory Peck. Well, at least like he did in his heyday. Even Ken is pretty glamorous in a Mafioso sort of way. Mr Faulkner could be absolutely gorgeous – and I think we're just about to find out.'

A car had pulled into the yard. Georgia peered over Trish's head. 'You could be right – unless it's Gran back from lunching with Spence, which I very much doubt. Do you want to tell him about the Southampton run while I go and grab something to eat – seeing as you've had most of the sand-wiches?'

'No.' Trish smiled sweetly. 'You're the boss, Miss Drummond. I'm sure he'd rather speak to the organ-grinder.'

Georgia hurled a handful of paper-clips across the office and straightened out the front of her sweater. This one had ducklings wading through puddles in bright red wellingtons. 'Do I look suitably boss-like and impressive, then?'

'Not really. More sort of juvenile and yobbish.'

Georgia was thumbing her nose and poking her tongue out when the office door opened and something large and shaggy stepped inside.

'Oh, bugger.' She tucked the mules hastily out of sight beneath her chair and knew she was blushing. 'Hello.'

Trish had perked up considerably. 'You must be Mr Faulkner? From Brimstones'?'

He nodded, pushing his hair out of his eyes. 'Good afternoon.'

Georgia fixed a professional smile and tried to control the blush. 'We meet again.'

'Do we?' He peered down at her from his six foot plus. In the daylight the shaggy hair was fairer and the eyes were darker. He didn't look quite so intimidating, and the sudden smile was a revelation. 'Oh, yes – so we do. The other night . . . no wonder you knew all about the best routes, working here.'

Georgia was aware that Trish had stopped inputting and was watching the exchange with blatant curiosity.

'And you obviously found Milton St John.' Georgia frowned. 'But, surely – you were driving a lorry from somewhere in London? How come you're now signed on with the Brimstones' Agency?'

He shrugged and smiled again. It was the sort of smile, Georgia thought, that should be issued only on prescription. In very small doses.

'I was tramping. You understand tramping?'

Georgia nodded. Of course she understood tramping. Her grandfather had told her stories of how he'd tramped before Diadem – driving a lorry to a destination for one company and then hanging around waiting for a return trip from another.

'There was nothing else doing.' He sighed. 'So, I thought I'd sign on for some agency work, look for digs, try my luck round here . . . you know?'

Georgia nodded again, this time with more sympathy. She had heard the story many times. The transport industry was notably precarious.

'And you've found suitable accommodation, have you?' She would hate to think that he was dossing down on someone's floor. 'Only, Jessie at the post office does B and B, and –'

'I'm nicely fixed up, thanks.' He shifted his weight from one hip to the other. 'It's very kind of you.'

'Maybe Mr Faulkner would like to sit down,' Trish hissed.

'Oh – er – yes, of course. Please –' Georgia indicated the squashy armchairs dotted around the office.

'Well, yes, I'd love to stay and chat – but I was told to report to the boss for an immediate start. Is he around? George, I think they said . . . yes, George Drummond. Is he in?'

There was an infinitesimal silence before Georgia spoke. 'Yes, he is. Only it isn't a he. I'm Georgia Drummond.' Her eyes challenged him to contradict her. It wasn't the first time it had happened and she was sure it wouldn't be the last. It certainly didn't annoy her any more but she really wished she'd been christened Rosie.

'Good God.' They stared at each other for a moment then he shrugged. 'Sorry. It's just that –'

'Yes?'

'I thought – well, you know, that you were a sort of secretary.'

Trish sniggered.

He seemed to be having difficulty in keeping a straight face. 'No. Sorry. That was very rude of me. I simply didn't expect –'

'People don't.' Georgia stood up. 'I'm a co-director of Diadem, Mr Faulkner, along with my grandmother. We even employ female drivers.'

He grinned at her. 'I take it that I've been awarded the MCP of the month badge?'

'I've heard worse.' Georgia moved round to his side of the desk. He towered over her. 'And as long as you've got a licence to drive LGVs and can cope with tachographs, your opinions are of no interest to me. Shall we go out into the yard?'

'Of course. Am I allowed to hold the door open for you?'

She glared at him. He was smiling again, his eyes trawling down her body. They reached the mules and he laughed openly.

'Actually,' Trish had given up all pretence of work, 'could I make a suggestion before you show him the lorry, Georgia?'

'Be my guest.' Georgia wished that she was wearing her cream Laurèl suit and the brown pigskin shoes that she kept for entertaining customers. She felt that his eyes were now riveted on the bosom-waddling ducklings.

'I just thought that we ought to establish Christian-name terms. Spencer didn't mention it – and we're very pally here at Diadem. We don't stand on ceremony.'

'So I noticed.' His eyes skimmed the crumpled tinfoil, the crumbs, the half-eaten biscuits. 'It's Rory.'

'Oh, as in Rory Gallagher? Was your mum a fan of wild Irish guitarists?' Trish sighed. 'All tangled hair and piercing blue eyes?'

'Nothing so romantic, I'm afraid. It's just Rory. It was the first name she stuck a pin in in the baby book. She thought I was going to be a girl. She'd chosen Rosie.'

Georgia didn't meet his eyes in case she laughed. 'Yes, well, fine. I'm sure Trish will be able to spell Rory. Now, the lorry is out in the yard. Here's the collection sheet and –'

'Don't forget *The Greatest Hits of Box Car Willie*,' Trish sang out sweetly, inserting a new driver file as Georgia ushered him out of the door. 'And I think Rory is a lovely name.'

The wind was blowing bitingly across the yard from the north. It numbed Georgia's toes as she walked towards a Mercedes in the black, gold and silver Diadem livery and held out the keys. 'It's a collection of small machine parts from Lennards on the industrial estate to go to their main factory in Southampton. They're one of our regular customers so it should be straightforward. There's a phone in the cab of course, if you get lost.'

'I wouldn't dare to, Miss Drummond. Not again. After all, I wouldn't have you to guide me, would I? And this phone? Will I recognise it? Or is it heavily disguised as something else?'

Georgia laughed. 'OK. But I didn't know you. I was pretty scared.'

'Understandable.' The wind was blowing his hair about his face. It was like a lion's mane. 'And very sensible. And your wagons are wonderful.' He cast an appraising eye across the yard. 'Any chance of driving the Magnum?'

'Every chance. Tomorrow morning.' Georgia glowed. She loved it when people praised the lorries. They were her babies. 'We've got two Magnums that we usually use for trans-European runs – one's in France at the moment – and two Mercedes and a Scania.' She suddenly remembered that she was supposed to be professional, and stopped gushing. 'I do hope you'll enjoy working for Diadem.'

'I'm sure I shall.' Rory Faulkner opened the Mercedes's door and turned to face her. Georgia felt suddenly hot despite the arctic blast. 'I'm so glad we bumped into each other again. I thought about you a lot that night.'

Georgia was relieved that her face was veiled by her hair. A blush would have been catastrophic.

'You were obviously scared of the situation but you were prepared to help me. And then, of course,' his eyes rested once more on the mules, 'I'd never met anyone driving an MG and wearing purple slippers in the middle of nowhere. It was just like one of those 1950s B-movies. Very surreal. Anyway, thank you for pointing me in the right direction that night – and I am sorry for leaping to the wrong conclusions earlier.'

'Don't grovel. We're very democratic here. We're all equally rude to one another.'

He laughed with her, slammed shut the door and coaxed the lorry into life with a deft hand. Georgia watched his exit from the yard as she walked towards the office.

'Well?' Trish was copying details from the blue-edged Brimstones' card. 'We know his name, his temporary address, his age – he's thirty-six – so what else did you find out?'

'Nothing.' Georgia switched on the kettle and crunched a chocolate digestive. 'Except that he likes the lorries and he's funny.'

'Peculiar?'

'No, the other sort. He can't be married.'

'Why not? Damn.' Trish deleted furiously.

'Well, tramping and then taking agency work and digs. It doesn't sound like the lifestyle of a committed family man.'

Trish paused. 'I'd say it did. He's probably working at anything to pay off the mortgage arrears. I mean, looking like he does and being in his thirties, he's bound to have some pouting baby-faced wife tucked away.' She warmed to her theme. 'She's probably very understanding, and hates having to let him wander, but she knows he's only doing it for her and the children.'

'Where on earth did the children spring from?'

'Sit down, dear,' Trish sighed, 'and let me explain . . .'

'You know what I mean.' Georgia flicked at a pile of magazines on the desk as she deposited two cups of coffee. 'You spend too much time reading this stuff and believing it.' She suddenly brightened. 'Maybe he's divorced.'

'Maybe he's gay.' Trish dunked a chocolate digestive in her coffee. 'Maybe his mum was right with Rosie all along. Maybe he's not glad to be gay, so being a lorry driver would compound the pretence. A rufty-tufty job and a butch name. Maybe –'

'And maybe it's about time you abandoned those psychology evening classes.'

CHAPTER 5

'I'm just leaving.' Cecilia's voice echoed up Georgia's stairs. 'We're having a committee meeting before we kick off – with the recasting and whatnot. You'll be there by nine won't you?'

'Umph,' Georgia muttered, tugging a multicoloured jumper over her head. 'Yes. Alan said he'd be here at eight.'

'I simply can't think why you haven't press-ganged that glorious man into auditioning.'

'Which man?' Georgia freed her hair from the neck of the jumper. 'Have I met him? Have you asked him to be your grandson-in-law?'

Cecilia had caught the merest glimpse of Rory as he'd dropped gracefully from the Magnum's cab the previous day, and had been waxing lyrical ever since. He'd become her main topic of conversation – even replacing Claude Foskett's shocking lack of solidarity in selling out to the enemy.

'Don't prevaricate, Georgia. You know perfectly well who I mean. If Rory Faulkner,' Cecilia cherished the name with her tongue, 'was our leading man, Marie would be trampled in the crush – especially in that steamy bit in the third act.'

'I'm pretty sure amateur dramatics wouldn't interest Mr Faulkner, Gran.' Georgia wriggled into her tightest jeans. 'But, of course, you could always ask him – if you wanted to risk breaking Alan Woodbury's heart for ever. He's word-perfect, apparently.'

'Good God, is he? What a bore. Oh well, the divine Rory would be wasted on Marie anyway. She's used to being mauled by Barney. I must dash. I'll see you later, darling.'

'Complete with the star of the show.'

She heard Cecilia's heavy sigh and the clicking of her high-heeled shoes across the hall. It looked as though the Poges Players were just about to inaugurate their most unlikely romantic lead to date.

Hastily applying what she always thought of as her 'facing the world but not serious seduction' make-up – one coat of mascara, brown eyeshadow and a slick of bronze lipstick – Georgia closed the bedroom door and hurried downstairs. She wanted to be ready when Alan arrived. Inviting him in might look too much like a date. The doorbell rang.

'Sod,' Georgia muttered, hobbling across the hall in one boot. 'Oh, hi, Alan. You're early – I'm nearly ready.'

Alan, dressed in ginger cords and a puffa jacket with the hint of a cravat, nodded as he stepped inside. 'Nerves. I couldn't eat a thing. This could be the most important night of my life.' He bent down to stroke a bevy of curious cats who were weaving themselves sinuously through his legs. 'Is Cecilia joining us?'

Georgia wound a voluminous tartan scarf round her throat. 'No. Is it snowing?'

'Not yet.' Still squatting, Alan looked round the hall. 'This is very cosy. And what unusual colours for a hallway. I didn't realise you were self-contained. I assumed you and Cecilia lived together.'

God forbid!

'We each have two bedrooms, a bathroom and kitchen. I've got a sitting room – Gran's got three other receptions and the cellar. The door over there divides the house.' She pulled on the missing boot and prayed that he wasn't going to ask for a guided tour. 'I did the decorating myself – Gran's part is far more conventional. Right. That's me done. Let's go.'

It was another diamond-bright night. The air was ice cold. Georgia cast a quick glimpse across the yard. The lorries slumbered in huge shadows. The office was in darkness.

'It's like a little village, isn't it?' Alan unlocked his car. 'The house, the yard, the office, and then all the Diadem workers living in the cottages. Snug.'

Georgia smiled at him. 'That was how Gran and Grandad wanted it. That's why they bought the farm. It was always their intention to offer homes as well as jobs – they'd been through the mill a bit in their early days. They knew how important security was.'

'A proper little family.' Alan sighed as he steered the car out into the lane. 'No wonder you don't want to be the next on Vivienda's shopping list.' He turned to her in the darkness. 'Georgia, would you do me a favour?'

Georgia held her breath.

'Would you hear my lines before we get to the pub?'

The Seven Stars was quiet. There were a few after-work stragglers still nursing restorative beers against the mahogany counter, and a collection of elderly men playing crib in a low-beamed corner. A log fire spat happily in a cavernous grate.

'Grab a seat,' Alan motioned towards the fireside alcove, 'and I'll buy some bevvies.'

Georgia shed her scarf and woolly gloves and stretched her hands towards the blaze. Even without Jed and Claude, the Poges Players were going to be pretty depleted tonight. Trish had gone to the hospital and Ken Poldruan – much to Cecilia's delight as Spencer Brimstone was the Am Dram's director – was driving a night trunk to Barnsley. No doubt the remaining scene-shifters and bit-parters not involved in the committee meeting would arrive soon. She hoped they wouldn't think she and Alan were an item – and felt instantly guilty.

'I got you a brandy and ginger.' Alan slopped the glasses on to the table. 'Mikey couldn't remember how he'd made the Blue Lagoons so I got a pint of this instead.'

'What is it?' Georgia was intrigued. The tall glass swirled with various colours.

'It's a Winter Warmer.' Alan took a mouthful and immediately turned puce. 'It's – um – very good. Very – euch – warm. Would you like a sip?'

Georgia shook her head. 'I'll stick to brandy, thanks. And I should be careful how many of those you drink –' Alan was already halfway down the glass '– after all, you're driving.'

'I'm fine,' Alan spluttered. 'Practically non-alcoholic, Mikey says. Most of the kick comes from the cloves and the ginger wine.' He finished the rest of it in one gulp, his eyes watering. 'I think I'll have another to steady the old butterflies. Same again for you?'

'God, no. This'll last me all evening.'

She relaxed into the cushioned chair as Alan returned to the bar. Various villagers had drifted in, waving to her. She waved back.

'Lovely fire, isn't it?'

The voice made her jump. Brandy splashed on to her fingers. She turned her head and stared up at Rory Faulkner. 'Oh, hello . . . I didn't know you were here.'

'I was having a meal in the lounge bar. I thought I'd bring my drink over to the fire.' He looked at her almost accusingly. 'I didn't realise the table was occupied – you can't see from the door.'

'No – well, sit down, please.' Georgia knew her face was crimson. She hoped he'd think it was the fireglow. Poor man. He obviously had no cooking facilities in his digs – and precious little heat either. 'We won't be staying long.'

He sat, stretching his legs towards the ash-strewn hearth. His fair hair was almost tidy, and the black sweatshirt made his eyes very blue. The leather jacket laid across his lap was soft and well-worn.

Georgia knew Rory was back because she'd seen his paperwork in the office. She had even sneaked a look at his tachograph – the spy in the cab, the circular disc compulsory in every lorry to register speeds, distances, rest periods. Rory's had been one of the few she had seen that was correctly completed first time. The man was a professional. She sipped her brandy. 'I saw your tacho in the office so I knew you were back. Did everything go OK?'

'Very well.' His fingers curled around his beer glass. 'And I got your message about tomorrow's run. I'll pick the trailer up at Lennards, shall I?'

Georgia nodded. 'It's their regular trunk. Ken's on it tonight. You're – er – all right with nights?'

'Whatever. I'm easy.' Rory smiled at her. 'It's a very well-organised company.'

'Lennards?'

'No. Diadem.'

'Considering that it's run by women? I'm glad you're – um – happy.' She had been going to say satisfied, but thought better of it. 'Has my grandmother mentioned that this will probably be a fairly long contract?'

'I haven't had the pleasure of meeting your grandmother, but Trish did say that her husband would be off for some time.' He leaned forward and Georgia caught a waft of lavender-based cologne. 'I'm more than happy to stay as long as you want me.'

This was her cue to enquire solicitously – as all good employers should – about whether it would interfere with his domestic arrangements, his wife . . .

'Are you – ?'

'Oh, nice. Company.' Alan rocked slightly against the table before sitting down. He squinted at Rory. 'Have we met?'

Rory shook his head and started to get to his feet.

'Please don't feel you have to go.' Georgia's voice rose a little too quickly. 'Alan Woodbury – Rory Faulkner. Rory's our new driver. Alan will help you if you ever do the Kon Tiki deliveries.'

46

They shook hands as Rory resumed his seat and Alan started to chat happily. He was a sweetie, she thought. He always made everyone feel at ease. People really shouldn't laugh at him. All he needed was a woman in his life – as long as it wasn't her.

'Why don't you come along with us?' Alan was saying. 'If you've nothing better to do. We have a lot of fun – and Cecilia's always looking for new blood.'

'Thanks for the offer, but I don't think amateur dramatics is really my scene.'

'I used to feel like that, but there's no need to be shy – and anyway you won't get roped in for playing anything this time. All the casting has been done. Actually, I'm the leading man.'

'Congratulations.'

Georgia shot a look at Rory but he seemed genuinely pleased.

'Tell him, Georgia,' Alan persisted. 'We could do with some more muscle to shift the scenery and –'

'If Rory says he's not interested,' Georgia hissed, 'let's just leave it at that. Anyway, we ought to be going. It's nearly nine.'

'God! Is it? My butterflies are doing somersaults.' Alan drained the second pint of Winter Warmer. 'Still, I suppose Kenneth Branagh had to start somewhere.'

Georgia's eyes met Rory's in a fleeting moment of shared amusement. It made her mouth dry. She stood up and started to wind the tartan scarf around her neck. Rory's eyes were again fixed on her sweater. 'I'm going to have to ask you – do you knit them yourself?'

Georgia shook her head, smoothing down the front of the unicorns leaping over rainbows. 'Sadly, no. I'm no knitter. If you gave me two pointy things and a lot of wool I'd manage to have my eyes out and strangle myself at the same time. Jessie Hopkins at the post office knits them for me.'

'On request?'

'No, not exactly.' Georgia pulled on her gloves. 'She used to knit everything for her children – she had seven and decked them out in identical jumpers, hats, scarves, you know. Then, when they grew up and married, she continued the tradition with the grandchildren . . .'

'Who were less than impressed?'

'Exactly. Poor Jessie. They wanted distressed denim and studded leather. So I said what a shame and the jumpers were lovely – and Jessie started knitting them for me instead.'

'And you were too nice to refuse?' Rory was shrugging into the leather jacket.

'Well, a bit – but I loved them anyway. I like bright colours.'

'I've noticed.'

'Georgia's house is like a child's paintbox.' Alan hiccuped gently. 'Isn't it?'

As if suddenly remembering that Alan was there, Rory smiled at him. 'Well, I mustn't keep you. I hope the rehearsal goes well.'

'Thanks.' Alan was almost cross-eyed. He staggered to his feet, clutching the table which rocked alarmingly. 'Oh do come with us. I could do with some moral support.'

He could do with *any* support, Georgia thought. He seemed to be having difficulty in sorting out his feet.

'Have you got far to go?' Rory asked.

'Just across the road. Masonic Hall.' Alan beamed. 'Come on – oops . . .'

Rory caught him as he pitched forward. 'Maybe I ought to see you safely inside.'

'Yeah.' Alan breathed clove fumes in Rory's direction. 'You're a pal. I'm not usually like this – it must be stage-fright.'

Jesus, thought Georgia, as she grabbed the other arm of Alan's puffa and helped to manoeuvre him through the public bar's obstacle course, Gran is going to love this.

*

48

Luckily the two-minute blast of ice-cold air seemed to sober Alan considerably, and by the time they pushed into the tropical fug of the Masonic Hall, he was walking unaided.

The Poges Players were either scuttling about self-importantly on the dimly-lit stage, or lounging inelegantly on the tip-up chairs.

'He seems to be fine now.' Rory watched Alan striding towards the lounging groups. 'I'll see you tomorrow evening when I pick up my tacho, maybe.'

'Probably.' Georgia wanted him to stay. 'We always man the office until everyone is safely on their way. And thanks for your help with Alan.'

'Don't mention it.' Rory looked at the Poges Players with amusement. 'Have a lovely evening. Good night.'

'Darlings!' Cecilia, dressed in sinuous bottle-green bouclé, came towards them. 'How lovely to see you! Mr Faulkner,' she held out her hand, 'I'm delighted that my granddaughter managed to persuade you to join us this evening. And, of course, delighted to welcome you, albeit belatedly, to Diadem.'

Rory took the proffered hand as Georgia was about to launch into explanations.

'It's a pleasure to meet you, too.' He looked straight into Cecilia's eyes. 'I've heard so much about you.'

'If it's from Georgia it's probably untrue.' Cecilia flirted wildly. 'Still, now you're here, please come and meet the others.'

'He's not staying,' Georgia said. 'He's –'

But Cecilia had linked her arm firmly through Rory's and was leading him towards the group that contained the Brimstones and other committee members. Her voice echoed around the Masonic Hall's gilded cherubs. 'Now, Rory, tell me. Are you married?'

Georgia closed her eyes.

'No, I'm not,' she heard him say.

'Not gay, are you?'

Georgia wanted to die. Rory laughed.

'No, why? Do you have some prejudice against homosexuals?'

'Of course not,' Cecilia said. 'I just wanted to know. Although in your case it would have been such a terrible waste. So, why aren't you married? Not found the right girl yet?'

'Something like that. Is that a proposal?'

For once Cecilia was silenced. Georgia shook her head in sheer admiration.

'Lamb to the slaughter.' Marie giggled beside Georgia. 'Mind you, I wouldn't mind inviting him for breakfast.'

Nor would I, Georgia thought. She grinned at Marie. 'Oh, I think Rory will be able to take care of himself. I reckon Gran has met her match there. So, how did the meeting go? Is Alan Woodbury to be the new romantic lead?'

'Yeah, sod it.' Marie sighed. 'You'd think with Barney stuck in France the least they could have done was give me some real tasty fella to get me teeth into. We're going to have a run-through in a sec. Are you staying?'

'I'll have to. Alan's driving me home.'

As the lights dimmed, Georgia found a chair in a discreet corner, well away from Beth Brimstone and the other committee members. If Beth saw her she knew she'd be roped in for the teas. Cecilia looked like a bright, darting bird, Georgia thought, as she watched her grandmother move gracefully amongst the crowd, pausing to place a hand on an arm here, or give a twinkling smile there. Beth Brimstone, by contrast, was solid and po-faced, her straight, cropped hair only emphasising her blunt features. Like Cecilia she was wearing a jersey dress and high-heeled shoes; unlike Cecilia, Beth had chosen maroon which did nothing for her muddy complexion, and the almost-cashmere clung unflatteringly to her robust figure. It was no wonder that Spence was so smitten with Cecilia.

The Poges Players gathered on the stage as Beth and Cecilia

furnished everyone with fresh scripts. Georgia was concerned to notice that Alan seemed to have resumed his swaying. She hoped that it was simply nerves and not a resurgence of the Winter Warmer.

'May I join you?' Rory dropped into the chair beside her. 'I've been instructed to stay.'

'I'm so sorry. About Gran.' She was glad he couldn't see her face properly in the gloom. 'She's very outspoken.'

'She's adorable.' Rory sounded as though he was describing a Persian kitten. 'Everyone seems to love her.'

'They do. They probably have,' Georgia muttered disloyally. 'She's so embarrassing sometimes.'

'I think you're all great.' Rory turned his faint-making smile towards her. 'I consider myself lucky to have been accepted so readily. Especially by such a close-knit community. It isn't always easy.'

'Have you always travelled? Always been on the road?'

'More or less. Ever since –'

'Excuse me!' Beth Brimstone clapped her hands and glared towards them. 'Less chattering at the back there, please!'

Georgia and Rory sat with shaking shoulders as the play wobbled into its run-through. *Inherit My Heart* had been written by Janey Hutchinson from neighbouring Tiptoe, and Cecilia had enthused wildly over the script.

'It's got some real raunch in it, Georgia. Almost like one of those Black Lace efforts. Super stuff.'

Georgia settled back in her chair and felt a pang of pity for Marie.

'So,' Rory whispered, casting a careful eye in Beth's direction, 'I gather this isn't your hobby any more than knitting. What do you do in your spare time?'

For a fleeting moment Georgia thought he might be going to ask her out. 'Actually, I love horse-racing. Being so close to Milton St John and Lambourn everyone round here gets sucked in.'

51

'I can well believe it. The night I spent in Milton St John convinced me that I'd strolled into *Gulliver's Travels* and got the Lilliputians and Houyhnhnms rolled into one. They were all either midgets or neighing.'

Georgia laughed. 'I take it you're not a fan, then?'

'I've never been to a race meeting in my life. Maybe,' he looked at her, 'maybe you could introduce me . . .'

Georgia held her breath. Tread carefully, he's only passing through. This is the last thing you need. 'I'd love to. I've got a horse in training in Milton St John. We – er – we could go and see him work if you like.'

'Great. That's even better. I'd have a foot in the door from the professional side.' Rory smiled. 'Isn't it very expensive, though? Owning a racehorse?'

'Drew Fitzgerald – my trainer – is an angel over fees. And I bought Tumbling Bay for twenty-five pounds.'

'Christ! Even I know that that doesn't usually buy a hoof! How come?'

'He was in a field off the M40. I used to pass him every day and he worried me. He always looked so thin and sad and hungry and cold. So one day I stopped and asked some travellers if he was theirs. He wasn't, but they'd been feeding him. They reckoned he'd been abandoned – so I gave them the money and loaded him into the lorry.'

'You stole him?'

'Rescued,' Georgia said firmly. 'I took him to Drew because his girlfriend Maddy is a chum of mine . . . and he's come on in leaps and bounds. Literally. We're hoping to jump him next month.'

'And Tumbling Bay? Is that because he's brown and falls over?'

'No!' Georgia laughed again, immediately clapping her hand to her mouth and shrinking beneath Beth's glare. 'It's the name of an old swimming pool in Oxford. Gran told me all about it. It was a natural place formed by the Thames, all overhung with willows and fronded with reeds. Of course, it's been gone for ages now that everything has to be hygienic and safe. I just thought it sounded beautiful.'

'It does,' Rory assured her. 'I can't wait to meet its namesake.'

A howl from the stage, a mass intake of breath from the audience, and a screech from Beth Brimstone rudely shattered Georgia's brief euphoria.

'That isn't in the script, Marie Davis!' Beth rustled through her pages. 'This is a scene of love and tenderness! We don't have any physical violence until Act Three!'

Marie and Alan were facing each other beneath the spotlights. Alan was clutching his cheek. Marie, quivering with fury, swung round and glared at Beth. 'Maybe we don't. But he didn't stick to the script, neither! I never had a moment's worry with Jed. Jed was a real gent – even in the clinches – but him . . .' She withered the already shrinking Alan with a blowtorch look of disdain. 'He was trying to get his hands into me bra!'

CHAPTER 6

'It was an accident!' a sweating Alan protested as he was led from the stage between Beth and Cecilia. 'I sort of stumbled and lunged out for something to hang on to.' He turned his head and smiled sheepishly at Marie. 'I'm really most awfully sorry.'

'What the hell had he been drinking?' Cecilia snapped.

'Only some non-alcoholic concoction of Mikey Somerville's.' Georgia bit her lip. 'But he said he was nervous. It was more likely stage-fright.'

'More likely lust,' Beth hissed, her hand pinching Alan's underarm as she struggled to keep up with Cecilia. 'Fuelled by drink.'

Spencer Brimstone, looking very debonair, appeared at his wife's elbow and removed Alan from her ministrations.

Spencer's all-year tan owed everything to the Body Tonic's sunbed; his hair was entirely the work of Grecian 2000; his smile, Georgia knew, was the sole work of her grandmother. He jerked his head towards his wife. 'I'm sure Georgia is right. It's a very tense time, one's debut in a major role. Alan merely succumbed to the excitement. You get back on the stage, Beth, and calm Marie. Mrs Harkness and I will take Alan home.'

Mrs Harkness my foot! Georgia had read the faxes that Spencer had sent to her grandmother. They all began 'Darling Dinky Doo.'

Beth was reluctant to let go. She had a stranglehold on Alan's cravat, causing him to gasp for air. 'Georgia brought him – she can take him back.'

She made Alan Woodbury sound as if he was a party frock purchased in the rash heat of a sale and found to be a poor fit.

Cecilia almost snarled at Beth's one-upmanship. 'Can you manage him on your own, darling?'

'Of course,' Georgia said. 'And I'm sure he can stand unaided.'

Suddenly freed from any support, Alan wobbled wildly. Rory stepped forward with a steadying arm. 'I'll drive him home. Georgia can show me the way.'

Cecilia nodded. 'That sounds eminently suitable.' She turned to Spencer. 'What say, if Georgia takes Alan home, we ask Elizabeth to do a run-through of Scene Two with the others – Alan and Marie don't take part in that, do they? We wouldn't want this little glitch to spoil the whole evening, would we? Anyway, there are some slight alterations to the finale that I'd like to discuss with you.'

Spencer smoothed back his hair. 'Which? Ah, yes . . . Perhaps we should discuss them in the anteroom.' He smiled winningly at his wife. 'Much quieter there, my dear. We wouldn't want to disturb you.'

'Nothing Mrs Harkness does disturbs me.' Beth narrowed her eyes at Cecilia. 'And please don't try to take command. I'm producing this show.'

Rory seemed about to say something, caught Georgia's eye, and turned his attention to Alan instead. His shoulders appeared to be quivering.

Cecilia straightened her shoulders and tossed the blonde bob. Only Georgia was aware of the fury boiling just beneath the surface of the elegant façade. 'Good Lord, Elizabeth. It's Am Dram, my dear. Not a meeting of the European Court of Human Rights. Surely we can each have some input?'

'Not without my say-so.' Beth's face almost matched her dress. 'And don't try to pull rank with me, Cecilia.'

'Move!' Georgia told Rory, keeping her voice low. 'I don't

want to get caught up in this. Once they start scrapping for the high ground we'll all get dragged in.'

Obediently, Rory led Alan towards the doors.

'He didn't have one of them Winter Warmers, did he?' Bert Nicholson, an Am Dram stalwart, queried as Georgia passed. 'They'm pretty lethal. Old Nathaniel Batty had to have his stomach pumped after he'd had half a one. An' Nathaniel Batty could drink for England.'

'He had two.' Georgia paused in following Alan and Rory out of the hall. 'But they only had cloves and things in. Like mulled wine.'

'Mulled wine my Aunt Fanny!' Bert roared. 'Mikey Somerville wouldn't know mulled wine if it introduced itself personal! Them Winter Warmers is triple rum and triple brandy and a dollop of every liqueur on the top shelf. He adds the cloves and whatnot to hide the burn.'

Alan leaned against his car while Rory unlocked the door.

'So sorry . . . Can't think what got into me.'

'Half the contents of the Seven Stars.' Georgia's teeth chattered. The frosty stillness was being swirled around them by a vicious north-east wind. 'Here – get into the back. You can stretch out a bit better. Do you feel sick?'

'No.' Alan clambered into the back seat and curled up like a child. 'Just numb.'

'What about your car?' Georgia turned to Rory as they pulled away from the Seven Stars. 'I can drive him, if you like.'

'I walked.' Rory's mouth was twitching. He suddenly laughed. 'Oh, shit. Sorry, I know it isn't really funny – but . . .'

Georgia giggled. 'I wish we'd had a camcorder. Marie's face was a picture! Oh – take the next left – and I thought Gran and Beth were going to turn poor Alan into a wishbone.'

'How long has that power struggle been going on? Do I turn here?'

'Yes, just here – and then second right – oh, Beth and Gran have been daggers drawn for as long as I can remember. It's real pistols-at-dawn stuff between them.' She looked over her shoulder. Alan's eyes were closed. 'I try not to get involved. I do think the Poges Players should keep Alan's ad libbing in the script. They tend to take themselves very seriously. Oh, just here on the left. The house with the hedge.'

Rory slowed the car. Alan was singing quietly to himself in the back seat.

'Shall I just drop him off and make sure you get him inside? Or do you want me to run you home?'

'What on earth made you think I'd want to stay?'

'Nothing.' Rory shrugged. 'I thought – oh, well, never mind. Let's get him indoors then.'

They hauled the now giggling Alan unceremoniously from the back seat and Georgia went through his pockets to find his front-door key. Rory stared at the sky.

Sod it, Georgia thought miserably; now he thinks I'm some hard-hearted bitch who won't even stay and make sure her boyfriend survives the night. She found the keys and, leaning Alan between Rory and the porch, unlocked the door.

There was no way that she could explain her relationship with Alan without making it sound like an invitation to Rory. Any sort of denial at this stage was going to sound extremely contrived. She'd just have to work it in later.

'Do you want to go to bed?' she asked Alan. 'Or shall we make you some black coffee?'

'Bed.' Alan's eyes rolled upwards. 'Bed, Georgia. You know where it is.'

Christ!

Rory was tugging off Alan's puffa and loosening his cravat. She knew where Alan's bedroom was because she'd been there on several occasions with Jessie Hopkins to collect jumble for the Upton Poges Bring and Buy. Alan had left his keys at the post office and his contributions in bin-liners in his bedroom.

'If you're sure you can manage, I'll leave you to it.' Rory had straightened up.

'Of course, if you have to go . . .' Georgia could have happily stamped on Alan's throat.

'I do. It's only a short walk to my bedsit. I'll see you at work tomorrow.'

'Yes. OK. Thanks for everything. For your help.'

Quietly Rory let himself out of the front door. Georgia glared at Alan. 'I'm not lugging *you* upstairs. You'll have to stay there. I'll fetch the duvet.'

By the time she'd returned, Alan was fast asleep, cuddling a cushion and smiling beatifically. She had a sudden vision of him choking on his own vomit and dying alone. Maybe she should stay. Then she remembered Rory's abrupt departure and said angrily, 'Oh, to hell with you, Alan Woodbury! This is one battle you can cope with alone.'

Making sure that his head was firmly wedged on one side by the remaining cushions, and draping a towel across the arm of the sofa, she tucked the duvet round him, switched off the lights and stepped outside.

The wind sliced straight through the sweater. She wanted to cry. She had no transport.

It meant either an icy, dark walk back to the Masonic Hall, or an even longer walk back to Diadem. She glanced longingly at Alan's car, but his car keys were with his door keys where she'd left them, safely on the coffee table. Locked in with someone who would probably remain comatose for hours.

'Bugger!' She growled at the penetrating blackness of the sky. 'Damn and bugger!'

She wished she'd taken more notice of those television programmes on joy-riding. At least she might have learned about hot-wiring. Tucking her gloved hands under her arm-pits, she started to trudge back towards the town.

Within minutes her nose was running. Her hair was whipped by the wind against her frozen cheeks. Upton Poges, sensibly tucked up for the night, was deserted. She should have phoned for a taxi from Alan's – or at least rung the Masonic Hall; someone would have collected her, surely? She had never been afraid of the dark, never really given much thought to walking alone at night, but now every tabloid headline loomed in horrific reality.

Who would know? Alan was out cold. Rory had gone home. Cecilia wouldn't even bother to check her part of the house. Georgia stifled a sob, already reading her own obitu-ary. They'd be so sorry.

A car screeched to a halt beside her, making her jump.

'Get in,' Rory said tersely from the open window, his breath dancing in smoky plumes. 'Quickly.'

She did, and glared at him. 'Don't bark orders at me. After all, you were the one who swanned off and left me stranded.'

'Hardly stranded.' Rory changed gear with such ferocity that she hoped it wasn't the way he drove the lorries. They'd all need replacement gearboxes. 'It did occur to me when I got home that if you meant what you said and weren't staying the night, then you didn't have any transport. I was in two minds whether to come back and check. After all, he's your boyfriend and –'

'He is not!' Georgia wiped her nose on a rather crumpled tissue. 'I told you I wasn't staying. Alan and I aren't – aren't –'

'It's none of my business.' They slowed at traffic lights. 'I merely came back because I need the job. I thought that if you were hard-hearted enough to abandon him and walked home and something happened to you, I'd hardly be the most popular person on Diadem's books.'

'Thanks for nothing, then,' Georgia muttered mutinously. 'Just drop me off at the Masonic Hall. I'll go home with Gran

– and your job will be quite safe, Mr Faulkner. It's nice to know where your priorities lie. And don't think I'm not grateful. I am, but – hey, you've passed the turning . . .'

'I know.' Rory was staring straight ahead. 'I like to finish a job once I've started it. I'll take you home.'

They sat in silence. Georgia was beginning to thaw. Her anger wasn't. Arrogant pig. Feathering his own nest. Looking after number one. Eye to the main chance. The clichés tumbled over themselves. She simmered. At least he'd had the foresight to come back for her – oh, no, she reminded herself quickly. Not for her. For his job. Bastard.

They roared into Diadem's yard. Georgia was practically out of the car before it stopped. She wanted to get indoors, punch a few cushions and howl abuse at the walls.

'Thanks,' she mumbled. 'It was very kind of you.'

She slammed the door shut and slithered across the icy yard towards the house. Her fingers fumbled with the key, so she yanked off her woolly gloves and, holding them in her teeth, tried again.

'Let me.' Rory took the key from her and opened the door.

'Thanks,' she mumbled again, even less distinctly because of the mouthful of glove. She switched on the light and was immediately enveloped by cats. 'And please close the door. I don't want them getting out.'

He did. Behind him. And stood looking round in some amazement. 'Christ!'

'I like pink,' Georgia said defensively. 'And green.'

The cats, sensing an ally, were squirming round Rory's feet. He scooped up a couple and sat down on the bottom stair. Georgia allowed herself a look of sheer self-indulgence. It was a rare occurrence, having a devastatingly handsome man sitting on her stairs – even if he was angry. 'Well, don't let me keep you. And please charge the petrol to Diadem. Get Trish to take it out of petty cash for you.'

'No.' He deposited the cats on the floor and stood up. 'I

won't. At least I can do something for other people without having a price put on it.'

'What?' Georgia had been heading towards the kitchen and stopped dead in her tracks. 'What exactly do you mean by that?'

'Forget it.' Rory moved towards the front door.

'No, I won't. Do you think that – well, that I – um – with Alan Woodbury because he's Kon Tiki's distribution manager? That I – I *prostitute* myself to gain business for Diadem? Is that what you're hinting at?'

Rory shrugged. 'You've got to admit, it looks a bit iffy. You're with him in the pub. He knows all about your place, you know about his. You strenuously deny that he's your boyfriend – so what else can it be?'

'He's my *friend*. Not boyfriend, lover, partner – or anything else. We're friends. It has nothing whatever to do with business. And nothing to do with you, either! Yes, maybe it did seem callous to leave him like that tonight – but I made sure he was OK and I needed to get home. I have a company to run – something you obviously know nothing about – you being –'

She stopped, appalled, and wished the sky would fall in.

'An employee?' Rory's eyebrows had disappeared into his hair. His voice was quiet. 'Oh, forgive me. For a moment I'd forgotten my place. I'll just bow and scrape and tug my forelock, shall I? Hell, Georgia. I always thought I was a good judge of character – but I was wrong about you.'

Georgia wanted to scream. 'How *dare* you make assumptions! I think you'd better leave, don't you?'

'I couldn't agree more. And will I still have a job tomorrow?'

'Christ! Is that all that matters to you?'

'Actually, yes.' He paused with his hand on the door-latch. 'You're a privileged lady, Georgia Drummond. You should try walking in someone else's shoes for a change.'

61

Georgia swallowed back furious tears. 'You know nothing about me! You don't know what I feel! You don't know what I'm like! You've just formed a completely wrong opinion on the strength of one bizarre episode! At least I don't hang people without hearing the evidence first! Yes, you'll still have your bloody job – at least until you foul up on the professional side. Personally, I think we'd just better avoid each other, don't you?'

'Suits me.' Rory's face was expressionless. 'Good night, Georgia.'

Georgia rushed back into the kitchen and grabbed a haphazard handful of paper towels. If only she'd told Rory the truth about Alan at the Seven Stars. So what, if he'd thought she was angling to be asked out? It'd be better than this, wouldn't it? She heard the click of the door and buried her face in her hands.

'Georgia.' Rory stood in the doorway. 'There is one more thing before I go. Something I don't think we'll have the opportunity to discuss in the future. Not after tonight.'

Georgia rubbed her eyes. 'Wh – what do you want?'

Rory grabbed her and pulled her tightly against him. The kiss took her completely by surprise. Georgia tried to resist, twisting herself away from him. Rory merely held her tighter and continued kissing her with wicked expertise. Suddenly she was kissing him back with all the passion the row had engendered.

He released her quickly, pushing her back against the door jamb. 'If you fire me tomorrow it'll have been worth it. Good night.'

And he slammed out of the front door.

CHAPTER 7

A week later, Georgia shoved the last empty cage into the back of the Scania, secured the ties, and wearily wiped her dieselly gloves across her face. She loathed multi-drops. Especially these bulk food deliveries to institutions. The cages were invariably loaded wrongly, with the result that the Wild Poppies Rest Home was delighted with fourteen dozen portions of smoked salmon au poivre, while the Bear and Biscuit was wondering what the hell to do with half a ton of Horlicks.

Georgia swung herself out of the back of the Scania's trailer into the bitterly cold north-east wind, dropped to the ground, and tugged at the locking pins on the tailgate. As usual, this move was greeted with wolf-whistles and good-natured jeering. Normally, Georgia would have grinned and returned the compliment. Today she just glared. 'Get a life. You've seen it all before.'

The loaders looked at each other in surprise. They had long ago stopped asking her if she needed any help – they'd soon realised that she could organise her own fork-lift loading and unloading, and was as adept at handling the cages as any of them – but she'd always joked with them.

'What's up, Georgia? Lost yer Yorkie?'

'PMT, luv? Or is it HGV in your case?'

Georgia yanked open the cab door and tried to swing up into the Scania. She'd done it thousands of times before. But today her Doc Martens slithered on the greasy step and she was left dangling in mid-air. She closed her eyes and swung again towards the cab. If she let go now she'd land in a heap in the yard.

Her feet slipping, she launched herself upwards at the steering wheel and clung on. Bruising her knees against the door-catch, she tumbled on to the cab floor.

The hoots of laughter from her audience swelled in her ears. Dragging herself upright, she crashed the door shut and leaned out of the window. 'If you'd been gentlemen, you might have helped me.'

'If you'd been a lady, we definitely would,' Wilf, the oldest loader in the Cannock yard, said tartly. 'But you've told us enough times you're one of the boys.'

Georgia set the gears, checked the brakes and turned the key. 'God, Wilf, I'm sorry. I'm just on a bit of a downer.'

'Ah,' Wilf yelled above the steady pulse of the diesel engine, 'the M6 can have that effect. Mind, it don't usually get to you like this.'

'Apologise to them for me,' Georgia motioned her head miserably towards the loaders who had been her friends for ages, as she started to pull out of the yard. 'Please, Wilf.'

Wilf shook his head, still shouting. 'Nope. You can do that yourself, next time. An' I'll get them to lay off the lady-trucker jokes – some of the younger ones still find it a bit of a laff.'

'I wish I did . . .'

They were still staring after her as she pulled out of the loading bay and headed for the motorway. Georgia caught sight of her face in the wing mirror and groaned. She'd got diesel smears across her cheeks and her bleary eyes were dark-shadowed. She looked like an extra in a Catherine Cookson adaptation.

Sod Rory Faulkner, she thought angrily, as she headed for the M6 and home.

Irritatingly, Diadem's office was functioning in party mode. Trish and Marie were wearing matching Cheshire cat grins and Cecilia looked stunning in what appeared to be a new

Jacques Vert suit. Even more surprising, Ken Poldruan, who was usually employed as the spare driver when he wasn't buried in the innards of a lorry in the workshop, was checking tachographs over a Moët-et-Chandon-filled ice bucket.

Feeling like a death's head, Georgia frowned. 'What the hell is going on? Have we won the lottery or something?'

'Miles and miles better than that, darling,' Cecilia purred. 'Jed is coming out of hospital this afternoon, Barney has just telephoned from Dover, and *we* are just about to pull off the biggest coup in Diadem's history.'

'We are?' Georgia sat at her desk and eased off her Doc Martens. 'Have I been caught in a time-warp, then? It is still Wednesday, not quite eleven o'clock? I *have* only been gone for seven hours?'

They all laughed uproariously. Georgia found their good humour extremely irksome. Trish and Marie were understandably delighted at their husbands' return but – pleased as she was for them – Georgia failed to share their glee. Since the débâcle on Am Dram night, she and Rory had avoided each other. No one else would know whether by accident or design, but Georgia had worked out the rotas carefully so that they shouldn't meet. Now, with Barney back on this side of the Channel, one of the temps would have to go – and she was sure Rory would ask the Brimstones for another job.

'Lennards.' Cecilia was collecting up her handbag and car keys and avoiding Ken's hands. 'They telephoned an hour ago. They've got a major new contract in the North-East – something to do with the Japanese car industry – and they're looking for a permanent carrier. Tom Lennard has just told me that it's between us and Ionio – well, Vivienda as they are now.' She licked her lips. 'Tom is taking me out to lunch to discuss things.'

'Oh.' Georgia smiled for the first time. 'And you and Tom were quite friendly at one time, weren't you?'

'Exactly, darling.' Cecilia fluttered a please-forgive-me glance towards Ken. 'I'd like to see those leeches from bloody Vivienda outplay me on this hand.'

'That's why we've got the champagne.' Ken, who was still beaming over his temporary elevation to desk-duty, tapped the ice bucket with a swarthy finger. 'We should be celebrating this afternoon, unless –' he patted Cecilia's apple-green rump, 'your gran has lost some of her powers. Which, of course, she hasn't.'

Cecilia dropped a kiss on the top of his gangster's head. 'Kenny, you're a sweetheart. I only hope I don't let you down. So, Georgia, if you can be back in the office this afternoon – complete with party hat and the semblance of a smile – I'd be very grateful.'

Georgia looked quickly at her grandmother. She had underestimated Cecilia's perspicacity.

Trish grinned hugely. 'I've got the afternoon off to collect Jed – and Marie is going to drag Barney straight into bed and wipe away the memories of all those Fi-Fis and Estelles and Nicoles – so you'll have to celebrate for us.'

'I'll only get Barney upstairs if me mum'll have the kids,' Marie said tartly. 'So I'd better be off and sort it out.' She looked across the office at Georgia. 'And you can put me back on the Kon Tiki run if you want. Old Alan the Groper won't try nothing now my Barney's back.'

The day after the rehearsal, Alan Woodbury had sent Marie an entire florist's shop of an apology. She had still not been completely won over, but at least the peace negotiations were under way. It augured well for a reasonably amicable performance of *Inherit My Heart*.

As soon as Cecilia had gone, Ken dropped a pile of tachographs on Georgia's desk. 'I've been through them – but no doubt you'll want to make sure that everything's in order. I'll go and check the Scanny. No problems?'

'None.' Georgia frowned. At least, not with the Scania.

The only problems she'd encountered were certainly not mechanical. 'And it's good news about Lennards, isn't it?'

'If it comes off, it could be the best news we've had for months.' Ken was whistling cheerfully as he closed the door behind him.

Left alone in the office, Georgia finished her paperwork, cast an expert eye over the next day's runs, and gazed at the heavy sky. The snow, which had been threatening across the Downs for weeks, had somehow missed Berkshire. She'd driven through piles of slush in the Midlands, and parts of the West Country were cut off, but as yet, it hadn't caused too much disruption.

Rory should be out all day, driving in central London, a job which he seemed to enjoy, and as everyone else hated it, she'd had no complaints. His kiss had disturbed her greatly. It had kept her awake at nights. Remembering. However much she told herself that it was just skin on skin – she'd dismissed flesh on flesh as straying too near the truth – her reaction had been volcanic. How strange that some men could fumble and paw for ages and not raise the merest twinge of excitement, while others . . .

Georgia pushed the chair away from the desk and stood up quickly. That was a dangerous road for her mind to travel. Any hopes she'd had in that direction were now strictly off-limits.

'Ken!' She leaned from the window and yelled across the yard. 'Can you listen for the phone, please? I'm going to be out for an hour.'

'Sure.' Ken emerged from the guts of the Scania and waved an oily hand. Georgia hoped he'd wash it before he came anywhere near Cecilia's Jacques Vert. 'No sweat.'

Milton St John was grey and windswept as Georgia drove the MG across Peapods' cobbles. The few villagers she'd passed had been muffled like Siberian peasants against the cutting wind.

She parked beneath the clock arch, and smiled as Drew Fitzgerald, Tumbling Bay's trainer, hurried across the yard to meet her.

'Sorry I'm late. I got held up on the motorway this morning. Have I missed the session?'

'Almost.' Drew blew on his hands. 'We didn't expect you at all, to be honest. Not with this weather. I hope the snow keeps off for a bit longer. We're right on course so far. Charlie's just putting him over the hurdles in the paddock – but he went great on the gallops this morning. I reckon we've got an all-time bargain on our hands.'

Georgia grinned as they walked towards the brushwood jumps. 'Gypsy horses are usually pretty good, aren't they? I'm just glad he's happy.'

'All my horses are happy.' Drew leaned against the fence. 'But Tumbling Bay is ecstatic. Maddy will be sorry to have missed you. She's at work.'

'Still?' Georgia watched the huge dark-brown horse, gleaming with health, thundering across the fences with ease. 'I thought she'd give it up now.'

'Not a chance.' Drew didn't take his eyes from the horse and rider. 'She'll still be working when she goes into labour. I've told her she must be distantly related to some African tribe – the ones who squat down and give birth in the fields and then carry on. Maddy will have the baby surrounded by Mr Sheen and J-cloths and then get up and polish the floor.'

'And will you be getting married? Oh! That was good, wasn't it? He jumps like a stag! Bless him.'

'We'll get married as soon as my divorce comes through.' Drew's eyes were laughing. 'The baby was a bit of a mistake, but a lovely one. Oh, yes! That was brilliant.'

They watched the horse for another five minutes. Georgia fleetingly recalled that she had invited Rory to come with her today. Of course, that was before. She sighed. It was a pity that Maddy wasn't at home. Maddy would have understood.

The schooling session over, Charlie Somerset and Tumbling Bay, both sweating, both impossibly handsome and Charlie knowing it, made their way towards the fence.

'You'll be leading him into the winner's enclosure at Aintree yet.' Charlie grinned crookedly at her. 'He's a natural.'

Georgia basked in the adulation on Tumbling Bay's behalf and hugged him before feeding him a handful of Polos.

'Jesus. I wish I got that treatment.' Charlie had dropped to the ground and removed his crash hat. 'After all, I did half of the work.'

'I'm sure I've got another packet of Polos somewhere.' Georgia giggled, feeling, as always, a slight shiver of lust. Charlie Somerset simply oozed sexuality with his taut, athletic body and his hair the colour of a wet fox. She was dismayed to discover that this pleasurable pang was absolutely nothing compared to the tidal wave of desire Rory had created.

Charlie ruffled her hair, kissed her cheek, and then got down to the far more important task of leading Tumbling Bay out of the wind and back to his box.

'We're entering him at Windsor at the end of next month,' Drew said as they walked back towards Peapods. 'If that's OK with you.'

'Oh! Yes! Brilliant!' Georgia almost clapped her hands. 'Goodness! Me in the paddock with all those people in top hats and furs and –'

Drew put his hand on her arm before she could actually pirouette. 'Georgia. This is a February afternoon at Windsor we're talking about. Either the first or last race on the card. It'll be tweed caps, padded jackets and boots. However, I want to see how he does, because I thought I'd put him in at Newbury at the end of March. That will place him against some of the big-timers, of course, and be a real test. Are you agreeable?'

'Absolutely.' Georgia nodded. 'Unless he falls at Windsor or doesn't like jumping. I don't want him to be forced to do anything he doesn't want to do.'

'No one could force Tumbling Bay into jumping.' Drew grinned. 'Our difficulty is stopping him. Oh, I do wish all my owners were as amenable as you. It would make life so much easier. Are you coming in for coffee?'

Georgia glanced at her watch and shook her head. 'I'd love to but I'm going to have to get back. I'm supposed to be visiting customers and Gran wants me to man the office later. Give my love to Maddy.'

'You'll have to come over for dinner.' Drew held the car door open for her. 'Give Maddy a ring and fix something up. You could bring your current man – or, of course,' his eyes laughed down at her, 'I could invite Charlie.'

Georgia urged the MG into growling life. 'I thought Charlie's speciality was bed and breakfast – not dinner.'

As she pulled on the brake in Diadem's yard, the first snowflakes started to fall. Whipped by the wind, they danced and swirled like bonfire ashes against the yellow sky. Georgia shivered and scuttled inside.

Ken stood up from her desk and stretched. 'It looks like we're in for a bit of a blizzard. Thames Valley Radio just said the gritters are out on the M4. Would you like some coffee?'

'Please.' Georgia slid into her chair. It was lovely and warm. Ken must have been there ever since she left. 'Thanks for holding the fort. Any messages?'

'I dealt with them all except one. It was personal.' Ken poured two beakers of coffee from the percolator. 'I left it on your pad.'

She looked at Ken's sloping writing with a dart of disappointment. 'Who's Samantha? I don't know any Samanthas. Did she say where she was calling from?'

'No.' Ken put the coffee on her desk and Georgia wrapped her cold hands round it. 'That's all she said. "Thanks for the invite. I'm on my way. Samantha."'

'It must be something to do with Gran.' Georgia shrugged. 'Or maybe she got the wrong number. No doubt we'll soon know.'

She soon did.

Half an hour later, when the snow was tumbling in fat goosefeather flakes, making it impossible to see the other side of the yard, a taxi groaned to a halt outside the office. Georgia peered through the window. It was probably Cecilia. She'd most likely had one too many glasses of champagne at lunch and decided to leave the car at the restaurant. Georgia was already reaching into the petty cash tin for the fare. Cecilia, like royalty, never carried any money.

The door blew open bringing a billow of snow gusting on to the carpet, rapidly followed by a battered suitcase, three carrier bags and a collapsible pram.

'Bugger me!' Sabrina Yates swept her yellow-and-black-streaked fringe from her eyes. 'It's enough to freeze your bollocks off!' She grinned at Georgia. 'Always assuming we had bollocks, that is. Maybe we should be thankful we're women on days like this, eh?'

Stunned into silence, Georgia watched open-mouthed as Sabrina deftly assembled the pram with a flick of the wrist and two kicks, and gently laid the sleeping Oscar in amongst the covers.

'Sorry it took us so long. I had a few things to sort out with the Social – and they don't shift themselves. I thought they'd never work out me giro – and then there were forms to fill in, and questions – so many bloody questions, you wouldn't believe. I thought you'd forget all about us. Still, we're here now.' Sabrina was shedding a donkey jacket and various scarves. 'It was really ace of you to invite us. I nearly cried

71

when I got your note, honest. I've kept it in my purse – and every time I felt down, I read it. I told Oscar that before long we'd have a proper home – and now,' she beamed happily at Georgia, 'we have.'

'Er –' Georgia swallowed, completely at a loss to know what to say. 'Um – have you paid the taxi driver?'

It must have cost a fortune from Oxford.

'Nah. The Social did that. They were chuffed to bits to see the back of me, I reckon. Well, it's one more off their books, innit?' She looked around the office admiringly. 'This is really smart. And all them lorries. Do you reckon I could learn to drive one? I've driven a van before, so I s'pose it's not that much different.'

Georgia, playing for time, gave a weak smile. 'No, I suppose not. Um – would you like a cup of coffee?'

'Yeah. Great. Then if you just show me where we'll be living, I'll get out of your way.' She kicked one of the carrier bags. 'I've brought some food. Just basics – but enough to see us through for a bit. Oh – you really are kind.'

Georgia handed Sabrina the mug. 'Er – that note – could I just have a look at it?'

'Yeah, here . . .' Sabrina fished into a grubby patchwork shoulder-bag and produced a very crumpled Diadem card. 'But can I have it back?' She dropped her eyes. 'I'm not usually soft or nothing, but it's the first bit of kindness anyone's shown me in ages. Well – ever since I found out Oscar was on the way. I'll keep it for ever.'

Georgia read her own scribbled message with a nasty feeling of impending doom. She really should have phrased it more carefully.

Sabrina.
  I looked after Oscar at the JR last Saturday night. Remember me? You really can't go on living like that. I'm sure I can help you. The address is overleaf.
  Georgia Drummond.

She handed the card back to Sabrina. 'Look, just sit down for a moment. I've got a couple of things to do.'

Sliding across the yard, almost blinded by the snow, Georgia skidded into the workshop. Ken looked up from a back axle. 'Your gran back, then? Time for the old bubbly, is it?'

'No. Not exactly. Ken, I need your help. I've done something dreadful.'

Quickly, she explained the situation. Ken's eyes alternately widened and narrowed with each part.

'So,' she finished, 'what sort of state is that flat in over the barn? The one that we put those students in last summer? I know it's more or less fully furnished and got a kitchen and a bathroom, but is the heating on? Is it clean? Jesus, Ken – help.'

Ken nodded slowly. 'I reckon it's warm enough – the heating works off the office system – and we gave it a bit of a spruce-up at Christmas when your gran had a house full and they were all too pissed to drive home. It should do nicely for Samantha and the kid – but,' he looked worriedly at Georgia, 'what the hell are you going to tell your gran?'

'Christ knows.' Georgia was already slithering back towards the office. 'No doubt I'll think of something.'

By the time Cecilia, shaking snowflakes elegantly from her astrakhan coat, had returned, Sabrina and Oscar had been installed in their new home on the far side of the yard. Sabrina had burst into tears, wandering round the tiny rooms in a state of joyous disbelief. Georgia had cried with her.

'Congratulations are in order!' Cecilia beamed. 'Fetch the fizz, darling! We've done it! The first of many contracts snaffled from beneath Vivienda's greedy snouts! We start daily Tyneside runs for Lennards next Monday. It's worth absolutely oodles of money, darling! Tom Lennard was a complete angel.'

As they hugged each other, Ken winked above Cecilia's blonde head and Georgia blushed. Cecilia poured three flutes of champagne and they clinked glasses.

'I also took the liberty of popping into Brimstones' Agency to have a little word with Spencer. I've worked it out with Tom Lennard, and now we've got Barney back we could really let one of the temps go.'

Georgia's teeth clamped on the wafer-thin glass.

'So, I've arranged with Spencer that Adenoids should stay on until Jed is fully recovered.'

Georgia could feel the tears forming a painful lump in her throat. She gulped at the champagne. It hurt.

Cecilia walked to the window and stared out at the whitening yard before turning to them again with a smile. Georgia wanted to hit her.

'*And* I've agreed with Brimstones' that we should have someone permanent on this new contract. It's good economic sense because of course we do pay over the odds for agency drivers. Spencer was a complete poppet and extremely understanding, although of course bloody Elizabeth put up all manner of objections. So, I'm going to ask Rory Faulkner to become a full member of staff. Won't that be super?'

CHAPTER 8

It was the middle of the following week before Cecilia made her offer to Rory. A week in which most of the country was swept by blizzards and shivered in subzero temperatures. A week in which Britain's transport system almost ground to a halt, and Sabrina and Oscar came out of the closet – or, at least, the flat above the barn.

Cecilia, agitated by the disruption to the business, had taken the news fairly philosophically.

'I suppose I should consider myself lucky that you didn't bring them back with you that first night.' She'd smiled gently at Georgia. 'I rather expected you would. And you must think I'm extremely hard-hearted if you thought I'd tell them to leave. This place is yours as much as mine, and God knows, there were times in the past when Gordon and I would have killed for a warm bed and a roof over our heads. Of course they can stay.'

Georgia had hugged her grandmother and promised that Sabrina would become an asset to Diadem – she simply knew she would.

'Maybe.' Cecilia had crossed elegant black ski-panted legs. 'That remains to be seen. I must admit I'd been toying with the idea of introducing a sort of same-day local courier service. I'm sure that we can organise baby-sitting rotas in the office if Sabrina is out in the van. Still, that's all in the future. The only drawback I can see is the flat.'

Georgia had protested that the flat was used so rarely that it was surely better to have it occupied, wasn't it?

'Of course.' Cecilia had leaned forward. 'But I was going to offer it to Rory – along with the job. I really couldn't see him lodging in that bedsit on a long-term basis. However, as the situation has altered, I'll up his salary accordingly and give him the chance to find a place of his own.'

Georgia had rocked a bit at this. For a fleeting moment she imagined what it could have been like having Rory living just across the yard. She'd shaken her head. 'I don't somehow think Rory Faulkner is the type to take sweeteners. He wouldn't care if you threw in Buckingham Palace. He'll accept the job if he wants it – and refuse it if he doesn't.'

'And do you want him to take it?'

Georgia had surveyed her grandmother in silence.

'Only,' Cecilia went on, 'I thought I'd detected a bit of a chill between you.'

'There's a bit of chill between everybody at the moment. It's to do with the weather.' Georgia had forced the joke. 'And you'd have to be a super-sleuth to detect anything between Rory and me. We've hardly seen each other since . . . since . . . Well, hardly anything at all. And being honest, yes, I'd be delighted if he took the job. But somehow I don't think he will.'

They used the remainder of the white-cold days selling Diadem to potential customers in the face of the new opposition, and securing their position with their regulars. Cold-calling took on a whole new meaning as Georgia, practically living and freezing in the cream Laurèl suit and the brown pigskin shoes, became very adept at extolling the virtues of Diadem's family-run efficiency and local-based knowledge as opposed to the distant corporate strength of Vivienda. She was uncomfortably aware that several customers, who had obviously already been approached by Ionio, were rather sceptical.

'That's all well and good,' the rather podgy transport

manager of Bradstock's Paints wheezed over his desk, 'but I've heard things . . .'

'What sort of things?' It was Georgia's third appointment on this particular trading estate. It was the third time she'd heard this uncertainty. 'I'm sure if you checked with our prestige customers – Kon Tiki, Lennards, Mitchell and Gray, Jeromes – that they would tell you we operate efficiently and quickly. We deliver when we say we will and our prices are lower than any of the big hauliers.'

'I know all that. But I've heard,' the transport manager leaned forward and breathed nicotine fumes across the desk, 'that Diadem has been known to sail a little close to the wind.'

'What?' Georgia was shocked. 'What exactly is that supposed to mean?'

The corpulent face grew weaselly and evasive. 'I'd rather not say.'

'And I'd rather you did.'

He sighed. 'Look, I don't know one way or the other – but I've heard a whisper that Diadem has been known to deliver on time only because they fiddle their tachos or disengage their limiters . . . that sort of thing.'

Georgia, itching to slap the smug piggy-eyed face, counted to ten. 'Who from?'

'I've no idea.' The gaze shifted downwards. 'I mean, no one has told me direct. I've just heard things in the rest room, you know.'

Georgia knew. Chinese whispers had been known to kill small businesses. She stood up. 'Then I trust you won't be repeating them. Please don't make unsubstantiated remarks about Diadem in the future, unless you wish to have letters from the company's solicitors – and please stress to whoever is spreading these rumours that they are total untruths. Diadem is a law-abiding firm built on integrity. And we can prove it. Unlike some. Do I make myself clear?'

'Crystal.' The transport manager lit a cigarette and blew a plume of murk towards her. 'But there's no smoke without fire, is there? Look, leave your price list. I'll give it the once over. Can't say fairer than that, can I?'

Georgia left the price list, but even before she'd closed the transport manager's door, she knew Bradstock's Paints would never become a customer of Diadem.

Cecilia had spent the week setting up the new Lennards deal. It became a round of visits to solicitors and accountants, frantic telephone calls and verbose letters to be signed in triplicate. Georgia waited until the dots and crosses had been made on the small print, the ink on the signatures dried, and Tom Lennard and Cecilia had celebrated their allegiance again, before sharing her doubts.

Cecilia didn't seem particularly concerned. 'It happens, darling; you know that as well as I do. This isn't a particularly friendly business. Gordon always said street gangs were more matey than rival transport companies. We'll just have to watch and listen and if things start to get completely out of hand then we'll take proper steps – but I honestly don't think we've got a thing to worry about.'

Georgia hoped Cecilia was right.

Two days later, however, Vivienda was the last thing on Georgia's mind.

'It's stopped snowing!' Cecilia called up the stairs in what Georgia thought was the middle of the night. 'There's not much sign of a thaw yet, but Radio Four says all main routes are open – not just the motorways – so we might just get back to work. Hurry up, darling. I've got the kettle on.'

Georgia, huddled in a cherry-red candlewick dressing gown, picked her way blearily down a staircase full of cats. The dogs, bored to distraction with being confined to barracks for so long, greeted her with wagging tails and lolling tongues.

'I'm going to put our proposition to Rory today.' Cecilia was already on fast forward, bustling round her kitchen in kilt and cashmere. 'Do you want to be there?'

'Uh?' Georgia was inhaling the tea steam, allowing her senses to unfurl one by one.

'Darling!' Cecilia was clipping on earrings and feeding the animals at the same time. 'I had great hopes of you and Rory becoming more than a working partnership. I had great hopes of you and that glorious Charlie What'shisname getting together. I even thought I could tolerate Simon Capley – but,' she frowned, 'if any of them saw you looking like that – well, they'd run a mile.'

Georgia opened one eye. 'Gran, I promise you, the next time I invite a man for breakfast, I'll practise the full Barbara Cartland bit. I'll be in frou-frou lace and batwing eyelashes even as I dish up his egg, bacon and fried slice. And yes, if I'm not needed on the road, I'll be there when you talk to Rory.'

She was. In jeans, boots and her absolutely favourite Jessie Hopkins jumper which had hordes of pastel cats stalking across a deep purple background. She'd even added two coats of mascara and a dark red lipstick, and had immediately gained Cecilia's approval.

Rory, arriving in the office at half past seven, looked at the welcoming committee in surprise. 'Oh, good morning. I hadn't expected anyone to be in. Is there a problem?'

'No problem – far from it. Come and sit down, Rory.' Cecilia oozed charm. 'The coffee pot's bubbling. We have something we'd like to say.'

Rory gave Georgia a murderous glare, which she returned, and sat down.

Cecilia handed round coffees, perched on the arm of his chair and explained the situation.

Georgia watched his reactions closely. Once he'd realised

79

that he wasn't being given the push, she decided, he looked far more relaxed. She closed one eye, like an artist, and skimmed over his profile. With some embarrassment she realised that Cecilia had finished speaking and that both she and Rory were looking at her.

'Something in my eye.' Georgia blinked rapidly. 'Ah! That's better. What were you saying?'

'I've just said yes,' Rory repeated. 'And your grandmother asked if you had any thoughts on the length of my contract.'

Georgia's mind was zooming off on an entirely different course. She quickly reined it in. 'Yearly?' she hazarded. 'Six-monthly? I mean, Lennards say this will be ongoing so it's really entirely up to you.'

'Six-monthly, then. That'll give both sides a bit of leeway. It'll make a change for me to put down roots. I'm really looking forward to it.' Rory spoke to Cecilia, smiling now. 'And the salary is more than generous.'

'Ah,' Cecilia patted his arm. 'That's because we had hoped to offer you accommodation. But, as we can't, owing to unforeseen circs, I thought it might enable you to start looking for somewhere more suitable to live.' She was clenching her fingers seductively into his soft leather sleeve. 'Have you met Sabrina and Oscar yet?'

Rory shook his head. 'Oh, you soon will. They're Georgia's latest good cause. My granddaughter has the softest heart in the world.'

Georgia winced and looked quickly down at her lap. Rory's face had displayed total disbelief. He coughed. 'Actually, I was thinking of moving anyway, so this couldn't have come at a better time. I've spent the last few days seeing properties to rent, and now, with permanent employment, I can go ahead. I'd like to thank you both very much indeed – and I shall certainly enjoy the challenge.'

Georgia lifted her head then. His lips were smiling; his eyes weren't.

'Well, welcome to Diadem, Rory.' Cecilia hugged him as she stood up. 'I'm sure you'll be very happy here.'

'I'm sure I shall.'

'One more thing – because I know you're both itching to get out on the road.' Cecilia wore her most persuasive smile and Georgia's heart sank like a stone. 'We've obviously been delayed by the weather, but Tom Lennard would like us to start as soon as possible. He has two trailers to go up to the factory straight away. One of ours and one of his. Ours will be the only one coming back, of course – ready for the trunking. It'll mean a double-manned run and I thought –'

'Put Barney and Marie on it,' Georgia said quickly, scrambling to her feet and promising herself she'd throttle Cecilia at the earliest opportunity. 'They could do with some time together.'

'No can do, darling. Sorry. Their domestic arrangements – the children – mean that one of them has to be on short runs if the other is on a long haul – you know that. And Kenny is tied up with Kon Tiki.'

'Adenoids. He's single. He –'

'Can cope admirably as far as Birmingham now, bless him. He's even become reasonably safe to send to Bristol. But, no. Not on this one. It's too prestigious for that. I'm sure you two will manage admirably.'

Georgia glared at her grandmother for pulling rank. 'So, when do Lennards want us to do this run?'

'Today.' Cecilia looked as if she'd just given broth to a beggar. 'You're both on local runs this morning – Barney can cover them for you.'

'The hours –' Georgia tried in desperation.

'You know perfectly well that you'll get up there without being out of hours, darling. You can take your break while you're there and be back here tomorrow.'

'But that means –?'

Cecilia's eyes twinkled. 'That you'll be having an overnight.'

*

Trundling up the M1 in the dark, snug in the Magnum's twelve-foot-high cab, with the wind buffeting the trailer and the sleet slicing across the windscreen, was definitely not Georgia's idea of fun. While the Magnum was possibly the most elegant and sophisticated lorry on the road, with every mod con known to man, including colour TV and a refrigerator – like the Ritz on wheels, Cecilia always said – Georgia would still have much preferred not to make this journey. The inside of the cab was air-conditioned, the specially designed air-suspended seats were the last word in driving comfort, and the gearbox with its eighteen forward gears and two reverse was computer-programmed to give the smoothest and safest journey imaginable. Georgia was still not happy.

She turned up the heater, fed Ella Fitzgerald into the CD player and concentrated all her attention on the tail-lights in front. Rory, driving the Lennards artic, was two vehicles ahead of her. He'd been polite and professional as they'd coupled up the trailers in the yard, asked her if she wanted to take the lead, and said he'd see her at the other end.

It was hardly the stuff of Mills and Boon.

The further north they travelled, the worse the weather became. The slush of Berkshire had remained hard-packed on the Oxfordshire borders, and now, almost in Northumberland, the sleet was accompanied by flurries of snow. Still, she thought, as the cab rocked rhythmically and the throb of the Renault engine played soothingly in time with Ella's smoky jazz, it was infinitely preferable to the forthcoming return journey when she and Rory would be closeted cosily together for hours. If they had another spat like the last one they'd make mincemeat of each other and someone would have to pick bits of them out of Spaghetti Junction.

Abandoning the motorway at the Newcastle turn-off, the Magnum was now on Rory's heels. The weather had deteriorated rapidly, fast-looming shadows deluging the stark whiteness with movement, making the visibility so appalling that Georgia had to lean forward across the steering wheel to be able to see through the windscreen. The phone rang and she tucked the receiver beneath her chin. 'Yes?'

'Georgia,' Rory's voice crackled in her ear. 'We'll be there in five minutes. Do you reckon they'll still be on site?'

The sound of his voice was so unexpected that she almost dropped the phone. She swallowed. 'God knows. I sincerely hope so – but I wouldn't blame them if they'd skedaddled. We'll just have to hope that they haven't all turned into icicles and someone is still around. I'll ring them and let them know we're on our way in.'

'OK. I'll keep going unless you get back to me.'

Georgia manoeuvred the phone more securely against her jaw and tried to force a detached expression. It proved difficult, as her lips insisted on curling into a smile while she punched out the number.

No one answered.

There was an unmanned gatehouse at the entrance to the site, almost entirely covered on one side by a blanket of snow like a lop-sided iced fancy. Following Rory's crawling tail-lights she drove the Magnum into what looked like a desolate moonscape, and pulled to a halt behind him with a hiss of the air brakes. As always, the hum of the engine still echoed in her ears. There was nothing else, just the silence of the swirling snow.

Oh, God, she thought. Cecilia would go ballistic if they'd fouled up. After all, weren't there several Japanese car plants springing up in the North-East? Suppose they'd got the wrong one? Tom Lennard's directions had been precise enough, but surely they'd made a mistake somewhere? Eskimos building deep-freezes wouldn't be working here.

Struggling into her padded jacket, buttoning it to the chin, she opened the Magnum's door and climbed out. Her lips were almost immediately numbed. The snowflakes had turned from gentle fairy things into spiky imps determined to inflict maximum pain. She stumbled forward along the length of Rory's lorry.

'Welcome to hell,' he grimaced, leaning against the cab, brushing snow crystals from his eyes.

'Hell's hot,' she stuttered. 'I wouldn't mind hell just now. There's nothing here. No factory, no warehouse, no bloody anything.'

'There must be something.' Rory squinted through the blizzard. His hair was already dusted with white. 'They've got a security fence and a gatehouse. Look – over there. What's that?'

Peering in the direction of his unsteady finger, Georgia would have clapped her hands if they hadn't been amputated at the wrists. On the far side of the lunar landscape, vaguely visible through the storm, there was an oasis of pale light in the darkness.

'Civilisation?' she lisped. Her teeth seemed to have gummed themselves together. 'Warmth? Shelter?' She wished she could think of less sibilant words. She blew her nose.

'I hope it's a Geordie–Japanese car manufacturer who is just longing to take delivery of two loads.' Rory was prosaic. 'Mind, warmth and shelter wouldn't go amiss either.' He looked at the snow-covered rubble beneath their feet. 'I don't think we ought to take the wagons any further, do you?'

She shook her head and, shoving her iceblock hands into her pockets, started to walk unsteadily towards the light. She knew Rory was close behind her; she could hear a constant stream of muttered curses.

'By!' A rich North-Eastern voice echoed from somewhere ahead of them. 'You picked a bobby-dazzler of a neet, didn't you? We've been waiting on you getting here.'

A stocky man, in oilskins and a balaclava, was powering his way towards them as though on skis. Georgia thought that perhaps they were more used to Arctic conditions nearer the Tyne.

'There was no one in the gatehouse.' She could have fallen on him and kissed him. 'I thought the place was deserted.'

'It is, pet.' The man nodded. 'Don, the security gadgee, is in the Portakabin with me. Along with the only other two silly sods stupid enough to be here, who are waiting to sort out your trailers hopefully before the pubs shut. I've got a Calor stove – and cable telly.' He surveyed Georgia and Rory with some amusement. 'Bet you thought you'd fetched up in the wrong place, huh? We're not even built yet – nor will be if this bloody weather doesn't let up. We've just got to take your trailers down to Wearside for the time being – there's an empty one for you to take back, I understand?'

Georgia nodded. Speech was beyond her. She'd never been so cold.

'I'll get the lads on to it reet away. There's a lav in the Porta – and a brew on. You go an' get yourselves a warm an' leave this to us.'

Georgia chattered out grateful thanks. Rory's were even less audible and she would have smiled if only her mouth hadn't frozen.

Restored to a state of semi-defrost, she and Rory sat in the Portakabin together with a Calor gas fug and a rather violently coloured American sitcom while the apparently weatherproof Geordie workforce sorted out the trailers.

'Nice tea.' Rory sighed over a pint mug of doubtful cleanliness.

'Nectar,' she agreed. It probably wasn't a full cease-fire, but at least neither of them had their finger poised on the red button. 'And if we've got to stay here tonight we'll have loos and running water.'

'The Savoy.' Rory gave the semblance of a smile which increased her rate of thaw no end. He stood up. 'We'd better go and give them a hand.'

Reluctantly buttoning herself back into the freezing dampness of her coat, she followed him outside.

'Oh, aren't they angels!' She grinned at Rory through the torrent of snow. 'They've taken the trailers *and* coupled up the Magnum for the return run. I was dreading all that shunting, and dropping the legs and fiddling with the air-lines in this weather. God, they deserve medals. I –'

'Georgia.' Rory's voice was strangely quiet.

'What?'

He trudged to a halt beside her. 'Yes, they have. Coupled up. Which is great. But –'

Their original rescuer skimmed towards them, his balaclava edged in white. 'All done then, pet. I'm off now. I've signed the paperwork. Here's the key to the washroom in case you need the lav in the night. I'm taking the stove and the telly home with me. Don locked the front gates on his way out so you'll not be disturbed.'

'But –' Georgia looked helplessly at Rory who was grinning. 'Where's the lorry?'

'Yours is there safe and sound, hinny. Ours is on its way to Wearside like I said. Oh, don't fret – I put yer man's overnight bag and bits and pieces up into the Magnum's cab.' He nudged her painfully. 'You two should be in for a reet cosy night.'

CHAPTER 9

'You might be quite happy to stand here turning into an iceblock,' Rory shuddered, 'but my sense of self-preservation is firing on all cylinders. Excuse me.'

Georgia watched with some dismay as he hauled himself up into the Magnum. Jesus! All night – in there – with him. Sniffing, her eyes watering, and cursing all workaholic Geordies to hell, she pulled herself up behind him.

The lorry cab had been specially designed for double-manning trips across Europe. There was tons of room for two people to take rest breaks quite comfortably. Georgia, wriggling behind the steering wheel, thought that the designers should have taken into account that one of them just might be enormous, snow-covered and not particularly friendly.

Rory, who seemed completely at ease with the situation, had already removed his leather jacket, turned up the cab heater, switched on the radio, plugged in the kettle, and unfurled a king-size sleeping bag across the double berth. Georgia eyed this last item with deep foreboding.

'If you pulled the curtains and started cooking supper I'd believe I was sharing with the housewife of the year,' she muttered, peeling off her padded jacket and unlacing her Doc Martens. 'I'm surprised you're not wearing a pinny.'

'I'm used to this.' Rory leaned across her and pulled the dark red side curtains. She held her breath, feeling the chill from his body, almost able to taste the mingled scents of faint cologne and diesel. His hair brushed her face. He straightened up. 'Although not usually in such luxury. And I was just about to suggest that we pool our resources for an evening meal.'

The Magnum was well equipped to deal with prolonged stopovers. There was no reason – absolutely no reason at all – why their law-enforced eight-hour break should be anything other than comfortable. Georgia thought longingly of huddling in the Portakabin and then remembered that the Geordie foreman had removed the Calor gas fire.

Moving as far away from Rory as she could, she unpacked her own provisions of coffee, sandwiches and a packet of biscuits. The snow was machine-gunning against the windscreen in the darkness, whipped into a fury by the crosswind which was softly rocking the cab. Rory looked at her meagre contribution with some contempt. 'Hardly enough there to fuel a hungry trucker.'

'It's fine for me, thank you. Why? Have you brought a three-course meal – or a full greasy spoon menu?'

He unpacked soup, a cold chicken, bread rolls and a mountain of potato salad. He'd also got fizzy water, orange juice, cheese and crackers, and two huge bars of chocolate. Georgia eyed them enviously.

'The soup and rolls will heat up, and I've got enough chicken and salad for two.' He produced two mugs. 'We can share your coffee and sandwiches and have the biscuits and chocolate for pudding. You're forgetting that I've spent a good part of my life with nowhere else to call home except the cab of a lorry.'

'Peripatetic,' Georgia said mulishly as the kettle boiled and Rory filled the mugs. 'The typical itinerant trucker . . .'

Except, of course, that he wasn't.

He handed her a mug. 'I do know the meaning of the word. I'm not completely ignorant. Or was that another reminder of my station in life? You rule – I serve?'

Georgia choked on the coffee. 'What the hell is your problem?'

'I don't have a problem.' He narrowed his eyes. 'I think you're the one who finds it hard to relate. I think being a woman in power has made it impossible for you to handle men on a natural level. You can't be friends with them, can you? You have to be in control – you have to prove that you're better, stronger, more capable than any man you may come in contact with. I think –'

'Crap.' Furiously, Georgia grabbed the door handle. 'I've had more men friends than – no – I mean, I've got loads of friends who are men. Dozens. So I'm not remotely interested in your half-baked psychoanalysis. Neither do I have to spend all night listening to it.' She waved the key to the Portakabin as she flung open the door. 'I'm going to spend the rest of the night over there.'

Siberia hurled itself into the cab as she leapt out on to the snow.

'Georgia!' The wind played with Rory's voice, tossing it like a leaf above her head. 'You haven't got –'

'Shit!' She sank painfully to her knees amidst the frozen debris, tears prickling her eyes.

' – your coat or your boots,' Rory finished, leaning down from miles above her, his hair blowing across his face. He jumped down beside her and pulled her unceremoniously to her feet, one hand under each armpit. Cold, wet, unbearably humiliated, she glared at him. He was laughing.

'Bastard! I suppose you think that's funny.' Her face was turning into ice, her hands and feet were numb. 'How dare you!'

He picked her up, pushed her bodily back into the Magnum's cab and closed the door behind them. 'This is something completely new for me. I've never had a woman hurl herself into a snowdrift to escape me before. You'd better take your clothes off.'

'What?'

'Your clothes.' Rory was re-boiling the kettle. 'Unless of course you want to add to Diadem's sick-list. Your jeans and sweater are soaking – and if you keep those socks on it's an invitation to frostbite – not to mention hypothermia. Go on, Georgia. Quickly.'

Her teeth were chattering and of course he was right, smug pig, Georgia thought. All her clothes were sodden and icy cold and unbearably uncomfortable. He fished out a huge towel from his bag. 'Pull the bunk curtains. Get dried off and changed up there. I won't look. I've never found watching a fellow trucker undress in the slightest exciting.'

'I haven't got any other clothes.'

'Tut-tut.' Rory shook his head. 'Not very professional. I always carry a spare set.'

'I bet you were top of your Boy Scout troop.' Georgia's teeth were like castanets.

'Actually – ' Rory began, before Georgia's groan of fury silenced him. He grinned. 'I've got socks and sweater. Sadly they're both black – hardly what you would have chosen – but as you're not in a position to be picky they'll have to do. Here . . .'

She grabbed the bundle and clambered inelegantly up into the bunk, pulling the curtains behind her. As she dried and changed she could hear him rustling and rattling about with the food, humming along to some ancient pop hit on the radio. She had never disliked anyone so much in her entire life.

'Oh, much better.' He gave her an appraising look as she climbed down from the bunk. 'At least you won't die on me now. I couldn't have faced your grandmother with the news that you were indulging in cryogenics in the North-East – not after she'd just given me the job. Coffee?'

His socks reached above her knees and flopped off her toes like pixie boots. His sweater would have wrapped round her twice, and nearly met the socks. She felt warm and snug – and extremely disadvantaged.

She took the coffee with bad grace. 'Thanks. Anyway, Gran would prefer to have reports of my death than reports of a failed delivery and Lennards changing allegiance. If we lost this contract to Vivienda I might as well be dead.'

'You underestimate her.' Rory was heating the soup and rolls and dishing up cold roast chicken and potato salad in a sickeningly accomplished manner considering the limited space available. 'She loves you very much. I do know how she feels about the business – but I've also realised how she feels about you. She is very proud of you – with good reason, and she loves you like a daughter.'

'Ten out of ten for observation,' Georgia laughed bitterly. 'It wasn't difficult. Morag, my mother, wasn't too hot in the daughter stakes.'

Rory said nothing for a moment. Georgia bit her lip. She very rarely mentioned Morag – and sometimes forgot about her for months at a time. Sometimes it was hard to remember that Cecilia and Gordon weren't her parents. Why the hell should she have mentioned it now? And to him of all people? She shrugged. 'Gran has always been my mother.'

'And your real mother? Er – Morag?' Rory had his back to her. 'I mean, don't talk about it if you don't want to. I've no right to pry. Was it an accident?'

'What?' Georgia studied her hands. 'Oh, no. My mother is still very much alive. I was the accident.'

'Illegitimacy isn't a crime.' Rory handed her a piled plate and a mug of soup. 'You shouldn't get hung up about something that is absolutely not your fault.'

She took the plate and looked quickly away. 'I'm not. Hung up – or illegitimate. My parents had been married for five years when I was born. They just weren't cut out for parenthood. It wasn't on their hippie agenda. They decided Gran and Grandad would give me a more stable home.'

'Good Lord.' Rory seemed shocked. Georgia suddenly wanted to giggle. He paused in the middle of his chicken. 'So, where are they now?'

'Playing at being the oldest New-Age travellers in the world somewhere in Wales I believe. They met and married at university, embraced the hippie way of life and parenthood would have severely curtailed it.' Georgia had practised the speech a million times in her head. She didn't often voice it and was surprised to find it no longer hurt. 'They usually remember my birthday – and they always send a Christmas card. I saw them last summer. They were passing through on their way to the solstice at Stonehenge.'

Rory seemed to be struggling to keep a straight face. 'And – er – do they come and stay at Diadem? With you and Cecilia? On a regular basis?'

'God, no. They don't seem exactly at home with running water and bathrooms and things. The last time they actually spent any length of time with us was at Grandad's funeral. They arrived in a purple van, all smocks and waistcoats and floppy hats. They brought a bunch of wild flowers and smoked spliffs throughout the whole service. They spent two days with us afterwards, getting stoned and crying a lot. I – I was quite glad when they went.'

Rory looked at her for what seemed like ages. She wanted him to say something. She didn't even know why she had shared the confidence. He pushed his hair from his eyes. 'It explains a lot. Your relationship with Cecilia and your fierce devotion to Diadem. You're very lucky, Georgia. Really. And I do appreciate you telling me – and I presume you'd like me now to develop instant amnesia?'

'If you wouldn't mind.' She felt embarrassed. After all, he hadn't asked for her life-story. It used to trouble her when she was younger; she had always wondered what she'd done wrong; why her parents didn't want her. It wasn't a problem any longer. She still loved them but she hadn't needed them for years.

He grinned and returned to his supper. 'I've forgotten it already. Are you happy with this schmaltz on the radio or would you prefer something else?'

Georgia glanced at her watch. Oh, what the hell. What did it matter what he thought of her now anyway? 'Would you mind if we watched *Coronation Street*?'

'Not at all. I always try to catch it myself.'

As he turned on the television Georgia couldn't fathom if he was serious or not. Filling the six-foot gap of seat between them with plates, mugs and food, she tried to concentrate on the programme. They huddled comfortably in opposite corners, only breaking the silence to pass the rolls, swap sandwiches, pour drinks. It was a treacherous peace.

With the wind spasmodically punching at the cab and the snow swirling from the darkness, it was the cosiest TV dinner Georgia had ever eaten. 'That was brilliant,' she said grudgingly after the news had ended. 'Thanks very much. I –'

'Since we're into soul-baring, I think I owe you an apology.' Rory collected up the plates and mugs. 'For the other night. Sorry is always the hardest thing to say – but I am – sorry.'

'You did rather jump to conclusions about my relationship with Alan, yes. But –'

'Not that.' He paused in the middle of packing all the dirty dishes neatly into a carrier bag. He really would make someone a wonderful wife. 'No, I meant kissing you. I took advantage. I'm sorry.'

Georgia's face flamed in the dim light. Her body tingled. 'Yes, well, you did rather. But – er – we were both over-wrought. Maybe we just ought to forget it.'

'Can you?' Rory wasn't looking at her. 'Because I can't. Oh, I won't be repeating it – don't worry. After all, you've made it very clear what my position is. But it was enjoyable.' He turned to look at her. He was grinning. 'Very enjoyable indeed. And you really seemed in need of being kissed. I obviously got quite the wrong signals. Still, power is quite an aphrodisiac – and I've never kissed my boss before.'

Struggling to think of something that would act as a cold shower – without actually resorting to flinging open the doors – Georgia shrugged. 'OK. I'll admit it wasn't an unpleasant experience ... but I still think we should put it behind us. And I'm not your boss – could we just get that clear? I apologise if I sounded like some jumped-up little prig, but I was angry. I hate being misunderstood. Alan Woodbury honestly isn't my boyfriend. Never has been and never will be. I certainly wouldn't have left him if he was – well, no, I mean – not in that state ...'

Rory nodded, glancing at the television screen. It was a violent thriller, with a backing track which marked it as at least twenty years old. 'Off?'

'Please. Try the radio again.'

He did. It was very comforting to hear the tones of Middle England interspersed with some fairly innocuous music. He settled back in the seat. 'We both accept each other's apology – and we know it won't be repeated – so we'll start again, shall we? As friends?'

'Friends.' Georgia nodded, quelling the little voice that was teasing her body, telling her that she'd really like Rory Faulkner to be more. Much more.

'So, if Alan Woodbury isn't a fixture, is there a man in your life?'

'No. Not really. There never seems to be time. Alan and I often partner each other from sheer convenience. There hasn't been anyone serious for ages. What about you?'

God. Trish and Cecilia would be delighted.

'Oh, a girl in every truck stop. Wherever I lay my hat and all that.' He smiled. 'This is the first permanent job I've had in five years, so who knows. Is there a lonely-hearts club in Upton Poges?'

Georgia laughed. 'No. Gran would snaffle all the contenders if there were.'

They lapsed into silence again. Georgia desperately wanted

to yawn – but that double bunk and the sleeping bag were far too close. She rubbed her eyes. 'I've told you about my weird past – so what about yours? Why have you been on the road? You must have family somewhere.'

'London.' Rory stretched endless legs into the space under the steering wheel. 'My father is dead. My mother lives in London – and my brother.'

'Oh?' Georgia caught the vibes. 'Older or younger?'

'Four years older.'

'What's his name?'

'Rufus.'

Georgia was enchanted. 'Does he have red hair?'

'No.' Rory's voice could have cut glass. 'He looks like me. That's why Mum wanted me to be a Rosie, you see. Rufus was – was, well, the son she'd always wanted. I should have been a girl.'

'That's not your fault any more than my birth.' Georgia picked at the last squares of chocolate, knowing now why he understood. 'And you don't get on? You and Rufus?'

'I hate him,' Rory said. 'I absolutely loathe and detest him.'

There was more. She knew there was. However, not wanting to snap the fragile thread of friendship, she managed to bite her tongue. He'd tell her if he wanted her to know. They had all night.

'There was someone in my life.' He was staring at the snow building in crystals behind the windscreen wipers. 'Stephanie. We lived together for four years. I – well, I came home early one day and found her in bed with someone else. Actually making love . . .'

'Oh, God.' Georgia almost reached out to comfort him but remembered in time. 'How appalling for you. How – ? What happened?'

'Not much. I wasn't sure that it was really happening. I remember standing there in the bedroom doorway just staring. Feeling nothing. Just looking at them. It was Rufus.'

'Your brother? Christ!' Georgia swallowed. 'Oh, I'm so sorry. Did you hit him?'

Rory shook his head. 'I wanted to kill them both – and I knew I was quite capable of it at that moment. They were scrambling around, making excuses, saying sorry. I didn't hear any of it. I could just see them. Together. And I knew I'd probably hurt them if I stayed. So I walked out and trailed round London for hours – just to give them time to disappear. I really couldn't take in the betrayal. I loved them both, you see.'

'Oh, yes.' Georgia touched his arm then. 'That made it so much worse for you. I mean, it would have been awful whoever it was – but your *brother*. And then what?'

'Nothing. I remember the numbness becoming a white-hot anger again – and the pain.' He gave a self-deprecating smile. 'I think I punched every wall in south London. It helped. I surprised myself. I'm not a violent person. I detest cruelty.' He shrugged. 'They'd both gone when I got back.'

'And are they still together?'

'God, no. Rufus only wanted Steph because she was mine. He'd always had everything. He couldn't bear it that I had something of my own. She came back, of course, after he'd lost interest. Asked me to forgive her.'

Henry Mancini played on. There was no other sound but the soughing of the wind. 'I told her to go to hell – and I've never seen her since.'

'Do you still love her?'

'No. But I'll never forget her – or what she did. The deceit. I'll never forgive her – or Rufus. I left the flat, and the family business, and took to the road.'

Georgia felt his pain and knew she was lucky never to have suffered that sort of anguish. Poor Rory. It explained so much. Especially how he'd reacted to her abandoning Alan Woodbury. If only she'd known. 'What about your mother? Did you tell her?'

'No. It wouldn't have done any good. The sun shone out of Rufus's arse as far as she was concerned – and she never liked Steph. She'd have thought I was over-reacting. So, now you know, Ms Diadem, why I became peripatetic – and why settling down again is something of an open wound.'

'It'll be different now, though. A fresh start. You'll just have to learn to trust people again. And, honestly, most people are OK. All the people at Diadem – however different – are brilliant. You'll make some good friends.'

'Cecilia was quite right.' He linked his hands behind his head and leaned back against the bunk. 'You're very generous-hearted – and I was a fool to think otherwise.'

It was the sort of remark guaranteed to make golden butterflies flutter inside her. She hugged it to herself, turned a few mental cartwheels, and stretched lazily. 'Shall I tell you about all the other people at Diadem?'

She did. And about Tumbling Bay's progress, and how Sabrina and Oscar had joined the fold. By the time she'd finished Rory had at least a thumbnail sketch of every character he was likely to meet in Upton Poges. 'Hell! Look at the time!'

'We really should be thinking about bed – er – getting some sleep,' Rory said. 'We ought to be on the road as soon as possible in the morning with the weather like this.'

'Yes – I suppose so.' Georgia peered through the windscreen. 'I'm going to have to risk a dash to the Portakabin for the loo and to clean my teeth.'

'Me too.'

They struggled into jackets and boots, scarves and gloves and, taking a deep breath, plunged into the storm.

Returning to the Magnum's cab was like taking a bath in warm jelly.

'Ooh! Bliss!' Georgia sighed, dispensing with her outdoor clothes. 'I always feel guilty on nights like this. When I'm warm and dry and others aren't.'

'I know.' Rory was tidily folding everything away. 'You have to try not to think about stray animals and homeless people, don't you? I always vowed that if I won the lottery, I'd buy a huge estate and scour the country just taking in everyone and everything that needed a home.'

Georgia beamed at him. For a moment she could see them running this venture side by side, kindred spirits. 'Oh, well, down to basics. Who's having the bunk?'

He looked at her steadily. Her heart was thundering.

'You are. And the blankets. I'll have the sleeping bag on the seat. OK?'

'Fine.' She wasn't sure whether to be pleased or disappointed.

She'd spent overnights in the Magnum before, doubling up with Jed or Barney, with no problems. But, she admitted to herself as they sorted out the bedclothes, Rory Faulkner was a different proposition altogether. She scrambled up into the bunk and tugged the blankets to her chin. Rory paused in pulling the curtains across. 'Good night, Georgia.'

'Night . . .'

In the soft red darkness she could hear him settling down, stretching out along the seat just beneath her. Her body tingled again. The wind rocked the cab. Deliciously snug, Georgia slept.

She woke once in the night. She could hear him breathing, slow, steady breaths, and smiled. She turned over and heard him murmur. If she reached her hand down she could touch his hair, stroke his face. She sighed and slept again.

The journey back to Upton Poges became easier as they travelled south. Sharing the driving, taking breaks in the service stations, chatting like friends now, it seemed to fly. The weather improved greatly, and by the time they reached the Midlands there was very little trace of snow. Having deposited the trailer at Lennards, they made good time back to the Diadem yard.

'I'll diesel up and hose the tractor,' Rory said. 'You take the tachos and the paperwork in to your gran. And Georgia –'

She turned. 'Yes?'

'Thanks. It was great.'

'It was, wasn't it?'

She skipped into the office. Trish, as usual, was tapping away at her keyboard. Cecilia was on the phone. It was another world.

'How did it go then?' Trish's eyes were huge.

'Very boring and grown up.' Georgia dropped the delivery notes and the tachos on the desk. 'Thank you. How's Jed?'

'Brilliant.' Trish grinned.

'You'll burst his stitches.' Georgia giggled.

Cecilia replaced the receiver. 'You made good time, darling. That was Tom Lennard on the phone. Absolutely ecstatic. He's thrilled to bits at the way you handled it, so I must thank you both. Where's Rory?'

'Dieseling up,' Georgia said. Her grandmother was the ultimate professional. Business always came first. There'd be hours of probing over the sleeping arrangements later. 'Good heavens!'

Sabrina Yates, sitting at Georgia's desk studying a lorry manual, grinned. 'Hiya! Whatcha reckon? Your gran arranged it. Her hairdresser came in this morning. Brilliant, huh?'

'Brilliant,' Georgia echoed dully.

Sabrina looked sensational in her tight jeans and one of Cecilia's cashmere sweaters. Her once-variegated hair now feathered in gleaming dark layers.

'It was the least I could do.' Cecilia walked across and flicked at Georgia's black hair which hung in unbecoming strands after the rigours of the last twenty-four hours. 'I mean you'll never let me tart you up, will you, darling? And you have to admit it is a vast improvement.'

It was a transformation. Georgia closed her eyes. Beside Sabrina's pert, pale prettiness she felt as alluring as a humpbacked troll.

Rory opened the office door. Trish stopped typing again. Cecilia held out her arms. He looked at Georgia and winked. Suddenly she felt beautiful.

'Hiya!' Sabrina's eyes sparkled from beneath the glossy fringe. 'And *who* is *this*?'

CHAPTER 10

Some days later, on a February evening when everything was sodden and grey, Cecilia poked her head round Georgia's kitchen door. 'Am I interrupting?'

'Only microwaved fish and chips.' Georgia removed a cat from the breakfast bench. 'Are you hungry? It'll stretch to two.'

'Kenny's taking me out to eat. At Leon's. After the rehearsal.'

'You don't mind me not coming to Am Dram tonight, do you?' She'd rather die than admit to her grandmother that she wanted to stay in just in case Rory phoned. Their friendship was flourishing nicely into shared chats and easygoing flirting.

Cecilia shook her head. 'I quite understand, darling. And that wasn't why I popped in. There were two reasons, actually. I've just had a phone call from Barney. He's had a blow-out on the M25.'

'He isn't hurt?'

'No, thank heavens. He's pulled on to the hard shoulder and he's waiting for the fitters. But he's going to be very late.'

'And he's delivering to Jeromes?' Georgia paused. 'And our last delivery to Jeromes was late because Marie had a problem with the gearbox.'

Cecilia nodded. 'I know we've had hiccups before. You can't run a haulage company without having mechanical problems, but two in two days – on runs to the same company . . .'

Georgia closed her eyes. The implications loomed large. It would be brake pipes and fuel lines next.

'I've asked Kenny to be extra-vigilant on his checks and to

make sure everything is in order before the lorries leave the yard. Let's hope it is just coincidence . . .'

Some coincidence, Georgia thought with a sinking heart. 'And the second thing? Is that about industrial espionage, too?'

Cecilia brightened. 'Oh, no. Much more fun. I'm inviting the Brimstones to supper on Saturday night. I thought I owed them some small recompense for purloining Rory.'

Georgia tipped the fish and chips on to a plate and shielded it from the attentions of the cat with her elbow. 'Poor Beth.'

Cecilia tutted. 'Not *just* the Brimstones, darling. Kenny will be there, of course, and you and –'

'Not Rory.' Georgia removed the cat. 'Don't matchmake, Gran, please.'

'You do like him though, don't you? I thought you and he were –'

'We are. I just don't want to rush things.' She shrugged. 'There are reasons. Look, I'll ask him myself.'

'As you wish.' Cecilia sighed. 'But don't shilly-shally, Georgia. I recognise sexual attraction – and it's very exciting – but it can be short-lived. Don't play it so cool that he thinks it's disinterest.'

'Pack it in, Gran.'

'At least you won't be partnered by Alan Woodbury this time. He always puts me off my food, simpering and gushing.'

Poor Alan. 'And how is he shaping up as leading man?'

Cecilia rolled her eyes. 'Totally over the top, bless him. Marie is being very stubborn about it. She doesn't want him anywhere near her – which is rather unfortunate as they're supposed to be the hottest lovers since Antony and Cleopatra. I'm taking Sabrina along with me tonight. I thought she could do with a break – and the Poges Players could certainly do with another pretty girl.'

'And who's baby-sitting Oscar?'

'Trish. She's had full instructions on bottles and Pampers, and says it'll be good practice. Well, I'll skedaddle, then. Remember to invite Rory on Saturday.'

Georgia shared her fish and chips with three of the cats, washed her hair, and was just stretching out on the sofa which she'd covered with a turquoise and magenta throw, when the phone rang.

Play it cool, she told herself, and count to ten before picking up the receiver. She reached three before snatching it up.

'Hi, Georgia. It's Maddy. I was sorry to miss you the other day. Drew said he'd invited you to come over one evening so I thought we'd firm things up.'

Georgia groaned. Normally she'd love a chat with Maddy, but not tonight – not when Rory might be trying to dial from his cab phone. She sank back on to the sofa. 'It's lovely to hear from you. How's the pregnancy?'

Maddy and Drew had recently moved in together after a whirlwind romance, and Maddy's pregnancy was still red-hot gossip. They talked about the baby, about Drew, about Tumbling Bay, about Charlie Somerset's latest bed-hopping adventures, and finally settled on Georgia eating at Peapods after Tumbling Bay's debut race at Windsor at the end of the month.

'. . . I might bring someone with me. Will that be OK? I'm not saying who in case I don't. No, you'll just have to wait and see. Take care. 'Bye.'

The phone rang again almost immediately.

'Georgia. I've been trying for ages.'

'I'm sorry. It was a mate. Well, Tumbling Bay's trainer's girlfriend, actually. Where are you?'

'Hull. It's raining. Will you be in the office tomorrow when I get in?'

She did lightning calculations. 'I should be. I've got the early Kon Tiki run. Why?'

'Because I want to be able to say that for you I've been to Hull and back.'

Georgia realised that she was in serious danger of falling in love. 'I've got something to say to you, too.'

'I'm all ears.'

'Gran's having a supper party on Saturday. For the Brimstones – to apologise for pinching you and losing them money. Actually, I reckon it's merely an excuse to flirt with Spence under poor Beth's nose, but –'

'I know. I'm looking forward to it. Sabrina asked me this morning. She needed a partner, and she said you'd be with Alan Woodbury.'

Georgia felt sick. Bloody, bloody Sabrina. Rory's voice echoed in her ear. 'Georgia? Are you still there? What did you want to ask?'

'Oh, just if – if you were coming on Saturday and – er – if you were going to bring a bottle. Gran likes dry white.'

'Fine. It should be a nice evening.'

It should have been. But it wasn't going to be now. She said goodbye quickly and sank despondently on to the sofa.

Dispensing with her Burberry to reveal a Jacques Vert suit almost identical to Cecilia's latest, Beth Brimstone glared at Spencer across Cecilia's elegant hall. 'I told you we'd be too early. I said half past seven for eight meant just that. I hate being first.'

Spencer, suave in fawn Sta-Pressed and a cord shirt, glared back. 'And I told you that it was informal. Cecilia won't mind. Oh, hello, Georgia. Don't you look lovely?'

Georgia smiled as she took the coats. 'Ken's dispensing alcohol in the living room. Gran's still in the kitchen. It's a horrid night, isn't it?'

'There's flooding on the Milton St John road.' Beth powered her way towards the living-room door where a flickering fire and Mantovani welcomed warmly. 'Has Cecilia got any vodka?'

Leaving the Brimstones to Ken Poldruan's ministrations, Georgia headed back into the kitchen.

'Your first guests. Beth's looking like you, only two sizes bigger, and Spence is doing his David Niven bit. You go and chat – I'll finish here.'

Cecilia wiped her hands and removed her apron from the little black Jean Muir. 'OK. It's all under control. Georgia –'

Georgia lifted a saucepan lid. 'It doesn't matter, honestly.'

Cecilia hugged her, the Joy mingling with the delicious smells wafting from the oven. 'I thought you'd be pleased. Poor little Sabrina has probably never had a family and I thought she'd enjoy a bit of social life. I really thought she'd ask Adenoids. I had great plans . . .'

'Look, Rory and I aren't an item. Anyway, it's only making up numbers – they haven't announced their engagement. Did you give Sabrina the run of your wardrobe, too? I wouldn't have thought she had a suitable dress.'

'Oh dear.' Cecilia fluffed at her hair. 'Actually, I gave her a salary advance to go into Newbury or Oxford and buy something.'

'*What* salary?' Georgia clattered a wooden spoon on to the draining board.

'Well, you know, the little idea I had about the courier service – with Sabrina driving the van? I thought she could start next week. Trish can mind the babe in the office between trips and –'

Georgia dug her nails into her palms. Just what sort of worm had she invited into Diadem's apple? It was her own fault. With a twinge of self-hate, she knew that she was jealous.

Sabrina arrived next. Alone. Georgia peered out into the driving rain. 'Isn't Rory with you?'

'Nah.' Sabrina unbuttoned her donkey jacket and deposited her umbrella in a corner. 'He said we'd meet here. It wasn't a date or anything. More's the pity, I says, because Rory

Faulkner is one juicy guy. I'd roll on my back for him any time.' She looked at Georgia with Goldie Hawn eyes. 'Sorry if I'm late – I had to give Trish last-minute instructions about Oscar and then he wouldn't go to sleep. Ooh, you look a bit tasty. What do you reckon to mine?'

She twirled in the hall. The dark layered hair was set off to perfection by a skimpy crimson dress. The addition of black opaque tights and high heels made her look leggy, innocent and very sexy all at the same time.

'Is it OK?' She grinned at Georgia. 'Only I never got to eat out much in Barford St Mary.'

'It's lovely. You look perfect.' Unfortunately it was true. 'Go through to the living room. They're all having drinks.'

'Ta.' Sabrina turned at the end of the hall. 'I'll never be able to thank you enough for all this, y'know. It's wicked.'

It made it difficult to dislike someone when they were so damn grateful. The doorbell rang again, followed immediately by a welcoming canine volley.

Rory loomed in the doorway. The rain had darkened his hair.

'Come in. Oh, thanks – when I said dry white, I didn't expect champagne. Gran will be delighted.'

Rory hung the leather jacket on the hall stand and smiled at her. 'You look stunning.'

Her dress, in varying shades of purple velvet, was one of her favourites. It flattered all her best features and disguised her worst ones. She had coaxed her hair into a sleek pageboy and had put on unusually dramatic make-up. 'Sabrina has just arrived.'

'And Alan Woodbury?'

'Isn't coming.' Georgia held the champagne bottle. 'He never was. I think Sabrina just assumed . . .'

Rory looked amused. 'So am I escorting you both? Or was I invited to keep your gran and Beth apart? Either option seems to have all the makings of a fun evening.'

Following him towards the living room, Georgia could see that his hair was different shades of dark blond in the light of the hall. 'Gran and Beth seem to be best buddies at the moment – and I've got a partner.'

Did she imagine it, or was there a tightening of the shoulder muscles?

Cecilia had swapped Ken's choice of Mantovani for a loin-grinding blast of Barry White. Everyone swooped on Rory and the champagne. The room was snug and warm and filled with laughter.

'Rory looks divine,' Cecilia whispered to Georgia. 'Doesn't he?'

He did, Georgia thought. She was relieved to notice that he'd greeted Sabrina with a smile but no kiss – not even on the cheek – and was now talking to Ken and Spencer. The doorbell chimed through the noise. The dogs barked again as she hurried along the hall.

'Christ! I'm sorry I'm late. I practically aquaplaned down the road between Milton St John and Tiptoe.' Charlie Somerset stepped inside, drenching the wallpaper with scattered raindrops. 'And Drew had an emergency.'

'Not Maddy! Not the baby?'

'No.' Charlie hung up his jacket. 'Equine – and not your baby, either. Tumbling Bay is fine. It was Solomon – Drew's special horse. A touch of colic. I hung on until the vet had given the all-clear. You look amazing! Come here.'

He enveloped her in a hug, pressing the length of his athletic body against hers.

'Charlie!' She giggled. 'We're friends. We're not supposed to snog in the hall.'

'Oh well, maybe later,' Charlie said good-naturedly.

Georgia made the introductions and, after a while, they all trooped into the dining room.

With its faded red walls and gleaming furniture, its glowing fire and its starbursts of table lamps, the dining room endorsed Cecilia's ability as a home-maker. Ken fussed busily, seating people, placing Spencer and Cecilia – Georgia noticed with amusement – as far apart as possible round the circular table. She was sitting between Charlie and Rory.

They demolished the first course – crisply baked potato skins with bacon and black pudding – with cries of delight and much clashing of glasses.

'You eat a lot for a jockey.' Sabrina fluttered her eyelashes at Charlie from the far side of Rory.

'That's because I have enormous appetites.' Charlie grinned, displaying crooked teeth. 'As Georgia will tell you.'

Cecilia dished up huge platefuls of chicken cooked in red wine and tarragon, with mushrooms and baby onions. As she had never scaled down the gargantuan lorry-driver-sized meals she used to cook for Gordon, her supper parties were frequently robust. Anyone who ate at Diadem found it difficult to move afterwards.

'Help yourself to veg,' she said as she heaped mashed potato on to Spencer's plate. 'Now, Spencer, tell us how Vivienda are doing. Badly, I trust? Cheer me up. I know we've snaffled the Lennards contract – but are they struggling in other areas, too?'

'No more potato for Spencer!' Beth interrupted, leaning across her chicken. 'I don't let him have too much.'

'I'm sure you don't,' Cecilia purred. 'In fact he's told me so himself. Many times.'

Spencer flashed her a warning look, and proceeded to give her the low-down on Vivienda. Georgia watched Ken edge nearer to Cecilia. At any minute all three would be sharing the same plate.

Charlie launched into a highly-embellished tale about the disputed ownership of this year's Grand National favourite. Halfway through, Georgia realised that Rory wasn't listening.

'I thought you wanted to know all about horses?' she whispered.

'Oh, I do. But from you, not Charlie. Anyway, I was trying to hear what Spencer was saying.'

'Were you? I never thought anyone – except possibly Gran – ever listened to Spence seriously.'

Refusing all offers of help, Cecilia gathered up the plates and swept towards the kitchen. 'See to some more drinks, Kenny, there's an angel. Spencer can put some more music on. No, Elizabeth, you stay and chatter. Sabrina and Georgia would love to hear about your herbal cure for warts, wouldn't you, girls?'

Beth's upper lip curled. 'Sabrina? That's a name you don't hear much. Mind, there used to be one in the fifties. Flaunty chest. You've got a baby, I understand?'

'Yeah. Oscar.' Sabrina was leaning a little too close to Rory for Georgia's peace of mind. 'He's a poppet.'

'Oscar?'

'Yeah. His dad used to read Oscar Wilde to me in bed after we'd had a sh – er – made love.'

Charlie and Rory laughed quietly.

'Good Lord!' Beth took a huge mouthful of wine.

'Just as well it weren't Dickens,' Sabrina continued. 'Or the poor little sod'd've ended up being called Pickwick.'

'Oh, I don't know.' Beth shook her head. Her hair, which had been lacquered into a rather dismal copy of Cecilia's bob, stayed put. 'Dickens had some lovely boy's names – Pip, Oliver Twist, David Copperfield, Tom Sawyer –'

Hardly daring to look at Rory, Georgia escaped to help her grandmother in the kitchen.

'Anything I can do?'

Cecilia was counting pudding bowls. 'Grab the trifle. What have I missed?'

'Nothing much.' Georgia picked up the trifle dish. 'Beth was just getting a little confused about her literary heroes.'

'Elizabeth Brimstone is a foolish woman all round.' Cecilia gathered spoons. 'I can't see how she hopes to project a professional image when she doesn't even know what size clothes to wear. Look at tonight's outfit. Someone should tell her that it's no good trying to squeeze a quart into a pint pot. No wonder Spencer draws comparisons.

Georgia frowned. 'Gran. You *promised*. You absolutely promised not to upset Beth.'

'Upset Elizabeth? Impossible. The woman has a hide like a rhino. And I've been exceptionally pleasant to her – so far.' Cecilia laughed at the outrage on Georgia's face. 'Look, darling, Spencer enjoys our little *affaire* as much as I do. He's hardly going to risk blowing it by flaunting it under his wife's nose, is he? He's been telling me some really riveting things about Vivienda, that's all.'

Georgia hugged the trifle. 'What sort of things?'

'Well, if what Spencer tells me is true, we're going to have to call a board meeting soon. Apparently, the Vivienda people who are running Ionio have approached Brimstones asking about our contracts. Very off the record, chatty-chatty, but they want to know which firms Spencer supplies drivers for, length of contracts, costs – everything. I don't like the sound of it at all.'

Georgia frowned. Neither did she. Of course, now that Vivienda had bought Ionio, it would make sense for them to try and close down their only local rival. A shiver of apprehension twitched along her spine. 'Can they undercut us on anything?'

'Not as far as I know – but they're a large company. They might be prepared to make regional losses initially that can be shored up by their head-office millions. We beat them at Lennards – but that was their first attempt. They'll probably be wiser next time. That was what Spencer and I were discussing over dinner, darling. Honestly.'

'Did you tell Spence about our suspicions over the Jeromes runs?'

'Yes, but as there hasn't been anything else since, he thinks it may have been coincidence. He says Vivienda are above that sort of thing.'

'And the rumours on the industrial estate? Did you mention those to him?'

'He's heard them too. It's quite worrying, actually. I think we ought to visit Ionio as soon as possible.' Cecilia smiled. 'Still, let's not worry about it tonight. We may be quite wrong – and we've got far more amusing things to concern us. How's it going? Do you think Charlie will seduce Sabrina?'

'I sincerely hope so. In fact, I'm banking on it.'

There were very few signs of seduction going on in the dining room. Ken had refilled glasses. Beth and Spencer were holding hands. Sabrina was leaning back in her chair, nodding her head in time to Irving Berlin. 'Ooh! Trifle!' She glanced at Charlie. 'Can I have yours as well – if there are too many calories in it for you?'

Charlie, who ate everything and always managed to retain his riding weight, nodded. 'Of course. But only if you let me lick your spoon.'

'Charlie's been riding at Sandown today.' Sabrina poured cream over her hundreds and thousands. 'He had a winner. I've never been to a race meeting before.'

'Neither have I,' Rory said.

'Really?' Sabrina's smile was guileless. 'Maybe we could go together some time? It would be nice to share an experience, wouldn't it? Sort of like both being virgins . . .'

Leaving the debris on the dinner table with Cecilia's happy cry of, 'Oh, don't worry about it tonight! Georgia and I will see to it in the morning,' they carried their glasses into the sitting room.

Sabrina nestled on the sofa between Rory and Charlie. 'Rory was telling me all about his new house,' she announced.

Georgia forced her face to remain politely interested. 'And where's that?'

'Dunno.' Sabrina stretched out her long slim legs. Charlie and Rory watched.

'Windwhistle Cottage. It's on the Tiptoe road,' Rory said. 'I was going to mention it to you. I'll have to change my address on the files and everything, won't I?'

'Trish'll see to that.' Georgia felt cold. Why had he told snaky Sabrina? 'When do you move in?'

'Next week. I've taken a six-month lease to go with my contract at Diadem.'

'We'll have a house-warming!' Sabrina said happily. 'A proper party – not like this. Oh, I mean, not that this ain't smart and that, but we could have dancing and games . . .'

Georgia simmered. 'It all sounds lovely, but actually, if you'll excuse me, I think I'll make a start on the dining room. I don't think I'll be able to face it tomorrow.'

She walked out of the room with carefully controlled nonchalance. As soon as she'd crossed the hall and closed the dining-room door behind her she kicked the table. 'Bugger! Damn! Sod!'

The tape on the stereo was still singing *Songs from the Shows* to itself. One of the cats had sneaked in and was snuffling cream from the jug on the table. It raised its round tabby head, cream drops on its whiskers.

Georgia lifted it down, viciously scraping leftover trifle into one bowl and clattering spoons into another. She screwed the napkins into tight balls and felt slightly less murderous. Then, as she heard the dining-room door open, she started singing along with Rodgers and Hammerstein. 'I don't want any help.'

'I'm not offering help.' Charlie closed the door behind him. 'I'm offering my body.'

She turned and laughed. Charlie could always make her feel better. She almost wished she could fall in love with him and have a joyous affair. He squatted down and stroked the cat. 'You really like Rory, don't you?'

'Yes, I do.' Georgia flicked crumbs into a pile.

'Do you want to tell me about it?'

So she did. Eventually Charlie shrugged. 'The trouble is, you treat everyone like your best mate and, without wanting to sound laddish, blokes are looking for a bit of a signal that you don't just want to be one of the boys down at the Seven Stars discussing diesel and drawbars, and that you'd like – at some point – to be tumbled into bed. Rory probably doesn't know what you want.'

'Whereas Sabrina is making it only too clear?'

'Exactly.'

Georgia stacked glasses. She couldn't just tumble Rory into bed for a fleeting affair. However unfashionable, she needed it to be love. A girl like Sabrina – offering sex and giggles and no strings – was obviously far more inviting. Damn and blast her.

'Am I unfeminine, then? Because I'm a lorry driver?'

'Christ, no.' Charlie lit a cigarette. 'Quite the opposite. It's a hell of a turn-on, actually. I just think that you need to have a sort of demarcation zone when it comes to Rory. I mean, you do the same job that he does, equally as skilfully. It's like having a female jump jockey beating all the guys in the Gold Cup. It's a blow to our fragile masculine ego.'

'So – should I crash gears and stall and whimper about early-morning starts and freezing brakes?'

Charlie ruffled her hair. 'Just don't make him feel emasculated. Men still want to have that slight edge. That feeling that when the sky is caving in they can be the protectors – even if the woman they're protecting is as tough as old boots and scares the shit out of people in the boardroom.'

Georgia scooped up an armful of dirty crockery. Charlie followed her into the kitchen. 'Can I give this to the animals?'

Georgia nodded and opened the scullery door. Immediately, the kitchen was a seething mass of wriggling bodies and wagging tails. Charlie fed them. 'If you really are serious about Rory, don't play it too cool. I'm sure he likes you but Sabrina is offering relief on a plate. She'll have him into bed before you know it.'

Rory opened the door. 'I wondered if you needed a hand. You obviously don't.'

'Oh, she does.' Charlie looked at them both. 'Two if you can manage it. I'll go and keep Sabrina company.'

Georgia put the bowls into the sink and turned on the taps. Rory picked up a tea towel. They worked in silence for a while, then Rory crashed a plate on to the draining board. 'Sorry if I interrupted . . .'

'You didn't. How's Sabrina? Has she chosen your curtains for you yet?'

'The house is part-furnished. It's already got curtains.' Rory looked apologetic. 'I was going to tell you. I mentioned it to Sabrina and Beth and Spence while you were in the kitchen. I had to make some sort of neutral conversation.'

Georgia continued to slosh about in the soapsuds. 'It's not really any of my business.'

'But I'd like to have been able to tell you first. After all, you know why I haven't put down roots before. I thought you'd understand what a big step it was for me.'

She turned, soap dripping down the front of the purple velvet dress. 'Yes, I do. And I'm very pleased. Is it – um – as nice as it sounds?'

'Perfect.' Rory hung the tea towel over the radiator. Two cats immediately tugged it off. 'I'd like you to see it.'

'At the house-warming party?'

'There won't be one.' He shuddered. 'I thought we could go out – maybe to the cinema or something. Then I could cook you a meal.'

Walk on eggshells, Georgia told herself. Don't leap. 'A date?'

He nodded. 'You'll have to organise the rotas so that we both have an evening off. As long as Charlie doesn't object.'

'Charlie won't object at all. What about Sabrina?'

The kitchen door opened and Cecilia beamed at them. 'Oh, you are angels! I do hope I'm not intruding.'

They shook their heads.

'Good-oh.' Cecilia looked very much as if she would have liked to have been. 'Everyone has had far too much to drink to drive and it's such a filthy night. Spencer and Beth are staying with me. Ken is putting up Charlie on the camp-bed in his bungalow – so that just leaves you, Rory, darling.' She picked up a cat. 'Don't think I'm playing Cupid, but Georgia has a spare room . . .'

Georgia's glare would have silenced a lesser mortal. Cecilia continued to beam happily. Rory looked at Georgia for a moment. 'Oh, what a shame,' he said. 'I wish you'd mentioned it earlier. Sabrina has already offered me the use of her sofa.'

CHAPTER 11

'You look like you've just chucked away a winning lottery ticket.' Trish paused at the filing cabinet as Georgia hurled her tachograph and delivery notes on to the desk, then pulled off her jacket, scarf and gloves. It was four days after Cecilia's dinner party. Rory was driving in Scotland.

Trish found the file she wanted and closed the drawer with her hips. 'Georgia? Have you been threatened?'

'Of course not. Why?'

'Oh, nothing.' Trish pushed her hair behind her ears. 'It was something Marie said when she came in. She stopped off at South Mimms for a cup of tea, and one of the Ionio drivers got a bit lippy.'

Georgia stared at her. 'What did he say to her? Marie should be used to handling sexual innuendo from dumbos by now.'

'It was professional. This guy had heard about the problems we've had – two blow-outs, the gearboxes, you know. He said that Marie would soon be looking for a new job because everyone knew the skids were under Diadem. And that Ionio had plenty of jobs going if she was interested.'

Georgia closed her eyes. They'd been complacent for too long. 'Have you told Gran?'

Trish shook her head. 'It didn't really seem worth it. I'm sure it's just the usual rivalry thing. It'll all settle down when the new Ionio drivers realise that we've worked in harmony for years.'

Georgia was doubtful. She'd had a letter from the managing director of Jeromes that morning. Diadem were being given one last chance. 'What's Gran doing?'

'She's in the yard with the coach painters.'

'But it's dark. And all the wagons are out except mine. They won't be able to see anything.'

'They're in the workshop, silly. Cecilia's keen to get that van liveried so that Sabrina can start the courier job as soon as poss. Which means,' Trish returned to her desk with a satisfied sigh, 'that I'll have to look after that gorgeous baby. Oh well, it's gone six, so I'm off. Jed's cooking tonight so I must remember to buy some Remegel on the way home. Jesus, Georgia. You were looking like a sick poodle before I told you about Marie's run-in. What's your problem?'

'Nothing.' Georgia tugged her hair from its ponytail and eased off her boots. 'What do you think of her?'

'Who? Marie?'

'Sabrina Yates.'

'Oh, she's a scream!' Trish flicked through the computer files and logged-off. 'And Oscar is just adorable. Don't you like her?'

Sliding her feet into the comfort of her slippers and straightening the pastel cats sweater, which she'd worn despite it reminding her of the night in the Magnum, Georgia sat on the edge of Trish's desk. 'I think she's a dangerous, two-faced, lying little tart.'

'That's a bit strong isn't it?' Trish opened a packet of biscuits with her teeth and offered them to Georgia. 'Go on. I was saving them for Jed, but this is obviously an emergency. They've got chocolate bits in them.'

Georgia crunched into one without thinking.

'This must be serious.' Trish spoke through the crumbs. 'You normally go on about calories and dental decay. So, what's poor Sabrina done to you? I thought you liked her – after all, you were the one who invited her here.'

'That makes it worse.' Georgia groaned. 'I really must learn not to interfere in people's lives. I should stop thinking that I can make people happy.'

'But you do!' Trish held Georgia's hand. 'Bloody hell, you can see the change in Sabrina in just a few weeks! You should be proud –'

'She spent Saturday night with Rory. All night. Until Sunday morning. He stayed in her flat.'

Trish began to button her coat. 'I didn't realise it had got to that stage. They came back from your gran's do together, but I didn't think anything of it. I told her Oscar had been fine and then I went home. I assumed Rory had just walked her across the yard. You should have told me straight away – not kept it all bottled up. I'm sorry, Georgia – and you really fancied him.'

'No I didn't! Well – yes, I did. But it sounds so tacky like that. Fancying. I just thought that we might, well, get together.'

She sighed, ate another biscuit and told Trish about how Sabrina had inveigled the invite.

'But would you have asked him to stay with you?'

'Perhaps. But not bed. He'd just asked me out as well.'

Trish picked up her car keys. 'So? Go out with him. Have you asked either of them about their sleeping arrangements?'

'That's why he's on the long haul to Scotland. I swapped it over with Barney. And I haven't seen Sabrina. I can't *ask* them, for God's sake. And it would hardly be ethical to mention it to Rory during a debriefing.'

'I would try to forget it.'

'How can I? They're bound to have slept together, aren't they? Under the circumstances?'

'Look, I don't really see the problem. You're not going out together yet. Start worrying if he dives under her duvet when you are.' Trish swept out of the office into the darkness of the February evening, leaving Georgia munching a third biscuit and feeling more depressed than ever.

By the time Ken Poldruan had taken over the evening shift in the office, Cecilia had returned from doing deals with the coach painters. She frowned at Georgia. 'Still here, darling? Have you decided to keep Ken company?'

'Not really.' Georgia was linking paper-clips into a daisy chain. 'I just wanted to have a word about Ionio. Jeromes are getting very jumpy – and Marie was hassled by an Ionio driver. I think it's time we did something about it.'

'So do I.' Cecilia's face was weary. 'This whispering campaign is getting to everyone. I'll call a shareholders' meeting. Don't look so grim, darling. It's not the end of the world.'

Maybe not, Georgia thought, but it was beginning to feel like it.

Georgia fed the animals, showered, changed into jeans and the inebriated elephant sweater, and cooked herself cheese on toast. It was slightly burnt and leathery and tasted foul, but she ate it as a sort of penance. Nearly eight o'clock. Georgia wandered around her sitting room, finding no comfort in the familiarity. At ten past eight, she pulled on her boots, grabbed her jacket, and headed for the stairs.

This was a serious depression if a night at Am Dram with Cecilia held more allure than an evening at home. She had always had more than enough to occupy her leisure hours before. Now, every waking minute was occupied with worrying over Rory or Ionio.

She knew she would never be able to concentrate on the television or the new novel she'd bought last week. She also knew that her eyes, ears and all other faculties would be straining towards the phone. But what was the point of sitting by a phone that wasn't going to ring?

It did, just as she'd reached the foot of the stairs and opened the communal door into the hall.

'Oh, blast it,' she muttered. 'It's probably only Trish checking to make sure I haven't committed hara-kiri with the cheese knife. Or Maddy wanting to drool about Drew.'

Either way, she could do without ego-boosting chats or platitudes.

She let it ring.

As usual, the Masonic Hall was bustling. With six weeks to go before the performance, the Poges Players were feeling very confident. Georgia had been assigned the job of programme seller and front of house. She perched on one of the tip-up chairs to watch the rehearsal.

'It's going to be wonderful.' Alan Woodbury sat beside her. 'Are you staying for the whole run-through?'

Georgia nodded. She hadn't got anything better to do. She felt angry with herself for behaving like a wimp.

Alan beamed. 'Smashing! It hasn't been the same since Barney's been doing our runs again – not that he isn't excellent, of course – but I've missed you.'

Georgia was glad someone had. Alan's moustache had sprouted in sparse patches and the anticipation of stepping once more into the Am Dram spotlights had made him perspire excessively. She patted his arm. 'I've missed you, too. How's your love-life?'

'Dismal. I went out with Barbara from the library. Twice.'

'That sounds hopeful,' Georgia said kindly. 'Are you seeing her again?'

Alan shook his head. 'The first time we went to a concert in Newbury. She invited me in afterwards for a cup of decaff. It was pretty daunting because her parents were sitting on the sofa between us. I just managed to kiss the side of her nose on the doorstep. The second time, I invited her back to my house for a meal. I spent all day cooking chicken fillets in Cointreau for starters and beef in red wine. I bought a tiramisu. And I'd got Frascati and Valpolicella and Courvoisier . . .'

Jesus! Georgia thought, an alcoholic's dream dinner. 'And –?'

'And she turned up with a bottle of Aqua Libra and some

tofu in clingfilm.' Alan bit his lip. 'Teetotal. Vegan. Green-peace, Women's Lib, Hands Off Our Heritage, Ban Every-thing. And –' he swallowed, 'not only does she not use deodorants because of the destruction of the ozone layer, but she doesn't wash much either because of water conservation.'

Georgia tried hard not to laugh. 'Oh, Alan! Poor you. So, you're still looking?'

'Advertising.' Alan stood up as the principals gathered on the dimly-lit stage. 'In the *Evening Post*. The singles column. How about you? Are you seeing that nice guy we met in the Seven Stars?'

'Oh, look. Gran and Spencer are waving at you.'

Alan grinned. 'A superstar's life is never easy. I bet Mel Gibson never gets a minute to himself, either. I'll have to go. Maybe we could have a drink later.'

'Maybe.' Georgia smiled at him. 'But not a Winter Warmer.'

'No. I'm steering clear of anything Mikey concocts in future. Oh, I haven't mentioned this to Cecilia, but maybe you should. Ionio sent me a price list this morning. They've undercut you on everything.'

God! Georgia shrugged. 'I'm not surprised. They're just starting up. They'll be after all the new business they can get. So, are you going to give them a try?'

'Goodness, no. I'm not a turncoat. I place loyalty and reliability above everything else.'

Thank goodness someone does, Georgia thought with deep gratitude, as she watched him walk towards the stage.

The Poges Players, directed by Spencer, chanted woodenly through their lines. Georgia was glad that Janey Hutchinson, the playwright, wasn't there to witness the massacre. It concerned her slightly to notice that Barney was lounging against a pile of chairs very close to the stage. He and Marie rarely socialised together owing to their hordes of children. Barney had never been to Am Dram before – she hoped he merely wanted to admire Marie's performance.

As Act Three limped into action, he raised his hand in greeting across the hall. Georgia waved back. 'All right? No problems?'

'None tonight. Marie had a bit of a set-to with one of the Ionio lot at South Mimms, though. She soon put him straight.'

'Yes. I'd heard. No one has said anything to you?'

Barney shook his head. 'Not yet. And they better not start. I finished the Brum run early, so I thought I'd take Marie to the Seven Stars later. You coming over?'

'Probably.'

'Shush!' Beth Brimstone, clipboard crushed to her tightly-angora'd bosom, clapped her hands. 'We can't hear Alan.'

'Bloody good job an' all.' Barney turned back to the stage. 'Hey! What you think you're doing?'

It all happened very quickly. Alan and Marie, their arms round each other's necks but reading their lines looking more like contortionists than lovers, stopped and stared. Barney had leapt on to the stage and was bearing down on them with Spencer and Cecilia in hot pursuit.

'Get yer hands off her!'

'It's in the script!' Spencer bleated. 'It's in the – ouch!'

'Good Lord!' Cecilia had joined the mêlée. 'There was no need for that, Barney, dear, now was there?'

Marie, wailing like a banshee, watched as her husband lifted Alan off his feet and then grabbed her arm. 'You get your coat, my lady! I don't know what your mum'd say! He was mauling you!'

Marie wriggled free. 'He wasn't! We've been through all that! Be your age, Barne! We're acting!'

'That weren't no act, my girl! You was smirking at him like you smirk at me of a Saturday night!'

'So what if I was?' Marie stood, hands on hips, glaring at her husband. 'I acts every bloody Saturday night, too. I should get a sodding award for it!'

Georgia realised that her mouth was hanging open. The rest of the Poges Players were in a similar state of suspended animation.

'Right.' Barney became even more aggressive. 'That's it. We're off. You're not having nothing more to do with them.'

'Oh, but, I say –' Spencer was rubbing his jaw. 'Marie is our leading lady.'

'For God's sake, stand up to him,' Georgia whispered to Marie. 'Don't let him bully you. You drive a lorry. You run your home and your kids like other people run huge companies. Don't turn into a pussycat now.'

'I'm not,' Marie hissed back. 'But it shows he cares, see. It's like a declaration of love.'

Georgia shook her head. She'd never understand some women. 'But you've just said he was crap in bed.'

'Nah.' Marie grinned wickedly. 'He ain't and he knows it.' She gave a gleeful shudder. 'I've got what I wanted – an' so will he when we get home.'

And with arms linked they walked out of the Masonic Hall.

'This puts us in a complete quandary, my loves, doesn't it?' Spencer said, still tenderly touching his jaw.

On either side of him, Cecilia and Beth nodded their agreement.

'But who's going to play Jocasta now?' Alan straightened his cravat. 'Marie didn't have an understudy. Does it mean we'll have to recast?'

Cecilia, always at her best in a crisis, peered out into the hall. 'Georgia, darling?'

'Not a hope in hell.' Georgia was adamant. 'You'll never get me on that stage. What about Beth?'

Cecilia frowned. 'Good God, no! Jocasta is supposed to be a beautiful young thing with a body to die for.'

Spencer, who had been nodding heartily, caught his wife's eye and stopped. 'Oh no, not you, Beth my love. You're absolutely indispensable in your present role. After all, anyone can play a tart – but without you on the organising side, the show simply would not gel.'

'If it's tarts you want –' Beth looked beadily at Cecilia, 'you don't have to look too far.'

'Ladies. Ladies.' Alan rubbed his palms together. 'There must be someone else.'

The Poges Players gazed glumly at each other. Georgia felt the noose tightening round her throat.

'I don't mind giving it a bash.' Sabrina was standing in the doorway. 'That's if no one has any objections. I'm sure I'll soon pick it up.' In black ski pants, Cecilia's cashmere sweater and her own oversized donkey jacket, and with her dark hair ruffled, she looked absolutely stunning.

You've been pretty nifty at picking up everything else, Georgia thought bitterly. Why should this be any different?

'Sabrina! Angel! Oh, yes! Perfect!' Cecilia was effusive. 'What do you think, Alan? Wouldn't she be an absolute dream?'

'Dream,' Alan echoed. 'Absolutely.'

Sabrina sat next to Georgia and hugged her. 'Oh, this is so exciting. Georgia, you're mega. I'll never be able to thank you enough.'

Struggling free from the embrace, Georgia hoped her smile looked fairly genuine. 'But what are you doing here – and where's Oscar?'

'Oh,' Sabrina fluttered her ridiculously long eyelashes, 'I was in the office talking to Ken and Oscar was asleep in his carrycot. Ken said if I fancied a couple of hours off he'd mind little 'un – so here I am. Lucky, huh?'

'Very,' Georgia agreed. 'Did you get the bus?'

'Nah.' Sabrina shrugged off the donkey jacket and straightened the cashmere over her breasts. 'Rory brought me.'

'But he's in Scotland.'

'Nah.' Sabrina laughed. 'He came in just as I was leaving

the office. Ken told him where I was going, so he gave me a lift. He's outside parking the car.'

'No he isn't.' Rory loomed over them.

'Oh, hiya.' Sabrina patted the seat beside her. 'Guess what? I've got the starring role!'

Rory looked across Sabrina at Georgia. 'Hello.'

Georgia felt light-headed. She hadn't seen him for four days. She'd forgotten how gorgeous he was. 'You made good time.'

'Sabrina!' Cecilia was beckoning from the stage. 'Come up here, poppet. We're going to read through from the beginning.'

Sabrina winked at Rory. 'Next stop Hollywood,' she said, and drifted towards the stage.

Georgia gazed straight ahead. A thousand opening lines were forming themselves in her head, but they all faltered into banality before she could utter them. They all seemed to revolve around Rory having slept with Sabrina. 'I didn't think you'd be back until the morning.'

'I made such good time on the last drop it seemed silly not to come home tonight.' He leaned across the gap. 'I tried to ring you. Ken said you were here.'

'And as you were bringing Sabrina anyway –'

'I wasn't. I wanted to see you. She wanted a lift.'

Oh, joy! Georgia wanted to kiss everyone in the Masonic Hall – even Beth. For a nanosecond. Then she remembered, he'd slept with Sabrina. Only four days previously. The bastard. 'Why did you want to see me?'

'To ask you out again. It got a bit fouled up on Saturday.'

You can say that again, Georgia thought. How cool should she play this? Should she be affronted and say loftily, 'Tough, Mr Faulkner, you had your chance and blew it', or 'I'm sorry? I thought you and Sabrina had something going' or –

'When?' The word almost shocked her.

'Now, if you like.' Rory looked amused. 'I'm totally exhausted, but I'd kill for a drink. Can they spare you?'

Georgia was already on her feet. 'I don't have to do anything until the actual show. I only came tonight because – er – well . . .'

'Your gran needed a chaperone?'

'Something like that,' Georgia said, hoping that Sabrina was watching them go.

The Seven Stars was almost empty. Upton Poges was either strutting the boards or snuggled up with *Sportsnight*. They sat in the alcove by the fire, nursing lagers.

'This isn't it.' Rory stretched his legs under the opposite chair. 'The "out" bit, I mean. I still want to take you out properly. For a meal or something.'

She wanted to ask about Sabrina, but didn't want to hear the answer.

'I'd love to. When?'

'Well, I'm moving into my new place at the weekend. Some time at the beginning of next week? When we're both off the road.'

'I'll have to doctor the runs.'

'Sounds slightly distasteful.' He leaned towards her. 'I've been longing to do this for ages.'

His mouth brushed tantalisingly against hers. She could almost taste him. 'You said there wouldn't be a repeat performance.'

'I did, didn't I?' he murmured against her parted lips.

CHAPTER 12

'. . . so I suggest that Georgia takes on that task.' Cecilia tapped the top of her biro against her notepad and looked around the group gathered in Trish's bungalow. 'And the sooner the better. All agreed?'

They were. Cecilia coughed, 'Georgia, darling. How about you?'

'Uh?' Georgia stared at them. 'Sorry?' She'd been miles away – or, at least, at the Seven Stars, and then afterwards, in Rory's car outside Diadem House.

The kiss in the pub had been truce-making, a promise of things to come. The sort of kiss you could just about get away with in the middle of the evening in the Seven Stars. It had been blissful. Then, later, after Am Dram, when he had driven both her and Sabrina back to Diadem and – joy of joys! – dropped Sabrina off first, he'd kissed her good night. Again, it hadn't been a kiss of unleashed passion, but it had been very thorough and she'd kissed him back with equal enthusiasm. She hadn't invited him in. It was still too soon. And they'd both been tired.

'Darling,' Cecilia frowned. 'This is a board meeting. Very informal, I grant you, but a board meeting nevertheless. We are fighting for our survival. Do try to concentrate.'

'I was. What have you just volunteered me for?'

'Infiltrating Vivienda – well, Ionio,' Cecilia said. 'We need some inside info on their plans before we fire warning shots across their bows. I thought you'd be perfect.'

They were all smiling and nodding. Cecilia and Ken, Trish and Jed, Barney and Marie: the Diadem shareholders. They looked, Georgia thought, slightly blurred at the edges and suffused in pink light. It was an odd phenomenon. Things had been like that ever since Rory had driven her home. It had made motorway driving really pretty.

'. . . so, just call in. Pretend you're a secretary or something, on your way home from work. Your boss wants quotes on deliveries to Luton and Darlington and – oh, you decide, darling. You've done this sort of thing before – and you're so good at it.'

'What?' Georgia returned to the present again. 'I mean, yes . . . lovely.'

Trish giggled, and stood up. 'I'll put the kettle on. I think we've got everything sorted. Georgia, come and give me a hand.'

Georgia drifted out into Trish's white and chrome kitchen. It was, as always, amazingly tidy and, beneath the harsh strip-lighting, looked like an operating theatre. Georgia, who was a very haphazard housekeeper, was rather in awe of it.

'Do you know what you've agreed to do?' Trish set out white Habitat cups and saucers on an even whiter tray. 'Do you know what day it is? Or shall we start with an easy one? What-is-your-name?'

Georgia leaned against the pristine table and smiled distractedly.

'Oh, God.' Trish filled a snowy teapot. 'Diadem doesn't have a hope of beating off Vivienda with you in this mood. Have you written his name on your pencil case yet? Has Sabrina been relegated to the second division?'

'Sabrina who?'

Trish laughed and emptied a packet of chocolate digestives on to a plate. 'Ten out of ten, Mr Faulkner.'

'When am I going to have to make this call?'

Trish handed her the tray. 'Can you manage without dropping this? Tomorrow.'

'Oh. Fine.' Georgia paused in the doorway. 'Do you know what tomorrow is?'

'If you're going to start quoting the *Desiderata* at me, or tell me it's the first day of the rest of my life, I shall probably hit you.'

'Valentine's Day.' Georgia grinned. 'And Rory has asked me out for a meal. Isn't that perfect?'

Georgia pulled the MG into Ionio's car park beside a top-of-the-range Jaguar at just after half past three the following afternoon. She had already done a short multi-drop run to Basingstoke in the Scania, and had gone straight home to shower and change into the cream Laurèl suit that looked more secretary than lorry driver.

There had been no thump of Valentine cards on the doormat – but that was no surprise. She hadn't expected anyone to send her a card anyway.

She locked the car and shivered. A biting north wind had chased the rain away, leaving a whistling greyness that rattled the branches of the trees and made paperchases from the litter in the gutter. Tucking her hair more securely into its secretarial bun, she walked across the yard. She couldn't, under any circumstances, reveal her true colours on this visit. She'd just have to keep her temper and not threaten to firebomb the company that was menacing her entire livelihood. She sighed. It wasn't going to be easy.

In Claude Foskett's day, Ionio had consisted of a shabby Terrapin office and a ramshackle corrugated-iron shed which housed his four lorries. Today, the faded navy and dirty white of Ionio had been transformed by the red and yellow corporate identity of Vivienda. The Terrapin was being replaced by a brick-built two-storey office block, and the existing lorries had been painted and joined by three brand-new Volvos. The whole place had an air of bustling prosperity.

Picking her way round a JCB and a cement mixer and ignoring the catcalls from a group of builders who were sheltering from the wind in the back of a van, Georgia headed for the office. The evidence of so much wealth was pretty daunting. Previously, Diadem and Ionio had co-existed in harmony, each knowing the other's contracts and not dreaming of encroaching on them. This was something completely different.

'Hello.' A glamorous black girl smiled from behind the desk. 'Can I help you?'

Claude Foskett had never bothered with the niceties of a reception area. Potential customers stepped straight into the Terrapin where he worked in a fug of tobacco smoke and, above the blast of Radio One, had shouted their requirements to a pink-haired bimbette.

'I hope so.' Georgia went into secretarial mode. She'd done this for Cecilia on two or three occasions and the script was easy to remember. Today's circumstances were much, much harder, though. 'I work for a small engineering company in Oxford and we're looking to expand into this area. We use carriers on an as-and-when basis at the moment, but we'll be wanting something more regular when we move. My boss would like to make an appointment with you, of course, for an in-depth discussion – but, as I was passing, he asked if I'd call in.'

The receptionist touched a computer keyboard with one hand and reached for a card index with the other. Claude had used an exercise book and a pencil. 'That sounds interesting. I'm sure we can help you. Do you have any transport of your own?'

'A small van. But we're going to need trailers as well.'

'Yes, of course. Please take a seat and I'll sort out some quotes.'

Georgia sat down and the girl sorted. She looked very elegant in her black suit with white collar and cuffs and her understated gold jewellery. Her blue-black hair was coiled elegantly into the nape of her slender neck. It was almost as if she'd been chosen specially to add to the air of new opulence.

The receptionist raised her voice above the whirr of the printer. 'I'm sure you'll find us very competitive. Have you made enquiries elsewhere?'

Startled, Georgia looked up. 'I think Mr – um – Markham mentioned another firm in – Milton St John? No, Upton Poges. Diamed? Diamond?'

'Diadem?' The receptionist raised her eyebrows. 'I really think it would be a waste of time contacting them. I understand they're almost bankrupt.'

Georgia glared across the desk. She had never felt so angry. The receptionist continued to smile. 'You know what it's like with these small companies – they can't afford to repair the vehicles, or keep up with the current legislation.'

Biting the insides of her cheeks to prevent any sound escaping, Georgia nodded. The receptionist peered at her. 'Touch of toothache?'

Georgia nodded again, sitting on her hands in case she grabbed the slender gold-chained throat.

'Shame. I always swear by oil of cloves. Ah, these are what you want.'

Jessica Sargeant, secretary to Gregory Markham of Markham and Peabody, who made machine parts – mainly for export – just outside Oxford, and who was suffering from raging toothache, was efficiently furnished with a full set of quotes for runs to docks, airports and to all the other places Diadem delivered on a regular basis.

'Please get Mr Markham to make an appointment with our Mr Woodhead when he's had a chance to skim through those,' the receptionist said as Georgia stood up. 'They're just basic quotes, but we can always offer substantial discounts on contracts.'

They smiled their goodbyes and, just as Georgia reached the door, a well-groomed woman in her late fifties emerged from the back office and swept past her, almost knocking her off her feet.

'I'm terribly sorry! I didn't notice you.' She nodded towards the receptionist. 'Field any calls for twenty minutes, Edel, then put them through to my mobile. I'll probably be stationary on the motorway by that time. Anything urgent, fax to London and I'll pick it up later.' And, in a whirl of expensive tweed suit and lowlighted fair hair, she headed for the Jaguar in the car park.

'Mrs Kendall. From Vivienda's head office in London,' the receptionist told her. 'She involves herself in all the new companies. She's been a great help – and she's ever so down to earth considering she's the chairman.'

Georgia watched as the Jag tore out of the car park and wished she had known that the whirlwind Mrs Kendall had been in the building. Vivienda must be taking the growth of Ionio very seriously indeed if they had sent the chairman in person. It didn't augur well.

Georgia hurried back to the MG. The builders had gone, and she huddled in the driving seat, leafing through the laser-printed sheets. They didn't make happy reading. Even without the discounts, some of the prices were far lower than Diadem's. There was, as Alan had said, some serious undercutting going on. Cecilia wasn't going to like it one little bit. And as for the smear campaign . . . Georgia pushed the papers into her briefcase and started the car.

The Scania and both Magnums were in the yard when she got back to Upton Poges. The threat of Vivienda receded a little in the joyous knowledge that Rory was home. Forgetting the suit and the unfamiliar high heels, she ran into the office.

'Oh!' A single red rose lay on her desk. She picked up the box with its intricately twirled ribbons and searched for a card.

'It's from Rory.' Trish came through from the back room carrying the inevitable coffee and biscuits. 'And, before you melt in a gooey heap on the floor, we all got one. Me, Marie, Sabrina, even your gran.'

Delight deflated like an overcooked soufflé. 'That was nice of him.'

'Yeah.' Trish plonked her mug on the desk. 'Your gran, of course, has had Interflora beating a path to the door all day. Flowers from Ken and Spence and Tom Lennard and Leon at the restaurant and various customers and God knows who else. I only got a card from Jed. How about you?'

'Oh, the usual. You know, sackloads of the stuff. I'll get my secretary to sort through it later.'

'So, how did your spying go?'

'Not good.' Georgia sat at the desk. 'Not good at all.'

She repeated the conversation later to Cecilia in the sitting room which now resembled a Mafia funeral parlour. Flowers tumbled from every vase and jug. Cards, embellished with satin hearts and garish roses, adorned the mantelpiece.

Screwing small diamond studs into her ears and hopping about on one of her high-heeled Pierre Chupins, Cecilia frowned. 'It all sounds mighty fishy. I've had a quick peek through the quotations and you're right. It looks as though they're deliberately undercutting us. I'm surprised you didn't punch the receptionist – I hope she realises we could sue for defamation. We'll have to watch them very carefully.'

'I wonder if we should be watching things closer to home.' Georgia surveyed her reflection in the looking glass above the fire. She was just visible through the Valentine salutations. 'Do you think that Ionio are working on information supplied by one of us – however innocently?'

'I shouldn't think so. And the prices aren't our main worry anyway, are they? We can deal with those. It's the rumours of unreliability and the breakdowns that could cause more damage. They're certainly not down to anyone at Diadem.'

Georgia bit her lip. 'God, this is so awful. Are we going to have to drop our prices across the board?'

'Not yet.' Cecilia picked up the astrakhan coat. 'We'll wait until one of our regulars squeals or defects. Jeromes being let down again, or Lennards starting to believe that we're inefficient or dishonest could be disastrous. But they're all hunky-dory at the moment. Oh, sod it – let's forget it for a bit. After all, it is supposed to be the most romantic night of the year. You look beautiful, darling. Is the outfit for Charlie's benefit? If so, it probably won't stay on for long – he always seems so delightfully physically inclined.'

Georgia shook her head. 'Not Charlie. Rory.'

'Wonderful! That's even better!' Cecilia hugged her. 'Oh, Georgia – I do hope this is the one.'

So did Georgia – and it came as something of a shock. After years of being perfectly happy to be single, Rory had made her think longingly of companionship and love, of home-making and babies. It was all rather disturbing.

Cecilia looked approvingly at the scarlet dress. 'And where are you going?'

'I've no idea. Out for a meal, he said. I'd rather hoped he'd invite me back to his new place.'

Cecilia picked up her handbag. 'Set all the ground rules first, darling. On neutral territory. Of course, I'll be awfully discreet in the morning if you invite him back here.'

'I won't.' Georgia shook her head. There was still the spectre of his night with Sabrina to overcome. 'Not this time. And – er – who are you being wined and dined by?'

'Kenny, of course. Bless him. At the Randolph. I believe he's booked rooms.'

Singular, Georgia thought. 'Oh, lovely. Enjoy yourselves.'

Cecilia kissed her expansively and swept towards the door. 'You too, darling. And don't worry about Vivienda tonight. Just be gloriously carefree.'

But she didn't feel carefree. Once Cecilia had gone and she'd returned to her own part of the house, she felt as nervous as a schoolgirl about to embark on her first date. The hands on the clock seemed to be slipping backwards. Her own were equally sticky – which more than made up for the lack of moisture in her mouth.

The dogs heard the doorbell almost before she did, and accompanied her down the stairs with their usual exuberance.

Rory, wearing a dark grey suit and a paler grey shirt and tie, stood in the porch. 'You look gorgeous.' He stepped into the hall. 'And these are for you.'

She took the bunch of white freesias and swallowed. 'Oh, they're lovely. Thank you. But, I thought – the rose?'

'Was my way of not drawing attention to anything.' He was stroking the dogs and cats with both hands and not looking at her. The hall light was spinning diamonds in his fair hair. 'Was it an unacceptable gesture to a group of militant feminists?'

'God, not at all. Everyone was delighted. Especially Sabrina.' She wished she hadn't said that. Bitchiness wasn't in the least attractive. She waved her hands around vaguely. 'Oh, you know. What with her success in the Poges Players . . . I think she's enjoying being swamped with flowers.'

Rory laughed and stood up. 'Yes, she rang me to say thank you. Apparently she had bouquets from Charlie and Alan too. Or am I not supposed to tell you that?'

Blast, Georgia thought, reaching for her jacket. Not that Charlie and Alan had sent flowers, but that Sabrina already had Rory's phone number. 'Alan is really nice – that's typical of him. And Charlie – well,' she put on her jacket, 'he's probably just setting out his stall.'

She peered at Rory as she freed her hair from the jacket's collar. He didn't look in the slightest put-out. Sabrina must have been a one-night stand. That didn't make it all right, of course, but it was better than the alternative.

'I'll just put these into water.' She buried her nose in the classic blooms. The scent increased her pulse rate. 'They really are heavenly.'

He followed her into the kitchen and leaned against the door jamb. Her hands shook as she placed the freesias into a vase. The last time he'd stood there they'd ended up kissing for England. 'Where are we going?'

'Leon's. I hope that's all right?'

'Brilliant.' Moving away from Rory, she shooed the animals back into the hall. The urge to recreate the moment was incredibly strong. 'I've never actually eaten there, just had take-aways.'

'Me too.' His eyes were roaming round the kitchen. 'I didn't take in the décor last time I was here. It's very –'

'Bright?'

He nodded. 'Cheerful. I had no idea there were so many shades of yellow.'

'Neither had I.' She smiled at him over her shoulder. 'I bought millions of those little tester pots of paint from B and Q and just kept daubing. On grey days it always looks sunny.'

'And on sunny days?'

'You can't even make toast without your Ray-Bans.'

They stepped out into the blustery night and he held the car door open for her. 'I'm never sure where chauvinism begins and good manners end. Is this acceptable?'

'Very much so. I've never believed in feminism on Valentine's Day.'

'So what do you believe in?' Rory started the car and they headed for the main road.

'Almost all of it.' Georgia snuggled happily into her seat. 'Fairies, Father Christmas, the Easter Bunny . . .'

He stared seriously ahead through the windscreen. 'Me too.'

Georgia thought it was probably the sexiest remark she had ever heard.

*

Leon's was crowded with happy couples. Red roses were on each table and obscenely chubby pink Cupids held the menus. Plinkety-plonk music echoed tinnily from behind garlands of entwined love-hearts and blowsy bows.

Rory gazed around with amusement. 'Are you happy with this? Are you sure you wouldn't have preferred damask linen and candlelight?'

'Goodness, no. Far too grown-up.'

They were still giggling when Leon, effusive as ever and displaying his yellow tombstone teeth, bore down on them with suggestions. They settled for taramasalata and humus to be followed by a selection of kebabs and salads.

'And drinks?' Leon whisked away the menu-holding cherub. 'Is it to be champagne?'

'It is.' Rory nodded. 'Although Georgia will have to drink most of it as I'm driving.'

'My brother – 'e will drive you 'ome if you gets too pissed,' Leon enthused. 'No problems. And Miss Cecilia? She got my flowers?'

'She did,' Georgia told him gravely. 'They were lovely. She'll be in to thank you personally, no doubt.'

Leon, who had been thanked personally by Cecilia in the past, blushed and bustled away. Georgia looked across at Rory and they both laughed.

They demolished Leon's mountain of food without much trouble.

'I do like to see someone with a good appetite.' Rory pushed the remains of his baklava to the side of his pudding dish. 'Most women pick at their food.'

'Have I been a pig?' Georgia spooned up the last of her ice-cream and wondered if he was referring to Stephanie. 'Because if I have, I'm not going to apologise. I'm a trucker, remember?'

'How could I forget? Anyway, after that night in the North-East I have no illusions about you eating like a sparrow.' His eyes softened. 'I'd like to do it again.'

'We haven't finished this one yet.'

'Not this.' He topped up her champagne glass. 'Although I'd like to do this again, too. No, I meant the double-manning. I really enjoyed it.'

'So did I. Maybe we could do Scotland.' She took a shaky sip of champagne, hoping that she hadn't sounded too eager. 'We've got another long haul booked in a few weeks.'

'That'd be great. God, I'm so glad I came to Diadem.'

'Are you? Even though it meant having to face up to things you'd rather forget? I mean, putting down roots and every-thing.'

He lifted his coffee cup. 'Well, they're only six-month roots at present. Hardly perennial. And no,' he reached for her hand, 'that hasn't caused me any sleepless nights. My new place is great – I can't wait for you to see it.'

She held her breath. Was he going to ask her to stay the night? He tightened his grip on her fingers. 'I'm not straight yet. I've – I've actually sent for some of my stuff from London. I suppose I'm thinking of making a proper home at last. When it's all in place – would you come for a meal?'

She exhaled, careful to keep the disappointment from her voice, conveniently forgetting that if he *had* asked her she was going to refuse. 'I'd love to. Although I don't mind a bit of mess.'

'Neither do I. But it's important that when you see Windwhistle Cottage for the first time it's exactly how I want it to be.'

'Just tell me when it's all *Homes and Gardens* and I'll be there. I've got something to ask you, too.'

He sat back in his chair, still holding her hand across the table.

'Ages ago, I invited you to come and see Tumbling Bay – and then, well, it didn't happen, did it?'

'No.' He grinned at her. 'There did seem to be some sort of a hiccup.'

'He's running at Windsor the week after next. Would you like to come with me?' She was holding her breath again. Please God don't let him say Sabrina had already asked him. 'I – I haven't told anyone else – not even Gran. I just want to see how he does. If he doesn't like jumping or gets frightened or falls, I don't want anyone there to laugh at him.'

'Of course you don't. Georgia, I'd love it. I know Sabrina mentioned going racing at your gran's supper party and I wondered if she'd been invited –'

'Oh, bugger Sabrina!'

Heads turned. Georgia knew she was blushing. Rory rocked on his chair. 'Obviously not the right thing to say. I only thought that she might be going as she and Charlie seemed to be so friendly now.'

'You'd know more about that than I would – after all, you spent the night with her.'

The plinkety-plonk music stopped. The neighbouring three tables gave up all pretence of eating. Rory folded his napkin. 'Yes, but we didn't discuss racing.'

'I'm sure you didn't.'

'Georgia, look at me.' He leaned forward and took both her hands. 'Oscar cried most of the night – and I wanted to. I slept fitfully on the sofa, kicking myself because I couldn't accept your invitation. I thought Charlie was bound to be staying with you. And I didn't sleep with Sabrina. There was never any question that I would. She is definitely not my type.'

'She's not?' Georgia wanted to clear the room and instigate wild dancing. 'Honestly?'

'Honestly.' Whisking his tie away from the ice-cream, he leaned forward even further and kissed her. 'And if she had been – my type, I mean, I still wouldn't have slept with her. I'm funny like that. And what about you? With Charlie?'

'God, no! He stayed at Ken's. Is that what you thought? That he was with me that night?'

Rory nodded and they laughed at each other.

'More champagne?' Leon glided towards the table. 'And my brother to drive you 'ome?'

'Absolutely,' said Rory. 'I think we're celebrating.'

Chapter 13

The morning was grey and motionless, misty and smelling of earth. Georgia, less in control than she had ever dreamed possible, smudged her mascara and laddered two pairs of stockings.

Three cats watched from the snug confines of her duvet. Then, becoming bored with the floor show, they tucked plump heads beneath sleek paws and slept. Balling up the ruined stockings, she pulled on a pair of opaque black tights – to hell with freezing in fifteen-denier anyway – and opened the wardrobe. Dress warmly, Drew and Maddy had advised. Windsor racecourse is near the river, they'd said; it'll be damp and chilly.

She rattled through the hangers. The customer-visiting cream Laurèl was far too flimsy, and would look wrong with thick tights and loafers. She had to look smart: firstly, because of her debut in the Paddock as an owner, and secondly, because Rory would be there with her.

She decided on a red suit, usually shunned because of the tightness of its skirt and its hip-skimming jacket, and tugged it on. She looked at herself in her dressing-table mirror. It was certainly glamorous but the amount of cleavage exposed would bring on hypothermia – or at least a nasty chest cold – before lunch. It needed something underneath it, preferably a Damart vest, and one of Jessie Hopkins's jumpers was out of the question. What did she have that was black and tight-fitting and warm?

Trish's body! With a cry that made all the cats open reproachful orange owl-eyes, Georgia took off the suit. Trish had lent her the body before Christmas for a party. And she'd never returned it.

Five minutes later, with her head and both hands between her legs, she managed to fasten the final popper. She wouldn't be able to drink anything all day, she knew, because a visit to the Ladies would take for ever. The sooner someone designed bodies that fastened with Velcro the better.

She pulled on her suit once again, checked her make-up, flicked her hair to her shoulders and picked up her almost-real Chanel bag which was crammed with packets of Polo mints. She felt she'd pass muster in the Paddock; she only hoped that she'd knock Rory for six as well.

Creeping down the stairs, she undid the latch on the front door.

'Darling!' Cecilia swept through the adjoining door almost as though she'd been hiding behind it for hours. 'Oh! Stunning! Now, you know I'm not one to pry, and when you said you were taking a day off, I didn't ask any questions, did I? Not even when I checked Trish's rotas and found that Rory was off too, but . . .'

'We're having an outing. Together.' Georgia cursed silently.

'So I gathered.' Cecilia's eyes glinted with excitement. 'Is he taking you to meet his mother?'

Georgia laughed. 'Not quite. I'll tell you all about it when I get back.' She kissed her grandmother's cheek, and tried not to notice the touch of disappointment in her eyes. 'I must go.'

It was almost like bunking off school, Georgia decided, as she drove the MG out of the yard. Knowing that everyone else was working; watching the comings and goings at Diadem and realising that for once she wouldn't be part of it. She so very rarely took time off work. And especially now that things were so grim, she felt deliciously reckless. Determined not to think about Vivienda, or smear campaigns, or industrial espionage for at least twenty-four hours, she turned up the Dinah Washington tape and headed for the Tiptoe road.

Windwhistle Cottage stood a little way back from the road: a proper cottage with bulging windows, uneven walls and a crazily-tiled sloping roof that looked like the frilly underside of a field mushroom.

Georgia stopped outside and gazed at it with pleasure. She couldn't wait to see what it was like inside. Even on this grey morning it had charm. She imagined it in the summer, when the old roses swarming round the door would droop with heavy heads and the garden would be shoulder-high with hollyhocks and delphiniums. The chestnut tree by the rickety gate would drip creamy pink candles, and the little path, just visible at the side of the cottage, would tread softly between beds of phlox and lupins and tunnels of soft fruit.

When Rory emerged and closed the front door behind him, Georgia gulped. He was wearing a dark grey suit, and – oh joy – a red-and-white-striped shirt and a red tie.

'Morning.' He doubled himself into the MG. 'You look wonderful.'

'So do you.' She smiled shyly. 'I only hope we don't look too Torville and Dean.'

'A matching pair,' Rory agreed, fastening his seat belt with difficulty. She was glad the journey wouldn't be very long. He was far too big for the car. 'Are you nervous?'

'Petrified.' Georgia eased the MG into first gear. 'God knows how Tumbling Bay feels.'

Because of work commitments, they'd met only briefly in the office since Valentine's Day, although there had been a mass of highly-expensive Vodaphone calls from various parts of the country.

Dinah Washington crooned about being mad about the boy, and Georgia blushed.

'Are we going straight to the racecourse?' Rory tried to fit his legs under the dashboard, gave it up as a bad job, and hugged his knees.

'Yes. Drew and Charlie'll be there early. Do you want to go back and get your car? I hate to see you all concertina'd like that.'

'I'll cope.' Rory grinned above Dinah Washington. 'I've always fancied having a chauffeur – or should that be chauffeuse?'

'Chauffeur,' Georgia said severely, heading for the M4. 'Don't start lapsing into sexism now. Not today.'

Looking like the entrance to a stately home with its curved gravelled drives and sweeping tree-fringed lawns, Windsor Racecourse was crowded with horseboxes, opulent limousines and muddied Land-Rovers. Following Drew's scribbled directions, Georgia rattled the MG across the cattle-grids and into the car park reserved for owners and trainers. She was sure that one of the sheepskin-jacket-and-trilby brigade of stewards would come across at any minute and send her over to the parking spaces allotted to visitors. It didn't seem right to be amongst the elite.

Rory scrambled from the car's confines and stretched with relief. 'Where to now?'

'I've no idea.' Georgia locked the MG and stood beside him. He towered above her and she almost wished she'd worn heels. 'We're very early.'

They stood beneath the bare black arms of the trees and watched horses in rugs being walked along the paths beside the stables, the hustle and bustle of stable lads diving in and out of boxes, and the bookmakers arriving with their satchels and boards. Ladies in hats and men in Barbours poured out of Discoverys and Volvos and disappeared into the scrum with an air of knowing exactly what they were doing.

Rory seemed fascinated. 'A whole new world. An industry carrying on like this every day while other people are stuck behind desks –'

'Or steering wheels.'

'Or steering wheels, building dreams for an afternoon and moving on. Like a circus.'

She nodded, sharing his delight. 'Would you like a drink?' Too late, she remembered the body. She'd just have to sip something slowly.

'I'd adore a cup of coffee. Do you think there's anywhere open?'

'Sure to be. I've got these badges. Drew said they'd open doors.' She handed one to Rory and, having tied hers to the chain on her shoulder-bag, watched him fasten his badge to his lapel with the confident air of one who had graced the higher echelons of racing for a lifetime. 'Shall we go and investigate?'

They found a large canteen serving fry-ups to ever-starving stable staff and sandwiches to early visitors. Too nervous to eat, Georgia and Rory secured coffees and a window-seat and surveyed the increasing excitement.

'Look!' Georgia waved her racecard across the table. 'I can't believe it.'

Rory smiled at her delight. Among the seventeen runners listed for the first race, Tumbling Bay's name stood out proudly: owner, G. Drummond; trainer, D. Fitzgerald; jockey, C. Somerset.

'Does it seem real now?'

'Mm. And scary.'

Fortified, they set off in search of Tumbling Bay. Drew found them first and, introductions made, led the way to the stables. 'He'll be out in a minute. He's fine. We'll take him round to the pre-parade area, and you can be there for the saddling-up.'

Georgia jigged up and down like a child. 'Is Maddy here?'

Drew shook his head. 'No. She sends her love and apologies. Her ankles are swollen and her back aches and she's feeling fed up. She says she'll have all her extremities crossed though – at least all the ones that she can reach.'

Georgia caught hold of Rory's hand. 'You'll love Maddy. You'll meet her later.'

'I will?'

'When we go back to Peapods. We're invited to dinner. Didn't I tell you?' Knowing that she hadn't, she pulled him forward. 'And this is Tumbling Bay.'

The horse nuzzled against her, searching for Polos. 'Later.' She kissed his long bony nose. 'After the race you can have as many Polos as you like. Just get round safely and if you don't like it, just stop.'

Drew laughed. 'Those are not the usual sort of instructions I hear from owners.'

'I mean it.' Georgia looked at him fiercely. 'I'll tell Charlie, too. If he hurts himself, I'll never forgive you.'

'Don't worry.' Drew hugged her. 'Now, are you ready for your debut?'

The saddling-up procedure was completed in open-fronted boxes, watched by an interested crowd. Georgia, all fingers and thumbs, left the tricky bits to Drew and the lads. Tumbling Bay seemed calmer than any of them, blowing foamily down his nostrils and rubbing his head against Georgia's shoulders.

The tannoy crackled, announcing the runners and riders, and the crowd – quite large for a minor meeting – flocked towards the Parade Ring. Still clutching Rory's hand, Georgia followed the rest of the owners beneath the archway of sagging branches.

The horses stalked round the ring, their hoofs muffled. Georgia stood in the middle of the grass wanting to burst with pride.

'How are the butterflies?' Rory asked.

'Aerobic,' Georgia whispered.

The other owners looked extremely blasé. They were a mixed bunch: corpulent business syndicates in suits and sheepskins, county types with waxed jackets and snug hats, debs and chinless wonders, and one elderly couple who looked as though they'd been dreamed-up by Noël Coward.

'Here they come!' The shout echoed from the back of the crowd, and all heads turned towards the weighing room as the jockeys strolled jauntily down the steps and crossed the grass.

Taller than the rest, Charlie saluted Georgia with his whip and winked. She tried to smile back. A gaggle of jockey groupies swarmed round him brandishing autograph books and racecards. Charlie kissed everyone.

Rory leaned towards her. 'Even if I'd never met him, I'd know he was your jockey.'

'Why?' Her heart was somewhere in her throat, making breathing difficult.

'The colours.' Rory blinked exaggeratedly and she punched him. 'Everyone else is in brown or sludge green.'

'Don't you like them? I'd wanted a sort of multicoloured patchwork effect, but another owner had already got something similar, so I settled for a diagonal rainbow instead.'

'Well, it'll give him a hell of an advantage,' Rory conceded as the jockeys joined their connections. 'He should blind the opposition.'

Charlie shook hands with Drew and Rory and hugged Georgia. 'You look sensational. Dead sexy. Mind, I got the piss taken out of me something rotten in the changing room.' He pulled at his colours. 'The lads reckon I'm only wearing these so that when I fall off the ambulance will be able to find me quickly.'

'Jockeys, please mount,' the tannoy barked bossily.

Charlie swung himself into Tumbling Bay's saddle. For a second Georgia wanted to tell him to forget it; that it was a crazy dream; that she'd die if either of them were hurt. She licked her dry lips. 'Good luck. Just be safe.'

Charlie touched his cap and circled away. She sagged against Rory. 'I don't think I can bear to watch.'

'I'm not sure I can either.' His breath was warm against her cold cheek. 'Shall we go and take our minds off it for a second? We haven't had a bet yet.'

'Go and see what odds you can get,' Drew advised. 'I backed him yesterday at fifties but you'll probably do better here. Rising Sun is the red-hot favourite. I'll meet you in the stand.'

The bookies, still bellowing the odds to those punters who hung on until the last minute in the hope of a good price, were not optimistic about Tumbling Bay's chances. Georgia felt very indignant on his behalf.

'Bloody sixty-six to one. I know it's his first time out, but even so . . .'

Rory had already taken a twenty-pound note from his wallet and was advancing towards the bookmaker. 'Oh, damn it. Let's go the whole hog.' He pulled out more notes. 'Fifty pounds each way on Tumbling Bay.'

The bookie snatched the money from his grasp and put it into his satchel with the sort of benign smile saved specially for mug punters. Georgia was horrified. 'You can't afford that!'

'It's special.' Rory brushed his lips against her cheek. 'Like you.'

Georgia fumbled with the clasp of her handbag. 'And for me.' She glared at the well-fed bookmaker as if daring him to contradict her choice. 'Fifty pounds each way. Tumbling Bay.'

The transaction completed, she and Rory stared at each other. In the middle of the pushing crowds, beneath the grey sky, their relationship had shifted. And they both knew it.

Rory broke the silence. 'If he loses, we'll both have to do a lot of overtime.'

'And if he doesn't, we'll celebrate all weekend.'

'Either way, I can't wait.'

They hurried back towards the crowded stand reserved for

members and squeezed in beside Drew. 'We took sixty-six to one,' Georgia whispered to him. 'And I think I'm going to be sick.'

They watched the horses lining up on the screen, circling, forming and dissolving. The starter was growing impatient. The tension was unbearable.

'Oh, for God's sake get on with it,' Georgia grumbled.

They did. The tape flew into the air and the horses surged forward untidily. Drew had his field-glasses clamped to his eyes and was motionless except for a muscle twitching in his jaw. Georgia prayed under her breath as the ragged stream approached the first hurdle.

'I can't look.' She buried her face in Rory's arm. 'Tell me when it's over.'

The crowd screamed encouragement and Georgia could feel the thunder of the hoofs approaching the Grandstand. They had another circuit to go.

'Two fallers,' Rory said hoarsely. 'Not us.'

She loved the 'us'. 'Are they OK?'

'All on their feet.'

The horses streamed past. The brilliant rainbow colours were bobbing along in the middle of the pack. Georgia felt a surge of pride, which was immediately submerged by irrational fear. 'Oh, God. Please let him be all right. I'll never put him through this again. Never.'

'Yes, you will. He loves it,' Drew said, not moving the binoculars. 'I knew he would.'

The second circuit seemed to go on for ever. There were several more casualties, none serious. Rory kept up a running commentary, his voice becoming huskier above the roar of the crowd.

'Only three more fences to go.' She could hardly hear him above the general noise and the nasal ranting of the commentator. 'He rattled that one though. He's still on his feet – oh, God!'

'What?' She clutched frantically at Rory's sleeve and opened her eyes. She couldn't see anything, just a group of horses bearing down towards the finishing post. 'Where is he? What's happened?'

The roar of the crowd almost obliterated Drew's muttered curses as Charlie and Tumbling Bay came over to the grandstand side of the course for the final hurdle. They were practically obscured from view by a golden horse the size of a small house.

'He's going to win!'

'No,' Drew's teeth were clenched, 'he's not going to win. Rising Sun is stronger and he's got an edge – but unless Charlie fouls this last hurdle he should get a place.'

Georgia willed Tumbling Bay to leap as he'd never leapt before. Charlie gathered him up, urged him into two short strides, then, neck-for-neck with the golden Rising Sun, they soared over the brushwood. The blurred multicoloured arc was a garish slash against the low pewter sky and the thundering of hoofs on turf jarred her bones. Her rainbow colours streaked towards the winning post alongside Rising Sun's far more austere brown and cream.

Tumbling Bay finished second.

'That was bloody amazing,' Drew enthused as they pushed their way through the crowd to the Winners Enclosure. 'He jumped like a stag, and loved every minute of it. Just as well you took a good price today – the odds'll be right down at Newbury.'

Georgia did a quick calculation of her winnings and her share of the prize money. 'It'll take care of your training fees for a while.'

'I'll go and collect our ill-gotten gains. After all, we're disgustingly rich now, aren't we?' Rory said.

'Richer than we were ten minutes ago, but that's not important. He ran so well – and he's all right! Oh, look at him! He's such a darling!' She caught Rory's eyes. 'Are you laughing at me?'

'No, just sharing your excitement.' He laced his fingers even more tightly with hers, then swung her round and kissed her.

She sighed with happiness and kissed him back. Her icing of perfection had a cherry on the top.

Once they reached the Winners Enclosure, Georgia ran towards Tumbling Bay and hugged Charlie as he slid to the ground. 'Oh, you were both incredible. Thank you so much.'

Charlie, reeking of sweat and Paco Rabanne, kissed her as expansively as his lack of breath would allow, then panted at Drew as he tugged off the saddle. 'Christ, Mr F, he was brilliant. I knew he'd be brave and jump well, I just wasn't sure if he'd spook with the crowds and everything. He's ace at home, but I never dreamed he'd respond to the course like that. I think we're talking Cheltenham and Aintree here.'

'No, we're not.' Georgia lifted her face from Tumbling Bay's sweating neck. 'The fences are too high. I won't let him risk an accident.'

'Women!' Charlie teased, pulling a face as he dived off towards the Weighing Room. 'Your horse is a natural, Georgia. Don't deny him his rights.'

Georgia poked her tongue out at Charlie's back. Drew put his arm round her shoulders. 'There's loads of time to discuss Tumbling Bay's future. Right now, I think the gentlemen of the racing press want to talk to you.'

'Why?' Georgia gave Tumbling Bay a final kiss as his lad led him away. 'Surely they'll want to interview Rising Sun's owners?'

'Rising Sun is well-known. There's quite a story behind Tumbling Bay – and they love anything like that. Gypsy horse makes good. It'll be good copy.'

She wrinkled her nose. 'Shall I tell them I nicked him?'

Drew shook his head. 'Use a bit of poetic licence. You

bought him fair and square from some travellers. Expand on his run-down condition. You'll have to fudge his original ownership.'

'OK. Why's Rory taking so long?'

'Putting champagne on ice if he's got any sense,' Drew said. 'Now, are you ready?'

She was bursting to spend a penny, but by the time she'd got to grips with the body's poppers the reporters would have lost interest. She would just have to hope that they'd put her jigging about down to nervous excitement.

CHAPTER 14

The MG bounced across Peapods' cobbles in the wake of Drew's dark blue Mercedes, Charlie's red Calibra, and the horseboxes. The house loomed through the murky twilight, lights spilling across the yard like liquid gold. Georgia shivered and sniffed the chill night air.

Rory unwound himself and stretched. 'Well? Is it going to rain?'

'Probably. You can always smell it coming off the Downs. Still, it doesn't matter now, does it? It stayed fine today.' She curled herself into his arms. 'I'm so happy – and extremely hungry.'

'So am I.' His lips skimmed her hair.

She laughed. 'Good. Maddy likes people who do her food justice.'

Drew, on his way to bed-down the horses and check the other occupants of the yard, raised his voice. 'Don't hang around out here, you two. It's freezing, and Mad will be dying to hear our news. Tell her I'll be about half an hour – and that she's in serious trouble if she hasn't spent this afternoon resting.'

Georgia, knowing Maddy well, thought that she'd probably spent the entire afternoon cooking.

'Shame I'm not joining you,' Charlie called as he headed towards his bungalow at the back of the stables. 'I can smell the dinner from here.'

'I'm sure Maddy wouldn't mind,' Drew said. 'She always cooks for about three hundred.'

'I'm otherwise engaged,' Charlie grinned crookedly. 'I have a very hot date with a lady called Sabrina.'

Rory and Georgia exchanged delighted glances and hurried under the clock arch.

Maddy, looking gloriously fecund in a flowing green wool dress that skimmed the swell of her stomach and accentuated the russet of her curls, swooped on them in the hall. 'Georgia! Congratulations on Tumbling Bay! Drew phoned me on the mobile.' She looked over Georgia's shoulder and held out her hand. 'And you must be Rory. How lovely to meet you.'

Rory kissed Maddy's cheek. 'And to meet you. I've heard so much about you. I know that's very hackneyed – but it happens to be true. Georgia's always singing your praises, obviously with good reason.'

Maddy, about to lead them into the sitting room, looked over her shoulder at him. 'Have you got Irish ancestors like Drew? That was a superb bit of blarney.'

'It was nothing of the sort,' Rory retorted. 'And your house is great.'

'I haven't quite got used to it myself yet,' Maddy admitted, showing them into a vast sitting room with a roaring coal fire, huge sofas and gleaming furniture. 'I still think I'm going to wake up in my old four-roomed cottage and find that this is all a dream. Make yourselves comfortable. Drinks are over there – I hope you don't mind helping yourselves? It's just that I hate treating friends as though I'm the lady of the manor or something. Which is another reason why we're having supper in the kitchen. I haven't yet got to grips with eighteen sets of cutlery and candelabra.'

The evening developed into one of delightful informality. Grouped round the stripped pine table, with plates piled high, they talked and laughed, questioned and teased. They discussed horses and family; raked over Milton St John gossip versus Upton Poges scandal; wildly exaggerated the mayhem at the Am Dram and enthused over Maddy's pet project which she shared with the wives of other trainers and jockeys: a sort of soup run for Newbury's homeless.

Georgia was relieved that Rory seemed to be enjoying himself. He and Drew had become firm friends, and he made Maddy giggle like a schoolgirl.

He passed the whisky decanter across the table to Drew and looked enquiringly at Maddy. She shook her head. 'It's one of the drawbacks of pregnancy, I'm afraid. I'm having to go cold-turkey on the Glenfiddich. As soon as the baby is born I'm going to chuck my maternity knickers, support tights and a thousand bottles of mineral water into a skip and have a bonfire that will be visible in Newbury.'

'She means it,' Drew said. 'Ecstatic as we are to be having this child, it has seriously curtailed Maddy's previously disgusting social habits.'

Georgia, sipping a very weak brandy, leaned forward. 'How did it happen exactly, Mad? No, I don't want explicit details,' she said quickly, seeing Maddy's wicked grin. 'But I thought you were going to wait until after you were married.'

'We were.' Maddy smoothed the lump of her stomach. 'It was my fault. Well, you know how chaotic I am. We went to Drew's place in Jersey for a long weekend and I forgot to pack my pills. I thought it would be OK if I took five when I came back. It wasn't . . .'

They all laughed, and took no notice of the wind rattling angrily against the windows.

Eventually, Georgia stood up. 'I'm going to have to go to the loo. Shall I go upstairs or down?'

'Cloakroom. Bottom of the stairs.' Maddy struggled to her feet. 'No, you two stay there and keep the glasses topped up. I'm just going to sort out the pudding in the back kitchen.'

'We can't eat anything else.' Drew shook his head. 'We'll burst and make a mess on the floor.'

'It's sticky toffee pudding and banana custard.'

'Blow the floor, then.' Drew reached lazily for the decanter.

After a prolonged tussle with the poppers, Georgia left the

body unfastened. Luckily, her thick tights cut off most of the draught. Following the clattering noise, she headed for the scullery.

Maddy was heaping steaming sponge into bowls. 'You kept him very quiet, Georgia Drummond. I thought we shared things like that.'

'I don't share Rory with anyone.' Georgia thought happily of Sabrina, who was by now probably being seduced by Charlie.

'I'm not surprised. He's gorgeous.' Maddy poured thick custard into a jug. 'So, how did you meet him? How long has it been going on? Go on, this lot needs to cool down a bit.'

Georgia leaned against the dresser. 'Well, we didn't start off very well and it got progressively worse. Then we had a fight and hated each other.'

'Perfect. And now you love each other and you're going to live happily ever after?'

'No.' Georgia laughed. 'We haven't made any declarations – and you've spent your pregnancy reading too many Mills and Boons.'

'A girl can never read too many Mills and Boons,' Maddy said, piling spoons on to a tray. 'Now I've had the potted version, tell me the full-blown story.'

So Georgia did. Then, helping Maddy load the trays, they carried the pudding carefully across the uneven flagstones.

'But what happens when the six months are up? What if he gets itchy feet and goes back on the road?' Maddy paused outside the kitchen door.

'I'm trying not to think about it,' Georgia admitted. 'I suppose I'll face that when – if – it happens. I know Gran wants him to stay on permanently. I just hope he'll be part of my life for ever. I suppose I can't imagine him leaving. Not now.'

'I'm sure he won't.' Maddy smiled. 'He's wild about you. Just promise me one thing.'

'What?'

'That you'll delay the wedding until after the baby is born so that I can be a bridesmaid in something flouncy and tacky. Preferably in purple – and low-cut to display my nursing breasts to their full advantage.'

It was nearly midnight when Georgia realised that they should be making tracks. They'd taken their coffee into the sitting room and were grouped round the fire. Easing herself from Rory's arms and putting down her cup, she stretched. 'You should have kicked us out hours ago, Mad. Drew will have to be up at the crack of dawn and you need plenty of rest.'

'I am resting,' Maddy murmured from her prone position on the sofa, her head on Drew's lap. 'And you don't have to go home. We've got a guest bedroom made up.'

Georgia sneaked a look at Rory, then shook her head. 'It's very kind of you but we – that is – '

'We've got to work in the morning, too.' Rory came to the rescue. 'And if we stayed here we'd never get to work on time. And my boss,' he sighed, 'is a slave-driver.'

'So I've heard.' Maddy nodded. 'Pity, though. If you'd stayed I could have done a full breakfast.'

They groaned. 'You ought to be running a restaurant,' Georgia said.

'Sometimes I think we are.' Drew rose from the sofa. 'I'm always rather doubtful about the number of stable lads and chums from the village who "just happen to pop in" when Mad's dishing up. Of course, I'm only marrying her for her cooking.'

Georgia shivered as Drew opened the hall door and an icy blast of rain splintered against her thin jacket. 'Anyway, thanks again for a brilliant evening. You must come over to Upton Poges soon.'

They kissed goodbye, and Georgia and Rory hurried across

the cobbles towards the MG. The rain was slanting straight from the Downs and, as she fumbled with the door lock, Georgia thought of being snuggled up with Rory in Maddy and Drew's spare bedroom. She slid into the driving seat and opened the passenger door. It would have been absolutely blissful. If only she could have accepted the offer. Sabrina, of course, would have had no such reservations.

'They're great.' Rory tried once again to fit his legs into the car. 'We'll have to invite them back.'

'We? As in us?' Georgia peered through the misted windscreen. 'To Diadem or to Windwhistle?'

'Both.' Rory's hand folded over hers on the steering wheel. 'We could sort something out for after the Newbury race meeting. I'm not being too presumptuous, am I?'

Georgia concentrated on keeping the car straight on the twisting, unlit road. 'If you mean, is Tumbling Bay going to run at Newbury, am I going to tell everyone, and is there going to be one hell of a party afterwards, then the answer is yes. Are you hooked on racing now, then?'

'Completely. Thanks for asking me today, Georgia. It's been amazing. All of it.'

She smiled happily in the darkness. They talked about the day, about Drew and Maddy, laughing and reliving each moment, and she realised she was driving slowly not just because of the blinding rain but because she didn't want it to end.

'Can I ask you something? Seriously?'

He turned his head. 'Of course.'

'Have you heard any whispers? About Diadem going broke? About us being unreliable? Anything like that?'

'Only what you've all been discussing,' he said quietly. 'Nothing while I've been on the road. Is it getting serious?'

'It could be. I wondered if someone could be insider dealing.'

'But everyone at Diadem is rock solid, surely?'

Georgia sighed. 'I've always thought so. It's beginning to wear us down. Oh, I wasn't even going to talk about it today, but I'm worried that it'll get so that everyone is watching everyone else.'

'Which is probably the intention.' Rory's fingers tightened on hers. 'If I hear any whispers I'll let you know. But these things usually blow over.'

She knew something was wrong seconds before anything happened. She had had the MG for so long that even the slightest odd noise pressed her panic button. She peered at the dashboard as the car ground silently to an apologetic halt. She turned towards Rory. 'I'm not sure if you're going to believe this.'

'Try me.'

'I think we've run out of petrol.'

CHAPTER 15

Rory leaned back in his seat. 'OK. I surrender. Just be gentle with me. Although,' he looked at Georgia, 'there was really no need to go to these lengths, was there? We could just have accepted Maddy's offer.'

Georgia closed her eyes. 'Rory, listen – '

'And, let's be honest, this car wasn't exactly made for seduction, was it? Certainly not when you're my size and this harness is fastened as securely as a chastity belt. Look, it's late and cold and bloody wet. If you start the car now, I'll make you a nice mug of cocoa when we get back to Windwhistle. Ouch!'

'Rory!' Georgia thumped him in the chest. 'We really have run out of petrol. And if you breathe a word of this at Diadem, I'll kill you.'

'As if I would.' Rory undid his seat belt. 'You stay there – no point both of us getting wet. Where's the spare can? In the boot?'

Georgia swallowed. 'It's not exactly full.'

'How not exactly full?'

'Empty.'

They stared at each other. Georgia was sure that if Rory laughed she'd punch him again. He didn't. Neither did he appear to be particularly angry. More importantly, he didn't launch into an attack on scatty women drivers who ran their vehicles on the same lines as their handbags. The rain sounded like bullets on the roof and the wind whistled through every gap. She chewed the ends of her hair. 'I know. It's very unprofessional of me. I simply forgot – with all the excitement and everything – '

'We've all done it. Not usually in the back of beyond in the middle of a monsoon, of course, but then, you always do things differently. So, how far do we have to walk?'

Georgia mumbled.

Rory leaned forward. 'What?'

'About two miles.'

Rory looked at her in disbelief. Of course, she thought, he was used to streetlights and pavements and people carrying spare petrol cans twenty-four hours a day.

'I suppose we could stay here,' she said hopefully. 'At least until daylight. Someone might come past.'

'Not a chance.' He opened the door. 'Come on, we're going to have to face it. Have you got a coat or anything?'

'No.' Georgia picked up the bag and her torch and, taking a deep breath, slid out into the slash of the storm.

It was as cold as only an after-midnight British February downpour can be. Immediately the wind pierced the slightness of her skirt, and made her wish that she'd spent a little more time in Maddy's cloakroom fastening the body's poppers. Rory unbuttoned his jacket and pulled her underneath his arm. 'This might help a bit.'

She looked up at him through her wet hair and loved him.

They trudged in silence for more than a mile, knocked sideways by the punching force of the wind, saturated to the skin by the relentless rain and so cold that all feeling was mercifully numbed. How many times had she dismissed people who did this sort of thing as dumb-brains who shouldn't be let out with anything more technical than a bicycle?

Eventually, completely exhausted, Georgia stopped walking. 'Rory – I'm so sorry. I usually do all the cockpit checks as second nature. Water, oil pressure, air – petrol. It was just that I was in a rush to get away before Gran started her inquisition.'

'It's OK.' His teeth chattered. 'I'm getting used to being stuck in peculiar places with you, especially in foul weather. If this was a balmy summer night, with the bittersweet chirrup of

161

the cicadas – whatever they are – I'm sure it wouldn't be half so much fun.'

She laughed at him. It was difficult with her make-up trickling down her face and her hair stuck in soaking clumps to the collar of her red suit. 'Oh, damn it. I think my nose is running now.'

He produced a sodden handkerchief and handed it to her. 'Just go through the motions. It'll probably help psychologically at least – God! What was that?'

'A cicada?' Georgia hazarded, stuffing the hankie into her bag.

'Shine your torch over there – by that clump of trees.'

Georgia shone. The bushes, glistening blackly, bowed in the wind. She shook her head. 'Don't go and investigate. Not here. Just leave it – it could be anything.'

'It sounded like someone crying.' Rory prised the torch from her cold fingers. 'We can't just walk away.'

'There're some funny goings-on round here.' Georgia, divested of the protection of his jacket, shook uncontrollably. 'They may not thank you for interfering.'

But Rory was already forcing his way through the thicket. 'I hardly think we're going to catch someone *in flagrante*, do you? Not in this weather?'

Not wanting to be left alone in the darkness, Georgia followed him. The bushes seemed determined to jab at her eyes and catch in her hair, and the ground had turned into quicksand. Squelching behind Rory, trying to stay close to the bobbing beam of the torch, she stumbled into him as he stopped. 'What is it?'

'Bastards!' Rory's voice was quivering with anger. 'The bastards! Look!'

Georgia stared at the tiny bundle of dirty white fur huddled beneath the soughing branches, desperately trying to shield its emaciated body from the lashing storm. 'Oh, my God! Is it tied up? Give me the torch.'

Rory threw the torch at her and dropped to his knees amidst the rotting leaf mould. Kneeling beside him, hardly noticing the draught rattling up her skirt, she could hear agonised whimpers and Rory's voice dropping to a gentle soothing.

He turned his head, not raising his voice. 'Some callous sod has tied him up with a piece of rope. The more he's struggled and the wetter it's got, the tighter the knot's become. They didn't intend to give him a chance. I don't suppose you're carrying anything useful like a penknife?'

She shook her head, biting back tears. 'I left everything in the car. Oh, hang on,' she fumbled through her bag, dropping things in the darkness. 'I've got some nail scissors but they're very small –'

'They're fine,' Rory said, turning back to the dog. 'Come on, sweetheart, we won't hurt you. Just let me – don't struggle. There, nearly got it. That's it.'

Georgia watched as Rory hacked through the filthy rope with infinite patience, pausing every so often to calm the dog. Feeling sick with hatred for the people who had done this, she prayed under her breath.

Then she heard Rory's soft exclamation. 'Got it! Come on, there's a good boy.'

Scooping the terrified animal up and buttoning it firmly inside his jacket, he shone the torch on the ground. Georgia's winnings were scattered amongst the twisted roots and mildewy moss. Sniffing back her tears, she bent down and scooped up the notes. Somehow, they'd lost their importance.

They pushed their way back to the road and inspected the puppy gently. He was probably white, but his wiry coat had been slicked grey by the rain and caked in mud. The small, skeletal body shook and squirmed against Rory's now-drenched shirt. Too angry to speak, Georgia stroked the shaggy head. The dog flopped against Rory, opened big chocolate eyes and licked Georgia's hand with a tiny pink tongue.

Rory's voice was gruff. 'I think we ought to get home as quickly as possible. I'm sure Eric is dying for a warm bed and a good supper.'

'Eric?' Georgia said above the lashing rain as they staggered against the gale. 'Why Eric?'

'Why not?'

Nearly half an hour later they plodded up Windwhistle's twisting path. Eric's head, just visible from the top of Rory's jacket, lolled limply. Rory handed her the key. 'Could you unlock the door? I don't want to disturb him.'

She did, and fumbled along the wall for the light switch. They stood blinking at each other. Their former elegance had degenerated into wet and mucky dishevelment. Rory grinned at her. 'You look disgusting.'

He led the way along the tiny hall and into the living room. A log fire was laid ready in the hearth and he soon had it alight, the flames casting flickering shadows across the darkened walls. Rory gently placed Eric on the red and gold hearthrug and switched on two table lamps.

'Oh.' Georgia was entranced. 'What a heavenly room.' She knelt down beside Rory and stroked Eric's head. 'Is he going to be all right?'

Eric lifted one mud-stained paw and placed it on Georgia's hand. Rory nodded. 'I think so. We'll dry him off and feed him and let him sleep. I'll take him to the vet tomorrow – just to make sure. I'd like to get my hands on the bastard that did it to him, though. It's beyond me how anyone can do a thing like that.'

'I know. But they do – far too often. Two of our dogs were motorway dumps and one came from the animal shelter after being subjected to unbelievable cruelty. I suppose Eric was a Christmas present and had outlived his novelty value. Poor baby.'

They sat back like proud parents as Eric, sniffing at his unfamiliar surroundings, looked at them both and wagged his stumpy tail before stretching out in front of the fire with a contented sigh.

Rory cleared his throat. 'I'll – um – go and get some towels. Would you like me to run you a bath?'

'Don't go to any trouble,' Georgia said quickly. 'I don't even feel cold at the moment. We ought to sort Eric out first anyway.'

'I can see to that while you get warm and dry. The bathroom is just across the hall. I'll chuck in a pair of jeans and a sweater for you. This is getting to be a habit.'

The bathroom, white and dark glossy green, throbbed warmly to the hum of an ancient corrugated radiator. The bath had claw feet and huge towering taps. Georgia, who longed to strip off her clothes and plunge into the delights of hot Badedas, thought treacherously of Rory bathing in there – of Rory gloriously naked. She concentrated on the array of Guerlain toiletries on the windowsill. The scent of him was everywhere, subtle, understated, unmistakable. She peeled off the wettest of her clothes, which by now included the body, and made do with rubbing herself vigorously with a fluffy white towel.

Relatively dry, and certainly a lot warmer, she tugged on Rory's jeans and sweater. Even though the clothes were clean she could still smell him, the hint of cologne mingling with the freshness of the washing powder. She hugged herself, and wondered whether he did his own washing or used a laundry. She wondered a lot of things. She knew so little about him.

Not liking to share the intimacy of his dirty linen basket, she picked up the body, her tights and the red suit, and after much turning-back of legs and sleeves, came out into the hall.

Rory, who had shed his Windsor finery for black cords

and a dark grey sweater, was just emerging from the kitchen. 'I've got the kettle on for tea. Are you sure you wouldn't have preferred a bath?'

'No, really. It's lovely to be dry.' She followed him into the living room. 'Hello, Eric. Oh, look! He knows his name already!'

Eric thumped his tail in his sleep but didn't move.

'I've dried him and he's had some warm milk. We'll try to get him to eat a little later.' Rory cleared some newspapers and a trucking magazine from the sofa, and removed a dark green mug from the floor. 'I apologise for my subdued colours. I suppose if you're going to become a regular visitor, I'll have to invest in some candyfloss pink mugs with purple stars.'

'Yes, I suppose you will.'

Curled on the sofa, warm and cosy, with the rain lashing at the window, Georgia sighed. 'I'm exhausted, and you must be, too. I suppose I ought to go when we've had the tea. May I borrow your car? I'll come and pick you up in the morning with some petrol then we can drive out and I can pick up the MG and –'

'I'd rather you didn't.'

'What?' Georgia wrinkled her nose. 'You can't want to turn out just to drive me home tonight?'

'No, I don't. I want you to stay.' He raised his eyebrows. 'Will you?'

'It depends how many bedrooms you have.'

'One.'

'Oh.' She bit her lip. 'Look, Rory –'

'You can have the bed. I'll have the sofa.'

Blushing, Georgia pulled away from him. 'I'm sorry – I thought –'

'That I meant one bedroom, one bed, us together?' He smiled in the soft light. 'Yeah, well, maybe I did.'

They looked at each other. She knew very well that if she

stayed neither of them would sleep on the sofa. And what if he wasn't going to be a permanent fixture? She'd always played safe. Was it worth running the risk? Rory kissed the tip of her nose. 'I'll take that as a "Lovely, but maybe some time in the future when I know you better", shall I?'

'I'm really sorry.'

'Don't be.' His smile didn't falter. 'Everything good is worth waiting for. And I'll wait, Georgia, I promise you.' He stood up, pulled her to her feet, and kissed her again. 'I'll make the tea. Why don't you have a look round. Make yourself at home.'

When she could hear him rattling about in the kitchen, Georgia stroked the sleeping Eric then walked round the living room. How much of the furniture had come with Windwhistle and how much Rory had brought from storage in London she had no idea, because all the pieces were old and obviously well-loved. The curtains and cushions were dark green velvet, the chairs and sofas pale gold. Lamps were on every table, and photographs dotted the walls. Georgia studied them.

There were some of Rory at various stages in his life. He had always been good-looking. Not surprisingly there appeared to be none of Rufus, and there were none that she could see of the errant Stephanie. She paused in front of a picture of what must surely be his parents. It must have been taken on holiday because there were palm trees in the background and they were both wearing lightweight, colourful garments. There was a definite mix of their genes in Rory, Georgia decided. The thick fair hair and the wide, pale eyes came from his mother, the build and the beautiful bone structure was inherited from his father. There was something familiar about the couple. Had she seen them somewhere before? The photograph had to be at least twenty years old judging by the clothes and the hairstyles. Georgia shook her head. No, she was sure she didn't know them. They were just a handsome young couple who still loved each other if the easy way they were touching was anything to go by. And yet –

She peered closer. She was positive she had never seen Rory's father before. But what about his mother? There was something very familiar about her face. The hair was different now, of course, far less bouffant and not so blonde. But the eyes, the cheekbones, the air of quivering energy that was evident even in the frozen frame were still the same –

Georgia clapped her hand to her mouth in horror. She *had* seen Rory's mother before. Very recently. In fact, she'd been tearing out of Ionio and roaring away in a flashy Jag. Rory's mother was the chairman of the Vivienda Group.

CHAPTER 16

Georgia woke in darkness. Squinting at the clock radio, she sighed with relief. Not quite five yet. Ages and ages until she had to get up. She curled back beneath her duvet and closed her eyes. Then, with a punch of dismay, she remembered.

'Oh, God.' Groaning, she rolled her face into the pillow.

She had stared transfixed at the photograph for a long time, shocked and confused. Eric had continued to dream in front of the fire; Rory had continued to clatter in the kitchen; but neither of these things had really registered.

Was that Rory's mother? And if so, was she the Mrs Kennedy – no, Kendall – that she had seen at Ionio? And, if she was, why the hell hadn't Rory told her? Had she told Rory about her spying trip to Ionio? She tried to think back.

She had looked long and hard at the picture, willing herself to be mistaken. It was not a recent photograph. Was the business that Rory had mentioned leaving so abruptly none other than Vivienda? She wished she could recall what he had told her about his family that night in the North-East. Maybe they weren't Rory's parents at all. Maybe they were just friends. After all, his name was Faulkner, not Kendall . . .

She had finally turned away, knowing that she was clutching at straws. All manner of horrors surged to the surface. One thing was very clear: if Rory did have family connections with Vivienda, he hadn't wanted her to know about them. Because, she had realised with a shiver, it made Rory's presence at Diadem very sinister indeed if his mother really was the chairman of Vivienda.

Her first instinct had been to yank open the kitchen door and face him with a sarcastic smile and some comment like, 'Nice photos. Shame about the business.' That's what Cecilia would have done, no shilly-shallying. But then Cecilia wasn't already half in love with Rory Faulkner.

Shivering again, she had hunched beside the fire. Her whole world, the fragile new world she'd built up around Rory, was starting to crumble.

'Georgia!' His voice from the depths of the kitchen had made her jump. 'You're very quiet. You haven't gone to sleep, have you?'

'N-no.'

She had made her decision in that moment. She wasn't going to say anything. She wasn't going to face him with her knowledge – not yet. After all, there might be some very good explanation – although she didn't have a clue what it could be. She would wait for Rory to tell her – or at least give her the opportunity to say something about it. To rush in with accusations now could be disastrous, especially if it was a concidence. She had twisted her fingers in Eric's coat, seeking comfort. She didn't want to lose Rory. One day she would turn the conversation round to his parents again, ask him outright, and then she'd know.

'Actually,' she had called back, 'I just wondered if you'd disappeared to Ceylon for that tea.'

The door had opened and Rory had stood there, carrying a tray. 'You never let up, do you? I'm surprised that you haven't strapped a tacho to the teapot. I promise to improve my brewing technique in future. OK?'

She had looked away quickly, in case it weakened her resolve.

He had been so lovely, she thought sadly, cuddling her as they sipped the tea.

'I'll sort the MG out in the morning,' he had said, kissing her good night when, eventually, he had dropped her home.

'I'll get some petrol and run Ken down to bring it back if you're already out.'

She had turned to look at him. His face was kind, honest, gentle. There had to be some really simple explanation. 'Good night.'

He had kissed her again with slow, lethal practice, and she had bitten back her tears as she'd stumbled across the cobbles.

Now, in the dark and silent hours of the early morning, she lay plunged in turmoil. She was used to keeping her own counsel, and Rory would have to make the first move. Georgia was a great believer that if you didn't talk about it, it might go away.

Curling her knees up to her chest, she eventually drifted into a fitful sleep.

'Where the hell have you been?' Trish shouted above the whirring of the printer. 'You're hours late.'

'I overslept,' Georgia mumbled. 'I didn't hear the alarm.'

'You obviously didn't hear anything.' Trish reached for the coffee pot. 'Rory phoned ages ago and Ken has retrieved your car from the middle of nowhere. What the heck's been happening?'

'I ran out of petrol last night.' Georgia took a mouthful of scalding coffee.

'Oh yeah?' Trish gave an exaggerated wink. 'Very convenient. Anyway, you can tell me the details later. Right now we've got far more urgent things to discuss.'

'We have?' Georgia's heart sank.

Trish was grinning. It was extremely irritating. 'Yeah. Lennards have been let down by their TIR driver. They've got a load and a return pick-up to go out today. Cecilia's cock-a-hoop, of course, because it means we could snaffle their trans-European business which will be one in the Ionio for Vivienda. It'll probably mess up your love-life a bit, though.'

Georgia's heart plummeted even further. 'You mean that Rory's got to go to France?'

'I mean that he's got to deliver to Madrid and Lisbon and then drive back to Barcelona to wait for the return load.'

'But that'll be days –'

'Two weeks, Lennards reckon,' Trish said cheerfully. 'So who's the lucky one, eh? Rory gets a fortnight away from dreary old England and some lovely sunshine.'

Georgia wanted to cry. 'Can't someone else go?'

Trish shook her head. 'You know Barney's in Scotland which means Marie has to be local because of the kids. Ken's taken over the Lennards domestic runs and is on his way to Cardiff. Adenoids, bless him, hasn't even got a passport – and you, sweetie, are booked on Kon Tiki.'

'It's all Jed's fault!' Georgia stormed. 'If he hadn't got bloody peritonitis –'

'– Rory Faulkner would never have come to Diadem in the first place,' Trish reminded her.

'I'm sorry. It's just –'

'Yeah, I know.' Trish patted Georgia's arm. 'Do you want to go and tell Rory? He's out in the yard with Ken.'

Georgia sighed. 'I suppose I'd better get it over.'

The previous night's wind and rain had faded into a sullen mistiness that left iridescent pools amongst the cobbles. Feeling miserable because Rory was going and she'd miss him, and relieved because his absence would give her some space to sort out the tangle of her thoughts, Georgia slid open the metallic doors to the workshop.

Rory was standing with his back to her beside Ken who had his head buried in the Mercedes's engine. Ken looked up first. 'Have you come to take her out for the Kon Tiki run? I won't be a tick. I'll couple up the trailer when I've finished checking the oil. We're all a bit behind this morning.'

'Tell me about it – and thanks for collecting my car. Actually, I wanted to have a word with Rory.'

Ken resumed his checking as Rory, with Eric in his arms, threaded his way between the lorries, his face shadowed by the towering vehicles. 'It's OK. If it's about last night, I do understand. I told you I'd wait.'

She fondled Eric's head, not looking into Rory's eyes. 'I know. I just feel really miserable. I suppose it was because we had such a lovely day.'

He stroked her cheek. 'We'll have plenty of others.'

'Not for ages –'

'Why? We've only just started and we've got all the time in the world.'

'We haven't. You're going abroad –'

She told him quickly. It was awful. They stared at each other sadly. God knows, Georgia thought, how people survived lengthy separations in wartime. Two weeks seemed for ever.

Twenty minutes later, having promised to look after Eric and Windwhistle, and having kissed him goodbye, Georgia brushed away her tears as Rory drove out of the yard. There had to be some mistake, she thought wearily, crossing the cobbles to the office. There was absolutely no way that Rory Faulkner could be related to anyone from Vivienda.

'Hiya!' Sabrina, with her hair in a tendrilly topknot, grinned up from the desk. 'You look really pissed-off. Shame, innit? Still, he'll be back – as long as one of them Spanish girls don't get her claws into him.'

Georgia muttered something under her breath and picked up her tachograph folder. Sabrina sashayed from behind the desk. 'I'm just off to sort out me van. Your gran's looking after Oscar while I do me courier runs. Didya have a good night?'

Not as good as you, Georgia thought sourly, noticing a necklet of love bites just below Sabrina's jawline.

Sabrina giggled. 'Charlie's bloody amazing. Don't fink neither of us got no sleep. See ya.' And with the bounce of the sexually fulfilled, she shimmied out of the office.

'Bugger, shit and damn!' Georgia yelled, hurling the tachos at the door.

Cecilia chose that moment to make her entrance carrying Oscar and his paraphernalia. 'Good heavens, Georgia. Surely Rory's mother wasn't that bad?'

It was absolutely the worst thing she could have said.

'I didn't go to see his bloody mother!' Georgia howled, and promptly burst into tears.

Dumping Oscar's carrycot on the desk, Cecilia smothered Georgia in a hug of scarves and Joy. 'Darling! What is it? You can tell your old gran.'

'I don't want Rory to be a lorry driver!' Georgia choked. 'I don't want to be a lorry driver, either! I want a proper job. Five till nine – no – nine till – '

Cecilia patted her shoulders. 'Come and sit down, sweetheart, and tell me all about it.'

'I can't,' Georgia sniffed. 'I've got to drive to Bristol for Kon Tiki and – '

'Alan Woodbury and his frozen whatnots'll hang on if I explain things to him.' Cecilia reached for the phone and the coffee pot at the same time. 'I think we need to have a little talk.'

The little talk lasted half an hour, two cups of coffee and a nappy-change. By the time she left Diadem, Georgia had told her grandmother all about Tumbling Bay's debut, the evening at Peapods and Eric's discovery. She had said nothing about going back to Windwhistle and recognising Rory's mother.

'Don't worry, darling.' Cecilia had been gentle. 'The time will simply fly by. I used to hate it when Gordon was away. I got through it by making wildly elaborate plans for his return. You're not my granddaughter if you can't think up something exciting to welcome Rory home. And, anyway, we've got so much to look forward to, haven't we?'

'We have?'

'Oh, darling! Don't be such a grouch! There haven't been

any problems recently – touch wood. I'm sure we were all over-reacting.'

Georgia wasn't. But Cecilia had ploughed on. 'Jeromes have telephoned. They want a meeting. I've popped it in your diary for this afternoon. I really think things are looking up, darling. They've probably heard that Lennards have given us Europe and want to get quotes. I can't imagine why I got so worried. I knew this Ionio thing would be a flash in the pan.'

Georgia had regarded her grandmother with grave doubt. Cecilia, ever the optimist, had a very dangerous habit of seeing only what she wanted to see. Georgia, more cynical, was pretty sure that Vivienda still hadn't played their ace cards.

Cecilia beamed. 'So, with business on the up, and the performance of *Inherit My Heart*, and the visit to Newbury to watch that ill-tempered horse of yours win us a fortune, I don't think you have anything to be miserable about. Rory should be back in plenty of time for both the Am Dram and the race meeting. And, of course, darling Jed is going to be back at work next week. Won't that be super?'

Alan Woodbury was delighted to see her. 'No probs about being late. I understand. Cecilia explained that you were feeling a bit down. You should come to the Am Dram dress rehearsal, and cheer yourself up. It's going so well. When we're doing the smoochy scenes I think Sabrina really fancies me.' He walked behind her as Georgia supervised the loading of Kon Tiki's refrigerated trailer. 'She French-kissed me in the last rehearsal.'

'Really? Maybe she's into Method acting. I wouldn't read too much into it.'

'Oh, I don't.' Alan ducked under the wing mirrors and sighed. 'While I was seducing her on stage she told me she was seeing Charlie Somerset. I suppose he's a real-life lover while I'm only pretend.'

Georgia straightened up. 'The only difference between you and Charlie is that he is brimming over with confidence. I'm sure if he'd had your knocks he'd be just as unsure. Anyway, how are your lonely-hearts adverts going?'

'Not good. I got Judith from my first ad – a rather large lady with a lot of facial hair from Milton St John – not of course that I held that against her. The hair or the village.' Alan sidestepped the air-lines. 'But she was a bit odd, you know.'

'How odd?'

'She'd been married four times and none of them had lasted more than six months. She said it was because of her habit.'

'Christ, Alan!' Georgia was alarmed. 'Don't get involved with a junkie.'

'She's not into drugs. She's into garlic. She chewed it all the time. Said it would stop her having a heart attack.'

Georgia giggled. 'Was she the only one?'

'And then there was Beryl. She was older than me and very – er – predatory. She told me straight away that she was seeking physical satisfaction first and companionship second. She tried to jump on me the first night. I – um – failed to deliver.'

'I'm not surprised.' Georgia touched his hand. 'Don't worry about it. Neither of them were right for you. Someone will come along, you'll see. Probably when you least expect it.'

'Like Rory did for you.' Alan rubbed his fingers over his moustache. It was still motheaten. 'I'm sure you're right. I've put the ad in for another month anyway. And I'm so glad that you're happy. You deserve it. I always think it's a pity that we were never more than just good friends, really.'

'I don't.' Georgia swung herself into the cab. 'True friends are worth a million transitory lovers.'

'Ah, yes, but you've got a friend and a lover in Rory.'

But she hadn't, had she, Georgia thought as she drove away. They certainly weren't lovers – and the friendship was always going to be in doubt until she knew the truth about that photograph. A little voice niggled deep inside, pointing out that she only had to ask him.

'Go away!' Georgia yelled at it. 'I'm not going to ask him because I don't want to hear the answer!'

Eric snuggled down in his seat as they approached the A34 and she fed Peggy Lee into the cassette player. It didn't help at all. The soul-searing music and seductive words made her want Rory with a longing that hurt.

'Hell, Eric,' she looked down at his spiky white head. 'How on earth are we going to get through the next two weeks?'

But getting through the next two hours seemed to be more pressing, Georgia thought irritably, as she looked at the tailback of traffic on the M4. She had been late leaving Kon Tiki, and now she would be even later arriving in Bristol. It would seem very unprofessional. She prayed that Ionio wouldn't be on site to witness her tardy entrance.

They were, of course. She pulled into the line for unloading immediately behind a newly painted red and yellow ERF. Eric woke and looked at Georgia with his head on one side.

'OK. I'll let you stretch your legs in a sec. You'll probably want to spend a penny – I know I do. Let's just get a time for unloading.' She leaned from the window. The checker making his way along the line of lorries was not one she'd seen before. 'How long before I can drop this lot?'

Wearing the Kon Tiki overall, cap and wellingtons, the checker eyed her and the lorry suspiciously. Oh, God, Georgia thought, just what I need. A joker who thinks women should be in the bedroom or the kitchen – preferably both – and definitely not behind the steering wheel of a lorry.

He tapped his clipboard and looked at his watch. 'You're late. You've missed your slot. Could be an hour – two, maybe.'

And she still had the Jeromes appointment, which would mean showering and washing her hair and dragging out the

shoulder pads. The checker squatted down by the refrigeration unit slung beneath the trailer, squinted up at Georgia,
then disappeared round the back of the lorry.

'Stay there,' Georgia patted Eric's head. 'This is a new boy,
and he's going to take all day at this rate. I'll go and hurry
him up a bit.'

As she dropped to the ground, the checker was leafing
through his clipboard. 'I'll open up the back so that you can
check the seal numbers – ' Georgia knew immediately that
something was wrong.

The checker was peering over her shoulder into the cavernous depths of the trailer. 'What's your temperature?'

'Minus nine – er – no, eight.'

'Can't accept the load then,' the checker looked smug.
'You shouldn't be below minus fifteen for frozen goods.'

'I realise that,' Georgia muttered through gritted teeth.
'God knows what happened.'

The checker prodded the nearest cage. It squelched.
'Enough food-poisoning in there to wipe out most of
South-West England,' he said cheerfully. 'And it won't be no
good when you get it back to Upton Poges, neither. It'll have
to be scrapped. I hope your company's insured.'

Georgia closed her eyes. 'It's a Kon Tiki trailer. There must
be a refrigeration fault.'

A driver for Ionio, resplendent in a red and yellow uniform
that made him look like a holiday-camp entertainer, had
wandered along the length of the lorry to discover what was
causing the hold-up. 'The only fault was that you forgot to
put diesel in the unit.' He sniggered. 'What were you thinking
about, eh, love? Your boyfriend or what to cook for dinner?'

Georgia clenched her teeth. She wanted to punch him. She
also knew that if she did Diadem could kiss goodbye to the
Kon Tiki contract. And she *had* checked the diesel in the
fridge unit. She remembered doing it. After she'd told Rory
about the European trip, while Ken was still doing the ground

checks. She groaned. This was definitely another dirty trick – and Rory had been in the workshop.

Stop it! she screamed silently at herself. Just bloody stop it! You've got enough to worry about – like this disaster being witnessed by the very company who would dine out on it for months.

The Ionio driver continued to smirk. "Course, it's Diadem, isn't it?' He winked at the checker. 'A cowboy outfit. A two-bit firm run by women, for Christ's sake! Haven't you heard about them?'

Georgia shoved her hands deep in her pockets. The checker raised his eyebrows. 'Oh, yeah. Aren't they the ones who lost all those fags on that bonded run? Iffy business, if you ask me.'

'No one did,' Georgia hissed. 'And we have never – never – short-dropped cigarettes or anything else!' She swung round on the Ionio driver. 'Where did you get that slanderous piece of information from?'

Other drivers, bored in the unloading queue, had strolled up behind them and were watching with interest. The Ionio driver lit a cigarette and blew smoke into the air. 'It's well known. Everyone's talking about how you lot are on the slippery slope. Face it, love, your days are numbered.'

Georgia's voice quavered. 'I think I ought to warn you that I shall be contacting my solicitor. Diadem will not be put out of business by oiks like you, and – ' she swallowed, 'sharks like bloody Vivienda.'

The Ionio driver laughed. 'Ooh, I'm quaking in me boots. Come on then, show me what sort of a trucker you really are. Hit me. Go on – '

Georgia took a step forward. The checker warded her off with his clipboard. 'Ere! We don't want none of that. You might as well turn tail and head for home, lady. And I'll be contacting my superiors. I think they'll be speaking to your boss about this.'

Knowing that there was nothing else she could do, Georgia ran back to the cab and snatched the door open. Eric had peed on the floor. It was the least of her worries. Shaking with fury, she stalled, crashed the gears and made four attempts to reverse out of the queue. Blinded by tears, she eventually managed to swing the trailer round. The Ionio driver was practically doubled-up with mirth.

She opened the window. 'We'll still be trading when you're dead and buried. Make no mistake about it. You can try whatever dirty tricks you like. Our customers are loyal. They know what good service they get from us. They'll never listen to your smear campaign. Never.'

'. . . I'm really so sorry to have to say this,' Sandie Jerome leaned across her leather-topped desk four hours later. 'But under the circumstances, we can't afford to run the risk. We won't be requiring your services any longer.'

Stunned, Georgia sat and stared at the tall, grey-haired woman in front of her. She'd hurtled back from Bristol, made garbled explanations to Cecilia, even more garbled ones to Alan, and had arrived at the Jeromes meeting with minutes to spare.

Sandie Jerome continued. 'I know we've always gone for female solidarity, what with me being MD of the family firm, and you being in the same position. But really, Georgia, your record speaks for itself.'

'Yes, it does,' Georgia tried to stop her voice from cracking. 'We've given you good service at an excellent price. We didn't hassle you for payments a couple of years back when you were going through a difficult trading period. We have never let you down.' God, at any minute she'd be on her knees, and begging to be reinstated. 'We've always been there to back up your own transport system which means we've never shirked the less glamorous jobs. I simply don't see –'

Sandie shook her head sadly. 'I know. And I do appreciate

what you're saying – but you've been late on several occasions recently and, well, I've heard that one or two of your drivers aren't exactly averse to breaking the law to get things done. Apparently, there was a consignment of cigarettes that went missing. As you know, we transport a lot of wines and spirits. We simply couldn't risk – '

There was a roaring in Georgia's ears. 'Sandie – they're all lies. All of them. We've heard them ourselves. It's a whispering campaign to put us out of business.'

Sandie Jerome shrugged. 'It may be so, Georgia, it may not. These things happen. But you have been late for deliveries. And, honestly, Ionio have come in with such good rates.'

Georgia stood up. There was no point in staying. She blinked back angry tears. 'Very well. But when Ionio let you down, no doubt we'll be hearing from you. I'm sure we won't have to wait long.'

'I think you might,' Sandie Jerome said quietly. 'I feel Ionio are a force to be reckoned with and, with the backing of the Vivienda Group, a very marketable force at that. Close the door on the way out, would you?'

CHAPTER 17

'Good Lord!' Cecilia paused in the foyer of the Masonic Hall and ran scarlet-tipped fingers through her hair. 'It's practically a sell-out. We'll have them sitting in the aisles soon. How are the programmes going?'

'Very well,' Georgia answered listlessly. 'And the raffle tickets.'

'Good, good.' Cecilia's smile faded. 'I know how you feel, darling. I feel exactly the same. We've lost Jeromes. We've had more little accidents in the last few weeks than I can ever remember. And the whispers are getting worse. But tonight we really ought to think about something else. We'll worry about the business in the morning.'

Georgia sighed. 'If we've still got one. But you're right – the show must go on, I suppose. And at least we're doing this for a suitable charity. We'll probably all need help from Shelter before long.'

Cecilia almost laughed.

Georgia sold two more programmes. 'What's it like back-stage?'

'Bedlam. Alan's having a panic attack, which I'll allow him because he was such an angel over that defrosted load and refused to claim compensation – and, more importantly, denied that it had ever happened to anyone who enquired, and Sabrina has decided that the seduction scene would have more oomph if she was topless.'

'Christ,' Georgia blinked, 'Alan won't know what's hit him.'

Cecilia frowned. 'It's not Alan I'm worried about. It's

Spencer. He's at that strange stage – watching the girls at Upton Poges High playing netball, you know? And Elizabeth would disembowel him if he stepped out of line.'

'As long as that's the only part of his anatomy she goes for, then I don't think you'll have too much to worry about.' Georgia dished out programmes and tickets to a knot of latecomers with a scowl.

The two weeks had stretched to three. Rory had been held up in Barcelona waiting for some EC paperwork to be sorted out and then had had problems with his tachographs. Once on the road he'd been further delayed by lightning strikes. His telephone calls had become more agitated by the day as the laid-back Spanish authorities failed to understand the urgency of his deliveries.

Georgia, already stressed by the smear campaign, had become increasingly resentful of the enforced separation. The only plus was that Diadem were still suffering minor break-downs and the whispers were still rife – all while Rory was away. It offered her a shameful crumb of comfort.

'Darling, I know it's awful, but it won't be for much longer. Think of all the catching up you'll have to do.' A crash and a scream prevented her from uttering any further platitudes. 'Sounds like Mr Knebley's having a bit of a problem with the lighting gantry. I knew he'd never cope with it and his hernia. I'll see you again in the interval – and remember, no long faces tonight. You never know who might be watching.'

Marie and Barney, followed by a gaggle of brushed and gleaming children, paused in front of the desk.

'You saved us the front row?' Marie asked. 'Like you promised?'

Georgia pulled a face. 'Oh, God, sorry. I completely forgot.'

'Got your mind on other things no doubt.' Barney was sympathetic. 'We all have. Not to worry, I'll sort the seats out,' and he shouldered his way into the hall.

Marie smiled fondly. 'He won't take no nonsense, won't Barne. We promised the kiddies the front row – an' the front row they shall have.'

Georgia stopped dealing out programmes to the children, most of whom looked too young to read. 'Are you sure it's suitable for them, Marie? It's not Walt Disney, is it? And you should know better than anyone what Act Three is like.'

Marie opened an enormous packet of popcorn with her teeth and handed it to the eldest child. 'They've seen worse'n that at home. With the eight of us in that house, they just have to turn up the telly when Barne gets a bit frisky. Know what I mean?'

Georgia looked again at Marie's children. Extremely well behaved and happy, they didn't seem to have come to any harm. Marie clucked them into a tidy group. 'I don't envy Sabrina. Every time I kissed Alan Woodbury, I got hairs in me mouth.'

Barney waved imperiously from the door. 'All clear, Marie, babe. Eight seats in the front row free now.'

Intrigued, Georgia peered into the hall. Eight bewildered members of the Upton Poges Evergreen Club were gathered in a little group, all clutching vinyl shopping bags for the interval, and copious quantities of tissues and sherbet lemons.

Before she could rescue them, Beth Brimstone, in a Cecilia-clone outfit which, as usual, didn't quite come off, clipboard at the ready, bored her way through the closely packed chairs. 'No standing, ladies and gentlemen! Take your seats, please. There will be a comfort break during the performance.'

The Evergreens chuntered more loudly.

Beth glared at Barney and Marie and the popcorn-eating children, who glared back. Assessing the situation, she powered into overdrive. 'Right. Now, if everyone in row three becomes a little more pally with their neighbours we'll be able to squeeze everyone in. Come along! Quickly!'

There was a lot of shuffling and grating of chair-legs and a very loud oath.

Beth raised her clipboard. 'Oh, I say! Mrs Fountain! Language – please! What? Oh, bunions. You have my sympathy.'

Laughing for the first time in ages, Georgia returned to the front of house.

Sidling unseen into the back of the packed hall, Georgia perched on a fire bucket for the first half of the performance. There were a few fluffed lines, and one or two wrong entrances when over-eager thespians trotted on, realised they were half a page too early, and shuffled off again. It was probably giving Cecilia and Spencer coronaries, she thought, but the Upton Poges audience, not versed in the finer arts of the theatre, gave a rousing cheer each time.

As always, half-time was very well received and there was the ritual stampede for the bar and the cloakroom. Cecilia, clutching a gin-and-tonic and looking shell-shocked, joined Georgia on the fire buckets. 'Thank God Janey Hutchinson couldn't make it. Problems at home, apparently. She'd charge them all with murdering her script if she was here. And Elizabeth Brimstone must have been a cross between Mata Hari and Boadicea in a previous existence. She's alternating between dropping hints of traitors in the camp and threatening poor Alan with death backstage.'

Georgia gasped. 'What sort of hints?'

'Oh, absolute rubbish.' Cecilia downed her gin. 'Saying that we could learn a lot from Brimstones in matters of security. That we should vet our staff if we want to keep afloat, and then, when I cross-questioned her, she just smiled and said we had her sympathy! Smug bitch!'

'She didn't actually mention anything or anyone specifically?'

'Of course she didn't.' Cecilia sighed. 'Foolish woman. She

just wants to appear important. I'm not letting her rattle my cage tonight. Hello, Charlie.'

Charlie Somerset, his arm round a very pretty, very young girl, paused on his way to the bar and kissed them both. 'What a brilliant show. I haven't laughed so much for years. Sabrina's very good.'

'I thought,' Georgia whispered, 'that you and Sabrina were – well, together.'

'Yeah,' Charlie grinned lasciviously. 'We are. But I always like to keep a little something in reserve. This little something is Hayley.'

Hayley dimpled shyly. She looked as though she ought to be tucked up in bed with a teddy bear, not Charlie Somerset. 'Does Sabrina know?'

'Knows I'm here, yeah. Knows about Hayley? Nah. I'll face that hurdle later. Talking of which, you're all set for next week? Tumbling Bay? Newbury?'

'Of course.' Georgia nodded. 'We've organised the deliveries for a complete Diadem turnout. Do you think you'll win?'

Charlie shrugged. 'Good for a place, certainly. There's a fair bit of competition. Still, I never go down without a fight.'

Hayley seemed to think this was rather amusing and giggled. God, Georgia thought, she even laughs with a lisp. Charlie put his arm around her and pulled her against him. 'I must go. I've promised Hayley a crème de menthe frappé.'

And that's not all, Georgia thought ruefully, as, glued-together, they moved towards the bar. She felt a pang of sympathy for Sabrina.

The second half of *Inherit My Heart* kicked off without much delay. Cecilia, determined not to lose the high ground to Beth, had bustled off to oversee make-up and costumes, and to shout at Mr Knebley on the lighting gantry. Georgia abandoned the fire bucket for the comparative luxury of a shopping trolley belonging to one of the Evergreens, and tried not to think about Rory.

The action had become far more steamy. Alan as Irwin, and Sabrina as Jocasta, had just discovered that they couldn't survive another minute without declaring their passion. Sabrina, it seemed, had been persuaded to keep her clothes on.

At the point where Jocasta's husband, Burke, learned that his wife had been playing around with Irwin – who was really his twin brother, the elder by ten minutes, who had been whisked away at birth and had returned to claim his right to the stately home and its mistress – and had marched offstage to grab his twelve-bore, the Evergreens sucked excitedly on their sherbet lemons.

When Jocasta slithered on to the stage to confront her lover, Marie and Barney's children sat open-mouthed. Georgia closed her eyes.

Sabrina, having been coaxed reluctantly away from performing topless, had chosen to improvise. Undulating across the stage towards a gob-smacked Alan, wearing a scarlet basque, six inch stilettos and black fishnet stockings, she stunned the entire Masonic Hall into silence.

Entwining herself sinuously round her lover, Sabrina moved into the technique that she must have used on Oscar's father and probably on Charlie. Alan, after an unsteady start, hurled himself into his role as inflamed roué with no prompting.

The Evergreens, clutching their vinyl bags with tight-veined knuckles, didn't dare blink. Mr Knebley on the lighting gantry shook uncontrollably, plunging the star players in and out of the spotlight with a dizzying strobe effect. Trish and Jed had their faces buried in each other's shoulders, and Georgia glanced at Charlie. He was twitching.

Beth appeared at the side of the stage, still clutching her clipboard, as the Evergreens stamped their air-cushioned soles. Jessie Hopkins from the post office, who was in charge of the curtain, was riveted to the spot. Beth motioned to her that she should draw a veil over the whole unfortunate scene.

Jessie pursed prim lips and clung tightly to her cord. Her whisper carried to the back of the hall. 'I don't think so, Mrs Brimstone. I take my orders from Cecilia. I'm crew.'

By now, Alan and Sabrina had tumbled on to the chaise-longue and were kissing each other with extremely realistic enthusiasm. Beth, realising that she couldn't pull rank with Cecilia's followers, stormed off into the wings. The applause was tumultuous.

By the time Sabrina appeared for the next scene she was more modestly clad in a porridge-coloured shirtwaister that sat oddly with the tarty stilettos and fishnets, and *Inherit My Heart* rolled on to its conclusion without further incident. Georgia clapped absent-mindedly. The remainder of the audience were in raptures, however, as Jessie Hopkins pulled the final curtain and the Poges Players were buried beneath half a ton of maroon velvet.

'Wasn't that sensational, darling!' Cecilia was flushed with success as she hurried between the rows of upturned chairs. 'Gather your things together quickly. Were having an after-show party at the Seven Stars.'

Georgia groaned.

The Seven Stars was packed. Mr Knebley of the lighting gantry was playing a wheezy accordion in the alcove, accompanied by a tipsy-looking Mrs Fountain on the piano. Everyone was singing lustily, although not the same tune. Mikey Somerville was ladling out glasses of purple liquid called 'Inherit My Heartburn', and Sabrina, back in leggings and a cashmere sweater – but still teetering in the stilettos – was signing autographs.

Cecilia handed Georgia a glass of red wine. 'Alan Woodbury is explaining to everyone at the bar that he and Sabrina are now an item and the kissing was for real. I wonder what happened to Charlie?'

'Hayley happened.' Georgia finished her glass quickly. 'She

probably had to be in bed by ten. Oh, I think Spencer is trying to attract my attention.'

Georgia watched her grandmother cross the bar and wondered if she could go home.

'Georgia!' Beth Brimstone was looking concerned. 'I wondered if we could have a word?'

Georgia sighed wearily. She really didn't want to speak to Beth. She didn't want to speak to anyone except Rory. 'Yes, of course, but if it's about Gran – '

'It isn't.' Beth cast a dismissive glance towards Cecilia and Spencer. 'It's about the problems you're having with Diadem. I've tried speaking to Cecilia, but she's most unresponsive. Look, I know that the rumours are without foundation, but there are plenty who don't. And the accidents are real, aren't they? No one can deny that.'

No, Georgia thought tiredly, they can't. 'So what are you saying?'

'Simply this – be careful of spies and infiltrators. Someone is working against you.'

An ice-cold trickle of fear ran down Georgia's spine. She shivered. During Rory's absence she had been over and over the smear campaign and the accidents. They had all started after Rory had joined Diadem; and his joining the company had been such a coincidence, coming just at the time when Vivienda were moving into the area. But as the incidents were continuing while he was away, there was no way –

She shook her head. It wasn't Rory. She knew it wasn't. 'Beth, for God's sake stop being so bloody mysterious. If you know something, then spit it out. If you don't, then please stop all this hinting – '

Beth turned away towards Spencer and Cecilia. 'Just be very, very careful, Georgia – that's all I'm saying.'

CHAPTER 18

As March billowed towards April, the weather decided to apologise for such an inclement winter, and frothed into an early spring. The flax-blue skies and lime-green shoots coincided with a rash of purple crocuses and acid yellow daffodils. Georgia, who would normally have revelled in the rainbow colours, failed to even notice.

Driving the Magnum back to Diadem through the New Forest, much to the annoyance of company reps in souped-up Rovers who knew she should have stuck to the motorway, she was deep in thought. It was the day before Tumbling Bay's race at Newbury and Rory should be back that evening. She was absolutely longing to see him. There had been no further customer defections, and no increase in the smear campaign. She would have much preferred them to continue all the time Rory was away.

As she walked into the office, Cecilia's grim face only scratched the surface of her angst. Hurling a tacho on to Trish's desk and helping herself to a chocolate finger, she became aware that neither Trish nor Sabrina were speaking.

'What's up?' She paused, the biscuit clenched between her teeth. 'Why is everyone – It's not Rory, is it? There hasn't been an accident?'

'No,' Cecilia shook her head. 'Nothing like that. Rory is on his way back. He's hoping to board at Calais early this afternoon. He phoned in about ten minutes ago.'

Her heart still racing, Georgia slumped into her chair. 'So? Is Jed ill again? Has Ken – '

'Ken has had a small problem with his brakes,' Trish said

flatly. 'It made him very late for a pick-up at Mitchell and Gray. When he got there he found that an Ionio driver had called in – just on the off-chance, of course – and had taken the load.'

Cecilia spoke quietly. 'Jed has just had the same experience at Habitat – only his was oil pressure, not brakes. Marie had an electrical fault and missed a collection for Panasonic, and Barney has had yet another puncture.'

Georgia narrowed her eyes. 'God! They can't all be accidents. I mean, these things happen all the time – but all at the *same* time? We're really going to have to do something, aren't we?'

'Yes,' Cecilia said quietly. 'I'm afraid we are. It gets worse.'

'How can it possibly get any worse?'

'Lennards have phoned.' Beneath the veneer of Estée Lauder, Cecilia's lips were white. 'They don't want us to work for them after this month's contract. Apparently Ionio have offered them a package for both the UK and European runs that undercuts us by fifty per cent. Oh, Tom was very sorry, we've been friends for a long time and all that crap.' Her voice was bitter. 'But, of course, business is business. He actually had the bloody nerve to say that – to me!'

Georgia allowed the news to sink in. How long would it be before Vivienda came sniffing around the Diadem yard like jackals? Offering to buy out remaining customers? Smiling while they stabbed? 'But the other major customers are still OK? Kon Tiki?'

'Kon Tiki is about all that's left. Oh, we've still got masses of small business, but unless we get out there and start selling ourselves, we'll lose Kon Tiki for sure.'

'But Alan thinks we're great,' Georgia protested, clinging to her last fragile hope.

'For the time being.' Trish dismantled a paperclip. 'Alan Woodbury is loyal enough, but he doesn't make overall transport decisions, does he? He's only local. If the whole

Kon Tiki group changed policy and decided to nominate a national carrier – '

There was no need to finish the sentence. Georgia knew, as they all did, that if Kon Tiki defected, Diadem would disappear completely. She felt sick. 'Who else knows about Lennards?'

'Just us. And that's the way it's going to stay. I don't want one word of this breathed outside the office. I have an appalling feeling that Elizabeth Brimstone is right. Someone, somewhere, is leaking information – and I'm not risking it going any further.'

'Cecilia's dictated a strictly confidential memo to the shareholders which I'm in the middle of typing.' Trish pointed at her computer. 'So that Marie and Barney, Jed and Ken know what's going on. Otherwise, we'll all have to keep shtum.'

'Rory – ' Georgia began.

Cecilia looked tired and almost old. 'Rory won't be told anything. Neither will Adenoids. They're not shareholders. And if someone is leaking information, I don't think it was given. I think it was sold – for a very high price. And,' she picked up a piece of paper from her desk, 'I had this this morning.'

'What is it?'

'A letter from the Halifax Building Society. Apparently Rory is intending to buy Windwhistle when his six months' rental is up. They've asked for an employer's reference.'

Georgia blinked. He'd talked about making Windwhistle his permanent home. He hadn't mentioned buying it. 'So?'

Cecilia sighed. 'So, where would Rory, who admits he's been a drifter for years, get the sort of money required for a substantial deposit on his cottage?'

Georgia almost laughed. Of course, if your family owned the Vivienda Group, the price of a cottage would be peanuts. She looked round the office. She knew she should tell them.

Diadem was her life – and theirs. She owed them that much. She shuddered, knowing that she couldn't, wouldn't do it until she'd spoken to Rory.

'It can't be Rory.'

Trish chewed her lips unhappily and stared at her screen. Cecilia rubbed her eyes with a tired hand. 'Sweetheart, you're bound to say that. But your judgment may be a little clouded. We know so very little about him. I'm aware that Spencer was asked for this information and refused to give it, and everyone else working here is a shareholder – so –'

'You've just said that Adenoids isn't – and neither is she!' Georgia pointed at Sabrina who was sitting quietly. 'She's nothing to do with us, and yet she's here taking it all in, being privy to information that I'm not allowed to tell Rory and –'

Cecilia and Trish looked startled. Oscar sucked harder on his dummy and gurgled. Sabrina's eyes flashed. 'That's bloody rich coming from you! You was the one who invited me here! Anyway, why should I want to screw things up when I've got a home for me an' Oscar an' a job an' mates? Get real!'

'Money,' Georgia spat. 'Something you've probably never had.'

'No, I haven't, Miss High an' Bloody Mighty! But that don't mean I'd hurt the people who've given me everything, does it? Some of us have principles.'

'We haven't seen many of yours so far!'

'That's enough!' Cecilia frowned at them both. 'For Christ's sake – we've got enough problems without you two having a fight. Of course it isn't Adenoids, the poor boy can hardly write his name. He reads *Beano*, for God's sake. And it certainly isn't Sabrina.'

'How do you know?' Georgia was fuming. 'We don't know any more about her than we do about Rory. A bloody sight less in my case. She might be the sort to sell her granny – or mine – for the promise of a few Vivienda shares!'

Sabrina started to laugh. 'What do I know about shares? What would I want to sell information for?'

Georgia stood up, pushing her chair back so quickly that it toppled over. 'Vivienda will be in here like bloody locusts and take over lock, stock and Magnum. They'll put us out of business but keep the staff on for the resurrection, because that's the way they work. And wouldn't it be more attractive to have shares in a multinational company than a little local firm? Christ, which one of the Vivienda hierarchy did you pillow-talk the prices to? How many of them have you been feeding with information? You know the routes, the times, where the lorries'll be – how much did you get? Better rates than standing on a street corner, I bet.'

'Georgia!' Cecilia's roar woke Oscar who started to wail loudly. Both Sabrina and Trish leaned over the carrycot. 'Apologise for that!'

'Not a chance!' Tears burned Georgia's eyes. 'Diadem is my life. I'm not the one bed-hopping through Upton Poges and the surrounding area, am I? She's been to bed with more men in three months than I have in three years.'

'That's your loss, innit?' Sabrina held Oscar to her shoulder. 'An' I reckon that's what it's all about. You're just jealous.'

Clenching her fists, Georgia marched out of the office. She could hear Cecilia placating Sabrina before she'd even closed the door.

She spent a very miserable afternoon, trawling round the trading estates, visiting old customers, asking them to ignore all the rumours. Most, reassuringly, seemed quite happy to do so, but of course, Georgia thought as she drew up outside yet another glass and concrete distribution centre, they were all small firms who only used Diadem occasionally.

Cold-calling on a couple of new factories off the A34 she made appointments and left literature and her business card, but her heart wasn't in it so, switching off her mobile phone, she headed for home. She was torn between wanting Rory to ring her, and hoping he wouldn't because he'd know there was something wrong. Well, at least she'd made one decision. With the phone switched off she couldn't talk to him. As she drove towards Upton Poges it started to rain.

Questions squirmed like worms inside her head. If Rory wasn't connected to Vivienda, where on earth had he raised enough cash to buy Windwhistle? Cottages in Berkshire went for phenomenal sums. And why hadn't he told her? Was Beth hinting that Rory was selling information? No! Georgia slammed her foot on the accelerator and wished it was Beth Brimstone's neck.

Tearing through the rooms when she got back to Diadem, flinging off the suit and the crippling shoes, and pulling on jeans and the pastel cats, she decided to blitz the house. Hating housework with a passion, she found cleaning very therapeutic. It was like self-flagellation.

She was up to her elbows in Flash when the phone rang. She picked it up and said hello with trepidation.

'Hi. Is Sami.'

'Sami?' The Flash was running up her arms. 'Sorry. I think you might have the wrong number.'

'No. Right number. Sami. Leon's brother. Turkish Take-Away. You 'ire my minibus for tomorrow. Racing at Newbury. So no one 'as to drive and you all get pissed, yes? I just ring to confirm. I pick up at eleven, yes?'

Georgia gulped. How could she have forgotten? They couldn't possibly go now, could they? This would be the most gloomy work's outing of all time.'

'Is all right?' Sami repeated. 'I be there at eleven. Good fun.'

'Oh, yes. I – er – suppose so.' She hung up. 'It'll be good fun,' she echoed bleakly.

Bouncing along the A34 in Sami's minibus the following morning, sandwiched between a perplexed Rory and a silent

Cecilia, Georgia felt utterly miserable. The entire Diadem contingent, sitting in mute rows like schoolchildren who had been promised Alton Towers and now realised they were getting a museum, stared out of the windows. Sami's constant stream of Cliff Richard hits did nothing to alleviate the gloom.

Georgia had wanted to abandon the trip, but Cecilia had insisted that it should go ahead. For company morale, she had said, daring to be contradicted.

'Whatever you say. You're the one taking the decisions,' Georgia had retorted cynically.

Now she and her grandmother, who was holding Oscar, sat with inches of multicoloured plush and a hundred un-spoken accusations between them.

Rory was even worse. Bewildered by Georgia's reaction to his telephone call from Dover the previous evening, he seemed even more confused now. His fingers wrapped round hers, his thigh pressing against the skirt of the same red suit she had worn at Windsor, only compounded her misery.

Last night, feeling unable to talk to Rory about Lennards and the concentrated spate of disasters, and worried about his purchase of Windwhistle, Georgia had felt horribly guilty at his concern when she had said she wouldn't see him.

'I'm actually pretty knackered. And I've got loads to do if we're going to Newbury,' she had told him on the phone. 'I'll see you in the morning.'

'Yeah, sure. And thanks for looking after Eric. I've been dying to see you – I couldn't wait to get back. I'd imagined – well, all sorts of things. Georgia, you are OK? You're not ill or anything?'

'No. I'm fine, and I've missed you too.' She could have cried.

She didn't want to have secrets from him. She knew she would tell him when she felt less angry with Cecilia – less likely to say the wrong thing – but it would have to be face to face. She was certain that Rory was incapable of lying to her. She'd know in an instant if he had given information to Ionio.

Oh, God, she had so longed to be curled in his arms and to make love all night. Instead she had hung up and Flashed the kitchen until her knuckles were raw.

'Have I got rampant halitosis?' Rory hissed in her ear. 'What the hell is going on?'

'Nothing much.' Georgia sighed, watching Sabrina watching them. 'I'll tell you later.'

'This is slightly different from the last time.' Rory, trying to make conversation, stretched out his legs, colliding with Ken in the row in front who moved his feet away without speaking. He leaned towards her. 'Are you nervous?'

Georgia shook her head. She was too numb to feel anything. Rory stared out of the window. She reached out and touched his arm. 'It'll be all right. Really.'

'I'm glad to hear it.'

They continued the rest of the journey in silence. Georgia was racked with anguish. Diadem had always been happy and laughing – and a day out like this should have been riotous. They might as well have been going to a funeral.

Arriving at the racecourse far too early, Cecilia announced that she, Ken and Sabrina were going to have some lunch and would be in the grandstand later on. Jed, Marie and Barney made a beeline for the bar. A misty sun and a gentle breeze ruffling the banks of daffodils heralded a pleasant spring afternoon.

'I'll go and get a couple of racecards,' Rory said. 'Before we find Drew.'

'Can you get one for me?' Trish had hung back behind the others. 'And I'll pay you out of my winnings.'

Rory grinned as he walked away and Georgia could have hugged her. It was the nearest anyone had come to being light-hearted. Trish looked worried. 'I wanted to give you some advice.'

Georgia's heart sank. 'Go on then.'

'Don't tell him anything.'

'Do you think it's him as well? God, Trish, we're supposed to be friends! Thanks a bunch!'

'Of course it's not Rory. That's why you shouldn't say anything to him. To be honest, Jed and I both feel that Ionio are working in the dark. We don't think anyone needed to supply the information. They could have worked out the prices for themselves and just kept cutting until they got a deal. And as for the rest of it – well, it *could* be just one huge coincidence. We've had them before – blow-outs, sump problems, all of it. We're getting too jittery. Christ, we've got enough real problems without getting screwed up over imaginary ones as well.'

Georgia felt deeply grateful. 'I know. It all just kept going round and round in my head last night – I mean, what's to stop our customers supplying the information on our prices? I mean they might want to be loyal, but if someone came along offering a better deal, loyalty would fly out of the window, wouldn't it?'

'Exactly.' Trish nodded. 'Cecilia is leaping to conclusions – aided and abetted by Beth. You know what a pair of old drama queens they are. I'm aware of the seriousness of the situation – but please, Georgia, don't let it foul up your relationship with Rory.'

Georgia blinked back tears. 'Thanks.'

''S all right. It's what friends do. Stick together.' And waving at the returning Rory, Trish tottered off on her high heels.

Georgia wondered if Trish would have changed her tune if she'd known about the photograph of Mrs Kendall on Rory's wall.

'You're in the third race,' Rory said. 'Did you agree to meet up with Drew and Maddy earlier? Hell – are you crying? Have you had a row with Trish? Georgia, what the fuck is going on?'

She winced at the harshness. 'Trish was being nice – and it made me cry. Look, could we get a drink, please? We can go into Owners and Trainers. The others can't.'

'OK.' His eyes were worried. 'Then can we talk?'

She snaked her hand into his. 'Yes. I promise.'

The bar was already filling rapidly, the rise and fall of conversation mingling with the tinkling of glasses. Rory carried Courvoisiers to a small table. 'I didn't bother with ice. I thought the atmosphere was frosty enough.'

Georgia pushed her hair behind her ears and took a mouthful of brandy. It was raw on her dry throat and made her eyes water. 'Are you buying Windwhistle?'

Rory paused in lifting his glass. 'Yes. Is this what it's all about? Are you getting cold feet?'

'No!' She spluttered and put her brandy back on the table. 'Of course not. Oh, God. Whatever I say is going to sound wrong – '

'Probably.' Rory looked grim. 'Do you want me to do it for you? You thought that we could have a fling for the duration of my contract. That when the six months was up I'd slide conveniently out of the way. That I'd be like all the other men in your life – filling in time but not constant. Because the only thing you really want is Diadem.'

'No!' Her cry made several Savile-Row-suited trainers turn and stare. 'You've got it all wrong. For the first time in my life I've found something that's more important to me than Diadem.'

'How reassuring.'

'Stop it!' This time the partners of the Savile Row suits turned to stare as well. 'Please, just tell me the truth.'

'I always have.'

Georgia looked down at the brandy in her glass. 'Why didn't you tell me you were buying the cottage?'

'I did.' He frowned. 'I told you I was putting down roots for the first time since – well, you know – and that it was because of you. I didn't actually spell out that I was buying Windwhistle because I didn't think I needed to go into that sort of detail. I'd always assumed that we were on the same wavelength. I did tell you I was going to make it my permanent home even if Diadem didn't extend my contract. I like Upton Poges, and I – I love you. Look, Georgia, if you're trying to give me the push, just do it.'

She reached for his fingers across the table. The watchers were agog. 'It's not that. It's just – ' She took a deep breath, teetered, and fell back on the easy option. 'Can you afford it? The mortgage, I mean?'

'Is this a pastoral care concern on behalf of the Diadem management? Of course I can bloody afford it. I wouldn't be doing it otherwise. Oh, I see. You want to know how, do you? Checking up on my financial status to see if I'm worthy of your bank balance. Or if I'm merely a gold-digger?'

'Don't be so insulting!'

'Then don't try to humiliate me.' Rory's voice was as stony as his eyes. 'Yes, I can afford it. My father left me some money. I've never touched it before because I didn't need anything. Now I do – or thought I did.' He took a huge slug of brandy. 'I've offered to put down a substantial deposit which makes the monthly repayments easily affordable – even for an itinerant trucker. OK?'

'I'm really sorry.' Trish's advice screamed through her brain. She raised her eyes. 'Gran told me yesterday she'd had a letter from the Halifax. She also told me that Diadem isn't doing too well at the moment. I didn't want you to saddle yourself with a debt you couldn't repay if –'

'How considerate,' Rory snapped. 'But don't let it concern you any further. I am quite able to pay my mortgage, thank you, and unlike you I don't need Diadem for total support. I can always find other driving jobs. And I'm not sure that concern over my financial standing would cause this much stress. I mean, it isn't just you that's upset, is it? The rest of them were acting like they'd just received a death sentence, too. It would be extremely flattering to think that the entire workforce was having a panic attack over my ability – or lack of it – to pay my mortgage, but somehow I can't quite believe it.'

Georgia realised that she should never have underestimated his intelligence. 'It's because of the business. They're all worried.'

'I understand that.' Rory looked like his patience was being severely tested. 'I know Ionio are playing dirty – but you must have expected that. But it surely can't be that bad? You must have had blips before. All companies have them. You and Cecilia have been running Diadem for long enough to – '

'We've lost Lennards to Ionio.'

'Oh.' Rory nodded slowly. 'In that case, I can see the problem.'

Georgia finished her brandy. 'Gran will no doubt use her powers of persuasion on Tom Lennard – but I don't think that they will work this time. Also, yesterday was a bad day for everyone. Breakdowns and things. We didn't do ourselves any favours, and everyone is feeling threatened. So,' she raised her eyes to his. 'Do you understand now? Why everyone's so pissed off, and why I was – er – distracted?'

Rory placed his empty glass beside hers and squeezed her hands across the table. The Savile Rows and their ladies lost interest and started to surge towards the Parade Ring for the first race. 'Sure – but even if the worst happens and you can't get Lennards back, you'll just have to tout for new business, won't you? At least you and Cecilia have the advantage of being intelligent, beautiful and hard-nosed. It won't be long before you capture more work.'

For an instant Georgia didn't care about Diadem. She had come perilously close to losing Rory. If she'd voiced her fears about the photograph and his family connections he might never have forgiven her. She should never have doubted him.

Determined not to let the moment slip away, and jubilant that the money for Windwhistle hadn't been gained by nefarious means, Georgia smiled properly for the first time. 'Anyway, we'll still have enough business to keep you on. Maybe Adenoids'll have to go back to Brimstones', but you'll stay.'

'So I can keep up my mortgage payments?'

Just in time, she realised that she was being teased. 'Yeah, because of the mortgage payments. But, more importantly, because of Eric. I couldn't bear to see him homeless.'

'Whereas I,' Rory stood up and held out his hand, 'could be on the streets and you wouldn't turn a hair?'

She snuggled against his side. 'Precisely.'

They walked from the Owners and Trainers Bar hand-in-hand and Georgia lifted her face to the sun. It was blissful. There was no way on earth that Rory would want to destroy either her or the business.

Having watched the first two races and gambled recklessly on horses with pretty names who chose to dump their jockeys at early hurdles, they made their way through the crowds to the saddling boxes. Tumbling Bay, glossy, gleaming, and dancing in his eagerness to be off, blew down his nostrils as Georgia kissed him.

Drew straightened up from fastening the girths and ran a practised hand along the conker-coloured flanks. 'He's never been better. Have you seen the prices?'

'Ten to one was the best we could get,' Georgia said. 'Which we considered a bit tight for a horse with no pedigree and only one run.'

'Hell of a run, though.' Drew fondled Tumbling Bay's nose. 'So, where's the rest of the contingent? I thought they'd all be here.'

'They are. They've sort of scattered. It hasn't quite worked out as I expected.'

'It rarely does.' Drew felt Tumbling Bay's restless legs, then gave him a friendly slap as though he was no bigger than a labrador puppy. 'I've got consortium owners who squabble like kids when they're all on a racecourse together.' He gestured towards Rory who was talking to Tumbling Bay's lad. 'Everything's all right with you two, though?'

'Brilliant,' Georgia said fervently. 'I must tell Maddy. Where is she, by the way?'

'Raised blood pressure. Swollen ankles. Resting – and extremely angry.' Drew grinned. 'I've got half of Milton St John popping in to keep an eye on her so that for once she does what she's told. She swears that when the baby's born she's going to abandon it to a wet nurse and go on a month-long rampage.'

Rory joined them. 'According to young Olly, you're going to beat the arse off Martin Pipe today.'

'Crikey.' Georgia giggled. 'How flattering – and very unlikely.'

Drew raised his eyebrows as the horses for the third race started to make their way to the Parade Ring. 'You never know – stranger things have happened.'

Deciding to peace-make between the warring factions, Georgia tugged Rory towards the grandstand as soon as Charlie and Tumbling Bay had cantered down to the start. 'They'll have been fed and watered by now,' she said. 'And they might have had some winners. Maybe they'll have cheered up a bit.'

Rory kissed the top of her head. 'Just as long as you have.'

She smiled up at him. 'But I've got you. They haven't.'

The Diadem contingent certainly seemed to have mellowed, Georgia noticed with relief. It was amazing what a couple of bottles of good wine and a satisfying lunch could do. She took a deep breath and drew her grandmother to one side. 'I wanted to say sorry. Today is very important to me, and I've wanted you to share it for a long time. It would be so sad to let a quarrel spoil it.'

Cecilia picked imaginary fluff from the sleeve of her Jacques Vert jacket. 'I'm sorry, too. Oh, what a difficult thing to say! Sorry . . . really is the hardest word. I think we all over-reacted. Darling,' she pulled Georgia to her, 'we've never had a serious fall-out and I don't want to start now. And you know I think Rory is a darling man. I'm sure he isn't – well, you know.'

'He isn't. Windwhistle is being purchased through his inheritance from his father.'

Cecilia's eyes widened. 'Oh, that's such a relief. But you didn't tell him – ?'

'No. I wouldn't be that insulting,' Georgia said shortly. 'But I'd appreciate it if you could let the others know. Discreetly, of course.'

Cecilia, who had never been on friendly terms with discretion, nodded. 'Now is this horse of yours going to win?'

'According to his stable lad,' Rory said, joining them, 'he's a cross between Arkle and Desert Orchid – with a bit of Pegasus thrown in.'

Sabrina, with Oscar in a baby-sling, slithered to Georgia's side. 'Did you speak to Charlie? Did he say anything?'

Bloody nerve, Georgia thought. Yesterday you were slagging me off. Today you want me to pass on messages from your one-night stands. Tough. 'Oh, loads. Shame you weren't there.' She stopped. Being in love with the whole world again, she suddenly felt sorry for Sabrina with her woebegone face. 'He sent his love.'

'Really?' Sabrina's saucer-eyes sparkled.

Blast, Georgia thought, why did I say that? It was probably more cruel than the truth. In all likelihood, Charlie had cut a swathe through at least half-a-dozen jockey groupies since they'd last met, not to mention the lisping Hayley. She shrugged. 'Maybe you'll see him later.'

'I hope so.' Sabrina cuddled Oscar ecstatically. 'An' I'm dead sorry for what I said yesterday. It was out of order. I was shit-scared, though.'

'It's OK.' With Rory's arm around her shoulders, Georgia could afford to be magnanimous. 'Oh, they're off!'

The tape flew into the air and the twelve horses rocketed away on their two-circuit trip of the course, with Georgia's neon-bright colours bobbing somewhere in the middle. The rush and thunder as they clattered through the brushwood in front of the grandstand was tangible. Breathing was audible. Curses were panted. Hoofs hitting turf jolted the body.

Watching through the field-glasses, Georgia bit her lips and prayed every time Tumbling Bay soared through the air. Cecilia was jumping up and down with very little regard for the heels of her elegant Carcavelos courts. 'Goodness! I never dreamed he would be so impressive, darling! This is almost as exciting as sex!'

They were almost at the end of the race. Ten horses remained, including Tumbling Bay. Georgia was relieved to watch both the casualties scramble to their feet unscathed. Rory, sharing the binoculars, seemed to be as excited as she. 'He's third now – and gaining. Only two more to go, and one of them's Martin Pipe. Maybe Olly was right.'

The roar as the leaders hurled themselves towards the grandstand sent shivers down Georgia's spine. Her palms were damp, her mouth, cardboard dry. Charging at breakneck speed towards the penultimate fence, Tumbling Bay took off level with the second horse. The Diadem screams of encouragement should have raised the roof.

A sickening grunt as horse collided mid-air with horse was followed by an eerie splintering and a shuddering breath. Tumbling Bay and Charlie became a terrifying windmill of silent, flailing legs. Landing with a nauseating thud they rolled over and over on the emerald-green turf.

CHAPTER 19

For a terrible suspended moment nobody moved, then an ambulance bounced to a halt beside the fence and people were running. The roar for the finishing horses was lost in the panic-stricken scramble.

Rory dug his fingers into Georgia's wrist and tried to drag her back as she hurtled towards the rails. 'They won't allow us on the course. There's nothing we can do. Oh, Christ!'

Through her streaming tears, Georgia could see the huge conker-brown hump of Tumbling Bay lying across the track. The other horse had staggered to its feet and was idly cropping grass, unaware of the pandemonium. Both jockeys were still lying flat out with the ambulance crews bending over them.

'Tumbling Bay's dead!' Georgia stuffed her hand into her mouth to stop herself screaming and shook away Rory's restraining grasp. 'I know he's dead! I've got to go! Don't you understand?'

Rory, white-lipped, wiped his eyes. 'Yes, of course.'

Not bothering to find out how the rest of Diadem were reacting, Georgia stumbled forwards. Drew was running across the course as Charlie and the second jockey were stretchered into the ambulance. The crowd was silent.

Followed by Rory, Georgia ducked under the rails, angrily shaking off the constraining hands of the stewards. 'Get out of the way!' she yelled. 'He's my horse! I should have left him where he was! It's all my fault!'

She dropped to her knees beside Drew on the damp turf, mascara and tears burning her eyes. 'I've killed him.'

Rory knelt down, encircling her with his arms. His body was

shaking as Georgia cradled Tumbling Bay's huge head against her face. 'I'm so sorry, baby. I'm so sorry.'

'He's still breathing.' Drew's words were almost inaudible. 'He's not dead.'

Relief surged through her. She rubbed her tears from her cheeks and stroked Tumbling Bay's inert ears. 'Oh, thank God! Drew – are you sure?'

'He's alive but it's not good, Georgia. I think he's had it.' Drew dashed his own tears away. 'Look, they do it very quickly –'

'Do what?' Georgia, her arms round the huge brown neck, could feel the fluttering pulse beneath the rope-like tendons. 'What's happening?'

The racecourse vet had arrived. Screens were being erected.

'Fuck off!' Georgia screamed, leaping to her feet. 'You're not going to shoot him! You'll have to shoot me first! Rory! Tell them!'

The elderly, kind-eyed vet shook his head. 'It's his leg, my dear. It's kinder to put him down. He'll never race again and –'

'No, he won't!' Georgia spat. 'He'll live in comfort until he's a hundred! Don't you dare kill him! I don't care what it costs.'

Drew and the vet exchanged glances. Rory sighed heavily. 'Can he be saved?'

'Possibly,' the vet said. 'It depends on the severity of the fracture and whether there are any other injuries. We'd need to get him to the equine unit. At the moment he's stunned and not feeling anything. We usually just destroy. We can do X-rays, of course, but I'm not sure . . .'

'Like Georgia said,' Rory spoke gruffly, 'do whatever it takes.'

'I'll give him an anaesthetic now,' the vet produced an enormous intravenous syringe and yards of tubing, 'and we'll get him back to the unit. The cost,' he looked at Georgia, 'could be horrendous, and even then there's no guarantee –'

'Just do it.' Drew and Georgia spoke together.

Rory nodded. 'Whatever the cost. It's not a problem.'

The vet mobilised his troops. Georgia bent down to plant a final kiss on Tumbling Bay's motionless forehead. 'Whatever happens, whatever you find, you won't put him down without talking to me first?'

'I promise. There would be no one happier than me if we can save this fellow.'

'I want to go with him.'

The vet paused in his ministrations and gave her a sympathetic smile. 'That's impossible, I'm afraid.'

'But you don't understand.' Georgia bit back the fresh tears. 'He's not a business proposition – he's my baby. I rescued him. I love him.'

The vet turned to Rory. 'Give her a large brandy and then take her home. I'll get all the details from Drew and I'll telephone as soon as I can.'

Feeling violently sick, Georgia allowed Rory to lead her away. Drew, grey-faced, followed them. 'I'd better get to the hospital now and check up on Charlie.'

Georgia realised that she'd forgotten all about him. 'Oh, God, yes. Shall I come with you?'

Drew shook his head. 'You go home with Rory. Sit by the phone. They won't hang about once they get Tumbling Bay on the operating table. They'll need you to give the go-ahead.'

Her teeth were chattering. 'OK. Give Charlie my love.'

The Diadem workforce were silent when she and Rory rejoined them. Trish was holding Oscar in his sling. There was no sign of Sabrina.

'She and half the women on the racecourse were trying to get into Charlie's ambulance,' Cecilia said, gathering Georgia into her arms. 'I think she might have made it. Oh, darling, what an absolutely ghastly thing to happen. That poor, sweet horse. Is he – ?'

Georgia burst into tears again. Rory explained briefly what was going to happen.

Cecilia patted Georgia's shoulder. 'In that case, darling, I think we should send the men scouting for Sami and get home *toute suite*. Everyone agreed?'

Alone in Windwhistle's sitting room, her teeth rattling against a treble Courvoisier, Georgia paced up and down. Eric was curled in a corner of the sofa regarding her sorrowfully with melted-chocolate eyes. She could hear Rory in the kitchen making comforting clattery cup-of-tea noises. She stared hard at the photograph again and knew she'd been mistaken. The woman in the picture was absolutely nothing like the Mrs Kendall from Ionio. Rory's mother, maybe; chairman of Vivienda, definitely not.

Why didn't the bloody phone ring? She itched to lift the receiver to see if it was still connected but didn't dare in case it was at that split second that the vet was trying to get through. Rory placed a tray on the coffee table, poured two cups, then wandered to the window, wiping his hand tiredly across his eyes.

They both jumped when the phone trilled into the silence. Rory looked at her. 'Do you want me to – ?'

She shook her head, her throat tight, and snatched up the receiver. It was Drew. 'Charlie regained consciousness in the ambulance. He may have broken his leg.' He gave a hollow laugh. 'I asked if they were going to shoot him, but apparently not. He's in X-ray now.'

Georgia could feel her eyes filling with tears again. 'Poor Charlie. That'll put paid to him riding for the rest of the season, won't it?'

'Riding didn't seem to be the thing that was worrying him most,' Drew's voice was still attempting to be light. 'You haven't heard from – ?'

'Nothing.' Georgia licked her dry lips. 'I was waiting.'

'I'll get off the phone, then. Ring Maddy at Peapods as soon as you hear. I'm staying at the hospital for a while.'

'Of course. And give my love to Charlie.'

The phone rang again as soon as she'd replaced the receiver. With closed eyes she listened to the gentle voice and croaked Yes and No and Thank you. Letting the phone fall back with a clatter the tears welled from beneath her lashes and fell fatly on her cheeks.

Rory encircled her with his arms, stroking her hair. 'Just cry, darling. Oh, hell, I wish there was something I could say to make you feel better.'

Georgia turned in his arms and sobbed into his shirt, her whole body shaking. Then, sniffing and gulping, she looked up at him. 'He's – he's going to be OK. They're going to be able to pin the bones. He'll be a bit lame and they said he might get rheumaticky when he's older – but they can save him.'

Rory swallowed, his eyes suspiciously bright. 'Oh, that's wonderful.'

'I know.' Georgia burst into tears again.

It took the rest of the brandy and two cups of tea before her tremors subsided. Having phoned everyone and passed on the news, Georgia felt as exhausted as if she'd completed a marathon.

'I'll run you a bath,' Rory said, 'then I'll take you home and you can get some sleep.'

'Would you mind awfully if I stayed? More than anything in the world I'd love a cuddle. I really don't want to be alone.' She smiled wistfully at his expression. 'Yeah, I know. Miss Independence doesn't want to be Greta Garbo any more –'

'Are you sure? What with all this on top of the Lennards thing and all the other problems?'

Georgia pushed her hair from her eyes. 'This has put things into perspective. So what if Ionio are trying to scupper us? So what if Vivienda have captured Lennards? So what if we have to scrape the bottom of the barrel for a few months? We've done it before.' She put her arms round his neck. 'This is all that matters. You and me, and Tumbling Bay being OK.'

Rory kissed her gently. 'I'm not sure that Cecilia will see it that way. Oh, she'll be delighted that Tumbling Bay and Charlie are going to be all right, but I expect the threat to Diadem will take precedence in the morning.' He unclasped her hands from his neck. 'Still, we've got all night to worry about that. Now, before I get sidetracked, I'll run the promised bath. Badedas and an Asti chaser OK?'

Georgia wanted to sidetrack him very much indeed. 'Sounds like something Mikey Somerville would offer a lady.'

'I never said you were a lady, did I?' Rory frowned. 'If I did, I apologise. I've been away from you for far too long. I keep forgetting the ground rules.' He pulled her towards him. 'God, Georgia, you'll never know how much I've missed you –'

He kissed her with a soft butterfly kiss that she found utterly arousing. Squirming with unashamed delight, she ran her fingers underneath his shirt. His body was warm and muscled and trembled beneath her touch. Holding her eyes with his he unbuttoned her red jacket. She shook her fringe out of her eyes and watched in fascination as his long fingers stroked her breasts through the white broderie anglaise bra. It made her shiver.

'Incredible,' Rory whispered softly, unzipping her skirt. 'You are so beautiful.'

She wriggled the skirt from her ankles and stepped out of it, thanking all the gods of seduction that her knickers, for once, matched her bra, and that she was actually wearing stockings. Rory removed his hands just long enough to discard his shirt and undo his trousers. 'Are you cold?'

Georgia gazed at him with huge luminous eyes. 'No.'

He smiled gently. 'Still, in the absence of a roaring log fire and a goatskin rug, I think we ought to go to bed.' His fingers closed around her wrist as he led her across the hall and into the bedroom.

He switched on a small brass lamp which illuminated the

pale room in gold. The high bed had a brass bedstead and was made up with white sheets, blankets and an eiderdown.

'Have you been in here?' Rory pulled off his socks and removed his trousers and rather snazzy boxer shorts in one easy move. 'On your visits?'

Georgia shook her head. Naked, he was more glorious than she had imagined. He lifted her up and sat her on the bed, removing her underwear with swift expertise. 'Jesus, Georgia – ' he sank into the downy softness of the quilt, pulling her against him, 'I want you so much.'

He kissed her hard, seeking her response and finding it. She shivered with pleasure and her body curved into his with an elemental force over which she had no control. This time there would be no going back; this time Rory was going to make love to her.

She trailed her hands over his body, exploring, stroking, arousing. His breath became more ragged. He kissed her, discovering the hidden places that made her writhe ecstatically. His tongue hardened, thrusting into her mouth, imitating the final climactic act of love. Georgia moaned, biting his lips, knowing that he'd make love with this same lethal eroticism. Rolling together, they nibbled and licked and tasted each other's flesh, devouring each other with hot kisses of exploration.

Whispering huskily, Rory pushed one thigh between her legs and the body-kisses increased in urgency. Georgia thought she was going to burst as the sensations burned and melted together. He was a skilled seducer, using every part of his body to drive her incoherent with lust. She clutched at him, digging her nails into his solid shoulders, pulling him even closer. She couldn't wait. She needed him. Now.

At last he was there, his body fused with hers, and she enclosed him greedily, wrapping her thighs around his as they moved together. Delicious and delirious, the feelings mounted and spiralled until, helped on by his expert timing, her body erupted in a seismic wave of pleasure. The tidal surge seemed to last for ever, throbbing and growing, then she was floating downwards, still enfolded in his arms, panting, shivering, crying. Rory's body, fulfilled, sank softly on top of hers.

Incapable of speech, Georgia turned her head on the pillow and smiled at him. She felt incredibly shy. Rory stroked her cheek. 'I love you.'

He pulled the eiderdown over them both and wrapped himself around her. 'You are quite the most amazing woman I have met. Do you want to go to sleep?'

Exhausted, sated, very much in love, Georgia shook her head. 'Just hold me . . .'

He was still holding her when she woke up. His long legs were curled around hers.

'Have you been to sleep?' she asked.

'No, I was watching you.' Rory propped himself on one elbow and stroked her hair away from her face. 'You smiled a lot.'

'I'm not surprised.' She stretched languorously. 'What time is it?'

'No idea. You haven't been asleep very long.'

'Actually, I'm starving.'

Laughing, he peeled himself away from her and reached for his dark green dressing gown. 'Whatever happened to romance? You've had your way with me and now I'm discarded like an empty husk. It's always the same with you business-women. I really should have learned by now.' He caught her hands in mid-air and kissed her. 'I'll go and run myself a bath – because, however alluring you find the smell of the working man, I really can't sleep with it. And why don't you try and find something to eat in the kitchen?'

Georgia sat up in bed, drawing her knees up to her chin. 'Is there something I can wear? Only I don't fancy frying bacon naked, and I really don't want to get dressed again.'

'It'd be a complete waste of time.' He threw her a voluminous sweater that looked very like the one she'd slept in that night in the Magnum. 'You'll soon have more of my clothes than I have.'

The feather mattress billowed on either side of her as she struggled to the edge of the bed. Giggling, she dangled her legs over the side. 'Is this a sort of lust trap? Like a spider's web?'

'Hell!' Rory put his arms round her. 'You've sussed it.'

Curling up against him, she rubbed her cheek against his unshaven chin. 'Is it new? The bed and everything?'

'Just the bed and the bedding. Thank you for participating in the christening ceremony.'

'My pleasure.'

Rory kissed the top of her head. 'And mine.'

'Why sheets and blankets, though? I thought everyone had duvets?'

She felt him sigh slightly. 'I had proper covers when I was a kid. My father used to tuck me in, kiss me good night, read to me, you know. I was happy then, and very secure. I suppose I was trying to recapture that part of the past.'

'And have you?'

'No.' He held her away from him, then kissed her gently. 'I think I've captured the future. Now, go and rustle up roast swan and suckling pig while I have a bath – otherwise I'll drag you back to bed again and we won't be seen for weeks.'

The kitchen was as delightfully old-fashioned as the rest of Windwhistle, with free-standing cupboards and an over-loaded dresser. A bottle of duty-free Moët bobbed in a sinkful of cold water. Opening various doors, Georgia discovered that Rory had cast-iron cookware and a fine assortment of mismatched crockery. She turned on Radio Two, and rooted through the fridge and the larder. Not a roast swan to be seen, and as for suckling pig –

She pulled the sleeves of the sweater up above her elbows

and padded to the bathroom. 'If the eggs haven't gone off, I think I can do Spanish omelettes. If they have, it'll have to be risotto. And there's no bread.'

Rory's voice was muffled from behind the door. She leaned closer. 'What?'

'Open the door. I wasn't preserving my privacy – merely keeping the heat in.'

Georgia was immediately engulfed in evocative clouds of Guerlain. Rory was practically submerged in the huge bath, but the bits of him that were exposed were absolutely gorgeous. Swallowing, she repeated the menu.

His head emerging from the foam, Rory grinned. 'We'll give the salmonella a miss then. Risotto would be fine – if you want to bother. I'll be quite happy with toast.'

'Toast is difficult without bread.'

He nodded. 'True. Do you want a bath?'

'Please. Leave the water and I can top it up again later.'

'Actually I was thinking of heeding Thames Water's advice on conservation.' He shot out a long wet arm and caught her round the waist. 'We shouldn't waste valuable resources –'

'Rory!' Georgia screamed as he dragged her to the edge of the bath and hot water slopped down her legs. 'Your sweater! It'll get all wet.'

'Sod the sweater,' Rory said, pulling her giggling on top of him.

Ages later they were eating the world's largest risotto at the kitchen table with Radio Two singing happily in the background. Cooking had become a joint operation and after emptying various tins and dried herbs and recycled bits of vegetable into the bubbling rice, they'd made love again on the kitchen floor.

'I suppose this is supfast – as opposed to brunch.' Rory had a fork in one hand and a glass of Moët in the other.

'Or brupper.' Georgia giggled. 'Either way it looks like it'll have to be Alka-Seltzer for pudding.' She dragged her eyes away from his for a moment. 'You're very domesticated – for an itinerant trucker, I mean. You've even got an ironing basket.'

Rory shrugged. 'Yeah. Embarrassing isn't it? Lorry drivers are supposed to be butch and macho and filled with Yorkie – and I even know the right setting for silk.'

'Who taught you to iron?'

'We were always encouraged – ' he paused, obviously not wanting to mention his brother's name. 'Well, to be able to do everything. Does it gladden your feminist soul?'

'I'm not that militant.' Georgia forked up rice. 'I mean I'm not a lorry driver as a sop to the sisterhood. I'm a lorry driver because it was what I was brought up with. What about you?'

Rory leaned back in his chair. 'Because it gave me freedom. Even before I ever dreamed of leaving the family business, I wanted to be in control of my own destiny. Lucky, really, considering what happened.'

Georgia held her breath. 'So the family business isn't transport?'

He shook his head. 'Buying and selling. Mum carried on with it when Dad died, and we were expected to join her.'

Georgia counted to ten. 'What sort of things did you buy and sell? Old things? Did you have shops?'

'Yes and yes. Mostly things people didn't want. Dad was red hot at striking good bargains.'

Biding her time, Georgia washed down the risotto with a mouthful of delicious champagne. 'And did your dad do the ironing and cooking and things as well?'

Rory seemed to find this amusing. 'God, no. He would have botched anything like that. He was far too impatient.'

'Do you miss him?'

'Yeah.' Rory trailed his fork across the plate, making patterns in the rice grains. 'A lot. We didn't see eye to eye on everything, but we were good friends. And he had principles.

I'm sure he would have understood why I left. I approved of the way he ran things – he was always fair. It changed so much after he died. Anyway he always thought – ' he rubbed his chin ' – he always thought that Rufus was a spoiled brat.'

Georgia swirled the remains of her champagne. 'Unlike your mother?'

Rory nodded. 'Exactly. Anyway, that's all in the past. My father is dead and thankfully my mother is out of my life.' He looked at the devastation of the kitchen and grinned. 'Shall we leave all this until the morning – I think the rest of the Moët would like to go to bed.'

Georgia was woken by a frantic tongue licking between her fingers. Smiling, she rolled towards Rory. The licking increased. Rory's breathing was steady. She opened her eyes. Eric was prancing up and down beside the bed, desperate for attention.

'Shush,' Georgia whispered, sliding out from beneath the covers. 'You'll wake him – and I haven't found out what he's like first thing in the morning – yet.'

She pulled Rory's dressing gown round her and followed Eric to the front door. 'OK. Go and spend a penny. I'll wait here.' She lifted her head and smelt the fresh spring day.

'Morning!' The cheerful voice made her jump. 'Lovely, isn't it?'

'Brilliant.' Georgia beamed at the postman and took three letters. Eric was sniffing excitedly round his feet. 'Don't worry about him – he's very friendly. C'mon, Eric . . .'

She closed the front door and Eric scuttled alongside her. 'OK, breakfast.' She leafed idly through the letters. Junk mail. The three envelopes all had company addresses printed on them. Georgia wondered what she'd have done if they had been pink scented envelopes with scrawled writing and SWALK on the back.

Moving a candlestick to anchor them to the mantelshelf, she froze. The uppermost envelope had a London postmark and a vivid red and yellow Vivienda logo.

CHAPTER 20

Georgia slid back into the MG and looked over her shoulder at the impressive sprawl of Williams Grand Prix Engineering. On a scale of Monday mornings, she thought, this one registered minus zero.

There wasn't a hope in hell that Williams would be using Diadem's next-day delivery service, of course. They had a fleet of lorries to rival any in the world, and Diadem would be as much use to them as a dictionary to a dyslexic. But the receptionist had said that they might – might – be interested in the courier service and, yes, she'd pass the literature on.

Georgia managed to start the MG at the third attempt and exhaled deeply. She still had appointments in Wantage, but her heart wasn't in it. Rory had left for a two-day haul to Felixstowe the previous evening and she was itching to get to Windwhistle. She needed to find that letter.

She had woken him with a cup of tea, with the post tucked under her arm. Ignoring both, he had grabbed her and tumbled her on to the bed. Eventually, he'd emerged, flicked through the envelopes and tossed them into the wastepaper basket.

'Aren't you even going to open them?' Georgia had to restrain herself from retrieving them. 'They might be important.'

'They're rubbish,' he'd grinned at her. 'Promises of instant wealth.'

'But one was from Vivienda.'

'Was it?' His eyes had teased her. 'Good heavens.'

'Rory!' She'd almost stamped in her impatience.

He had reached for her again and kissed her lovingly. 'Yes, it was. And as I know what it contains, I don't want to read it.' She had held her breath as he stroked her hair. 'It's an offer of work.'

She'd jerked away from him. 'A what? How do you know?'

Rory had kissed the tip of her nose. 'Apparently, now that they're into transport companies in a big way, Vivienda are sending circular letters to every registered LGV holder. A lot of the drivers on the ferry had had them. I knew mine wouldn't be long coming. Any further questions?'

'Hundreds,' Georgia had said happily, getting into bed with him, 'but they can all wait.'

They had spent Sunday visiting the invalids. Tumbling Bay and Charlie were both 'stable' – a word which she found far too apt under the circumstances. Both the hospital and the equine centre had been fairly sniffy over her hoot of laughter. Tumbling Bay had been sore and groggy but sleepily delighted to see her, and they'd left a ton of Polo mints with the vet for the minute he felt better.

They had then fought their way through a horde of jockey groupies to see Charlie, who was also sore and groggy but much cheered by the news that he hadn't broken any bones. He had been even more cheered with their gifts of the *Sunday Sport* and a bottle of Lucozade laced with Smirnoff.

Georgia sighed as she drove away from the Williams' headquarters and headed for Wantage. She had believed Rory about Vivienda on Saturday morning, and she still wanted to. But she was definitely going to read that letter.

She parked outside the reception area of Dearlove's Carpets on the outskirts of Wantage and wondered if Diadem's reputation had got there first.

Robert Marshall, Dearlove's depot manager, tall, blond, and looking totally out of place in the rather scruffy industrial block, ushered her into his office.

'I'm new,' he said without preamble, sitting himself down on a chair with legs still wrapped in corrugated paper. 'The whole set-up is new. We relocated from Wigan last month and we're looking for local transport. As yet we haven't nominated a local carrier. We have two artics of our own doing night and day trunks, but we'd like to involve local companies. I've read your literature, sounded you out, and I'd like to talk prices.'

Georgia blinked. 'Great. Of course it would depend on whether we were going to be contracted, or on an as-and-when basis.'

'Contracted.' To Georgia's surprise, Robert Marshall began to snap matchsticks in half. 'I like what I've heard about Diadem. I'll give you a month's trial to see if you can come up with the right prices. If I still like you, we'll carry on from there.'

'Great,' Georgia said again, rather at a loss without her sales patter. 'Well, we'll tailor our prices to suit you, of course. At least, as far as we can without risking bankruptcy.'

Robert Marshall started folding the edges of his blotter. 'I've also heard that you've had problems.'

Georgia's heart sank. 'Yes, well, I suppose you would. But – ' she glared at him, 'they're without foundation. We don't sail close to the wind, employ drivers with DR10s on their licences, lose loads, fiddle limiters and tachos, or – '

Robert Marshall smiled for the first time, abandoned the matchsticks and blotting paper, and started to chew his fingernails. 'Actually, that wasn't what I'd heard.'

Georgia closed her eyes. Robert Marshall leaned back in his chair. 'I approached Ionio first because they had the backing of the Vivienda Group. They came to me with an extremely impressive package. They also told me that if I was approached by Diadem – which, of course, I had been – not to touch them with a bargepole. They said you were expensive, inefficient, small-time, and – ' he leaned forward and riffled through the sheaves of paper on his desk, 'run by a mad nymphomaniac.'

Georgia winced.

Robert Marshall grinned and looked quite human. 'I decided that I had never heard anything quite so spiteful – so I took it upon myself to do a bit of investigating.'

Georgia held her breath. He put his papers to one side and sighed heavily. 'I had excellent reports from most of the people that have used you. I also felt that an enterprise such as yours should be encouraged in these days of monopolies and mergers. So, as I never like to be told what to think, or what to do, I've decided to give you a try. If it's only for a month, then I don't see what I've got to lose.'

Georgia could have kissed him. 'We won't let you down. And I'm very, very grateful.' Deciding that he would dislike bitchiness, she added, 'I won't pretend that it's been easy since Ionio were taken over, but I'm sure that there is plenty of room for both companies. When would you like us to start?'

'Tomorrow. Three a.m. Here to Bradford.' Robert Marshall gnawed his thumb. 'Can I ask you something?'

Anything! Georgia nodded.

'Are you the mad nymphomaniac?'

Georgia laughed. 'God, no! That's my grandmother! Er – no, well, it isn't – She isn't –'

'And, Miss Drummond, one last question.' He gripped the edges of the desk until his knuckles were white. 'Do you have a cigarette on you? I gave up yesterday morning and I'm going to kill somebody if I don't get some nicotine.'

Georgia drove into Diadem's yard, still smiling. She'd telephoned Cecilia from Wantage, arranged for Barney to be at Dearlove's in the morning, then rushed into the nearest Spar and bought twenty Benson & Hedges. Robert Marshall had actually kissed her before ripping off the cellophane with his teeth. If only all bribes were so easy, Georgia thought. And now they had got a new, important customer, surely the defectors would start returning? Ionio were about to get a taste of their own medicine.

Having pulled on leggings and the waddling ducklings jersey, fed the animals, and taken Eric and the Diadem dogs for a brisk run, she glanced at the clock. Surely it was too late to go to Windwhistle now? Maybe tomorrow . . .

'Wimp!' she shouted at herself, dropping down on to the sofa. 'You're behaving like a child who believes something's invisible if it closes its eyes!'

Eric settled himself on her lap as she flicked through the *Radio Times*. A thrice-repeated sitcom, the final part of a thriller, and yet another celeb chefette doing amazing things with capers, offered very little interest. Maybe she'd read the latest Terry Pratchett, which she'd pinched from Windwhistle's bookshelves, and chuckle herself to sleep instead. Anything rather than go to Windwhistle. Anything rather than face the truth.

The echo of the doorbell sent Eric scrabbling from her lap. Cursing, Georgia followed him. If it was someone selling double glazing, she thought as she opened the door, she'd probably scream.

'Hiya.' Sabrina, pale and dishevelled and clinging on to Oscar's buggy, looked hopefully into the hall. 'Are you busy?'

'Yes,' Georgia said, grabbing hold of Eric's collar before he ran out into the yard. She hadn't completely forgiven Sabrina for the slanging match. 'Is it urgent?'

'A bit.' Sabrina chewed her lip. 'Are you on your own?'

'Of course I'm on my own. You know that Rory's away and – ' She stopped. 'Is that why you want to talk to me? Something to do with Rory?'

'Nah,' Sabrina shook her head. 'I really need a mate, and you've always been great to me.'

Georgia almost laughed.

Sabrina dropped her voice, looked down at the sleeping

Oscar, then leaned towards Georgia. 'See, I think I'm pregnant again.'

'Good God! You'd better come in.'

In the living room, Sabrina uncoupled Oscar from the buggy and put him in Georgia's arms. 'Hold him a sec, would you? He's probably starving. Just bounce him around for a bit.'

Oscar was plump and sweet-smelling. However scatty Sabrina was, she certainly doted on her son. Georgia held him close to her, breathing in the clean scent of talcum powder, shampoo and baby skin. 'So – er – what makes you think you're pregnant?'

God! Georgia thought. She sounded like something out of a Victorian melodrama.

Watched expectantly by Eric, Sabrina was busily spooning brown sludge into a miniature plastic bain-marie. 'Oh, that was a bit of a fib. I *know* I am. You can't mistake it – even if you try really hard to ignore it and hope it'll go away, you know?'

Georgia did.

Sabrina hooked Oscar under one arm and tied a bib under his deliciously fat chin before spooning the goo into his mouth with swift no-nonsense strokes. 'I got one of them kits from the chemist this morning. It's a right pain. I mean, I love him to bits, of course,' she scooped dribbles from Oscar's chin and fed them back into his mouth, 'but he's only seven months. I'd've liked a bit of a breather. Still,' she gave Georgia a dazzling smile, 'it'll give him someone to play with, won't it?'

Not sure what to say in the face of such equanimity, Georgia found herself nodding in agreement.

'See, I reckon I'd manage fine with two kids as long as I've got a roof over me head and me little courier job.' She looked sternly at Georgia from beneath her long eyelashes. 'That's why you were wrong to think I'd give away Diadem's prices.

You lot have given me everything I've ever wanted. Nah, my problem again is the father.'

Georgia was confused. 'Er – just how many contenders are there?'

'Only one really, well, two – but I know who it is. Oh, do you reckon I slept with Rory that night after your gran's do? Not a hope – more's the pity. I tried me best, wandering around in a T-shirt, bending over, sitting on the end of the sofa with me legs all anywhere . . .' She gave a happy sigh at the memory. 'But he's only ever been interested in you.'

Georgia felt ridiculously happy, then remembered Sabrina's problems. 'So, don't you think you ought to speak to Charlie straight away? I mean, it's not fair for you to carry this alone.'

'Yeah, well . . . I slept with Charlie loads, but only the once with Alan – the night after the play. He was magic. Bloody brilliant.'

'Charlie?'

'Nah. Well, yeah – but then I expected him to be. Nah, Alan was a real turn-up – or turn-on,' she giggled. 'He didn't look like he'd know where to start but – ' she shuddered in delight, 'he was wonderful.'

Georgia was stunned. Alan Woodbury? Stammering, sweating, apologetic Alan? A demon beneath the duvet?

'But how can you be sure which one of them it was?' Georgia winced. She was in serious danger of sounding holier-than-thou.

Sabrina giggled again and propped Oscar back in his buggy with a bottle of orange juice. Eric was polishing off the remains of the brown goo with obvious relish. 'Charlie was always stocked with enough condoms to supply an army. But Alan,' she shook her feathery dark head, 'that were really torrid. We couldn't wait to get our hands on each other. See, we'd both got really gee'd up on stage an' well . . .' She shrugged. 'You know how it is.'

'So it's Alan's baby?'

Sabrina nodded. 'But I'm scared to tell him. I think he'll do a bunk like Oscar's dad did.' She twisted a tendril of hair round her finger. 'That's why I was sort of wondering if you'd tell him . . .'

'Me?'

'See, I know Alan's not drop-dead gorgeous like Charlie, but he's so kind. He makes me feel warm and safe – like my dad used to. Alan'd give us safety and security and – ' she searched for the words, 'well, proper happiness. You know, the sort of things that last for ever.'

'But do you love him?'

'Love?' Sabrina shrugged. 'That's what everyone says when they go to bed together. Nah, I've had that sort of love – it don't last long. I'd like to give the other sort a try – '

Georgia felt almost humbled. 'Of course I'll talk to Alan for you. But I'm sure you won't have to worry – he'll be fine about it.'

Sabrina threw her arms round Georgia's neck. 'Ace! I knew you'd be my best friend from the minute we met! Will you go tonight?'

And she had meant to, Georgia thought afterwards. She really had meant to. It was just that, when she'd started driving away from Diadem towards Upton Poges, the Tiptoe road had sort of beckoned to her. Windwhistle was only five minutes away, and Rory's keys were burning a hole in her pocket.

She unlocked Windwhistle's door and turned on the hall light. It wasn't breaking and entering, she told herself. After all, she had promised that she would keep an eye on things. The cottage oozed Rory from its pores. The smell of him – leather, diesel, Guerlain – was everywhere. Georgia swallowed and crept into the bedroom.

The bed was unmade, the covers tousled as they had been all weekend. She dragged her eyes away. She wanted him.

The letters were still where he'd thrown them in the wastepaper basket. Georgia almost gave up. Surely, if there had been anything incriminating he would have destroyed the evidence? But then, he had no idea she suspected anything, had he? He trusted her. He wouldn't expect her to be sneaking in to go through his rubbish bins like someone in a second-rate spy film.

The Vivienda envelope crackled in her fingers. Slowly, slowly, she pulled out the letter and unfolded it.

It was certainly a circular – but not to lorry drivers. It was a very healthy quarterly statement. Rory Faulkner was a shareholder in the Vivienda Group.

Too stricken to cry, too devastated even to move, Georgia replaced the letter in the envelope and shoved it deep into her pocket. She stared at the tumbled bed and wanted to die.

It all made sense now. Every single bit of it. Especially Mrs Kendall at Ionio. Why, oh why, hadn't she confronted him with that at the beginning? Because, she admitted to herself, this was exactly what she'd feared.

It was so clever. And he had never exactly lied to her about any of it, the conniving, cruel, calculating bastard. Everything had been fudged and blurred, and she, falling more and more in love, had believed every treacherous word. Rory must have been feeding information back to his family right from the start. Rory, with his sweet-talk and his lethal love-making, had infiltrated his way into Diadem and done his best to ruin them.

A vicious knot of pain was punching its way up her windpipe. Rory had betrayed her. Worse than that. She swallowed. He'd beguiled and dazzled her and taken her for a fool.

Georgia paced up and down the bedroom, anger temporarily blotting out her grief. Rory Faulkner – the itinerant trucker, drifting in and out of companies in the best disguise since G.K. Chesterton's postman! The family business –

buying and selling! He'd told her so much and, with the genius of all good spies, had managed to make it sound entirely plausible.

Realising that before long her fury would be swamped by the agony of loss, she stumbled to the telephone. She had to make sure. Her hands were shaking so much that it took ages to punch out the right number. The digits swam in front of her eyes.

'Hellair.' The exaggerated voice barked into Georgia's over-sensitised ear. 'This is Brimstones'. How may I help you?'

'Beth,' Georgia's voice was a strangulated croak. She coughed. 'Beth, it's me, Georgia Drummond. Sorry to call so late but I'm catching up on some paperwork, and – er – I wondered if I could check on something?'

'Of course.' Beth had reverted to a more acceptable shout. 'You know us, Georgia. Like the Windmill, we never close.'

Georgia knew only too well that Brimstones' Agency was manned twenty-four hours a day to satisfy the vagaries of shift-working employers. 'Could I come over and go through a few things with you?'

'Now?' Beth sounded surprised. 'Yes, if you wish. Spencer's not here though – he's at a meeting in Newbury. Will I do?'

'Yes.' Georgia bit her lip. Cecilia was at a meeting in Newbury, too. 'I'll be with you in twenty minutes.'

She was. Icy cold and stiff with shock, she pulled the MG to a halt outside the Brimstones' four-storey Victorian villa. Beth and Spencer ran the agency from the ground floor and lights flooded out across the severely pruned front garden. The evening was still and dark and seemed to press in on her.

Beth, resplendent in ski pants and a tight angora sweater, beamed at her as she opened the door. 'Women workers of the world unite!'

Georgia slunk into the harshly-lit office with its austere wall charts and gun-metal filing cabinets. 'I – um – was just updating the drivers' records and I know that when you sent us Adenoids – er – Brian and – ' she took a deep breath, 'Rory – we never actually saw their original driving licences. I know you check all that before you allocate them, but – '

Beth pulled her painted eyebrows together. 'Are you suggesting that we sent you people who were not adequately qualified for their positions?'

'No – no. Nothing like that.' Bile was rising in Georgia's mouth. At any minute she'd start to panic. 'It's – er – just that Trish didn't take down details of their full names and you know what the DTI is like for spot checks.'

'Yes,' said Beth, who luckily didn't.

Georgia blundered on. 'So, I thought if you had taken copies of their driving licences and – '

'Of course.' Beth clattered open a filing cabinet drawer. 'Here we are. Brian Dickson.'

Beth waved Adenoids' file at Georgia who didn't want it and only remembered just in time. She'd never make a good spy. Unlike – she gulped and took the file.

Beth paused as she flicked through her alphabetical dividers. 'Are you feeling under the weather, Georgia? You look peaky.'

'I'm fine.' Georgia riffled through the papers, noting without interest that Adenoids had been christened Brian Aloysius Cassius.

'I heard about your poor horse and Charlie. Nasty business.' Beth clanged the cabinet shut. 'No wonder you're so pale. You could do with a holiday. Spencer and I are considering the Ballyricks this summer. Minorca, of course. Not one of the common ones. Here you are, Rory Faulkner – '

Georgia took the file as though it was a coiled cobra. She opened it, and the feeble hope she had been harbouring died.

Rory James Kendall Faulkner.

There was nothing to say. Dragging her face into a grateful gesture she handed both files back to Beth.

'Is that all you wanted?' Beth tossed them into the filing tray for the day-release girl to deal with in the morning. 'You're very thorough, Georgia. Coming all this way just for that. A gel after my own heart. Business before pleasure. Cup of herbal tea before you go?'

Georgia shook her head. Gathering what was left of her wits together, she thanked Beth for her time and headed towards the door.

'You didn't take notes,' Beth shook her rigid bob. 'Did you not want to write anything down?'

'There's no need,' Georgia said grimly. 'I'll remember.'

'Clever girl.' Beth thumped back behind her desk to wait for anguished calls from the all-night supermarket warehouses. 'And is your grandmother also working late this evening?'

'No – she's . . .' she remembered about Cecilia just in time, 'she's having an early night.'

'Ah.' Beth was transparently relieved. 'Good idea at her age.'

'Beth, can I ask you something?'

Beth, still poised over the telephone, looked round. 'Of course.'

'You hinted that the information that was being given to Ionio had come from inside Diadem. Did you *know* who was doing it? Don't pretend, Beth, please. You knew, didn't you? About Vivienda?'

The phone rang and Beth pounced on it. Georgia wanted to snatch it away. Beth put her hand over the mouthpiece. 'I warned you for your own good, my dear. That's all.' She turned back to the phone call. 'What say? Fork-lift drivers? Two? Now. Yes. Yes. I'll have to make phone calls, of course. I'll get back to you in ten minutes.'

'Why didn't you tell me?' Georgia was nearly in tears.

'Ten minutes, yes.' Beth put her hand over the receiver again. 'I like you, Georgia – it's your grandmother I can't stand.' She smiled sadly and resumed her call. 'Yes, they'll be certified. All my people are certified –'

Georgia drove home on autopilot. There was a jabbing pulse throbbing in her temples and her eyes kept misting over. The bastard! The gnawing pain under her ribs had slipped to her stomach and settled there. She wanted to abandon the MG and run crying through the black tangle of the Upton Poges countryside like a wounded animal.

The joyful reception she received from Eric and the cats only increased her despair. She felt as though someone had tied weights to her ankles. Pouring herself a haphazard measure of Courvoisier, she wandered to the window and stared at nothing. Rory had spent the previous evening in her flat and everything now reminded her of him. His clothes were in her room; the smell of his cologne was in her bed, on her cushions, floating on the air; his laughter was ringing in her ears, and she could still feel the touch of his hands on her body. The white freesias he'd bought her – long dead – were dried and standing on the television set. Downing the brandy, she swept the freesias and the vase on to the floor.

Eric and the cats dived for cover as she picked up the *Radio Times* from beneath the debris. With tears streaming down her cheeks, she laughed out loud. The date flashed from the top of the page as though it was illuminated in neon. April 1.

All Fool's Day.

CHAPTER 21

Slitty-eyed through lack of sleep, Georgia waited outside Windwhistle the following morning. Huddled in the MG with a mist of drizzle sweeping from the Downs, she crossed her arms round her inebriated elephant sweater and tried to stop her teeth from chattering.

She had telephoned the office and told Cecilia that she was going to spend the day drumming up more new business. Then she had slapped blusher on to her sallow cheeks, given up mascara as a total waste of time and wiped off the lipstick that made her face look like a clown. Her grandmother, greatly buoyed up by the evening with Spencer in Newbury or the Dearlove's business or both, had agreed happily that a bit more successful cold-calling was just what the company could do with. Georgia had bitten back her tears. There would never be a colder call than this one.

Rory would be back from Felixstowe and in Diadem's yard by nine, and allowing for the ritual dieseling up and hosing down of the lorry, Georgia had estimated that he should return to his cottage about an hour later. She had wrenched the phone from the hook last night, muffling the squawking alarm with a patchwork cushion so that she wouldn't have to talk to him. This, their last meeting, had to be in person.

She hunched over the steering wheel, frightened by how angry she felt. And how alone. The stabbing in her stomach had intensified. Grief and betrayal had become a gnawing, nagging, physical pain.

When Rory's car eventually turned into the road she felt a frisson of excitement leap through her body, followed immediately by black despair. She clutched at the sight of the long denim clad legs, the broad shoulders in the brown leather jacket, the tousled hair. She'd never see them again.

Rory had spotted the MG and was grinning as he locked his car door. 'Fantastic! Just what every lonely trucker needs after a trip away. A beautiful lady to welcome him home and – Good God, Georgia,' he frowned as she stumbled from the car, 'you look appalling. What on earth has happened? Is it Tumbling Bay? Charlie? I thought there must be something wrong. I tried to ring you all last night. What is it?'

He was moving towards her, his arms outstretched. You cool, clever bastard, she thought, still loving him madly. She backed away from the temptation. 'Don't touch me!'

'What the hell's going on?'

Georgia laughed. It hurt her throat. 'Christ! You really should have joined the Poges Players! Very nicely done. Now, do you want to talk out here, or shall we go inside? Whichever way, it won't take long.'

Rory looked as though he'd woken from a bad dream. 'Georgia . . .?'

'Unlock the door.' She ground her teeth together to stop herself crying. 'I really don't want this to be public.'

She followed him into the hall. The bitter knife continued to slash at her stomach. Taking a deep breath she looked into his eyes. 'Good morning, Mr Faulkner. Or should I say Kendall? What else do they call you in your family – apart from Judas? How long did you think you'd get away with it?'

'With what?'

'Don't waste my time!' she snapped. 'We both know what we're talking about. All I want you to do is leave Diadem. Now. Today. Before you can ruin us further.'

'I haven't –'

'Crap!' She wanted to attack him. 'You have one thing in your favour and that's the fact that I don't want to look more of a fool than you've already made me. So, tell Gran that you're moving on. Tell her that I've OK'd you not completing your contract. Tell her whatever you like, but don't, for God's sake, tell her the truth.'

'Which is?' His eyes glittered.

'That you're part of Vivienda.' She spelled it out sarcastically. 'I suppose you have to be reminded from time to time. After all, you're so good at slipping into your alternative role.'

Rory took off the leather jacket and stormed into the kitchen. Above the noise of running water and kettle-filling, he said, 'I'm not part of Vivienda. My brother is a director. I merely receive payments from the shares my father left me, that's all.'

'That's all? That's all?' Georgia's voice had risen, and she fought to control it. 'How much more can there be? Your mother *is* the chairman, I take it?'

'Yeah.' He appeared in the doorway again. 'And two uncles, one aunt and several cousins are on the Board. How did you find out?'

Georgia's eyes were filling with tears and she turned her head away. Crying was for later. When she was alone. 'The letter on Saturday morning.'

Rory started to head for the bedroom but Georgia shook her head. 'Don't bother. It's in my pocket.' She'd read it over and over again. She knew it by heart. Rufus was a majority shareholder. So was Stephanie Kendall. Stephanie, who had broken Rory's heart . . .

'Christ,' Rory seemed taken aback. 'I shouldn't have underestimated you.'

'Why the fuck didn't you tell me when you got the letter? Was it something that just slipped your mind? The name of the family business you told me so much about? You two-faced shit! And Rufus must be so much like you that Stephanie was confused enough to marry him –'

Rory bunched his fists for a second, then let them fall wearily open again. 'That must have been quite recent. She wasn't on the previous statement. So, do you want me to explain? Are you going to listen?'

She shook her head so violently that her teeth rattled. 'What's to explain? What's to listen to? More of your carefully-rehearsed lies? I've told you what I want you to do. And I want you to do it now. Go back to Diadem and tell them you're quitting. Then leave.'

'OK.'

His quiet compliance shocked her. She pointed to the photographs on the wall. 'I even knew that was your mother! And I didn't say anything because I wanted to be wrong!'

'My mother? How the hell did you know she was – ?'

Georgia's face was contorted as she continued to point at the photograph. 'I met her at Ionio – '

Please, please, she prayed silently, please tell me I've got it all wrong.

But he didn't.

She let the tears run down her cheeks. 'God, I've been so stupid. I should have realised – the signs were all there, weren't they? At Windsor, when the press appeared you were nowhere to be seen. Did you think they'd recognise you and blow your cover? And I actually told you that Vivienda had got the Lennards contract and you didn't say anything! Because,' she was almost incoherent now, 'because you already bloody knew!'

'No, I didn't.' His face was tired and filled with pain. 'But it didn't surprise me. They were determined to take over all your prestige accounts. And I've never run away from the press, either. I've never run away from anything in my life, and I'm not going to run away from you. I'll walk. Quickly.'

She couldn't have been more shocked if he'd hit her. He continued to stare at her with blank, cold eyes. 'I'll come and collect my things straight away, shall I?'

'Yes. And get as far away from here as possible before you do any more damage. If you go, we might just survive.'

'And Eric?'

Georgia swallowed a fresh clutch of tears. 'Eric belongs to you.'

Rory had snapped off the electric kettle and picked up his jacket. 'Very well. There's no point in saying anything else. You've got me hung before I've even been accused.'

'You hung yourself,' she hissed, 'by being a traitor.'

She followed him miserably outside and climbed back into the MG. There had been a tiny spark of hope glimmering inside her, the faintest belief that he might deny everything and tell her it was all a mistake.

But he hadn't. Because it was horribly, terrifyingly true.

Leaving the phone off the hook and smothered by the cushion, Georgia lay dry-eyed and shaking on her bed. Time and silence merged together. Nothing would ever be the same again. The room grew dark. The darkness didn't take away the scent of Rory from the pillow.

She heard the soft footfall up the stairs and her heart gave a thump of joy.

Cecilia pushed open the bedroom door. 'Darling –'

Georgia couldn't hold back the tears. Too devastated to cry as long as no one was being nice to her, she knew that once she started she'd probably never stop. 'Go away, Gran. Please.'

'In a minute.' Cecilia's shadow came into the bedroom, followed by the familiar waft of Joy and a swish of silk jersey. 'I just want to make sure you're all right.'

Georgia wiped her eyes with the back of her hand. She'd never be all right.

Cecilia sat on the end of the bed and reached out for Georgia's hand. 'Do you want to talk about it?'

'No.'

'Right. Then we won't. I'll make you a cup of tea swimming in brandy instead.' She stood up and paused in the gloom of the doorway. 'I just want to know one thing.'

Georgia's lips were trembling. 'What?'

'Was it my fault?'

'No!' She dashed the tears away again but they welled up and trickled painfully down the inside of her nose.

'Oh, good.' Cecilia's sigh was audible. 'Only I realise that I tend to go over the top at times – and Trish and I wondered if you and Rory had fallen out because you'd mentioned the inside information thing.'

'No – I didn't – I didn't – ' It was all so farcical that Georgia started to laugh. Then the laugh got caught up in a fresh wave of tears and turned into shuddering sobs.

Cecilia flew back to the bed and cradled Georgia against her thin shoulder. 'Oh, darling, don't. Please don't. There are always lovers' tiffs, sweetheart, and, invariably, you think they're the end of the world. But it'll work out, believe me. You and Rory were so perfect together. Whatever silly thing you've quarrelled about will seem like nothing in a few days' time. Why, we haven't even taken him off the rotas – just pencilled in two weeks' leave and – '

'Take him off everything!' Georgia hissed, sitting up for the first time and glaring at her grandmother through puffy eyes. 'I mean everything! Obliterate him from our records! Rory Faulkner does not exist,' she started laughing again. 'He never did. He never bloody did.'

Shaking her head, Cecilia stood up and made the promised tea and brandy. Georgia, still sitting in the dark, muttered her thanks, knowing that she wouldn't drink it.

Cecilia shrugged. 'I don't like to leave you like this.'

'I'm better on my own.' Georgia's lips were swollen and her nose was sore. 'Put it down to inexperience. If I'd had dozens of relationships, I might be a bit more adept at handling the end of them, mightn't I?'

'But it seems to be more than that.'

'Of course it isn't,' Georgia lied through her chattering teeth. 'I'm not pregnant. He's not married. He hasn't run off with my best friend – or the family silver. It's just over.'

The most horrible, final, words in the world.

Doubtfully, Cecilia left the room. 'Just shout if you need me, darling. Promise?'

'Promise,' muttered Georgia, who only needed Rory.

Cecilia turned round on the landing. 'Do you want me to tell everyone else? It might save you some embarrassment –'

'Trish was obviously in on his exit,' Georgia said, 'so no doubt the whole of Upton Poges knew by lunch-time.'

'That's not very nice.'

'True, though. But, yes, if there's anyone still left in the dark I'll leave it to you to post the announcement. You can say whatever you want . . .'

Cecilia obviously had, Georgia thought the next day when, white-faced and red-eyed from a further night without sleep, she appeared in the Diadem office. Marie, Jed and Barney, all sorting out their run sheets, stopped laughing and began to talk to each other in hushed voices. Ken scuttled out of the door and leapt into the Magnum as though the hounds of hell were at his heels. Trish suddenly found it necessary to bury her head in the pages of the PC manual she hadn't touched for years, and even Cecilia sloped off into the outer office with an excuse about topping-up the coffee pot.

Only Sabrina, nursing Oscar, actually met her eyes. 'Georgia, I'm dead sorry. He was a lush guy. It hurts, don't it? If you want to talk or anything –'

'Thanks.' In spite of everything, Georgia was touched. 'How are you?'

'I guess you never got to see Alan?'

Georgia shook her head. If she had, none of this would have happened.

Marie, Jed and Barney shuffled out of the office, giving her the scantest smiles. God knows what embellishments Cecilia had added to the parting, Georgia thought. It looked as though it may well have contained terminal illness and murder as two of the lighter ingredients.

'Say something,' she hissed at Trish as she slumped in her chair and tried to concentrate on the paperwork in front of her. 'Say anything. Just talk to me.'

'I don't know what to say.' Trish was flicking across the keyboard. 'I thought it was going to be for ever. I thought I was going to be the oldest bridesmaid in Christendom. I couldn't believe it when he said he was leaving. Is there any chance – ?'

'None at all.' Georgia wondered if she'd ever get used to this awful feeling of drowning in despair. 'Oh, Christ. What on earth am I going to do?'

CHAPTER 22

Three weeks later, Cecilia waved farewell to Diadem's accountant who had been for his monthly ritual of book-checking and knee-squeezing, and closed the office door on a grey and blustery afternoon. Georgia, who had been doodling distractedly on a notepad throughout most of the discussion, didn't look up.

'Well, that was cheering, wasn't it?' Cecilia slipped off her loafers and rubbed her fine-deniered toes. 'I knew we'd start improving as soon as Ionio slapped up their charges. Lennards' defection could have been fatal. But now, with Dearlove's business on a regular basis and a lot of our old customers back, I think we'll need another driver.'

'No!' Georgia's pen skittered across the page. 'Don't even think about it!'

'Sweetheart,' Cecilia's eyes softened, 'I didn't actually mean Rory –'

Georgia bit her lip. The mere mention of his name nipped at her with red-hot pincers. 'Sorry. I thought –'

Cecilia looked at her granddaughter with affection. 'I know. No, I meant how do you feel about taking Adenoids on full-time? As a replacement for Rory, if you like. We can afford him, and now Jed's fully fit we can put him back on long hauls.'

'Whatever,' Georgia said wearily. 'Yes. I'll leave a note for Trish to draw up a contract.'

She retrieved the pen and resumed her doodling. The pain hadn't lessened. In fact, she missed Rory more each day, and her continual apathy frightened her. Three weeks could have been three years. She almost wished he'd left her for another woman. At least that way she could have won public sympathy. As it was, she suffered alone.

To give him his due, Rory had told Cecilia that their parting was a mutual decision due to insurmountable differences. Intrigued, Cecilia had assumed sexual difficulties of Herculean proportions, and appeared disappointed that Georgia had refused to elaborate.

Georgia wiped her hand across her tired eyes and added stars to the doodle. Her thoughts wandered along the same barren track. When she had first fallen in love with him, she'd weighed up all the risks, but had secretly thought it would be for ever. Sad, romantic fool that she was! The sooner she faced the truth, the better. Rory had never intended staying longer than was necessary – and now he was gone. No doubt he was finagling his way into the affections of some other small business at this very minute without giving her a second thought.

And since he'd left, the customers – with the exception of Lennards – had returned. They still suffered from the same minor breakdowns and hiccups, but no one was reading anything sinister into them now, and the Ionio drivers merely sneered rather than actively threatened. She didn't need any further proof of Rory's allegiance to Vivienda.

She shook her head. Surely he had felt *something* for her – or for Diadem, at least? Maybe he had rushed back to the viperous bosom of his family and told them that Diadem was simply not big enough, not efficient enough, to pose a threat – and certainly not worth taking over. She could imagine the smug expressions on the faces of the handsome Rufus, who she had decided through torturous sleepless nights must be exactly like Rory but without the warmth, and Stephanie whom he had once loved, and his mother – the chairman he'd simply forgotten to mention . . .

'Why don't you get glammed up and have a night out?'

Cecilia was collecting her handbag and briefcase. 'You haven't been out of that house since – well, for ages. You should contact your friends, or come along to the Am Dram meetings. We're planning the summer show already. It's a comedy.' Sensing she was playing a losing hand, Cecilia hurled in all her aces. 'At least we've got the Brimstone Ball to look forward to.'

'Jesus,' Georgia muttered. 'Is it that time of year already? I can't think of anything worse. I don't want to do anything – least of all sit through an evening of acute embarrassment with Beth and Spencer and a lot of free-loaders.'

Cecilia stretched out a hand in a helpless gesture. 'Sweetheart, I know how you feel. You're probably too young to remember, but after Gordon died I didn't want to go on living. I only did because I had to care for you. I'm sure if you hadn't been there I would have slunk off to bed with a bottle of whisky and a handful of pills. Oh, yes, don't look so shocked! I thought about killing myself several times. But I'm very glad I didn't.' She smiled. 'Gordon would have been absolutely furious!'

'It's not the same.' Georgia's eyes filled with tears. 'I'm not suicidal. R-Rory's not dead. This is completely different.'

'But you're not eating properly. You're certainly not sleeping. And your mind isn't able to concentrate on anything. It's grief and shock, Georgia, and it's making you very depressed. You really need to cope with it. The Brimstone Ball is usually jolly good fun. But if you really don't feel up to it, why don't you have a little holiday, maybe, or –'

'I don't want a holiday!' Georgia stood up quickly and hurried towards the office door before Cecilia started on her 'find someone else' or 'plenty more fish in the sea' routines. 'I don't want to tart myself up and do awful dances with Spencer. I'll be fine if everyone will just leave me alone! I've made a fool of myself, and I'm the one who's got to live with it!'

She slammed the door and stood shaking on the cobbles. She couldn't face another night in the house with the reproachful eyes of the dogs and cats wondering why she didn't want to play any more, and Trish or Cecilia or Maddy ringing every half-hour 'just to see if you're OK.'

She couldn't face another night of a joyless bath followed by television programmes she hardly watched because there wasn't any alternative, or reading the same page of her book thirty times over. But going out? Going away? She wanted to cry out loud. What was the point without Rory? Without Rory, what was the point in anything?'

Knocking on Alan's conventionally brown front door two hours later, the visit didn't seem like such a good idea. Maybe he'd be entertaining one of his lonely-hearts ladies? Georgia shrugged. So what? She would pretend to be selling a new soul-saving religion or something equally obscure. After all, she had become a very accomplished actress. Perhaps she should have phoned first? She shook her head. If she had planned the visit she wouldn't have bothered to do it. The inertia had really dug deep.

Alan opened the door and peered out into the darkness. Judging by the rather ill-fitting grey jogging suit and a pair of plaid slippers, he was in relaxing mode. Georgia, trying very hard to imagine him as a sexual athlete, failed miserably.

'Georgia! I was just thinking about you. Come in – or isn't it a social call?'

'Well, it's not business so I suppose it must be.' She stepped inside Alan's relentlessly beige hall. The last time she'd been here was with Rory. 'I'd sort of meant to go to Peapods to see how Charlie was getting on and I thought – er . . .'

He ushered her through into his very neat, very beige living room. 'It's lovely to see you again, whatever the reason. It hasn't been the same since Jed's been doing the deliveries.

Not that he isn't good, I mean, but – ' He plumped a cushion in the chair beside the electric fire. 'Sit down. It's turned really chilly. Tea? Coffee?'

She shook her head. What the hell was she doing here? What was she supposed to say? 'Sabrina's pregnant and you're the chief suspect'?

Alan sat opposite her. 'I was so sorry to hear about you and – um – Rory. You poor thing. You seemed so happy. Why don't the really wicked people in this world get hurt? Why is it always the softies?'

'That's why.' She flickered a smile. 'How are you doing with your advertising ladies?'

'I've given it up as a bad job.' Alan stroked his moustache with his thumb and forefinger. 'To be honest, my heart wasn't in it. Oh, God, you probably don't want to hear this – especially not now – but I couldn't give my full attention to anyone else when I realised I had met the only woman I would ever love.'

She stretched the smile to interested. 'Oh?'

'Yes.' He sat back in the chair and looked dreamy. 'You know, the way you realise something's been under your nose for absolutely ages and you don't recognise its significance until it's gone. That's how it is with me – '

Georgia trawled around in the murky waters of her dull brain to find something illuminating to add. If she had been with Rory she would have joked that the only thing under Alan's nose was his weedy moustache. 'Oh?' she said again.

Alan leaned forward, crossing one grey furry knee over the other. He wasn't wearing socks, Georgia noticed. His feet looked very white in the slippers. 'Still, it'll keep. I'm sure this isn't what you want to talk about at the moment. How's Tumbling Bay?'

Georgia tried to shield her legs from the relentless heat of the electric fire. 'Getting better, thanks. Visiting him is one of the few things that's kept me going. When he eventually comes out of the equine centre, Drew's going to have him back to convalesce at Peapods. He's got a pool and these heat-therapy things. Then I'll probably take him back to Diadem for his retirement. We could do up the stable block – '

They talked about Tumbling Bay, about Charlie, about the forthcoming Brimstone Ball, about work, about the Poges Players' next production, and about Maddy's pregnancy and imminent baby.

Sensing this was the only opportunity she was going to get to raise the subject, Georgia pushed her lank hair behind her ears. 'Er – yes, I know Drew's really excited about being a father. Maddy says he's been to all the classes. Does it appeal to you?'

'Fatherhood?' Alan's face was shiny with enthusiasm. 'Goodness, yes. My wife – ex-wife – didn't want children. Said it would damage her career structure. It was one of the reasons we parted,' he sighed sadly. 'Still, there's not much hope for me in that area, is there?'

Georgia felt hugely relieved. 'Just now, when you said you'd fallen in love – were you talking about Sabrina?'

Alan's eyes misted over. 'Yes. She's wonderful. Gorgeous and funny – and so beautiful. Like a dream. And I adore Oscar. But I don't think she's the slightest bit interested in me. I mean, she'll always compare me with Charlie.'

'She has,' Georgia nodded. 'And you came out on top. Oh – er – I didn't actually mean – Alan, Sabrina fancies you like mad and she's also – '

'Really? Honestly?' Alan's grin was ear-to-ear. 'Sabrina? Oh, that's super. Totally unbelievable.' He paused. 'She's also what?'

'Expecting your baby.'

There was a stunned silence. Then Alan leapt to his feet and punched the air in triumph. Georgia, whose right leg had been char-grilled by the electric bars, stood up and grabbed his hands. 'She was frightened to tell you. She thought you'd leave her like Oscar's father did.'

'Me?' Alan was almost running towards the telephone. 'God, no. There's only one thing I'm going to do.'

Georgia hobbled through the beigeness towards the front door. 'Oh?'

'Ask her to marry me,' Alan grinned, clutching the telephone. 'As soon as possible.'

Still reluctant to return to the loneliness of Diadem, Georgia drove through the blustery night. Sabrina and Alan. An odd couple, but who was to say they wouldn't be happy? Most of her wanted them to be, of course. Most of her . . .

She swallowed the permanent lump in her throat, and turned the MG in the direction of Milton St John.

Parking at the back of Peapods' stable block, and praying that Drew and Maddy wouldn't see her, because she knew she would disgrace herself if they showed her any sympathy, she knocked on Charlie's front door. If he was alone it would be a miracle.

The door swung open. The hall table was piled with back copies of the racing papers and a stack of envelopes. Get Well cards were pinned to the walls and dangled from the picture rails. Letters written on deckle-edged paper in different-coloured inks with heavily underlined telephone numbers, littered every available surface.

Georgia raised her voice above the thud of Motorhead. 'Charlie? Are you decent?'

Motorhead diminished slightly. 'Come in. Who are you?'

Opening the door with trepidation, Georgia peeped into the living room.

'Hi,' Charlie grinned crookedly from the sofa. 'Have you brought me anything?'

'Not what you most obviously need.' Georgia couldn't help grinning back at him. He was wearing boxer shorts and a T-shirt and looked amazing. His bruised and battered leg was resting on cushions. 'You're looking much better. Have you started the physio?'

'Yeah.' Charlie was delving through Georgia's visiting pack of girlie magazines and two bottles of gin. 'Her name's Fiona.'

'You're hopeless.' Georgia perched on the edge of a chair. 'I only came to get a progress report.'

'You could have done that on the phone – not that it's not great to see you.' Charlie was dispensing a hefty measure of Gordon's into a glass. 'I won't offer you anything alcoholic because I know you'll only snap at me. There's Coke in the fridge. Well?'

Georgia shrugged. 'I didn't want to stay at home. I had to go and see Alan, so – you know.'

Charlie leaned back on his cushions, his fox-red hair glowing against the calico. 'I get the picture. Georgia, you look terrible. Don't you think you and Rory could sort it out?'

'Not a hope.'

Charlie took a swig of gin. 'Pity. He was a nice bloke. You were really good together.'

'Can we change the subject?'

'OK. Why did you go and see Alan Woodbury? Not that I'm really interested, of course, but lying here I'll gossip about anything. I've even got into daytime soaps. Hell, you weren't asking him out or anything, were you?'

Georgia shook her head.

'Thank God for that. I mean, he's a nice guy, but wasted on you. If you hang on until I get out of here, I could sort you out some therapy. I'm very good with broken hearts.'

'And all other parts of the female anatomy.'

'You've been reading my mail.' Charlie finished his gin and poured a refill. 'So, is that what you want to discuss? Whether shacking up with Alan Woodbury would be a good way of getting over Rory?' He levered himself up the sofa. 'Not a great idea, Georgia, to be honest. In fact, pretty bloody lousy.'

'Actually, I went to talk to him about babies.'

'Babies?' Charlie's eyebrows climbed towards his hairline. 'Christ. Why? Is that what you're going to talk to me about too? Do you want to have my children?'

'Of course not! I thought Sabrina might, though. But she seems to think that Alan – '

'Sabrina's pregnant?' Charlie splashed gin over the sofa. 'And it's drippy Alan's baby?'

Georgia, knowing she had been indiscreet, groaned. 'Yes, but don't say anything yet. I mean, it's not for public broadcast. I – um – thought it might be yours, actually, but Sabrina says you – er . . .'

Charlie rocked with laughter and then flinched. 'Shit. I keep forgetting the leg. What? That we used enough condoms to keep the Durex shareholders in champagne for a year? Yeah, we did – but as we're both being indiscreet tonight, and you need cheering up, I'll let you into a state secret.' He leaned towards Georgia and kissed her cheek. 'It's all for show. I fire blanks. I was kicked in a very delicate area when I was an apprentice.'

CHAPTER 23

Deciding that getting away from Upton Poges was probably a wise move, Georgia volunteered, much to Cecilia's delight, for a four-day trip in the Magnum to Scotland.

The weather was glorious, the scenery breathtaking, and Georgia hated every minute of it. Weary and dirty on her return, she plonked her paperwork and tachos on Trish's desk. The office was almost deserted.

'Where is everyone?'

Trish waved her hands expansively. 'Your gran has gone into Newbury to buy a frock for the Brimstone Ball. Ken's gone with her to supervise – although I think the frock will be more for Spence's benefit than anyone's. Everyone else is driving – except Sabrina. She's sick.'

'As in not well or throwing up?'

'The latter.' Trish shuddered. 'If that's what pregnancy does for you, then I'm glad I'm giving it a miss.'

Georgia sat down heavily. 'What about your IVF?'

'Coffee?' Trish was already reaching for two mugs. 'Biscuits? Don't shake your head at me – you've lost over a stone already. You look like a calorie-deficient rake. Chewing a biscuit while we talk won't be like proper eating. Here – '

Enjoying being bullied and mollycoddled for once, Georgia dunked the custard cream in her coffee. She'd eaten two before she realised it.

'I thought I'd be really jealous of Sabrina, but I'm not. After all those years of praying for pregnancy, imagining the symptoms, crossing my fingers every month, it's something of a relief not to have to bother. And thank God the baby is Alan's and not Charlie Somerset's. At least Alan is going to do the decent thing. Charlie must have a string of illegitimate kids across the country.'

Giving a noncommittal shrug, Georgia concentrated on her third custard cream. Trish leaned forward. 'Anyway, it's partly because of Sabrina that Jed and I have decided not to go ahead with the treatment.'

'But I thought you liked Oscar?'

'I dote on him! He's an angel! And I adore baby-sitting and looking after him in the office when Sabrina's out driving. But,' she looked fiercely at Georgia, 'I can always give him back. Being so close to him has made me realise what a tie babies are. Jed and I have worked our lives round each other and we're really not sure if we could take all that disruption.' She sighed. 'So we've decided to let nature take its course.'

Georgia shook her head at the offer of a further biscuit. After so many weeks of self-imposed starvation, she was beginning to feel sick.

Trish whisked the packet away. 'It's lovely about the wedding isn't it? Oh, God – sorry. Wrong subject. Do you still hate her?'

'No. I never really did. At first, I think I was jealous because Gran seemed so besotted. And then I thought she was after – after Rory. But now, well, she's just a bit of a madcap kid who seems delighted to be here. I've got no regrets about that particular rescue mission – but I'm certainly not planning any more.'

'Look, about Rory – I know everyone agreed not to say anything to you, but don't you think you ought to talk about it? Get it out of your system –'

Georgia drained her coffee. 'Please, Trish. I really don't want to discuss him. Not even with you. Have you told Dr Hodgson you're cancelling the IVF?'

Looking slightly miffed, Trish nodded. 'Yeah. I explained that I was terrified I might turn into one of those gruesome professional mothers. You know, someone who's forever banging out action rhymes on the piano and hanging ghastly paper things round the walls. And then there's the mess. Until I saw Sabrina's flat I'd never realised. And at the moment me and Jed can have sex at any time. With kids you never know when they'll appear beside you, pointing and saying "Ooh, what's that?", do you? And then –'

'OK. OK.' Georgia held up her hands in supplication. 'I get the picture. What did Dr Hodgson say?'

'I think she thought I was a bit odd, actually,' Trish conceded. 'And Jed's sure I'll change my mind. But I won't. If I become pregnant it'll be because it's meant to happen. And it'll leave the IVF programme free for someone who wants it more than me. If Sabrina hadn't been here, I could have made a terrible mistake.'

She started to clear away the biscuit packet and coffee mugs, leaving Georgia to ponder on the vagaries of human nature. But not for long.

In a flurry of Camp Hopson bags, Cecilia flew into the office.

'Oh, super, darling.' She beamed at Georgia who was pouring out a cup of coffee from the inexhaustible pot. 'I'm gasping. Pour one for Kenny, too, there's a love. He'll be in in a minute. How was your trip? You look tons better.' She delved into her carrier bags. 'Tell me what you think of this for the Brimstone do? I know turquoise isn't usually my colour but I really didn't think my little black could stand a further outing.' She pulled out a swathe of silk and flapped it around the office.

'Oh!' Trish enthused. 'That's fabulous! Handkerchief hems always look so gypsyish, don't they?'

Georgia stared. It was more slash than dress and very see-through. 'Are you sure . . .?'

'Never more certain,' Cecilia said, stowing the frock away amidst a crinkle of tissue paper. 'With the right shoes and some rather flamboyant Cabouchon baubles it'll knock 'em for six. Now we'll have to get your outfit sorted, won't we?'

'I'm not going.'

'Of course you're going. We're all going – even Sabrina if she's feeling better and we can persuade Marie's mum to add Oscar to her baby-sitting list. So, what do you fancy? Something slinky? Or maybe something wild and sexy? You could wear your hair up and –'

'I'm not going,' Georgia repeated. 'I'll only be a complete misery and wreck everyone's evening.'

'No you won't,' Cecilia frowned across her coffee cup. 'You'll go and you'll enjoy it. And one of the joys of the Brimstone Ball is that, because everyone knows everyone else, you don't have to have a partner. You might meet someone and –'

Georgia stood up. 'I'm definitely not going if you're going to spend the entire night playing Cilla Black. It will *not* be a lorra, lorra laffs, OK? And I do not want to be paired off with Wayne, Shayne, Warren or Darren, who work in personal fitness centres and have IQs smaller than the Tories' popularity figures and spend their leisure time clubbing and beating up rival football supporters and –'

Cecilia swallowed a mouthful of coffee the wrong way and spluttered. 'Hallelujah! You're getting better. A week ago you couldn't even be bothered to argue with me! We'll have an absolutely super time and – where are you going?'

'To see if Sabrina's feeling better.' Georgia paused at the office door. 'Then I'm going to have a shower. A warm shower. And then I might, just might, sort out something to wear for Beth and Spence's party. But,' she glared at her grandmother, 'I'm not promising anything, so don't hold your breath.'

Sabrina's flat was as chaotic as ever but Alan, who was holding Oscar, seemed completely unaware of the devastation. Georgia looked at him closely. There was something different about him. She shook her head. Maybe it was just the air of radiant happiness. 'I won't stop. I thought Sabrina might be on her own and I know she's off-colour.'

Alan grinned sheepishly. 'Poor love. Every time she's sick I feel so guilty. She's wonderfully brave though. Like a little lion. We've set the date.'

'Date?' Georgia picked her way through a trail of toys and clothes.

'For the wedding.' Alan beamed. 'We've got a special licence. Wantage Registry. The day after the Brimstone Ball. Not ideal, I know – but it's the earliest they could fit us in.'

'Lovely. Oh – ' Georgia suddenly noticed. 'You've shaved off your moustache!'

'Sabrina didn't like it. Said it made me look old. We'll be inviting everyone, of course, and your gran has been brilliant about putting on a bit of a party at Diadem afterwards. Oh, Georgia, I know how down in the dumps you must be feeling, but I'm so happy.'

Georgia hugged him. She was delighted for them both. She just wished it didn't hurt quite so much. 'Alan, would you and Sabrina be awfully offended if I didn't come to the wedding? I – I really don't think I could face it. If I burst into tears at the reception I can always disappear upstairs – but I'd hate to make a scene on your big day.'

Alan patted her shoulder. 'I understand. We'd both love you to be there, of course, but you do what you think is best. If you change your mind, you know you'll be more than welcome.'

Hearing a gurgle from the bathroom and a door being slammed, Georgia deduced that Sabrina was feeling better and decided to make her getaway before she was deluged in descriptions of wedding dresses, flowers and honeymoons.

'Give Sabrina my love,' she said, letting herself out. 'And I hope you'll always be happy.'

They probably would be, she thought, crossing the yard. She should be ecstatic. Two of her lame ducks nicely sorted out, living happily ever after. She just wished that someone would take her under their wing and whisk away her despair.

The light on her answerphone was winking as she closed the door. She groaned. She hadn't switched it on for ages – in case Rory tried to ring. Cecilia must have put it on while she was away. She pressed the play button, ready to erase the message if it was Rory – yet hoping treacherously that it might be.

'Hi, babe! It's me. Morag. Just to let you know we'll be dropping in some time soon. Not sure when. Henry sends his love. Let Mother know. See you.' The message ended with a lot of blown kisses.

Georgia turned it off, not knowing whether to laugh or cry. A visit from her parents was all she needed.

CHAPTER 24

The annual Brimstone Ball was second only in social importance to the Chamber of Commerce Dinner Dance. Beth, wearing a frock of lime-green rhinestones which looked as though it might have had a touch of Vivienne Westwood in its pedigree, and Spencer in his twice-yearly tuxedo, welcomed the guests in the foyer of the Upton Poges Manor Hotel with much bonhomie and a glass of warm Asti.

Feeling about as miserable as it was possible to get without calling the Samaritans, Georgia slunk in behind Cecilia and Ken.

'God!' Trish breathed in her ear. 'You look amazing. I must say the funereal garb sets off your pallor a treat.'

'Cheers.'

'I mean it.' Trish clung unsteadily to Jed's arm. Mikey Somerville had been roped in to supervise the bar and had produced an ice-breaker called 'Brimstones' Bomb'. Trish had had two. 'We're so used to seeing you in butterfly colours that this is something of a stunner. Isn't it, Jed?'

Jed, who'd had three cocktails, was cross-eyed. He nodded. 'Yeah. Really knockout.'

Georgia tried to smile. She had left her outfit-buying until the last moment and the tight black satin leggings with matching long coat and black court shoes had been Camp Hopson's choice. All the brightly coloured party frocks and ball gowns had hung limply from her shoulders like paper-chains on Twelfth Night.

'We do have this,' the assistant had produced the black suit. 'All the rage in Paris.'

'I don't wear black,' Georgia had said wearily.

She'd bought it and the shoes in five minutes flat, and driven back to Diadem feeling more dejected than she could ever remember.

Scraping her hair back into a schoolmistress bun at the nape of her neck and applying dark make-up, she'd gazed bleakly at the gaunt, austere figure in her bedroom mirror.

'Wonderful!' Cecilia, perched on the bed, had enthused. 'You look like a cross between Angelica Houston and Cruella de Ville. Deliciously sexy, darling. Especially now you're so thin. Good heavens, you'll have to fight them off.'

So far, Georgia thought morosely, she hadn't needed to throw even the slightest punch. Several people had turned to stare, not recognising her at first. Then they had realised that it was just jolly Georgia in a depressed state, and returned to their Asti and conversations.

Cecilia fluttered to her side, swirling in the diaphanous turquoise frock. 'Has anyone checked the seating plan?'

Georgia had. The Diadem contingent were sharing a table with Mallett's Fresh Fruits and three of Brimstones' Agency drivers and their wives, none of whose names Georgia recognised.

A portly man, glamorous in green and gold livery, struck a large gong. 'Ladies and gentlemen! Dinner is about to be served! Could the lowest-numbered tables take their places first, please! Table numbers one to six. Then seven to twelve.'

'What are we?' Cecilia was batting her eyelashes at Spencer.

'Five,' Georgia hissed. 'And Spence's on the top table, so pack it in.'

As they filed past the gong-banger, Georgia almost smiled. It was Ted Danbury who was more usually employed selling papers on the corner of Upton Poges High Street. No wonder he yelled so loudly, she thought. It was only surprising that he hadn't bellowed an encore of 'Sportin' Pink! Get yer Sportin' Pink!'

The banqueting hall was wood panelled and chandeliered. The tables were smothered in damask cloths, red roses, gold cutlery, and a diamond dazzle of crystal glasses.

'Typical Spencer,' Ken sneered. 'All fur coat and no knickers.'

Georgia was sitting between Ken and a Brimstones' driver, who was either Paul or Stan or Andy. Introductions were made across the table while everyone oohed and aahed over the grandeur. Georgia felt very much alone. The familiar ache crept under her ribs and her throat tightened. The desperately-missing-Rory moments hit at such times. She swallowed and stared determinedly around the room. She was not going to cry.

Ionio, represented by the gorgeous black receptionist, a couple of whizzkid salesmen, and several of the drivers Diadem had clashed with, were sitting at table eight. They were all, she noticed with malice, wearing ties sporting Ionio's red and yellow corporate colours and looking rather tacky. She hoped that the receptionist wouldn't recognise her.

Having chosen pumpkin soup as her starter because everything else was game and she couldn't reconcile herself to eating anything that had been hunted, she lifted her spoon. The crash of cutlery rattled against the tide of conversation. The pumpkin soup, sweet and cloying, stuck in her throat. Her eyes wandered – she dropped her spoon with a clatter.

'Here you are, duck.' Her neighbour, who turned out to be Paul, handed it back to her. 'Bit of a butter-fingers tonight, aren't we? Good God, gel! What's up? Soup isn't that bad, is it?'

Georgia couldn't breathe. Rory was sitting on the far side of the room.

Paul followed her eyes. 'Know him, do you?'

'He used to – er – drive for us.' Georgia's hands were trembling so much that lifting the spoon again would have been impossible.

'Still owe him for his last stint or summat, do you? He's a laugh.' Paul was ripping into his breast of pigeon with sharp teeth. 'Old Rory. One of the boys.'

Old Rory. One of the boys. Bit of a laugh. Spy.

Georgia was certain the entire room could hear the thumping of her heart. 'Does he still work for – er – Brimstones' then?'

'Yeah. On and off. Do you want me to catch his eye?'

'No!'

'You must owe him a hell of a lot, gel. You've gone as white as the tablecloth. Here – do you want the rest of that soup?'

Georgia shoved the bowl sideways. The rest of Diadem were scraping plates and bowls and didn't seem to have noticed her frozen expression. Why was Beth still giving work to Rory? Maybe she just fed him into huge conglomerates where he couldn't do any damage. She chinked her teeth against her glass of Pouilly-Fuissé, trying to drag her eyes away.

He looked more sensational than anyone had a right to, she thought angrily. In a dark suit and pale silk shirt he was still heart-stoppingly handsome. She curled her lips. He knew how to iron silk. He knew how to cheat and lie and inveigle his way into people's affections. How dare he sit there, calm, unruffled, *knowing* that she'd be there; *knowing* what he'd done or, at least, attempted to do to Diadem?

'Venison, boar or ostrich?' a camp voice echoed in her ear.

'Uh?' Georgia jerked her head round.

'Your main course.' The waiter was teetering as if on tiptoe. 'Venison, boar or ostrich?'

'Good God!' Georgia couldn't believe it. 'I donate pounds to wildlife charities to save all those! How dare you *cook* them!'

'I don't, dear. Chef does. Now which is it to be?'

Georgia looked at the bloodied mess being heaped on to other plates. 'Haven't you got a vegetarian alternative?'

'Wild mushroom plait,' the waiter sighed, 'but you should have ordered earlier. I'll have to see what Chef can do.'

'I'll have yours if you don't want it,' Andy, the other lorry driver, leaned sideways. 'I hate to see waste.'

Georgia stared at Rory again. She couldn't see what he was eating. She'd kill him if it was animal. Whatever it was, he didn't seem to like it much. He appeared to be too deep in conversation with the ladies on either side of him to raise his knife and fork very often. Trembling, the lump in her throat getting bigger by the second, Georgia wondered which one of them had taken her place. The tiny blonde in silver and black with big hair? Or the well-preserved forty-something in lilac who was practically gnawing his ear? Both, probably, she thought, feeling sick. Especially if they ran a transport company . . .

'Wild mushroom plait.' The waiter thrust a heap of grey goo in pastry over her shoulder. 'Veg as standard. You've got no objection to veg, I take it? You don't belong to the Veg Liberation Front?'

Andy and Paul eyed her plate hungrily. She pushed it towards them and sipped the glass of Shiraz in front of her.

Pudding, something whipped with raspberries, was accompanied by more Asti. Georgia gulped at it, praying for alcoholic oblivion. Looking round the table to see if anyone else had spotted Rory, she was slightly cheered to realise that they all appeared to be squiffy.

'Is this meths?' Paul peered at the fresh glass of clear liquid that had magically appeared beside each plate. 'It's got a slug in it.'

'It's Sambucca, sir.' The wine waiter hovered with matches. 'And that's a coffee bean.'

'Christ. Cutting down on the courses a bit, aren't you?' Andy looked doubtful. 'Hey! Cut that out!'

The Sambuccas were ignited simultaneously. Cries of delight rose from the other tables, but not theirs. Paul had doused the lot with a soda siphon.

Georgia wanted to cry. She and Rory would have laughed, their fingers entwining. She swallowed the watered-down Sambucca and shuddered.

'You don't eat much, but you can sure put away the alcohol,' Andy said admiringly. 'Do you want your After Eight?'

Ted Danbury, the gong-banger, bustled up to the top table and rapped smartly with his gavel. 'Ladies and gentlemen! Pray silence for your hostess!'

Beth reared to her feet, a myriad rhinestones glinting beneath the chandeliers.

'She looks like a Christmas tree.' Cecilia was licking the centre from her After Eight. 'Someone ought to hang her above Oxford Street.'

'Friends!' Beth bellowed down the microphone. 'I hope you've all enjoyed your meal. It's our way of saying thank you to you all: to our customers, our employees and our friends for your continued support of the company. We are greatly blessed. Now, I'm sure you'd all welcome some exercise – '

Cecilia caught Spencer's eye and smirked.

' – so,' Beth continued, 'there will be dancing in the Cavalier Ballroom. I shall, of course, be available myself for dances later. Once again, my husband and I hope you have a truly splendid evening.' She sat down to riotous applause.

Cecilia tisked. 'How on earth Elizabeth contrives to sound like a cross between the Queen and Margaret Thatcher completely eludes me. Kenny? Where are you going?'

'Seeing a man,' Ken gave a theatrical wink. 'Back soon.'

'Well, at least the old trout kept it mercifully short.' Andy inhaled his cigarette, but Georgia wasn't listening. Rory was staring at her, his eyes as bleak as a deserted seafront in a January gale.

Everyone crashed towards the ballroom, talking loudly. The Diadem contingent, now best buddies with Mallett's Fresh Fruits, were nowhere to be seen. The lorry drivers and their wives had left as well. Georgia sat still, pleating her napkin. She could see the shadows under his eyes. He'd lost weight too.

Rory looked away first. He stood up, spoke to someone on the other side of his table, then walked out of the room.

Knowing she couldn't stay a minute longer, Georgia hurled her napkin on to the table and hurried out of the banqueting hall.

The hotel's reception area was deserted as she telephoned for a taxi.

'Half an hour, love. All right?'

Georgia said yes, she supposed so, and wondered how she could kill the next thirty minutes without returning to the Cavalier Ballroom's jollity.

The waiters, still clearing the debris from the dining room, teetered past her with trays. Partygoers flocked in and out of the cloakrooms giggling. She had never felt so alone.

'C'mon, love.' One of the Mallett's Fresh Fruits ladies appeared from the cloakroom and linked her arm through Georgia's. 'You were on our table, weren't you? Had a squabble with your man? No point in sulking out here. Come an' join in the fun.'

'I'm waiting for a taxi. It'll be here in half an hour and –'

'They always say half an hour.' The Mallett's Fresh Fruits lady started to pull Georgia in the direction of the ballroom. 'You could be waiting all night. Might as well have a bit of a laugh in the meantime.'

Too depressed to explain, and knowing that if she started to struggle it would cause a scene, Georgia tried to smile.

'That's the ticket.' Georgia's rescuer, still tugging, took this as encouragement. 'You come and sit with us duck, if you want.'

Georgia shook her head. Being lonely in a crowd of happy people was far worse than being lonely in isolation. The Fresh Fruits lady beamed as they approached the ornately carved doorway. 'Sure you'll be OK?'

'Yes, thanks.' Georgia managed to extricate herself. 'I'll just wait here for the taxi – '

The Cavalier Ballroom echoed to a dying round of applause. All eyes were riveted on the stage. Spencer, looking pompous in front of the Glen Miller sound-alike band, was in the process of handing the microphone to Rory.

If he's going to sing 'I Will Survive', Georgia thought viciously, I'll hate him for the rest of my life. Well, I will anyway, of course. But it'll just make it easier.

Waiting until his capacity audience were all watching him, Rory spoke quietly. 'I won't take up much of your time, but there's something I have to do. Maybe I should have done it a long time ago. But now that everyone concerned is together, it'll make things easier – '

The wine waiter sidled up to Georgia. 'My, but he's masterful,' he said admiringly. 'This is all a bit Hercule Poirot, dear, isn't it?' He raised his voice. 'My guess is the butler, love!'

Rory silenced the wave of laughter with his hand. Cool bastard, thought Georgia, wondering why, if he was going to thank the Brimstones for the evening's festivities, he hadn't done it after Beth's speech at the dinner table.

'This may come as a surprise to some of you, though not all,' his unsmiling eyes skimmed the crowd and found Georgia. She shivered. Rory looked away. 'But I have been accused of industrial espionage.'

Georgia closed her eyes. He couldn't do this. There were excited whispers. Rory's voice rose above them. 'Unfairly, I may add. But mud sticks, and I was determined to clear my name. I won't bore you with the details – I'm sure you know them already.'

Heads nodded. Upton Poges was very insular. Opinions had been loudly divided over the smear campaign.

Rory moved towards the edge of the stage. 'I want to say that at no time during my employment with Diadem Transport did I tamper with vehicles, spread damaging rumours, feed information to rival companies or,' he stared at Georgia again, 'have any contact with the Vivienda Group.'

The Ionio contingent shuffled uncomfortably. Frantically Georgia searched the crowd for Cecilia. She was standing with the rest of Diadem and the Brimstones in a far corner, looking shell-shocked.

'However, during my employment by Mrs Harkness and Ms Drummond, I thought I knew who was responsible for attempting to bring about their downfall and, naturally, once I had been accused, I set out to prove that my theories were correct.'

Several people clapped. Rory frowned. 'For my sake – and for the sake of the businesses involved – I watched, listened, asked questions, and checked until I was certain who it might be. And, because my reputation has been publicly tarnished, this is why I've chosen such a public manner in which to clear my name.'

Georgia looked away from him, her eyes stinging. Why was he doing this?

'The whispering campaign which was so successful, was instigated by Beth Brimstone.'

Beth gave a little scream and swayed against Spencer. No one spoke. 'There were various reasons but,' he glared at Beth across the immobile heads, 'most of them were personal.'

'But Mrs Brimstone wasn't alone. She had a collaborator. A spy in the Diadem camp, as she was so fond of saying. She dropped none-too-subtle hints that this spy was me. Several of you, I'm sure, believed it. I was the most likely candidate, of course. The outsider.' He stared towards Cecilia. 'I'm really sorry about this. I think you ought to ask Ken Poldruan about his mechanical handiwork.'

'No!' Cecilia's whisper was clearly audible in the silent room. 'Why?'

Ken tried to shoulder his way through the crowd. The three Brimstones' drivers from their table prevented him from escaping.

'Because he was also jealous,' Rory said gently, speaking only to Cecilia. They could have been alone in the room.

Cecilia's face blanched. Georgia longed to run to her grandmother's side, but her feet wouldn't move. Beth was wailing like a banshee. The Ionio contingent had melted discreetly away.

Rory hadn't quite finished. 'I don't think there's any need to say anything else. Nor will I suggest retribution, legal or otherwise. All I wanted to do was clear my name. Thank you for listening to me.'

He left the stage to tumultuous applause. Half the guests seemed to think it was part of the entertainment; the other half – the half that it affected – were shocked to the core. Everyone noticed that neither Beth nor Ken had uttered one word of denial.

Georgia tried to force her way through the throng. She had to reach Rory. She had to say sorry – at least for suspecting him.

'He's gone, love.' The wine waiter caught her arm. 'Eyes blazing. Shoulders squared. Oooh – what a man!'

'Georgia!' Cecilia clutched her arm through the crowd. She was close to tears and looked her age. 'Oh, Georgia!'

Georgia shook her head. 'Don't say anything. Yes, that's why we split up. But – ' her anger surged, 'don't you realise that you could have ruined the business? You – playing around with Spencer, flaunting it under Beth's nose, goading Ken!'

'But what were they going to do?' Cecilia seemed be-wildered. 'When they'd ruined us? What on earth were they going to do?'

'God knows. Maybe hurting you was enough.' She looked at her grandmother with sympathy for the first time. 'I think you need a brandy.'

'I've been a bit of a fool, haven't I?'

'A lot of a fool – but you don't have sole rights to that.' Georgia spoke bitterly. 'Are you going to call the police?'

'Police?' Cecilia's voice quavered slightly. 'It's not a police matter. Thanks to Rory, everyone who needed to know the truth now does.'

Trish and Jed, Barney and Marie clustered round them, looking stunned. Jed sighed heavily. 'Ken's pissed off. I presume he's heading back for Diadem to do his packing. Do you want me and Barney to – ?'

'Let him go.' Cecilia dashed away her tears. 'As long as he's packed and cleared out by the time we get back and never asks for a reference –'

'I'd bloody kill him if I got me hands on him,' Marie said. 'I don't know how you can just let him walk away.'

'What else is there to do? He tried to destroy the company – but it was partly my fault. I really didn't treat him very well. Anyway, he didn't manage it – which is the most important thing. What about bloody Elizabeth? I should have slapped her face and really given her something to yell about. Where is she?'

'I think Spence took her home,' Barney said with some relish. 'Probably going to beat the livin' daylights out of her.'

The band trumpeted into action. Most of the guests were dancing. Georgia felt exhausted. She looked at Cecilia who was sipping her restorative brandy and starting to perk up. Her grandmother, Georgia was sure, would never fully admit her responsibility for Beth and Ken's desperate measures.

'Georgia,' Tom Lennard touched her shoulder lightly. 'I'm so sorry. I should never have believed – I'll be in touch tomorrow to make proper apologies to Cecilia and to offer you my business back, of course.'

'Er – thanks.'

Tom Lennard squeezed her shoulder more tightly. 'It's all a bit much to take in, isn't it? Still, no harm done. Diadem lives to fight another day, eh?'

There was a stream of similar platitudes. Georgia smiled and nodded at everyone above the roaring in her ears. Diadem would survive and prosper. But what about her?

What was going to happen to her?

CHAPTER 25

In the silence of the deserted Diadem office, Georgia bent down to lace her Doc Martens. The room swam alarmingly. Taking a deep breath, she straightened up. Light-headed through lack of sleep, she knew she had to concentrate. She had to get to Warrington and back with a Dearlove's run. It had been the only delivery they hadn't been able to reschedule, and Georgia had grabbed the chance to have a genuine reason for not attending Alan and Sabrina's wedding. Their total bliss would have been too hard to bear.

Everyone else had staggered off, nursing their hangovers, to the registry office. She had promised Alan and Sabrina that she'd be back in time for the last knockings of the reception. She had never felt less like celebrating in her life.

May drizzle swept damply across the yard. The curtains in Ken's bungalow were tightly closed. Jed and Barney had barged in there on their return from Upton Poges, but Ken had gone, taking everything with him. Cecilia had stood in the middle of the emptiness weeping copious and very real tears of grief.

Beth and Ken – conspirators in crime. No matter how many times she thought about it, it still seemed almost impossible. Georgia paused in the office doorway, and retraced her steps. She picked up the phone, her hands shaking so much that she misdialled three times. No one answered. She could visualise the telephone on Windwhistle's hall table, shrilling to itself. She just wanted to talk to him. She needed to say sorry.

Rubbing her eyes, she clicked the cradle and was just about to try again when the office door flew open.

'Georgia!'

Georgia let the receiver tumble from her hands and stared at the tall gaunt figure in jeans and a beaded waistcoat beneath an ex-army overcoat.

A pair of eyes sparkled through grey-streaked hair. 'Hi! Don't say you'd forgotten we were coming?'

'Of course not,' Georgia croaked, staring at her father. 'Hello, Henry. Mum.'

'Not Mum, babe, please. It makes me feel so old.' Morag, plump and jolly in tie-dyed velvet and a matted shawl, whisked away a purple fringe as she hugged her daughter. 'God! What's happened to you? You're like a rake!'

'Long story,' Georgia looked helplessly round the office. 'Look, the coffee pot's on, and there's tons of food in the house. I can't stop – I'm driving to Warrington.'

'No sweat.' Henry Drummond sat down in Georgia's chair and hauled his legs on to the desk. 'OK if I smoke, babe?'

'Yes. Oh, God, no.' Georgia cast an anguished glance at her father who was gumming together Rizla papers and emptying the dubious contents of a tin box on to the desk.

'Where's Mother?' Morag was drifting round the office touching things. Her bracelets jangled. 'I hope she's expecting us?'

'Not exactly,' Georgia sighed. 'But she'll probably be delighted. She's at a wedding. They all are. The reception will be here in about – ' she glanced at her watch ' – half an hour.'

'Ace,' Morag smiled dreamily, inhaling the incense-rich scent of dope and leaf-mould that was floating across the room from Henry. 'Anyone we know?'

'A girl who works here and one of our customers. I think Gran sees it as a good corporate match.' Despite her misery, Georgia smiled back at Morag. They had absolutely nothing in common except their genes. The relationship was as weird as it was possible to get and yet they were very fond of each other. Georgia always felt at least twenty years older than her mother. 'I'm really sorry to leave you like this. And in case Gran forgets to offer, please take some food when you leave.'

Morag shook her head. Twin chandeliers of ethnic earrings clanked beneath her aubergine hair. 'We don't need it, babe, thanks all the same. We're into self-sufficiency now. We've parked the bus on a bit of land in Brecon and claimed squatters' rights. We grow all our own veg, and we've got goats and chickens. What we can't grow we trade for round the markets.'

Georgia looked at her parents with something akin to admiration. They had probably found what most people were searching for. Love and peace could have been invented for them. She kissed them both. 'Promise you'll still be here when I get back. And if the phone rings don't worry, we've put it on divert for the rest of the day. Oh, I think the happy couple have returned –'

A procession of cars pulled up behind Henry and Morag's battered van. There were shrieks of laughter as the wedding party clattered across the cobbles. Georgia felt a punch of pain. They had plenty to celebrate.

Sabrina, looking gorgeous in gold and cream, was hanging on to Alan's hand. Alan was glassy-eyed and totally besotted. Trish was nursing Oscar.

Kissing them and mouthing congratulations, Georgia caught Cecilia's arm. 'I'm just off to Warrington. I'll be back later. Mum and Dad are in there – what's the matter?'

Cecilia pointed over her shoulder. Spencer Brimstone was clambering out of his scarlet BMW. 'Elizabeth has left him. Packed and gone. With Kenny!'

Georgia stared at her grandmother. 'So they were – um – as well as being traitors?'

'It looks that way,' Cecilia said briskly. 'Poor Spencer is going to need careful handling over this. He's totally devastated. Can you believe the cheek of the woman?'

'For leaving him or trying to wreck Diadem?'

'Neither!' Cecilia snorted, grabbing hold of Spencer's arm. 'For running off with my Kenny!'

'Come on. Come on.' Georgia squinted through the Scania's windscreen which was practically obliterated by torrential rain, at a winding, stationary queue of traffic on the M6. 'Get a bloody move on.'

She had driven to Warrington and was now on her way back to Upton Poges. She'd tried to phone Rory at every opportunity but there was still no reply. Suppose he's gone now, she thought in panic. He's cleared his name – what's there to stay for? Suppose I can never say I'm sorry . . .?

The cab phone rang and she snatched at it.

'Darling,' Cecilia's voice crackled, 'have you had a blow-out or something? You're ages late. Where are you?'

'Just past Hilton Park,' Georgia snapped back. 'Stuck in the usual queue. The radio says the tail-backs will probably last for up to two hours. It's dark and wet and I'm totally pissed off.'

Cecilia, whose broken heart had obviously undergone a miracle cure, had the nerve to chuckle. 'You sound just like your grandfather. Look, darling, you will try to be back before the end, won't you?'

'Yes.' Georgia couldn't wait to get Cecilia off the line so that she could try Rory again. 'Although I don't have a lot of sway out here. How's it going?'

'Magnificently! We've phoned round and invited the whole world. The house looks like a Mardi Gras. There's still oodles of food and drink left, and with ribbons and balloons and absolutely tons of confetti, it's all gorgeous. Morag and Henry are having a lovely time! And Spencer and I have been helping each other come to terms with what's happened.'

Surprise, surprise, Georgia thought. 'Save me a slice of cake and a vat of champagne, and I'll be there as soon as I can.'

Half an hour later the Scania had edged forward less than six feet. Practically tearing her hair out, Georgia glared at the string of lights that looked like garnets on her side of the carriageway and diamonds on the other. She used to find them beautiful, as they glistened and danced in the rain. But not tonight. Tonight they were merely obstacles that prevented her from getting home and finding Rory.

She'd go to Windwhistle. She'd camp on his doorstep. She'd make a complete nuisance of herself until he spoke to her. She laughed ruefully. If he'd left Upton Poges they'd find her sitting in the cab of the Scania covered in cobwebs like a trucking Miss Havisham.

Gradually, the traffic started to move. Inch by inch, tyres hissing, Georgia crept nearer to home.

Swishing along the M40, her eyes hypnotised by the rapidly flickering windscreen wipers, Georgia glanced at the clock on the dashboard and howled. Slowing, punching out Diadem's number, she cursed the Department of Transport and their bloody regulations.

Diadem's phone, like Windwhistle's, rang for ever.

'Jesus!' Georgia snarled, stamping on the air brakes as a Vauxhall Cavalier cut in front of her, happily oblivious to the damage that a forty-foot lorry could do. 'Answer the bloody phone!'

'Hi! We're having a party!' a voice slurred. 'Why don't you come and join us?'

'I'm trying to,' Georgia gritted her teeth. The noise in the background was ear-splitting. Cecilia hadn't exaggerated about inviting the world. 'Who's that?'

'Trish – I think,' the voice giggled. 'Oh, hi, Georgia! Where are you?'

'On the M40 – and it looks like that's where I'll be staying. I've run out of hours.'

Trish was shouting above the strains of 'Chirpy Chirpy

Cheep Cheep' and a dozen massed voices. 'What can you do? Can you get home?'

'Not without fiddling the tacho, and I'm not going to risk that. Look, Trish, is there anyone there who's sober enough to drive out and meet me? We could swap vehicles. How about Jed?'

Trish let this filter through the Krug-induced haze. 'Oh yeah. Well, no, actually Jed's been smoking something your dad gave him. He's dancing on the table wrapped in a curtain with the fruit bowl on his head.'

'Oh, brilliant. Surely someone must be sober?'

'Marie!' Trish shrieked. 'She's just got back from seeing to the kids. She's been on orange juice. Sit tight. I'll get Marie. Where are you?'

'I'm going to pull in to Warwick Services. I'll wait there.'

She waited. It seemed like for ever. The lorry cab, snug against the slanting rain, seemed very isolated. The thought of the party raging on without her only increased her loneliness. Rory . . . God, no, she mustn't start thinking of Rory. Not now. She wouldn't even try phoning again until she got home. If she ever did . . .

She switched on the radio and listened to a very sad local phone-in from people in bedsits who had been abducted by aliens or had Lord Lucan in their basements.

The rain trickled down the black windscreen like silent tears. She missed Rory so much. She wondered idly if she'd end up like Cecilia, rapaciously seducing every man in sight because she could never again seduce the only man she had ever loved. She pushed a cassette into the slot and Dinah Washington crooned silkily through the sadness.

When the headlights pulled up behind her, Georgia hardly stirred. She'd been jumping up for ages, only to sink down again when she realised it wasn't Marie. She pulled down her inebriated elephant sweater and peered in her wing mirror. Yes! Her MG was pulling up alongside.

She leaned across and flicked the passenger door-catch open. 'And about bloody time! God, am I glad to see you! Thanks, Marie – oh – '

'I'm not Marie.' Rory hauled himself into the cab and closed the door. 'Although in a bad light you could be forgiven for not spotting that immediately. Apart from the fact that I'm two feet taller, the wrong sex and – ' There was an excited flurry of wriggling white body and madly whirring tail erupting from beneath Rory's jacket. 'He's missed you.'

'Eric.' She held out her arms and her tears were licked away as fast as they appeared. 'Oh, Eric – '

Rory turned his head away as Eric leapt and scrabbled, yelping with excitement.

Hugging Eric, Georgia's tongue was suddenly far too big for her mouth. Her heart punched her ribs. 'What the hell are you doing here?'

'I'm driving the lorry home while you take the car,' Rory said crisply. 'Those were my instructions from Trish. So shove over.'

'But Trish said Marie – '

'Did she?' He was professionally inserting a new tacho. 'I can't imagine why. There, I'm all legal.' He smiled in the dark red gloom. It didn't reach his eyes. 'Off you go. You'll be home before they finish the cake. I must say, Alan and Sabrina getting it together came as something of a surprise – but then I've been out of circulation for a bit. Things seem to happen very rapidly in Upton Poges, don't they?'

Georgia longed to hurl herself into his arms, but was pretty sure that he'd just hurl her out again. 'It was a shock to everyone. Rory, about last night – '

'I vindicated myself – which was all I wanted to do.'

Eric scampered between them both, beside himself with

joy. She stroked his head. 'But you *are* a Vivienda share-holder. It *does* belong to your family. I know I shouldn't have leapt to conclusions, but you should have told me – '

He nodded, not looking at her. 'Of course I *should* have done. Easy to be wise after the event, though, don't you think? I tried to tell you, early on, and then when I realised what a threat Vivienda were to Diadem, I could never find the right time. I was afraid that you'd think – well,' he shrugged, 'what you did think, actually. But I didn't lie to you. I merely withheld some of the truth. Not that that's an excuse – I do realise that.'

They stared at each other. There was still no warmth in his eyes. Georgia turned away first and glared at the rain on the windscreen. 'So – what were you doing at the wedding reception? Did Gran invite you?'

'No, Spencer did. He seemed to want to thank me for getting rid of Ken – and for not pressing charges against Beth for defamation of character. Which I couldn't because she never actually said it was me, did she?'

'No.' She hadn't needed to. Georgia had added two and two together and made five hundred. 'But how did you know it was Beth? And Ken, for God's sake – '

Rory shrugged. 'I just watched Ken's disintegration. He loved Cecilia, but he knew she was playing fast and loose. I don't think he gave a toss about destroying Diadem. He just wanted to hurt your grandmother. As did Beth.'

Georgia nodded. It made sense. 'And, of course, Ken was always there, fiddling with the lorries – and he made sure he had his fair share of mishaps. I'm glad you exposed them.'

He didn't speak. Dinah Washington stopped crooning. The rain beat even harder. Eric curled happily between them, his nose buried in his paws.

Georgia knew she was going to cry. 'I – I've been trying to ring you all day.'

'I've been driving. I thought you understood about lorry

drivers – oh, no, I forgot. You don't think I am a lorry driver, do you? You still think I'm a director of Vivienda. Why were you ringing me?'

He wasn't going to make it easy. She bit her lip. 'To say sorry.'

'Don't bother.' He shrugged off the leather jacket and pulled up the sleeves of his silk shirt. 'By the way, I met your parents. They're great.'

'I suppose that's fair. I've met your mother, after all.' Georgia chewed her thumb.

'Now, are you going to leap into the MG and skitter off home to the biggest hoolie Upton Poges has ever seen, or what?'

'Or what,' Georgia said truculently. 'I want to know if you've been back to Vivienda.'

Rory exhaled deeply. 'After I'd left Diadem, yes. I met my mother and Rufus. I needed to find out if they could buy my shares. I also suggested that they asked Ionio to back off in what they were doing.'

Georgia flinched. She could imagine just how gentle his suggestions had been.

'They agreed pretty readily – especially when I told them that I knew Ken and Beth were dishing the dirt. That shocked them a bit. I hinted that people might assume that Vivienda were paying them to put Diadem out of business. Then they really panicked. Vivienda don't want to be dragged across the front of the tabloids. Rufus is hoping for a knighthood.' He leaned forward and rewound Dinah Washington. Georgia could see the ripple of muscles beneath the thin fabric of his shirt. 'I swear to you that apart from those bloody shares, I am no longer part of Vivienda. I'm my own man – or thought I was. But you didn't trust me, did you?'

She shook her head. The easygoing, laughing, loving Rory seemed to have left her. 'But you must admit it was a bit of a coincidence you turning up at Diadem just as Vivienda took over Ionio? Surely, anyone could be forgiven for wondering –'

'Not really.' Rory stared out into the blackness. 'You'd be pretty hard-pressed to go anywhere these days and not find a company that Vivienda is fiddling with. They seem intent on spreading themselves across the entire country.'

Georgia persisted. 'What about your name though? Where does the Faulkner bit fit in?'

'Faulkner is my correct surname. It was my father's name.' He was still staring straight ahead, watching the raindrops gathering in pools on the windscreen wipers. 'Vivienda came from my mother's side of the family. Her maiden name was Kendall. I've never used it. Rufus always has.'

'Oh.' She felt desperately ashamed. 'I really am sorry –'

'Stop saying sorry.' His eyes flashed. 'Actually, I think I was far more to blame than you were. I deceived you by withholding the truth. It was stupid of me. Stupid – but not malicious.'

'Rory,' she was about to sell her soul. 'Couldn't we start again?'

He still hadn't looked at her. Eventually he turned his head. He was grinning. 'I thought we already had.'

'What?'

'It's just a pity you're not wearing the purple mules.' His eyes glinted. 'They would have made the action replay – admittedly with role reversal – just that bit more authentic. I mean, we've got a lorry and the MG. The weather is appalling. You're even wearing the same jumper –'

Georgia squealed with delight as he pulled her towards him. Eric whimpered happily in his sleep.

'I've been to hell and back.' He kissed her throat.

The mingled scent of cologne and diesel fired every pulse. She giggled. 'And I've been to Warrington –'

'Georgia – please will you forgive me?'

Her answer was impossible. Rory kissed her with hunger and deprivation. A slow, erotic kiss. The only kiss she'd know for the rest of her life. Negotiating the steering wheel, Georgia squirmed ecstatically on to his lap and kissed him back.

'Christ, I've missed you,' Rory said eventually, surfacing. 'But I think we've got a party to go to.' He pulled the inebriated elephant over her head. 'We shouldn't be much later.'

'Gran's parties can go on for days.' Georgia was tugging at the buttons on his silk shirt.

'I didn't actually mean that one.' Rory dragged aside the bunk curtains. 'That one can wait. I meant a more exclusive truckers' party.'

'Oh, God, I do love you,' she whispered as they tumbled into the bunk. 'Oh, shush – don't wake Eric.'

'Eric'll have to get used to this.' Rory was butterfly-kissing her skin. 'I love you too. I think I always have. It was probably the purple mules. You'll have to wear them with your wedding dress.'

Dinah Washington crooned once more about being mad about the boy. Georgia's last coherent thought was that she wasn't the only one . . .